I0787995

# Behind Even The Shadows

## Unveiling Thorns

### Molly Moles

Scriverdea Publishing

Lewisville, Indiana

Scriverdea Publishing
4886 East 1100 North, Lewisville, Indiana, 47352
Printed by IngramSpark with permission



For additional information, contact Molly Moles using the listed address or email behindeventheshadows@gmail.com. Be sure to join @BEtheShadows on Facebook (with links to other social media platforms) for author updates and fan forums.

**Unveiling Thorns** first edition, 2020
Second in the *Behind Even The Shadows* Series of six novels.

*Cover artwork and illustrations by Bekah Koen*
*Photomanipulation, logos, and accents by Jacob Moles*
*Concept editing by Janet Hughes*
*Map created using Inkarnate.com with proper licensure*

ISBN: 978-1-951499-06-8 (paperback)
978-1-951499-07-5 (hardcover)
978-1-951499-08-2 (eBook)
978-1-951499-09-9 (Audiobook)

LCCN: 2020919217

Novels in the

# Behind Even The
# Shadows

Series:

**Cloaked Heart**

**Unveiling Thorns**

**Paradox Puzzle**

**Mental Tempest**

**Verity Pursuit**

**Callous Closure**

# ~ Dedication ~

*To The One Who gave me the ability to produce the work I do ~ my Lord and Creator, God Almighty. May He be glorified in all I do, and may this book — and series — be a reflection of young Christian adults striving, growing, renewing, maturing, and perfecting day-by-day to follow Him and be in the world but not of it. Standing up to the sinful nature of those who do not submit to God's commands, while at the same time, showing them they do not have to continue in hopelessness and sin.*

# ~ Acknowledgements ~

*Sometimes "thank you" doesn't do justice; and yet what else can I say except, "Thank you!" I've added a couple enthusiastic readers to this great team and am looking forward to this following growing:*

| | | |
|---|---|---|
| *Jay Moles* | *Bekah Koen* | *Evabeth Bailles* |
| *Janet Hughes* | *Jacob Moles* | *Amane Nixon* |
| *Linda Rogers* | | *Laurie Koen* |

# ~ Table of Contents ~

# ~ Pronuciation Guide ~

*NOTES: Underlining: "hard" vowel. Capitals: stressed syllable.*

## First Names:

Abril: <u>A</u>-bril

Anneque: ann-K<u>E</u>

Asdum: az-DUM

Graygoré: GR<u>A</u>Y-g<u>o</u>r-ey

Lenön: le-NEW-n

Olara: <u>O</u>-lar-ah

Redje: reh-J<u>E</u>

Yana: YA-on-ah

Yannabelle: Y<u>A</u>N-ah-bel-ah

Zelpha: ZEL-fa

## Last Names:

Benthvole: benth-V<u>O</u>L

Buhlg: BUL-g

Retoy: R<u>E</u>-t<u>o</u>y

Utree: Y<u>OO</u>-tr<u>e</u>

## Places:

Arable: <u>AIR</u>-<u>a</u>-bul

Indalla: IN-doll-ya

Pheafoul: F<u>E</u>-ah-fowl

Reeg: REG (short e)

Wyfal: WHY-fal

Yerlonga: yer-LON-ga

## Miscellaneous:

(Drug) Deplasterhine: D<u>E</u>-pla-stir-rin

(Drug) Deplasto: D<u>E</u>-pla-st<u>o</u>

(Title) Doyen: D<u>OY</u>-yen

(Disease) Fibromylophagia: fy-BR<u>O</u>-my-low-f<u>ag</u>-<u>e</u>-ya

(Title) Fidus: F<u>I</u>-dus

(Title) Haut Monde: <u>O</u> mond

(Title) Strigidae: stri-gi-D<u>E</u>

(Industrial Plant Name) Uloy: Y<u>OO</u>-l<u>oy</u>

(Language) Yeronich: yer-ON-itch

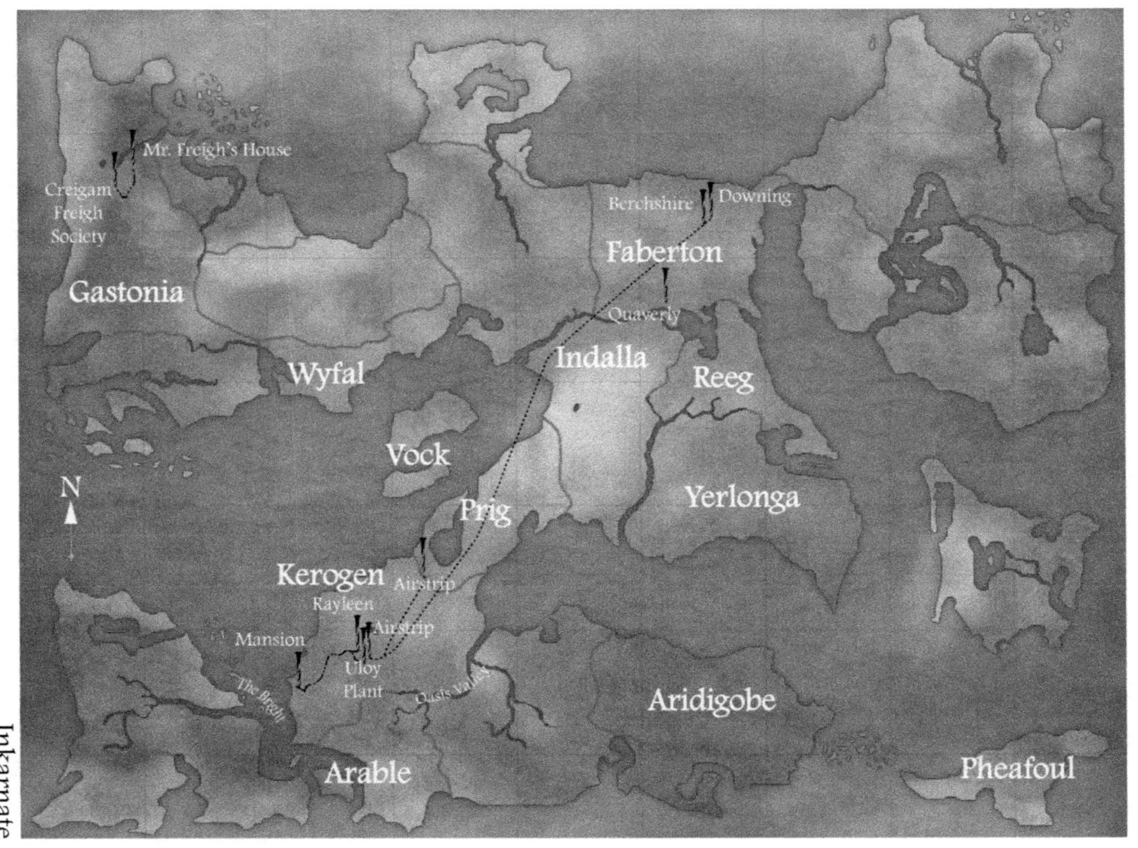

~ Map of Quidoria ~
Mr. Freigh's House
Creigam
Freigh
Society
Berchshire
Downing
Faberton
Quaverly
Gastonia
Indalla
Reeg
Wyfal
Vock
Yerlonga
Prig
Kerogen
Airstrip
Kayleen
Airstrip
Mansion
Uloy
Plant
Oasis Valley
The Brecht
Aridigobe
Arable
Pheafoul
N
Inkarnate

*In loving memory of the most encouraging editor this world will ever know: Janet Hughes. Her love for The Lord, first and foremost, as well as her sassy form of constructive criticism and encouragement molded the character — Mrs. Manning — who makes her debut in this novel. While this does not do complete justice to her memory, I hope you come to love her as your second grandmother like I did.*

$$\sim 1 \sim$$

Clouds lingered as Callimay leaned on the railing of the balcony. Technically, she was supposed to be in bed by order of Doctor Gerould… not just in the room. But if she did, she couldn't see outside; and it looked so nice out. Getting sunshine and fresh air were valid reasons to get up. These were important things the human body needed to heal. At least that was how she justified it.

She closed her eyes and looked toward the rising sun, taking a deep breath. The sweet-smelling breeze brushed against her hair and ruffled through her silk nightgown. It was cold, but the warm embrace of the sunshine made this minor inconvenience just that: minor. Everything felt calm and peaceful. What a change in such a short time!

"Callimay Rose Nevrille! What do you think—"

"I promise I'll go to bed in a minute." She pouted as she looked over her shoulder; the sunlight bathing her already glowing face. "Please?"

Destan nodded to Rocher who had followed him in carrying a tray; concluding his scolding remarks in a more painful and worried tone, "Why didn't you ask before I left? I would've carried you and made sure you had a chair. You're too weak to be up and about like this."

"This sniffle isn't anything. I was up and about yesterday and felt fine for the most part. — And I've been in bed for what… a month? I don't see how this could hurt any."

He sighed as he rubbed her arms, "That was different."

Unable to resist his offer, she wrapped her arms around his neck and let him carry her back. He leaned his forehead against hers for a bit and helped her settle. As he walked around the foot of the bed, she could tell he was favoring his right leg, "Okay. What's wrong?"

"I'm fine, Calli." He brushed off as he flashed his small smile to her. "It's nothing."

There was an awkward pause as he started getting her breakfast ready, but he slumped his shoulders in surrender after he hissed; mumbling, "You can tell, can't you?"

She nodded, her eyes bobbing to-and-fro with concern.

"I guess I shouldn't even try to act brave, huh?" Destan sighed as he sat beside her. "You saw most of what happened yesterday. … I'm sorry Calli. It's not that I was lying, I just— I don't want you to worry. You need your rest. Yes I'm in pain, but listen: I'm alright. I've been through worse." *Much worse.*

"I'm sorry about yesterday. I—"

"Calli, it's okay." He took a deep breath as he flopped onto the bed. "What's done is done. Lance said all I need is… rest."

Without saying a word, Destan knew she was telling him to practice what he preached. At least he figured that was the case since he caught himself and couldn't deny he was guilty. He made a face and rolled over to look at her; leaning over to kiss her, "I love you."

"I love you too." She replied sad; her eyes still having that worried, shaky look. "I'm sorry about your birthday being ruined."

*You never stop thinking about others, do you Calli?*

Destan knew she didn't understand what it meant for him to know she was alright. He did tell her, but this "sharing your emotions" thing was new to him. How was he supposed to tell her how seeing her eyes and hearing her voice gave him peace and comfort?

*Albeit she 'is' going a bit overboard with this apology, but I'm glad to know she's still herself after what I did. She hasn't said a word about it. ~ This isn't overboard. Not for her. You know that.* "You don't have anything to be sorry for. You didn't do anything wrong. In fact, you did everything that made my birthday the best one I've had in forever."

It was still an adjustment for Callimay to see this side of Destan for so long and so strong. There was a calmness about him she only saw twice: when he proposed and their first day "home". And yet this was different. Different and wonderful.

❦

Even though the horror of what happened just a day ago was fresh, life began anew that day. It was time to form a new and healthy routine. This "change" wasn't one for Destan, though. He'd done this for the past month. And yet, holding the woman he dearly loved felt nothing like it had.

The more time he spent with her, the more he began to realize and understand he was married. What Doctor Gerould told him was sinking into his head and heart in different ways; being reaffirmed and deepened by the Scripture passages he would read aloud to Callimay while they both rested. Destan now saw how there was so much more to a marriage than physically protecting the one you love.

And so, each day, he worked to find a new way to show Callimay he cared about and loved her. He put in the work necessary to find what she wanted and needed. These questions were coupled with awkward silence and rarely any eye contact at first, but they slowly morphed into what felt natural.

Much to his relief, Destan's frightening actions were but a bygone and forgotten mistake to Callimay… at least she never mentioned it. It touched him that she still contained the heart to let the past be forgiven and forgotten. But there were things he himself had to work through: feeling her hold on him fall away and seeing her eyes close when she would fall asleep in his arms. He understood how the past could only be forgotten in some ways. It unfortunately would find a way to manifest itself; making him face the facts and fight this fear now inside him: he was "dangerous".

As the days passed, he started following Doctor Gerould's advice: making himself uncomfortable and going through the pain of telling her about his past. He'd never included someone in such a raw part of his life, and Callimay knew it and was respectful about his wishes. Yet on the flip side, he was enjoying having someone to talk with… even though a part of him tried to deny it: *Why do I still have this hesitancy? ~ Really Boon? You know good and well~ That's not it.*

ЯÞ

Though it was something he dreaded, Destan knew he needed to get as much information from Toreon as possible… and as much as he could emotionally stand. The only thing was, Toreon was a good liar: he told enough truth that was well-known to sucker you in before leaving you with the impression that he was the innocent, preyed upon, helpless victim, "I know about your ties to the Syndicate. You're not just 'any' Falconer. Don't lie to me: 'Prince'."

"When have ever I denied my birthright? And am I to understand from your brutish tone that you are insinuating my being tied to the Syndicate — albeit in a very personal way — automatically makes me an evil person? Why I never! We are nothing less than the beacon of justice and order for Quidoria; the very reason Augury was the name given to this era we enjoy. We are nothing like the Shadows who grovel in the dark and break the Law. But putting all aside, let me put your ill-conceived accusation to rest: the Syndicate did 'not' have anything to do with this, Nevrille. I assure you. It was instigated and authorized by the Society. No. One. Else."

There was a tense moment of silence, Destan gritting his teeth and trying to keep himself as composed as possible: *Calli I know I need to stay calm but I need to get this frustration out.*

*I know it's hard for you to keep things in when—*

"If you just can't take a simple no for an answer, fine. I'll indulge you and shoot down your conspiracy theory: why would we utilize another entity to do what even 'you' know we are more than capable of doing ourselves? Using such a cover would create unnecessary ties and prove to be nothing but ill-spent resources. Money is a precious thing and we have bigger issues to address, which I am sure you are aware of. What the Society is doing is nothing but fulfilling some madman's science experiment to fix a fictitious problem 'they' fabricated." Toreon continued to defend, sounding as smug as ever. "What's this silence I sense from you? Oh don't tell me. 'You' fell for the 'Rogue' smokescreen they planted? … I'm disappointed in you, truly I am. I thought you to be above falling into line with propaganda and hysteria. But I guess that is what conspiracy theorists like yourself do. — Back to my point, let us look at the other side of this: surely you don't think a reputable organization such as the Syndicate would stoop to such chicanery as pulling from the lore of the Homeworld to bring down the Shadows, do you? Such cunning isn't necessary to take you simpletons down."

"Enough." Destan snapped back; clinching his fists in midair as he worked to listen to Callimay's loving and calming voice so he wouldn't come over the table and choke him. "You murder — yes, I said murder and I'd say it again under oath in any court — people on the grounds of being genetically different; not because of any moral truth. Laws don't determine what is right and true; people's emotions and money couldn't come close to finding righteousness. Man may try, but deep down he knows he can't play God. ... So with that said, you're no beacon of justice like you and your parents 'love' to claim. You are nothing but tyrants: selfish, power-hungry, scumbags. Last I checked, those characteristics have nothing to do with protecting or looking out for the welfare of others. — And don't put words in my mouth. Evil was a word you used, not me. But I guess you would know best whether or not you are. — Then on top of everything I 'really' can't believe you of all people got dragged into this. As much as it disgusts me to give you 'any' complement, I will acknowledge you're no idiot. ... So why did you blindly follow this? You did say you came after me because 'they' told you to; not because you wanted to."

"Since when was that an established fact?" Toreon began to smirk. "I do believe you're starting to put words in 'my' mouth, Nevrille."

"Everyone is under someone's authority. Even 'you' bow to it. It's just you've got the money and name to throw around so you can choose who that is." He folded his arms in front of him, eyeing the sorry excuse for a man sitting in front of him. "The way you and Baleck talked and acted after you threw Callimay over Lookout Point w—"

"First off: I didn't throw her. She ripped her hand out of mine and fell. I don't care what your 'precious' little wife told you. That's a bald-faced lie. I won't have my honor sullied by some half-brained nitwit... no matter how beautiful she is." He corrected in an irritated tone as he lifted his cuffed hands and pointed in what he assumed to be Destan's direction. "Second: I was merely being respectful and trying to find someone to take care of the..."

"Mess you made?"

"May I speak? Seriously! — It just so happened the scheduler was available and got in touch with him when I told them about Callimay. I only wanted them to be aware a medical professional's presence might

be necessary. I had no idea what his intentions were when we talked…
and honestly I still don't. — Why are you 'so' suspicious of him? Mr.
Freigh is the conductor. He is the one who has final say on all the
dealings at the Society. Why would Mr. Willgun be your target?"

"Well first off — to use your own methodology — Willgun isn't a
medical professional, so that lie about you contacting them for that
reason won't hold any amount of hot air even. Secondly, Callimay was
there when you were processed." Destan revealed, causing him to
flinch. "She heard 'everything' Willgun said concerning what he wants
done and what you know. — Freigh's probably in on it too; I never
denied that. But the fact remains that I know about Willgun for sure…
and I know about you."

"Pfft," Toreon brushed off as he leaned back in the chair. "He
probably knew she was there and was trying to place blame on me so
you'd keep your focus off Freigh; he is the go-between man. At least
that is the most logical reason I can think of since I honestly haven't got
a clue what's going on. I'm in the same boat as you: burdened with
abilities I didn't ask for and trying to use them for good."

"Quit lying, you filthy scum!" He fumed as he slammed his hands
on the desk. "You spoke with Willgun only to tell him you finished
your job and then went to the main school building that other night for
the express and sole purpose of being processed. You knew."

Ꮎ

Destan was always worked up after being around Toreon — which was
understandable and maybe even understated, knowing what they spoke
about and how Toreon acted. He didn't want to snap at Callimay when
she wasn't who he was mad at, so he would wait and "cool off" before
going to see her.

Time and time again he tried piecing together the deepening
conspiracy he was uncovering concerning Creigam Freigh Society.
Things began to make sense about a couple students Dakoe mentioned
being "operatives", but was it just them? Then again, were they even
connected to the Syndicate like he thought? Was he jumping to
conclusions based on past experience? Was there more than one "bad
guy" out there? Was what Toreon said about that the truth? There was

no way to deny what he said: the Syndicate could have done what the Society was doing without any front whatsoever. They were "the law of the land". Every governmental agency around the world automatically sanctioned anything they did. Granted, they would have to find the information his father had on the serums; but their reach was so far and wide it wasn't impossible for them to get their hands on it since it was already in the hands of someone whose moral compass was broken. — Every person like that had their "price". — And if it were them using it, they would have their people in charge. Toreon wasn't there in that capacity even though it felt like he ran the show.

But was Destan falling for a well-placed trap? Was the Syndicate trying a different approach to keep this under the radar? Why would they bother keeping it hidden? — And what about the Rogues? Was Toreon right about that, too? Was the information Destan found in his file fake? Was his gut instinct right that the possibility of there being two-thousand "super villains" out there just waiting to pounce on humanity nothing less than the most ridiculous tale ever told?

This "cooling off" time was supposed to help him calm down before seeing Callimay. Thinking about these scenarios was in no way helpful; the entire process not heading anywhere productive. He attempted to shift his thoughts, but they kept circling back to this. How could he put it aside? These questions and their answers had immediate effects on him and the woman he loved more than anything else. He had to know.

After hearing Toreon talking in circles and flat out refusing to answer questions — seeing how it all was affecting Callimay a little bit more each time — Destan had enough. Fighting with his own emotions was hard enough, but dealing with the likes of Toreon at the same time made things just about unbearable. He didn't want to repeat what happened when he lost his cool around Callimay the last time.

So, several phone calls were made and serious discussions had.

It was arranged for Toreon to be taken to Ferdinan where Destan had personal connections with federal and local government officials. He wanted to make sure Toreon would be found as far away as possible while somewhere he could trust those who would be detaining him.

On top of all this stress, he was a nervous wreck. Keeping Toreon in the same place as Callimay was making every nerve he had raw; he couldn't sleep, didn't eat much, and was becoming more and more distant. And as if he knew this, Toreon was in no way shy of how he talked about her. Even though he knew the comments he made weren't true and he was purposefully trying to get him to lose it; Destan still fell for the trap Toreon set each time. The mere mention of her name crossing his lips drove him up one wall and down the other.

♌

Not a day too soon the escort came. Destan was up earlier than usual and as serious as ever. He made sure there was breakfast for Callimay but refused any until he knew things were done and taken care of, "Stay with her."

"As you wish, Sir." Rocher nodded and went back in the room.

"They're here, Destan," he heard Doctor Gerould call out.

"We'll go down once everything's ready." He said monotone as he rushed down to the vestibule. "They sent two of their own detachments along with what we have, correct?"

"Yes."

"Do you have what you need to prep him for transport?"

"Destan, everything is fine." Doctor Gerould said light-hearted while at the same time retaining a serious undertone. "Don't—"

"Nothing's 'fine' until he's gone." He shook his head and stormed outside to meet with those who arrived.

♌

Callimay hadn't been awake for much time at all when she heard voices downstairs. Rocher calmed her to let her know what was going on; assuring her he wouldn't leave until Destan came back.

As she sat there, the voices she heard didn't sound familiar at all: *What are you doing? ~ They sound like male v~ Rose Petal! ~ What! ~ Stop! Why in the world do you think you'd recognize any of the voices? These people are from Ferdinan. ~ I… I don't~ Just stop, okay?*

The voices cut off, prompting her to rush to the door, "Milady, please stay h—"

"I'm just going to listen, Rocher. I promise I'll come right back in a minute." She put a hand out as she leaned against the door.

8

Sure, Callimay could have used her ability; but she didn't want to accidentally connect with Toreon… and she wasn't about to open the door and risk seeing him. She never wanted to see him again.

There were quick, methodical footsteps that she heard but no voices. The front door opened and then shut with purpose… and then silence.

They were gone. And with them, Toreon.

She leaned on the door for a while before she came back and collapsed on the bed; relieved he was gone from their lives… she hoped for what would be forever.

It was strange how Destan didn't "feel" relaxed when he came up a few minutes later. Why? Toreon was gone. Attempted murder wasn't a charge even he could walk away from.

By the end of the day — which Destan spent pacing the floor — the phone rang. He ran down to answer it; his emotions almost spiraling out of control. A few minutes later he returned and sighed, his voice sounding like the weight of the world had been lifted off his shoulders, "They're in Ferdinan, Calli. Toreon's halfway across the world where he's going to stay."

# ~ 2 ~

With this beautiful, emotional peace came the first hints of spring-like weather. March came and went, followed by April which ushered in the usual and refreshing change to the grounds of the mansion. The gardens were cleared of winter's lingering presence; and as if waiting anxiously, the birds flocked and fought for their spot by their closest source of freshwater which the fountains provided.

The sound of them coupled with how the wind softened and changed direction made Callimay's strenuous physical therapy much more tolerable. Doctor Gerould told her there was no reason her shoulder wouldn't heal, but wouldn't deny the road to that point was going to have its ups and downs… more downs at first.

Meanwhile, all the rosebushes arrived as planned and were mature enough to bloom that year; just as she requested. Destan had a few of the men make sure the fence line was prepped — when Rocher reminded him they were coming — so there wasn't any delay in getting them planted. They thrived in the salty air; their beautiful hues of red, pink, yellow, and white being one of the first splashes of color to the rugged landscape.

She enjoyed spending time outside and was doing little things all over to bring that small feminine touch to her new home; all the while making sure she had Destan's approval, "Calli it's alright."

"I just wanted to make sure."

He smiled as he brushed her face, "This is your home too. I want you to be comfortable; so do what you like."

Callimay glanced at the piano before looking down and away, him realizing he was sounding like a hypocrite, "I… I'm—"

"I didn't mean— well, I did. But I didn't intend t—"

"It's alright. I can't think of anything else I would call 'off limits'. And even if there is, I won't lose my cool like I did. I realize I can't hold you to my expectations when you don't know what they are. Promise."

ℬ

When the weather was dreary and there wasn't much to do, Destan would catch Callimay looking out the window by the fireplace on the main floor. At first he assumed it was because she was doing what she did so often while they were at the Society: look toward the sky and around at nature; but when he would go to look after she left, he was confused since it didn't offer the view like the sunroom did and more times than not it was overcast.

Then it hit him one day. He noticed her watching a couple vehicles coming to and going from the mansion: *So that's why. … Oh Calli. I—*

"I cannot deny how Milady's countenance has appeared to devolve and become downcast as of late, Sir." Rocher noted as he stood at the edge of the drive. "If I am allowed to inquire into such delicate matters: is she fairing quiet well?"

Destan sighed in agony, though part of him was relieved to know the answer now: *Why am I still so slow at picking up on things like this?* "She's restless. Even though she never asked me outright, I now know she wants to leave. Now I don't think it's a permanent thing. She seems happy enough… don't you think? … But I understand. Even 'I' have been a bit stir crazy the past week with the weather change. — But it's still too dangerous."

"Last report, if you will indulge my repetition, substantiated that the Prince has no recourse except to make restitution for his egregious acts stated in your deposition. No action originating from the Syndicate has surfaced concerning his state of incarceration. And no persons of the Falconer like have yet to be noted as frequenters in the vicinity of Kerogen's borders; or patrolling for said matter."

"I know. I just— I came too close to losing her, Rocher. You would think after so much loss I would be accustomed to the feeling of my heart being broken — which I even thought I had — but what I felt when I thought I lost Calli was something I hadn't felt since mother and father were taken from me. It was as if I gained back my ability to grieve; to feel. As if I found it in me to care for someone again on that deep, personal level; and understood what it was to lose them. … I realized I forgot what it felt like to have my heart break and it scared me as close to the grave as possible without actually putting me there. — I think you can attest to this more than anyone else: after mother and father were murdered, I allowed anger to scar me to the point I couldn't feel anything else when I lost someone close. … Am I right?"

Rocher never said a word, but an understanding sigh and nod was more than an adequate answer for Destan.

"I— it's hard to explain, but it's as if Callimay— as if she healed this brokenness in me. Of course I say that but I can't deny how she's only pointed me back to the truth I've already known."

"The unconditional love found in the fairer sex is beyond the comprehensive understanding of man at many a time, Sir. I've yet to cross such a path with one who contains the aptitude to explain it with much coherence. — It is splendid to hear your resolve to move straight ahead from the past. I might also add how I recall with great detail how it has been a tumultuous road for you to journey down."

As much as he was talking about his past, he wasn't willing to acknowledge Rocher's comments, "I just wish I could take her somewhere: anywhere. Somewhere she could enjoy herself and feel… normal. Right now I feel like I'm holding her hostage here. It hurts me to see her like this. But how do I do it?"

"Would your forbearance endure long enough for me to offer such a suggestion?" Rocher encouraged as he handed him a paper. "I fully understand and admire your concerns surrounding Milady's welfare. And the hurt you spoke of is in fact not hidden from anyone; Milady included. It stems, I believe, from the stark as well as pertinent odds of your wish to control and maintain your level of protection on one hand while your deep-seated desire to fulfill her wishes resides on the other. Could this, perhaps, be a small avenue available by which you are availed the occasion to spend recreational time outside the premises in each other's company — not paying regard to current situations — while still conforming to the control and protective nature you wish to conduct such outings for the comfort and sanity of your soul?"

"But I told you to inform them I wouldn't be attending?"

"Begging your unending forgiveness, Sir; but I took the liberty of withholding said annotation. I was of the conviction and earnest hope your devoted time at the Society would be short-lived while equally productive so you would retain the possibility to fulfill this office you are deeply passionate about. … I do recall how the decision to forego the Gregorian and table the Verde altogether were frustrating decisions which showed to be necessary to say the very least, Sir."

He replied under his breath as he folded the page, "It was."

"I have the utmost confidence that Milady would enjoy such an opportunity to support you and your efforts to honor such people by offering this service as is noted in Hope."

"Do you think so?" Destan noticed he caught her eye.

"The remedy to that inquiry is one you yourself hold. I will see to preparations at once unless you wish otherwise. … Sir?"

"Alright. That's fine, Rocher." He answered in somewhat of a daze as he continued to look at Callimay as she walked over; though to him she looked like she was gliding on the breeze that played with her hair.

"Good afternoon, Destan." She smiled while giving him a kiss on the cheek. "It's a wonderful day. How are th— are you alright? … Destan? Is something wrong?"

"Oh, I'm fine. I was thinking."

"Pulling a 'me'?"

"Huh?"

"Oh never mind. What were you thinking about?"

Putting two and two together, he smiled as he tickled her chin: *What do you mean by that?*

"I don't pay attention all the time." Callimay shooed his hand away. "Stop that! You know that tickles."

Destan chuckled a bit as he messed with her flailing hands, her slapping his a couple more times before he replied, "Rocher was talking with me— hey! Those long nails of yours hurt, woman."

"I'm sorry."

"Geez. … Maybe we 'won't' go out Saturday. Serves you right."

"Out? This Saturday? You mean outside the barrier kind of out?"

"I was thinking of it, yes."

"Why… I!" Callimay gasped as she looked toward the drive entrance, her eyes wide with excitement. "Where would we be going? Oh please let's go. I'm sorry."

"I'm just kidding," he let the paper unfold as he held the edge.

*Dear Mr. Nevrille,*

*We hope this letter finds you well from your frequent travels. On behalf of my wife and myself, I wish to send this thank you prior to the Ball of Hope in April.*

*It has been nine years now that you have been hosting this event and I…*

Callimay was reading aloud but faded off as she continued; her face looking more and more confused. Once she finished, she looked up to him with her eyes wide, "You've hosted a ball for the last nine years?"

"This one, yes."

"This 'one'? You mean there are others!"

"There are…" Destan paused as he looked up, muttering to himself; and then finishing, "Six I host individually and then a handful of others I sponsor in some fashion."

She dropped the letter, fumbling to find words that made a coherent thought and pertained to what was going on, "You… you mean to tell me, on top of everything else you know, you can dance?"

*Not what I was expecting your first comment to be.* "I never said that, Calli." He laughed as he leaned over and picked up the paper. "I only provide the venue and opportunity for others. I've never had a suitable partner. … I'm afraid Rocher just isn't my type."

"Oh, Destan." She shoved his forearm as she rolled her eyes. "You know what I meant. — So, what is this 'Ball of Hope' for?"

"Well. When going through my father's papers, I came across a series of correspondences he had with various charitable organizations that aided those with diseases he formulated drugs, treatments, and even cures for. He'd voiced his desire to host events for those who unfortunately were not helped; to give them a small escape from their daily struggles and to have an evening that offered encouragement. I didn't want his dream to die just because he did. … So I took it upon myself to get this ball, and others, off the ground."

Callimay wrapped her arms around him, snuggling herself close to his chest, "That is 'so' sweet of you to do all this for people in need. … Which disease is this one for?"

*She had to ask, didn't she? ~ You know how to say it. And even if you do butcher it, I doubt she would know if you said it wrong.* "You've heard of Fibromylophagia, right? … And its treatment?"

"Umm… it's something like Deplasterhine, right?"

*Deplasto. ~ Eh, close enough.* "My father is the one who formulated it. It was the first and still is the only known cure for this disease."

"So what do we need to do to get ready? This is a 'real' ball, right?"

"It's a 'real' one, yes." He mimicked her vocal stressing of that word. "And as far as getting ready, you don't need to lift a pretty little finger. Me? Thankfully everything should be done so I don't have to run back and forth. I'll have to get with Rocher about the speech when w—"

"You give a speech too!"

"Yes." Destan exaggerated even more this time; a bit annoyed by her constant questioning, but calmed the second he looked at her smiling face. "People here in Kerogen are 'very' immersed into tradition and formality since this was one of the founding countries." *A stark contrast to what's just across the Bright nowadays.* "And before you say anything, don't think I am the one who writes these speeches. Rocher is the one who takes care of it."

She smiled as she swung their interlocked hands back and forth, "Oh… I bet you could. From what I've read of your work, you write really well. Have you ever tried?"

"Believe me, Calli. It's best this way. — I know it might be shocking to know there's this… well this 'social' side to me." He scratched his head, looking away from her. "I do get out and 'play nice' as it were; but I'm very purposeful with when and where I go. My standards as far as the company I keep are very high."

*Isn't he so sweet when he says things like that? And the way he blushes~ Hush. Let me enjoy this. … It's endearing to see this side I never knew 'any' man had. And it's not fake or exaggerated. It's him doing it because he wants to. I love it so much. ~ He's a keeper, t—*

"Calli?"

"I'm sorry. I was talking to myself," they both said in unison; Destan laughing when they finished.

She wanted to be upset with him for making fun of and knowing exactly what she would say, but she couldn't stay mad, "I love you."

"I love you too, Calli."

"As far as what you said, who has time to be shocked? I'm excited! — You look like you're about due for a haircut. If we're going to a big fancy b— Destan?"

"Huh?"

*He is one distracted man today.* "I was going to say something last week but forgot." She hopped on a bench so she could reach his hair. "You're going to be mistaken for a homeless beggar with no wife to take care of you… and I can't have that even if we did stay here."

He nodded and tossed his head, "I guess it is a little long."

"A little? How can you see!"

"You're one to talk! … I'll have Rocher cut it tonight if he can."

Callimay smiled as he helped her down; a happy sigh rolling off her lips as she leaned her head against his arm, "Rocher can do just about anything, can't he?"

No answer.

*Oh dear me. I'm starting to ramble and lose him. ~ He might just be tired. He was up awfully late last night.* "So. … This will be the first time you get the: 'who is the young woman with you?' 'how long have you been married?' type of questions from people you k—"

"You're right. I hadn't thought of that." Destan stopped and stared out into the distance, sounding worried.

Seeing that look on his face hurt her. If she would have kept her big mouth shut then he wouldn't change his mind.

"But you know?" His face burst with his small smile. "We'll wait and cross that bridge 'if' it comes. — So! Would you like to go, Calli? Or do I need to ask?"

"I… I'd love to!"

"Then that settles everything. I'll go to Rayleen on Friday to make sure everything is ready to go."

## ~ 3 ~

For the rest of the week, Destan would spend an hour or so in the morning going over the speech. There were times he would speak with Rocher, but most of the time he would pace around the piano, practicing the flowery speech in solitude. Callimay would come down and watch, but kept her distance.

She was fully adjusted to how Rocher talked, but hearing such phrasing and vocabulary coming from Destan was comical — in a way. It's not that he was some hick who had poor grammar, but he didn't mince words either. Such flamboyancy didn't fit him at all.

But then she felt guilty for laughing when she would see him stop every so often and with a tender touch, lay his hand on the piano. He would bow his head and look over where his hand was for a moment, then take a deep breath and continue.

Her heart broke. With all he went through — let alone what they were still going through — this was obviously hard for him.

Callimay could tell it was a battle within him. One side knew it was done out of a sense of duty toward his father and others because of what he had been blessed with, while the other side saw it as being done out of the love for his father and wanting to help others. She didn't know how he had been able to do it this long on his own, and hated everything was made more complicated by her being around, as well as what the Society had done.

And yet she thought back: for practically the same amount of time he had been doing these balls and coping with his loss, she had been muddling through the same process. Callimay was humiliated because she shut everyone out; Destan — who had been hurt so much deeper

and longer than her on some levels — was doing all he could to put his best foot forward and do what he could to help those around him.

ℬ

Friday morning came and Callimay woke to find she was alone. She jumped out of bed, grabbing her robe as she ran to the door and rushed downstairs. The moment she got to the vestibule and looked over she stopped dead in her tracks. Destan was hunched over, as if burdened with a heavy load on his back while he sat at the piano. His left hand gripped the side of the instrument while his right hand was beside him, holding his speech. The pain was not hidden from Callimay, but as far as anyone else was concerned, he was merely deep in thought. There wasn't a sound of grief to indicate otherwise, and yet there was a steady flow of tears pooling on the fallboard of the piano; proving this silent grief was deeper-cutting than someone crying out.

After a few moments, Destan let the papers go; allowing them to dive for the floor. As if scared of him, they fled as far as the air could carry them and then made soft slap-pat sounds as they hit and slid across the floor. He put his head in his hands and wept silently.

Callimay wanted so much to fix everything, but what could she do or even say? He kept most of this part of his life from her. Yes, he told her some, but he rarely answered questions about his parents.

Deep down she understood what he went through was horrid, and that it was up to him whether he took hold of the way to move on and heal or stay wrapped up in the anger of what happened so long ago.

It was hard for her to stand there and watch. She wanted to fly over and wrap him in her arms and keep him safe, but how could she keep him safe from his own memories? How could she protect him from something that didn't physically exist?

She tip-toed over and kneeled to pick up the pages, hoping that if nothing else he would know she was there and trying to help without barging into his memories that were full of so much pain.

As she looked up, she saw him staring at her, his eyes bloodshot and weary. Callimay knew Destan hadn't slept much at all since he started working on the speech. In that moment she wished so much that she knew what he needed from her.

After gathering the pages, she took her handkerchief out of her sleeve and reached over to wipe the fallboard, knowing he wouldn't want it to have a watermark. Destan reached for her hand as his eyes began to look defensive and protective; all the while doing everything possible to act better than he had last time.

"Here. Why don't you do it?" She encouraged as she took his hand and put the cloth in it.

Just as he was about to say something, the door opened and Rocher walked in. Destan cleaned the spot and shoved the handkerchief back in her hand: *Not today. I understand.*

Without saying a word, he rushed over and spoke with Rocher for a moment before going upstairs. He came back down a few minutes later, looking around as he buttoned his suit jacket.

Knowing what he was doing, Callimay started over. The moment he saw her, he jogged over, "I'm having one of the other men drive me so Rocher can stay with you."

"Destan? Please d— don't stay too long." She tried to sound positive.

"I'll be back before you know it. Is there anything you would like me to bring back?"

"Yourself."

That small smile couldn't help itself; it jumping out to reply to her kind and loving answer, "You can put those on my desk. I'll go over them again when I get back."

"Oh… okay."

He could hear what she was thinking, but didn't want to sound heartless by telling her she couldn't go. Rayleen was well over a two-hour drive to the northeast on a good day — on that front alone it was going to be a long day — and there were countless details to iron out that she wouldn't know about. In short, it wouldn't be anything less than a starched business meeting. That and he knew her stamina wasn't up to par. She needed to save herself for tomorrow.

The risk of something happening while he was gone was there — more to himself since he wouldn't be in the barrier and she wouldn't be close by if something would cause him any sizable amount of anger or frustration. He knew she understood this all too well and in a small way even he was concerned.

Destan didn't know what to say to comfort her, so he turned and left… then stopped and stuttered as he looked at her out of the corner of his eye, "I… I love you, Calli."

"I love you too." She cried in a whisper as he turned and pulled her to his chest, her gripping his jacket tight. "I don't want you to go."

He was about to answer when he heard her answer herself: *I know you'll always be with me no matter what happens, but I'm not ready for this. Maybe I sound like a spoiled brat: 'I want to be with you no matter where you go or what is happening.' It's probably selfish of me to say… so many wives stay home while their husbands are gone each and every day. I just— I worry. I worry in a way I know no other wife ever would. I can't bear t— if it's your time to go then I want to go too. I don't want to be left alone. Not again. I know why you want me to stay — to keep me safe if something does go wrong — but Destan? I—*

"Oh, Calli. I wish I could make everything different. I wish I could make everything safe and carefree for you right now. I'm sorry I can't."

She could hear Rocher talking about "time becoming short", so she stepped back and stifled her sobs as she fixed his lapel, "Just… promise me you'll do everything you can to come home."

"I promise." He looked her in the eye and rubbed the side of her face. "Promise me you'll be waiting for me 'when' I get back."

"Promise." *I'm going to keep my eyes closed so I don't have the memory of you leaving.*

"Alright Calli." He whispered as he gave her a kiss.

"I love you." She replied under her breath as she felt him step back. "Come home Destan. Please."

ଈ

Rocher could tell he wasn't happy about being apart from her for so long by his umpteenth reminder to stay by her side. He did his best to encourage Destan, reminding him what to focus on while keeping in mind what the next day would hold.

Before long he was off, so Rocher began fulfilling his assigned task. As he opened the door, he looked over and saw Callimay sitting at the piano. He noticed she had several papers in her hand, which gave him an idea, "Milady?"

"Yes? I… I didn't mean to—"

"I did not have any intention of startling you nor reprimanding your actions. And I truly believe Sir would not in his present state of mind. Please forgive my intrusion."

She took a deep breath and started wandering toward the desk, "You're fine. I just wasn't— I wasn't paying attention."

"I have observed how Sir has been struggling, to say the least, with the speech. He makes a point to dedicate all his efforts so its delivery is of the same caliber concerning formality and its relationship to every point of purpose surrounding this event. To put it another way: by this point in time of preparation, the speech is all but memorized. — I have come to observe he is secretly unhappy with the finished product and does not wish to critique my work that he knows is nothing precarious nor subpar compared to years past. … Do you think you might find it within yourself to assist me in revising it, Milady?"

"I don't see why not. But I don't know how much help I can be."

"A fresh set of eyes can do nothing but benefit the finishing of any article." Rocher encouraged as he walked over to the desk in the parlor, a lively spring in his step. "Very well then. Shall we begin?"

ℬ

This served as the perfect distraction while fulfilling a much-needed purpose. At first Callimay would glance at the desk clock from time to time, but the more she asked questions about what the speech needed to talk about and reading what he had prepared so she knew what was "expected", the more time didn't matter.

It humored Rocher to hear her speech morph and begin to mimic his own, but he didn't say a word about it since he didn't think she was being impolite or rude. Her adaptability was something he noticed right out of the gate and attributed to her willingness to do whatever she could to include others.

He didn't withhold one word from Callimay's eraser; and by the end his face was beaming with pride. Rocher handed the finished work to her; asking if she would be willing to read it in its entirety.

As she looked at the single page that was in typed form, she bit her lip, "Destan told me earlier how this is an important aspect of the ball.

Since Kerogen is a society of tradition, I can't see how speeches carry any less weight at such an event. They 'need' to reflect the formality of the event. I'm not sure this is going to suffice, Rocher. The length of it—it's so short!"

"It is poignant and straight-forward in its message and delivery, Milady. I see no issues with it in the slightest. Length does not draw equality with quality, nor wordiness with formality. It speaks to the heart of the evening in a beautiful way."

"Are you sure? It's so different from its predecessor. I know editing and revising can weed out some lengthy passages, but this poor thing looks like I lopped off its head, arms, 'and' legs! What I've inserted doesn't say much about the disease itself. Maybe we should add that portion back? I know 'of' it but I'm not familiar with it like you and Destan are."

"It is quite ready for him to deliver the way it stands presently."

Once she glanced at the words again, she gasped, "But this is what I would say, Rocher. W… why there's nothing left of— this is all mine!"

He confessed as he pushed his chair back and stood, "That was the very point of this entire endeavor of mine, Milady. Sir has heavily depended upon me for the source of speeches over the years due to his 'disdain' shall we politely say, for such addresses? It was for so long the part of the evening's formalities that he saw as a duty compared to that of a desire. There was no emotional link or deep-seated devotion to it. This year though, I deciphered he wasn't pleased with it after its final polish — which bucked his well-established precedent. He said in his usual way he would 'make it work', but that conveyed to me there was something still amiss with the material… some box wasn't being ticked on his list. Alas, it was only after more time lapsed that I came to the conclusion he desired to 'make' this speech… it broke through and became more than a duty. He now desired to convey his father's wishes by channeling the evening's focus on doing good for others which stemmed from being concerned for their well-being; not for the money it brought him or the accolades the drug continues to bear of being 'the medical miracle'. He now sees this as an integral part of the hope given to so many people who suffered by no fault of their own. It has always been, but now even more so, the vocal mode of resolve to — above and beyond all else — help those who were not benefitted by what so many see as something not capable of failure. … As you penned, this event reminds them: good isn't enough. Life is not complaisant but a constant striving toward betterment."

"What you said is so beautiful, Rocher. Why didn't you rewrite it?"

"I am doing nothing more than repeating what you yourself wrote, Milady. … I do confess I felt the responsibility to deviate your focus on the time, but the more I considered it the more I began to view myself as unworthy to be the individual who would be attributed with the authorship of such a work. — Let it be known I hold no animosity toward his disdain of my style of words, nor your alteration of them. Tradition can at times hamper what is needed. Formality and proper words such as mine will only convey so much; and admittedly are older and somewhat cold in their tone than what is so widely accepted by society today. You, Milady, have such a special touch when the subject of words comes to mind; though let it not be said I infer that is the only area you excel in. To this end, you carry the special ability to reach a broader range of people and include their importance and involvement in this wonderful evening through the conveyance of emotions in words which speak with formality and properness. I would not ever find myself in a moment of hesitation when stating the well-known fact that women have the inherent, natural ability of carrying this strong emotional connection along with elegance and simplicity."

This overflow of praise floored Callimay and left her without a response. — It appeared she used all her words in the speech. Or maybe the fact she was now speaking in such a formal way as Rocher was she couldn't figure out how to respond in his caliber style.

Seeing this befuddlement on her face, Rocher offered yet more praise, "Sir has been in the presence of your beautiful speech long enough to understand nothing I, nor he, could pen had any prayer in relation to the capability of contending and overcoming what naturally flows from your lips. He struggled to accept what was in and of itself 'good' when he knew there lie a source so much better that he could freely utilize. Sir hadn't discovered the issue — or at least conveyed to me he had — but upon my realization, it did not take me but a few moments to perceive the connection. This is without doubt the most heart-felt speech Sir will have 'ever' relayed at any gathering of this kind. The only one which might rival it would be his confession of love to you, but alas I was not there to witness it, so my ability to make such a reference is quite open to criticism."

"But I just said what I would have to anyone in this situation. There isn't anything 'special' about this."

"I know it all seems but a fantasy and tall tale for me to suggest you disregard everything you may believe; but when you hear Sir tomorrow evening and see the array of those in attendance, you will understand why this needed to be altered." Rocher assured as he glanced out the window. "Now. If Milady will excuse me, I do believe that is Sir pulling up the drive. I will take my leave to see to finishing touches for dinner."

"He's home! So soon?" She exclaimed as she scrambled to her feet and ran to the window. "But he said h— it's dark out!"

"It is now a quarter of eight, Milady." Rocher commented as he took his pocket watch out.

♬

Callimay flew across the room and down the steps. She threw the door open and ran toward the vehicle without so much as stopping to grab a jacket. The sleek sedan stopped and Destan got out right as she reached him; her running full speed into his chest, "You're home!"

"I'm home." He comforted as she clamored to keep her hold around his neck. *It's so good to have you back in my arms. ...* "I'm glad your shoulder feels good enough so you can—"

"It is wonderful to see you and hear your voice. I missed you so."

He stood there for a few moments and then smiled as he leaned his head against hers, "I missed you too."

"Did everything go well?"

Destan started up the drive, her not giving any indication she was letting go, "Dull as ever. Well, there were a few things needing to be adjusted; but nothing spectacular. — Calli? Speaking of adjustments, could you do me a favor?"

"Oh! I'm s—"

"It's not that. Though if you don't mind I will put you down. I doubt your shoulder is ready to support your weight f— what I meant—"

"Pay it no mind." She patted his flushed cheek. "I understand what you intended. — Now. What is this about a favor?"

"Have we been talking with Rocher?"

Callimay tilted her head as she made a face, trying to understand his exaggerated comment, "What 'ever' do you mean?"

"'Pay it no mind.' 'Whatever do you mean.' ... You sound like Rocher." He laughed as he leaned back. "Oh, now don't get all fussy with me; you're laughing too. ... Back to what I was saying: it's about tomorrow's speech. Something isn't right. I usually have it memorized by now but I can't— something's wrong with it."

"Isn't Rocher the one who helps you?"

"Yes. But we've gone over it countless times and I'm still not happy with it; and I don't have a clue why. It sounds fine: just like every other one I've given."

"What are you doing?" Callimay asked as he got in the car.

"You didn't tell me what to get you, so I had to find something on my own."

She sighed as he put a small box in her hands, "Destan I told y—"

"I know," he exaggerated.

"You're spoiling me."

"You're driving me up a wall, woman!" He bantered while he reached for the box. "Are you just gonna stare at it or are you gonna open it?"

"Alright, alright!" Callimay batted his hands away.

Inside the box, which had been gift-wrapped with shimmering paper and an orange bow, sat a pink glass flask nestled in a bed of glitter-speckled tissue, "How did you—"

"I had one of the men ask in Rayleen about a perfume that smelled like roses. — He's probably still mad at me for that; but it was good for him. He said he has a girl, so it's best if he gets used to things like this. — I'm amazed how many people get the smell of roses so wrong when it comes to perfume. I can't remember how many I went through to find this. It's made in a secluded hamlet in Reeg by a family-owned business. — Your mother's maiden name was Buhlg, right?"

"Yes," she replied in a confused tone as she opened the bottle.

"I thought that's what you said."

The hesitation in his answer was too long, "Why do you ask?"

"That's the name of the family who owns the company."

"What?" She looked up with a stunned expression.

He shrugged his shoulders and repeated, "She's somehow part of the family that owns that perfume company. Buhlg isn't a 'popular' last name if you know what I mean. — Now I didn't ask since I couldn't remember what you said."

*Could that be where~ Anything's possible, Rose Petal.*

"Come to think of it, it's really a present for me."

"What do you mean?" Callimay asked as she sniffed her wrist.

"I've missed that fragrance. It reminded me you were close by my side while we were at the Society. I looked forward to smelling it every morning. … Now I'm not saying having you by my side isn't enough, I—" Destan paused, her brushing the side of his face that was even more flushed now. "Is it the same one?"

"It is. Thank you. It's a wonderful present… for 'both' of us."

❦

Destan spoke for a moment with the man who drove him, and then took Callimay by the hand and escorted her inside. As he reached for the door handle it opened, "It is a relief to see you returned earlier than anticipated, Sir. I take it that would suggest most if not all of the evening's arrangements were in order?"

"For the most part. There are a couple things which will have to wait until tomorrow, but other than that, everything looks like it's ready." He sighed as he looked around, his eyes quickly fixing on Callimay. "We'll be leaving around noon. No later than twelve-thirty."

"Very well."

"Oh. If you could push dinner back to… let's say nine? Callimay and I have something to see to first."

Once Rocher excused himself, Destan took her to the desk and picked up the papers on top of a stack. She tried her best to be calm and contain herself, but at the same time knew he wouldn't think much of her being fidgety since he'd been gone all day.

"Okay, I'm listening," she nodded after she sat down and brushed her skirt out.

"Hope is the foundation o— I must have picked up the wrong one."

"What do you mean?"

"This isn't the speech." He shook the papers in his hand as he scanned the desk.

"Well let me see." She took them while he continued to search. "Not all of them, but this top one is. … Yes, this is it."

"No. No it's not, Calli. That's not how it started."

"It is now." She grinned; her eyes closed as she tilted her head and clasped her hands in front of her. "Surprise!"

As cute as she looked, Destan couldn't lose his annoyed tone, "What does that mean?"

"Just read it."

"I'm telling you this isn't it." He huffed as he rolled his eyes.

"Please? For me?"

"Alright," he cleared his throat; giving the page a gentle shake.

Callimay laughed to herself, gaining unwanted attention from her husband who now had his eyebrow raised, "What. Is it?"

"Just read. I'm ready." She answered quickly, biting her lip.

"I leave for one afternoon…" he mumbled and then started.

*Hope is the foundation of all our dreams and desires. It isn't some lofty possibility that is unreachable or nothing more than a fantasy; it is something to be grasped so long as we strive to do everything within our power to reach the goal our desires and dreams have instilled in us. It only hinges on what our desires and dreams are in the grand scheme of life: realistic and truthful or impossible and sinful. Though sometimes I would wager what is sometimes seen as impossible is still something that is truthful and should be hoped for.*

*It is because of this powerful reason that hope was used in the naming of this evening's gathering. All of you here have shown hope in your unwillingness to succumb to the relentless hold Fibromylophagia has over you or your loved one. To stand against what was seen as impossible for so long and fight back with determination and faith.*

*And let it be known we refuse to give up as well.*

*My father did not want to give treatment opportunities and leave it at that. He wanted to create an environment of hope. It was never about what he could monetarily or socially gain from this treatment that he sought after; but rather: what help he could offer, what hope he could give to those — who by no fault of their own — had found themselves in a less than desirable place in life. He wanted to remind those still fighting: we are not going to stop or say good is good enough. His whole life was dedicated to protecting others and looking out for their best interests. He gave his life—*

His voice finally gave out. He couldn't go on. Destan couldn't believe what he was reading. It was what every speech these past nine years never said but he felt in his heart.

He looked up from reading and asked, "H… how did you know?"

She rushed to his side, worried he was upset with her including that detail. Unlike what she was expecting, he put his finger to her lips and then wrapped her in his trembling arms and held her. He cried for a good while and then gathered himself, sitting beside Callimay to finish.

*…He gave his life because he knew it was the only thing he had left to give so he could protect those he loved. In what was such a short span of time, he did what all selfless people do: put himself in the other person's situation, looked for what would help them, and then acted.*

*I know for a fact that those here tonight do the exact same thing on practically a daily basis.*

*Look around you right now and remember you are not alone. There are others who know exactly what you're going through: the sacrifices, pain, struggles, and even the victories.*

*Empathy is yet another powerful thing God has given to mankind. In one way or another, those of you who have benefited from this drug know exactly what those who are still fighting are going through. Know this also: you're able to give them courage to keep going like no one else can. Admire their resolve to refuse surrender. Share in each other's sorrows. But instead of dwelling on them, use them as stepping stones toward a brighter future. Encourage and give hope to each other in ways only you who have been in that situation can.*

*On behalf of my father — and even my mother — I want to convey that 'hope' is still alive and well. It can be found in all of you. My father's motto was: 'the greatest legacy anyone can leave is the good change they were able to help bring about in others.' I know for a fact this life-mission was fulfilled. God bless you all tonight and this upcoming year.*

He slumped over and stared at the page, still mesmerized by it.

Callimay waited for a bit and then said, "Rocher said he could tell you weren't happy with it, so he asked if I would be willing to help him fix it while you were gone. I thought it was to keep my mind off you being gone, but by the end I realized I was the one who wrote the entire thing. … He said he did it on purpose."

"Why you sly—"

"I only did what was of absolute importance." Rocher defended as he walked over, his eyes looking a bit glassy. "And I take it this meets with your full approval and does not lack what the other did?"

"There's one glaring problem." Destan shook his head as he wiped his face. "Calli forgot to include herself in the last paragraph."

"I believe you can even see at this time, Milady, how this change was necessary. — Will you still be taking dinner later, or since things are to your liking would you prefer to be seated now?"

"I think we'll be fine to go ahead right now." Callimay smiled as she offered her handkerchief. "Right, Destan?"

"Yeah," he snapped to as he took the piece of fabric that was being shaken in front of his face. "Yeah that's fine."

# ~ 4 ~

Under normal circumstances, Destan would be the first one up and about; but today was a special day. This was going to be the first day in about four months since Callimay was "out". How could she sleep in on such a day?

The second the sun poked its finger through the curtains, she was wide awake. This thin strip of light toyed with the dust in the air; Callimay noticing it was shining on Destan's face: *He doesn't like it when he wakes up and there's sunlight in his eyes.*

There wasn't a moment to lose. Yes, it was early, but she never knew what time he exactly got up. It could be any moment. She tip-toed over and overlapped the velvet fabric, motioning to it like she was telling an animal to stay still.

Now that she was up there was no going back. The only problem was: she couldn't see much at all. But it wasn't so horrible. She'd always wanted to know what it was like to be a spy: working to find the target while not tripping any alarms… all under the cover of darkness.

In no time at all, she proved to be the worst spy to walk the face of Quidoria. Callimay never recalled dropping so many things before or realized how loud opening the drawers of her vanity was until the room was "full" of silence, and another person was fast asleep only a few feet away. And to add insult to injury: the harder she tried to be quiet the worse she got.

Each time she would gasp and look back, afraid Destan would be upset. But he didn't move… not an inch: *At least he's a heavy sleeper. I wish I were. ~ Land sake, Rose Petal! Are you trying to wake him up? ~ Of course not, silly. W—*

31

"What in the…" a groggy voice called out. "How long is it going to take you to get ready, Calli?"

"Destan!"

He rolled over and picked up the bedside clock; putting it close to his face, "It's barely six in the morning. Why in the world are you up this early? … Why don't you have a light on? — Look, unless it's going to take you six hours to get ready, come on back to bed. It's going to be a long day. I don't want you pushing yourself. And don't worry. Rocher won't leave without us. He wouldn't go to something like that alone."

She picked up her brush and put it back, slipping into bed as quiet as possible. Callimay tried her best to go to sleep, but she couldn't help entertaining the thoughts running through her mind. — Well, more like bouncing. — If anyone could "see" her thoughts they would have thought they were watching an intense tabletop-pong match. They darted back and forth over pretty much every detail Destan must have finalized the day prior… or didn't give a second thought since it didn't matter. But that wasn't about to detour her.

First on the list was that she'd never been to a ball before… let alone being the hostess of one. What a way to jump into something! How big was this ball and how many others would be attending? Was it inside or outside? If it were outside, what about the weather? What was the report for Rayleen? Maybe it would be better if she wore something a bit warmer.

This was quickly abandoned for the fact: due to the sometimes painful and more oftentimes paralyzing nature of Fibromylophagia, she knew those who weren't helped by the drug would at least have some type of walking aid if they weren't already wheelchair-bound. Was this a "normal" type of ball? She'd always known those gatherings to have nonstop dancing. How could that be possible if this were the case?

And then what about food? Were they going to be served a meal? With Destan organizing it, food sounded like a logical addition.

Then hearing the birds singing outside on the balcony made her wonder what kind of music there would be. There would be at least background music… right? Would equipment be set up with recorded music or a small orchestra/band playing? The latter seemed to make more sense since Kerogen was all about tradition and formality.

Wait. Callimay didn't even know how long the ball was going to last. Destan said it was going to be a "long day". Did this mean they would quite literally be dancing until the sun came up?

A complete sidetrack led her down the wandering trail of: was what she wanted to wear going be "too" formal since there could be those there who would not be financially as well off as she now was? Then again, would there? Was this ball free-of-charge? She knew it was an invitation event, but did that mean only certain ones were invited? Or was every person who had the disease sent an invitation?

Come to think of it, the more she thought the more she realized she didn't know much at all. Not that it scared her, but she wanted to be able to "play her part" correctly and not look like some bumpkin who didn't know what fork to use or that shoes were required. Callimay was not too long ago the one who was out-of-place since she didn't have expensive clothes. But then she recalled meeting Destan and how he was genuine and unconcerned — to a point — with his appearance. And look at all the money he had! Maybe those who he socialized with were the same. He did say he had high standards: *Well he sure didn't appreciate Toreon's approach. ~ So you 'did' think they were mortal enemies from the get-go, didn't you? ~ Well… I guess so. I wasn't gonna say anything because I didn't know for sure.*

With fuzzy thoughts now occupying her mind, she rolled over and sighed, forgetting what she'd been mulling over since she opened her eyes. The man who was lying beside her — passed out yet again — had mussed hair as usual and his shirt collar was turned up. With a loving touch, she combed his hair with her fingers and then fixed his shirt.

Destan smiled a bit as he took her hand in his; him not opening his eyes: *Go to sleep, Calli. I don't want you being exhausted before we get there, okay? — And don't worry about every little thing. You'll be a wonderful hostess. I know you will.*

The next thing she knew, someone was calling her name. They were saying other things, but she couldn't understand it. It was soft and sweet, yet deep and full… it had to be Destan.

She opened her eyes and saw he was already dressed.

He smiled, his eyebrow raised in curiosity, "Are you ready to go? I know I told you to go back to sleep but come on!"

"Oh no! What time is it? … Eleven! Oh no! I've got to— and then— there's not enough time before we have to go! I… I'm sorry Destan! I know you said no later than—"

"Hold on there," he laughed in a boisterous voice as he grabbed her by the waist and pulled her back to him. "I'm just messing with you. It's only nine forty-five."

"The clock says—"

"I changed it." He showed her his pocket watch.

"That's not funny, Destan Nevrille." She pushed him away and pursed her lips while planting her fists on her hips.

*Stuck your foot in your mouth there didn't you Boon? ~ What? ~ She used your last name. ~ Oh. I guess I must be in trouble, huh? ~ No. Not at all. I was just being sarcastic— of course you are, you dummy. ~ At least she didn't say 'mister' or use my middle name. I'd be banished to a guest room if she—*

"You bet your sweet life you would be. And for a week! — Rocher? Come back here."

"I in no way meant to interrupt your… spirited, discord." He froze, and with some force, walked back in the room.

"We're not fighting, Rocher. I'm just having a little fun and Calli isn't awake enough to appreciate it."

"A little fun, huh?" She grabbed a pillow and threw it at Destan who had his back to her.

He jerked from the impact and then whipped around; snatching it off the floor, "That's it. No mercy, woman! Prepare yourself."

"Woman? What kind of name is that? 'Mister'." Callimay rebutted as she ducked and then threw another pillow.

"I will excuse myself from the front lines. Please notify me once you have an affirmative ceasefire or one side indeed does offer terms of surrender; laying down their weapons of… interesting choice." Rocher shook his head as he left, knowing no one was listening.

It took a bit of doing, but once every piece of ammo was littering the floor and out of reach, Destan was able to convince Callimay the real time was what his watch said. And by this time, it was a quarter after ten. Looking back, they both had a good laugh as he worked to get things cleaned up while she got ready.

The process of getting ready took Callimay quite a bit more time than she anticipated; but they soon made their way downstairs for brunch. Even though she only wore the orange dress that once, the memories of their first evening at the mansion were forever tied to it in Destan's mind; bringing to mind them meeting as well as other fond memories: *Everything was so different then. … So very different. So many things changed which shouldn't h—*

*Shh. It's okay. Things are alright now.*

They were poised and mature in their demeanor at the table. But even so, it gladdened Rocher to know they were able to let their guard down and enjoy where they were in life with each other. He knew for Callimay it was a nice break from the formality she now found herself part of. Adjusting to a new environment was difficult for anyone; and even though she appeared to be doing well, Rocher knew she enjoyed those moments where she didn't have to act or say things a certain way.

It didn't seem like much time passed before brunch was over and the clock sounded the fifteen-minute warning: eleven-forty-five.

"Oh! I almost forgot." Destan snapped his fingers as he stopped short of the front door.

Callimay tilted her head as she turned to him, "Forgot what?"

"Just stay there."

By the look on his face she knew nothing was "wrong", but she was equally sure something important — to him — was missing. Even after she did a rundown in her mind of what he said they needed, she couldn't think of one thing he forgot.

He soon came out of their bedroom, hiding something behind his back, "Close your eyes and put your hands out, Calli."

"Another present? … Oh alright. … Wha— Destan!" She gasped when she felt the lush fur in her hands.

"It's a bit nippy out still, so I thought you would like this."

"I don— it's not real is it? Fur costs—"

"Don't 'ever' think you need to worry about money." He rested his hands on her cheeks. "I'm going to be a good steward with what I have. I promise to only spoil you with what I have 'left over'. Deal?"

𝕯

Callimay flinched when Rocher turned off the drive. It was the middle of the day and yet there were deep shadows everywhere. What a reminder this gave her.

*I guess I forgot we're hiding. … But maybe since Toreon's gone things will change? ~ Let's not get the collar before the dog, Rose Petal. ~ I'm just asking.* "Des—" she stopped when she saw him passed out beside her; like the last time they were in the car. *So much for that, huh? ~ Why is he sleeping? ~ How should I know? … Is he, actually? ~ Oh please. Destan wouldn't be ignoring me.*

With the same wonder of seeing new places as she appeared to have been born with, Callimay's eyes were glued to the windows. Everything made a rather abrupt shift from the dense woods to the open, rolling plains Kerogen was known for. It looked like a different world!

The architecture found in the country lent itself to the older, more traditional style which was copied from the area of Europe on the Homeworld. This is one of the ways the rich heritage of tradition and formality in Kerogen was established. In addition, there were no crop fields; only the occasional vineyard or tree grove dotting the landscape. These rolling plains were left mainly untouched — no small towns or what were also known as villages anywhere to be seen. This truly was a different "world" to her.

Vast estates and manors they passed by reminded Callimay: Kerogen was a country of people who were financially stable. It wasn't just because they had more money — even though a vast majority of them did — but it was because their government was on firmer ground and a type which offered more opportunity… a stark contrast to what she was used to in Faberton. This security bolstered the confidence and freedom found in the average citizen of Kerogen so they would engage in commerce to make better lives for themselves. They, for the most part, saw the wisdom of taking care of what they had all while keeping in mind how others would be helped through industrious pursuits.

As they entered Kerogen's principal city of Rayleen, Callimay was left in awe of the huge skyscrapers and multiple-leveled roadways which crisscrossed the city. It was equally baffling and confusing to her how Rocher knew where to go in what looked like a chaotic mosaic of dotted and solid lines on the roads; not to mention the countless signs with arrows pointing in every which direction.

He could tell she looked confused and possibly curious, so he rolled down the window between the front and the back, "Would this venture be your first in Rayleen itself, Milady?"

"It's my first time in any city of this size, Rocher." She moved over and sat on the seat against the partition so she wouldn't disturb Destan. "The largest city I've ever been in is Quaverly, and I was on the skirts and only there a couple times for work. From what I saw, there weren't skyscrapers like these."

"But as I take it, you 'have' traveled through the heart of Crosswall. Whipple Grove boasts quite a bit of such architectural feats."

"I don't count riding a train through as being 'in' the city, but I do see your point. … Rocher? How do you know where to go?"

The laughing wrinkles at the corners of his eyes burst wide as his mustache bobbed up and down from him chuckling, "It would be from eons of experience, Milady. And as it would specifically pertain to this occasion, please take into account I have driven this exact route many a time over the years."

*I guess anything new and daunting like this would seem rather impossible to anyone.*

"The gateway coming up would be the one for the University of Kerogen." Rocher tapped on the window to his right.

"Where Destan's father worked?" She looked out the window and then back to Destan who was now awake; him nodding. "My goodness that was a drive! Did he do it every day?"

No response.

"I will be altering to Bickard Avenue because of a collision, Sir." Rocher cut off to a matter-of-fact tone, seeing the conversation wasn't going to continue and he was doing something out of the ordinary.

"We've made good time to this point so that won't be an issue." He sighed as he looked out the window and stared at the bustling traffic. "Figures something happened around the weave this time of day."

Rocher rolled the window up, causing Callimay to turn around and fold her hands in her lap. She looked at Destan and smiled, but it was quite apparent he wasn't in the mood. Now everything felt awkward and strained. She felt as if she'd ruined the day by saying what she did.

Callimay jerked to steady herself when the car started turning; Destan not budging an inch. Without looking, he tapped the seat next to him and opened his hand to her when the car came to a stop. She got up and took his hand, sitting exactly where he gestured. He let go and put his arm around her, pulling her closer to him as he sighed: *Not right now, Calli. I… I can't. Not yet. And not here.*

*I understand.* She laid her hand over his heart. *I'm sorry.*

The last part of the trip was choppy by Callimay's definition: all the stopping and starting. And then they were in close quarters with so many other vehicles; these drivers being focused on nothing but their own destination. She couldn't help but notice how there were some who weren't patient or caring, "Did that man just— oh no! Oh my, that was so close. He could've hurt the person in that other vehicle!"

"Don't bother watching, Calli. There's more road rage on the city streets than anywhere else. And Saturday's worse than others since it's an all-day thing and not just peak hours for normal shifts."

"Why?"

"They think these streets are the interstate, and so they take it upon themselves to discipline people who won't go the speed they want to."

She huffed; her pursing her lips, "That's just rude."

He shrugged his shoulders, looking like he was working to suppress some amount of laughter, "That's city driving for you."

"What's going on? We're not at an intersection and there's no traffic. Why did we stop?"

"Because we're here." He smiled as he kissed her.

♄

The glass doors swung open for them as they entered the extravagant reception area. A cheerful and well-meaning young lady who was a bit younger than Destan and Callimay turned to greet them, "Welcome to the Conflux. How may I— oh! Well my goodness. You're earlier than usual, Mr. Nevrille."

"It appears we are." He noted in an upbeat tone as he checked his watch. "I take it we are not too early though?"

"No! Not at all. The overlook is open if you would like. Just be aware the finishing touches aren't quite complete if you decide to head on in. They should be done in about an hour, last I checked." She waved her hand over a sensor on the desk. "I will call if you would like me to when things are ready."

"Thank you Sonnie. That would be great." Destan nodded as he brought Callimay forward. "And as promised, you are the first to—"

"Oh good! — What a pleasure this is, Mrs. Nevrille!" She popped up from her seat full of excitement and just about jumped over the desk to offer her hand. "It's so wonderful to meet you! I admit I thought he was joking at first, but wearing a ring did seem a bit too far to take such a charade… and Mr. Nevrille spoke so much of you yesterday that I couldn't help but start to believe him."

"Oh?" Callimay smiled as she looked back at him. "It is a pleasure to make your acquaintance, Sonnie. Correct?"

"Yes. If there is anything you need, please feel free to use the phone in the overlook to contact me."

"The last little detail we talked about before I left yesterday… could it be put in the overlook before we get there?" Destan sounded a bit vague and obscure with how he was wording his request.

"Oh absolutely. I will see to it right away."

*You talked about me? You didn't want to keep me a secret? Th—*

*Why would I want to keep you a secret?*

"How did you hear me!"

Destan began to laugh as the elevator door closed, "What do you mean by that? I can hear you whenever you talk to yourself."

"But I have to leave the channel open so you can. I had it closed."

"Are you sure?" He exaggerated.

"I'm serious, Destan. I made sure you wouldn't hear me."

His forehead wrinkled from curiosity, "Are you positive you did it right? I don't pretend to know how you do it, but did y—"

"Yes, I did. I'm sure of it."

"Well that's strange. — Oh well. This is our stop. After you."

Callimay looked down when she heard how loud her heels were clacking; gasping and grabbing Destan's arm in fear of what she saw. This drastic shift caught him off guard, "What's wrong?"

"Why is the floor made of glass!"

He said light-hearted as he looked down, tapping his foot, "Well what do you know. I can see 'all' the way—"

"Destan, please!" She whimpered as she buried her face in his chest. "I'm terrified of heights. You know that!"

"I'm sorry. I didn't mean— it's only in the hall. The overlook isn't like this, I promise. Here. Keep your eyes closed and I'll guide you."

She trembled the entire way, trying to be confident and trusting that it was okay for her to take the next step. A part of Destan became angry, but he was only making every attempt he could to keep the evening upbeat and relaxing… brother did that backfire!

"Let me just carry you. Okay?"

There wasn't any hesitation on her part. In fact, she gripped his hair and clung to him for dear life the entire way: *I'm sorry, Calli.*

♄

When they got to the open-plan common area, it took him a while to convince her to open her eyes; let alone let him go: *It's alright, Calli. I won't let you get hurt; I promise. Everything's okay. I'm sorry about poking fun like that. I— it wasn't even tasteful banter.* *What do I do? I don't want her to feel like she's trapped in the ballroom all night. ~ What do you mean by that? ~ This is supposed to be a getaway of sorts. She's supposed to be free to go wherever she wants while she's here. At least that's what I intended. But if she can't walk in the hallway because~ Easy, Boon.*

"Destan? Could they… I don't know. Is there some way they can fix it so I at least can't tell it's a glass floor I'm walking on? Am I asking for something impossible?"

"They'll put a carpet down here in a bit. … Would that be enough?" He asked unsure as he looked around. His eyes starting to sparkle and a smile spreading across his face as he finished in a much more confident tone that was still quiet, "I have another surprise for you."

"Destan, really. I don't need an apology gift. I know y—"

"This actually doesn't have a thing to do with that. I've had this surprise ready since yesterday. I wanted something to give you that said 'thank you' in a special way. … It's a fact that I'll never be able to do enough to thank you, but that doesn't mean I shouldn't do anything when I can. — And before you ask, I'm saying thank you because you're why I'm alive. That's a debt I'll never be able to repay."

Trying her best not to cry, Callimay soaked in the loving words he was saying. These tender moments were becoming more frequent and slowly stringing together… this was lasting. She didn't want it to take such a dangerous accident to change him, but knew she was willing all along to endure whatever it took to help him.

He stepped to the side to reveal what he was hiding, Callimay gasping as she jumped up and rushed over, "Where did you find these! Why I… I never knew these existed!"

"Orange was mother's favorite color." He slumped his shoulders and sighed; then continued more cheerful when he saw her face, "Even though father was a biochemist in the sense of working with humans, he did most of his work with plants in high school and still 'tinkered' with them after graduating. He wanted to make something very special for mother on their first anniversary. They'd been apart for most of the year, so he was trying to do something to make up for the lost time. — Any orange rose to that point was an artificially colored white one. Mother loved them, but they had no 'good' fragrance and they never lasted. So, father developed a naturally occurring orange rose with the same fragrance of the deep red but the full bloom of a white."

"Your mother?"

"You're more like her than you'll ever know, Calli." He smiled as he fiddled with one ringlet of her hair which wasn't pulled back.

She said a bit choked up as she ran her fingers over the soft, velvet-like petals, "Thank you, Destan. Thank you for everything."

"And just because," he reached behind the bouquet and pulled out a corsage and matching boutonniere.

"You thought of everything, didn't you?"

Destan sounded a bit nervous, fumbling to open the clear, plastic box, "I tried to, but this wasn't my idea. It was Sonnie's."

Callimay laid her hands on his and smiled, "Even without them it would still be a perfect day."

Once their outfits were adorned, they sat and looked out at the vast metropolis that rolled out in front of them, "I have a question."

"What is it?" He replied as she leaned her head on his shoulder.

"Is Sonnie… is she deaf?"

"Don't worry, Calli. She's not ashamed of it and isn't offended if people realize that because of how she speaks."

"How does she know what I said, though?"

"She reads lips. It's kinda like how you read people's minds. — I guess that's not the greatest example, huh?"

"Not really."

A while later they heard voices followed by someone knocking. When Destan opened the door, a middle-aged man with well-styled two-toned hair explained as a couple other men who were dressed in a similar fashion passed by him, "Pardon my interruption, Mr. Nevrille. I thought I would come and tell you myself that you could start your walk-through if you wish."

"Calli?" He turned and motioned for her to come. "They put the carpet down. Come tell me if this works."

She crept over and summoned all the courage she had so she could look out; nodding and relaxing a bit when she saw the caramel-colored velvet rug in front of her.

"Good." Destan sighed; and then stopped when he felt Callimay grab his arm, "Oh! I'm sorry, Graygoré. I forgot to introduce my wife. — Calli? This is Graygoré, my event liaison here at the Conflux."

"I figured as much. — It's a pleasure, Mrs. Nevrille."

"It's nice to meet you." She bowed her head in respect, but corrected Destan: *That's not why I stopped you. Why are you leaving me here?*

*I'm just going to make sure everything's ready to go. I'm not going to be staying in there. We'd just— oh why do I even try. Come on.*

🜚

For some reason, Destan felt awkward holding Callimay's hand when there were others close by. It made no sense though: *I love her. And I 'do' want others to see that. ~ Then snap out of it. ~ I'm trying!*

He put those thoughts aside and focused on the moment when he heard Callimay gasp. There was shock and surprise on her face, but his knee-jerk reaction was that something was wrong. His eyes darted back and forth as he jerked her to him. Once he understood, his shoulders

dropped and he took a deep breath. In front of them was a waterfall…
"in" a building nonetheless! Hearing her astonished voice reminded
him everything was alright.

After a few moments, he took a step closer to it. It parted at the
middle and then fanned out to the sides, revealing the room behind it,
"It's the door?"

"Sure is."

"That's— I've never!" Callimay fumbled, so shocked as he took her
hand. "Wait. What is that?"

He shrugged; barely being able to hear the sounds of a piano above
the rushing water, "Oh, the orchestra probably."

"No. That song. I— it is! I know that song!" She dragged him in the
room and looked around.

At the concert-grand piano was an elderly gentleman who was in
his mid to late seventies; his posture and fluid cadence showing his
passion and dedication toward what he had done for quite some time.

She swayed back and forth as she listened; Destan standing beside
her and watching. At one point, she began singing lyrics that
apparently accompanied the music. One line in particular caught his
attention, but he waited to say anything until the song was done. The
only thing was, the elderly gentleman turned and asked first, "How do
you know this piece, miss?"

"My mother played it quite often, sir. I know it is a very old song
and one not many know anymore… it's dear to me though."

"No one else in the orchestra knows it or has the desire to learn it,
which is why I always arrive early. Practice is never a lost cause when
trying to keep an old mind fresh." He smiled as he tapped his temple.
"It is good to see you, Mr. Nevrille."

"It is good to see you as well, Mr. Benthvole."

"Might I be allowed to ask who this beautiful young woman is with
you?" He turned so he was looking at them straight on.

Destan nodded as he gestured to her, "This is my wife."

"I knew that the bachelor's life you were leading wouldn't hold you
forever. — It is a real treat to be in your company, Mrs. Nevrille."

Their conversation went on for a while in this polite and formal
manner before Mr. Benthvole went back to playing.

As they turned and walked away, Destan recalled the question he had, "What was that song, Calli? The sun doesn't rise in the east. It rises in the north. You know that."

She began to laugh, but hearing her voice carry so easily caused her to clap her mouth shut with her free hand. After calming herself, she replied in a hushed tone, "I'll admit I had the same question for my mother when I first heard it. — The song was written on the Homeworld… where the sun rises in the east."

"Well, that would also explain why I don't know it." Destan chuckled; his eyes showing the tiniest of a sparkle as he gazed into hers. "It is a beautiful song. And the more I think— it's rather fitting. … Oh stop looking at me like that. Doesn't it sound familiar to you? The story behind it? At least what I heard, the song sounds somewhat like our 'story'."

"I… I guess you're right."

He flipped in his mood and asked preoccupied, not paying attention as he looked to the other side of the room, "Hey, Calli? I'm going to check on a few things. You can stay here. It's not very exciting and will only take a—"

"My home is beside you, Destan. I came to be with you. … So I'll follow you wherever you go."

The ballroom was organized with a dancefloor in the middle and tables set for eight people around the perimeter. The seating capacity seemed small, but just as she was about to ask, Callimay heard voices and looked up. There was a second-floor terrace that wrapped around the ballroom: *Glad I looked before I asked. ~ Why? ~ Destan's starting to tense up. I don't want to irritate him.*

*I'm fine, Calli.* He replied a bit perturbed.

Once she settled from the shock of him hearing her yet again, she turned her attention to the finer details in the room. The centerpiece of the table was admittedly the first detail which caught her eye. But what crystalline chandelier that "sat" on a table wouldn't? The sparkle alone was enough to gain her full attention. And of course it being accented with tapered candles and fresh flowers added to its appeal.

Destan was methodical as he looked over every, single, tiny, detail. He pointed toward a few things and nodded, but then growled under his breath as he snatched up a slender, crystalline glass; marching over to Graygoré. Voices weren't raised, but Callimay could tell there was quite a bit of tension. Graygoré nodded and took the glass without saying much of anything, motioning to someone nearby.

"What's wrong?" She asked when he came back.

"I specifically made a note yesterday about no wine or champagne glasses being set out." He grabbed his clinched fist with his other hand. "I don't get why— we've gone over this time and time—"

"Well it's fixed now. … What else is there to check? Can I help y— Destan? What's really wrong?"

"Just that."

"Destan. Tell me what's wrong."

"Why can't you believe me and leave it at that?" He pulled his arm away from her and stomped off. "Why do you pester me by asking the same questions when I've already answered them?"

Rocher jogged over, hearing and seeing the outburst, "Please find it within yourself to forgive Sir, Milady. He has a set routine for these events that he 'never' deviates from. I regret I neglected to share this information with you prior to this instant. … Rest assured, this eruption is not due to you. — It is rather inflamed from the usual, but it 'is' commonplace for him at about this time. — I believe the light dawns on him each time he steps foot in here as to 'why' he performs this service; and it causes his anger to be kindled with regards to what happened to his parents so long ago. Inasmuch as that is a hypothesis, I do know quite certainly that the recollection of his motivation is the root of why he arrives so early. With my previous statement of his emotions playing a roll, it leads me to contemplate whether or not he 'seeks' out something to be amiss so he has a reasonable excuse to expel his emotions and justify his subsequent disappearance to the outlook until guests arrive. — But as much as he may seek, this venture does in fact hold weight in and of itself. There always is one detail requiring amendment which is of vital importance to Sir: the glasses being this year's victim. I have no doubt he acknowledges human error as a reality in life, but like someone we both held dear, he holds people to the standard that he has been held to; be it flawed or not. — And his struggle against inebriation was one that was founded from his anger of past memories. I know for a fact how meticulous he is when keeping such temptation away; so that alone could be the entirety of this circumstance. — Have no fear, he will return in an hour or so, not showing any recollection of the 'altercation' but apologizing when informed. … I am afraid I instigated things today by mentioning what I did about the University. I take the full burden of responsibility for his actions, Milady. Please do not hold this against him."

"You said he goes to the outlook?"

Rocher nodded reluctant, sounding concerned, "I would not ad—"

"Calli?"

She turned and saw Destan, breathing heavy and having a terrified look on his face.

Neither of them said a word.

Callimay now understood somewhat of why he reacted like he did; but it wasn't an excuse. She wasn't his play toy he could push aside when he wasn't "in the mood". Let alone the fact: he shouldn't lash out like this because of some simple detail that was missed; no matter how personal it was. People made mistakes. It wasn't a sin for them to forget that those glasses weren't supposed to be there. And the only reason she asked was because she cared. Yes, she was being persistent, but he was beginning to let things get out of hand emotionally and did, in fact, need to be reined in.

"Calli. I…" he tried to explain; his voice stuttering and shaking almost as much as his hand he had outstretched to her. "I messed up again. You could tell I wasn't doing well. I know you only wanted to help. I wasn't thinking clearly."

Crushing silence.

"Would you come with me?" Destan pleaded as he offered his hand a second time. "Please Calli? I need you."

❦

The dull tone of the building's air circulation system was the only sound in the room; the silence soon drowning it out. Time passed by like a raindrop stuttering while sliding down a window. But soon the tense moments of resistance were over with and she felt him calm to a "normal level".

Callimay looked up and saw Rocher open the door, motioning to her in a subtle way. The only thing was, as she tried to get up, Destan grabbed her hand and pulled her behind him.

Rocher calmed, not appearing startled or defensive, "I was only intruding long enough to inform you that the first of your guests have arrived. Rest assured, they are merely making confirmation of and settling into their accommodations. Miss Vonn t—"

"Oh. … Do the servers know?" He loosened his grip and flopped onto the sofa, looking at the clock before rubbing his face.

"Yes."

"Do you know if they've—"

"Everything's been seen to as you originally mentioned. I saw to it myself, Sir. And upon my inspection I found nothing else askew."

"Alright. Tell Sonnie it's alright if they wish to come up once they are settled in. We'll be there in a bit."

"Very well, Sir."

"Destan?" Callimay whispered, almost scared to reach out her hand.

"I'm sorry I lashed out at you earlier. I don't 'ever' have a right to be cruel. And you asking questions isn't stupid or nagging. — This is a safe place. I wouldn't have brought you here if it weren't; but even so, I may have made the most reckless decision of my life by bringing you here." He said in anguish as he shook his interlocked hands. "I forgot about myself. My anger. I felt myself getting close to losing it in there and I remembered—"

*Destan look at me.* She fell to her knees and reached out to his face. *I'm right here. I'm not going to leave your side while we're here or anywhere else. I… I understand this isn't something free of danger; whatever the source. I could tell you were getting close earlier, so I said something to h—*

"But I didn't listen!"

"Destan Quinton! I— just because you made a mistake in the past doesn't mean you need to keep doing it now. … Please listen to me." Callimay watched while he paced the floor, his emotions beginning to spike again. "Rocher told me you have a routine; and as much as he says I'm not the reason for the change, I know things 'have' changed since I came along. You may be acting the same as before but you have got to realize you can't do that anymore. … Destan? You wouldn't say everything changed in a bad way. Would you?"

"You're right," he dropped to his knees in front of her.

"We need tonight, Destan. 'I' need tonight. I feel so selfish saying it but it's true. But it's not because I want to be around people to show off my wedding band and fancy dress. I need to see you for who you are in situations like this. Destan? I know this is a big part of you. Don't push me out, please. I want to help. I want to be part of this. … I want to be part of your life: your wife."

His sigh sounded painful and agonized as he let it out, his body hunched over even more.

"Oh, Destan." She comforted as she turned his face so he was looking at her. "Destan let everything go for tonight. Toreon's gone. We're alright. — Remember why you're doing this. The hope you're giving others? Enjoy tonight like you always have. … Can you do that?"

"No."

"Why not?"

He pushed her bangs back behind her ear, "I can't enjoy it like before because I have you. Compared to now? I never 'enjoyed' these balls. Now I know I will."

She slipped her arms around him, sighing, "There's my Destan."

The thought lingered in his mind about something happening at any moment to make this dream a nightmare, but he remembered what good had come from everything. A year ago when he was in this room, he was alone with his anger and vengeance; fighting to be happy and not put up a façade. — He hated lying just as much as he hated the memories he couldn't erase. — But now? Now he was in the warm and loving embrace of the most beautiful woman in the world; one who gave her love without reservation. She kept giving it beyond what he thought he deserved. Though the circumstances of how they came together were far from fairytale-like, or even what he felt she deserved; the life he now had was so much more than he could've ever dreamed. Whatever happened from this moment forward would be bearable and faced with honesty, love, and courage… no matter what.

In short: he wasn't alone anymore. He didn't have to fight the world off without a "comrade-in-arms" right beside him. Someone loved him.

"Are you ready?" Destan asked as he stood, sounding more relaxed but keeping a stern undertone.

Callimay said with joy; feeling giddy like a little girl, "This is going to be so exciting! I can't wait for it all to begin!"

"Then let's go greet our guests so things can." He cracked that smile she loved seeing.

⅁

At first it was a crash-course on "how to be a proper hostess", but she followed Destan's lead and in no time caught onto what was expected of her. She enjoyed every second and in retrospect remembered how worthwhile things were: *I might not have gotten much positive out of being at the Society, but my ability to socialize has certainly improved! That's probably the 'only' useful lesson I learned. … This is how it's supposed to be with differences in social or financial standing: you may be different but you embrace it as your individuality; not as a stepping stone to put others down.*

People from Wyfal, Yerlonga, the neighboring country of Arable — as well as others — were in attendance. Destan knew guests by either name or formal title; them striking up a conversation with ease. And then there always came that moment of pause. They knew without him saying a word that Callimay was new and was fulfilling the role saved for only the closest of relations to the host. He savored this moment before revealing their suspicions to be correct.

Each person responded with joy and started acting as if they were his family members: in no way shy when it came to speaking of Destan; recounting instances of his hospitality and care for others in need. He did so well, hiding he was embarrassed, but knew at the same time Callimay loved they were so open and willing to tell her who they "saw" when they saw him. This was what she wanted.

During one of these stories, without doing anything to gain his attention, she saw he looked over and smiled at her; the butterflies she had tickling her heart: *Who knew under your stern exterior would be such a soft heart? Well… I knew it was there. — I love you.*

*I thought I could keep it hidden, but you just wouldn't give up.* He winked at her as he walked over to the next guests. *I love you too.*

Rocher walked up beside her toward the end of their meet-and-greet session, commenting, "Sir seems well-recovered and relaxed, Milady; wouldn't you agree?"

"He does. — I don't know if he did, but 'I' want to say h—"

"Sir already made amends with everyone; I assure you. Do not let the thought linger in your mind concerning it… nor the thought that I bear the same ability as you. I only deduced such a question from the expression on your face. I take it I was correct?"

"You don't need abilities, Rocher. You can read minds naturally. — Is this how Destan usually acts? I mean, is he like this when he's talking and socializing with people. … Is this how he was last year?"

"Fundamentally, yes, Milady. His actions tick all those boxes. — He fully enjoys this type of interaction with others. — Though I wouldn't hesitate to add my observation that he is even more so this night."

She tilted her head as she turned to face him, "Why is that?"

"It would be due — not in part but in whole — to yourself, Milady. I grant him finding religion was a large aid, but it does stand out to my eyes how you have come to alter him for the better in a way I do not believe it did. Perhaps it is because your presence brought to light some areas of his religious beliefs that were previously hidden… but that discussion is better had at another time. Prior to now he was one to be segmented in how emotions were displayed to 'any' individual; be it an acquaintance or contemporary." Rocher continued to converse with her; something the two of them became accustomed to in the past while Destan was secluded and distant. "I know he is but a far cry from where he needs to or would even desire to be, but he has indeed progressed by leaps and bounds because of your very presence."

"I… I d— I haven't done anything, really." She wrung her hands.

"Just please do not grow weary of reminding him of your presence, Milady." He requested as Destan motioned to him. "He has told me just you beside him in a constant manner gives him strength."

If this wasn't going to leave her shocked into confusion, then the fact that everyone had been greeted and so her "job" was now done was more than happy to do so. — What was she supposed to do now? — Destan laid his hand on her shoulder while he whispered in her ear. She smiled as she looked up toward him, taking his hand.

Their table was on the midway landing of the grand staircase which connected the balcony section to the main floor. Hushed comments and smiles were exchanged as well as the occasional muted wave as Destan escorted Callimay. He agreed with them all: she was stunning.

As if they were at the mansion, he pulled her chair out and gave her a kiss and a quick embrace before he took his seat. But then he rolled his fingers over the table and contorted his face as he looked at the distance between their chairs, "Well this isn't going to work at all. … There. That's better, wouldn't you agree?"

"Of course I would." She tried not to laugh as she fixed the tablecloth he bunched up. "Is it time for your speech?"

He took her hand and rubbed it, looking hypnotized, "Not yet. I've got to relax and pay attention to you and then eat. I can't give a speech if I'm constantly wanting to look at you or if I have an empty stomach."

She shook her head as she rolled her eyes, "Oh. I see."

"Can you?" He exaggerated as he tried to mimic her face.

"Really Destan? Now? Here?"

"Why not?" He grinned as he gave her a quick kiss.

Servers all but popped out of the walls and began to take dinner requests while serving appetizers. Callimay was accustomed to the lavish food served at the mansion, but as she picked up the menu she became overwhelmed, "Grilled salmon, filet mignon, lobster t— Destan how am I supposed to choose from all this!"

"Just get it down to three. You can pick and choose what you want and Rocher and I can split the rest."

"I may be learning this whole 'formal dining' thing, but I do know that's not right: shoveling food off of plates onto others after it's been served. Why would you even suggest that?" She refused, trying to talk as soft as possible as she hid her mouth with the menu.

"Well if that's how it's going to be." Destan laughed loud and clear.

"What are you doing!" She whispered, looking embarrassed.

*Whatever happened to talking like this?*

*You're kidding, right? … No, you're not. Ugh!*

"There's my Calli." He smiled as he calmed down. "Don't worry about it. I'll explain and have those in the kitchen do it for us. Would that make you feel better?"

"But what if I pick something you don't like? And I'd still have to pick 'three' sides!"

Rocher chuckled as he took his seat across from them, "Oh, have no fear, Milady. Sir only constructs a menu of foods he prefers. He'll gladly eat anything you choose regardless of the arrangement. And I can whole-heartedly confirm the same can be said for myself… even if I do have a strong contender."

"Why don't you just pick something?"

"Good evening Mr. Nevrille, Mr. Jackman. And good evening to you Mrs. Nevrille. It's quite a thrill to finally meet you! You've been the talk for all of today. I admit I couldn't believe it — and I'll be out fifteen solera now; but don't be concerned." The server complemented as he put personal-sized plates with a couple small portions of appetizers at each setting. "What may I order for you all tonight?"

"Well. The lady will have the grilled salmon with duchess potatoes, risotto, and spiced vegetables." Destan dragged out as he looked at Callimay who nodded after each choice; finishing without looking, "I'll have the lobster tail with scalloped sweet potatoes, steamed broccoli, and Cobb salad with the pomegranate vinaigrette."

"Wonderful choices. — And you Mr. Jackman? What may I serve you this evening?" The server nodded as he finished writing down the order and turned his attention to Rocher.

"Nothing of any noteworthy alteration, Percivon. I'll have prime rib — medium rare — a healthy amount of sautéed mushrooms and onions over mashed potatoes; stringed onions and potato soup."

He smiled and nodded as he looked up from his notes, "I would expect nothing less. — Will you all be waiting to order dessert?"

"I believe so." Destan nodded as he looked to Callimay and then Rocher. "Yes, we'll wait."

Within the half hour, rich and full flavors of various meats, roasted vegetables, and other foods were filling the ballroom. The low roar of people talking was now hushed to allow the occasional clank and clatter of forks and knives to be audible.

When they were served, Destan waited for Callimay to try each part of her meal — as he always did — and then asked, "How is it?"

"It's wonderful. Your choices were perfect."

"Good," he nodded as he put his hand atop hers and then switched his focus. "Rocher?"

"Sublime as always, Sir."

It didn't take but a few minutes for Callimay to notice he sat there and watched everyone else with what looked like glazed-over eyes and a soft smile. He wasn't eating. She got Rocher's attention and motioned to the untouched plate; not wanting to bother Destan.

*Yet another of Sir's irregularities for such occasions, Milady. Have no fear. He is alright.*

She glanced at him once more, him noticing, "Is something wrong?"

"No," she shook her head as she reached for her water glass. "I just wanted to make sure you were doing alright."

"Oh. I'm fine."

The servers made their rounds refilling glasses and checking to ensure everyone's food was to their liking; then one by one, place settings were exchanged for desserts. This change in the air — the sweet and tart aroma of fruits as well as sharp and fragrant spices — livened everyone's chatter. In a way, this appeared to hint toward something special coming.

Destan reached for their dessert menu and handed it to Callimay, "What would you like?"

"Well let's see what is available first, shall we?" She sighed, almost dreading to look at it. "What is this? It's a sentence in and of itself!"

He leaned over and turned the menu so he could see it, "Oh! It's just chocolate cake filled with cherry sauce and topped with cherries; it all covered with fudge and edible gold."

Callimay sat there for a moment and slowly blinked, him throwing his head back, "I don't make the names, woman."

A perturbed sigh rolled off her lips as she looked back at the menu; but then she perked up a few seconds later, "Oh! Cheesecake!"

"You take a fancy toward it, Milady?"

"I got it once a year: on my birthday. It was so very expensive that it was a rarity and saved for that single occasion. The place mother would get it at— the place we ate at. Remember? It was like a slice of paradise: so creamy and silky. The crust was a rich butter cookie like I've never tasted before. And the fruit! Oh my. It was so fresh and tart that I…"

"What's wrong, Calli?" Destan asked concerned when she faded out and laid the menu down so she could fold her hands in her lap.

She shook her head and bowed it; avoiding his gaze, "Nothing. I just realized I was babbling on about—"

"Oh let it not concern you, Milady." Rocher encouraged as he leaned forward. "I rather delight in the opportunity to participate in your reminiscing. Pay Sir never mind if he does not. Please. Continue."

"Thank you," she began to blush. "But there's not much else to say. It was the only time my mother would splurge, by her standards. And yet she did it every year for my birthday."

After a few moments passed, Destan smiled as he took her hand, "What fruit do you want?"

"Cherries."

He looked over to Rocher and then back to Callimay, all while his emotions spiked in a strange way, "What? If they don't have them I'll just have it plain."

*Like I said: you're more like my mother than you'll ever know.* He answered in a tender voice as his eyes became glassy.

Percivon asked in his chipper tone as he adjusted his glasses, not knowing he was interrupting a conversation, "Have we decided upon desserts for the evening?"

"The lady will have cheesecake with cherry compote. I will have the Pavlova with wild berries. — Oh, Calli. Do you want tea?"

"Well. Umm. Would you happen to have a red tea? Endurance's Blush, by chance?"

"Indeed we do, Mrs. Nevrille. — Any for you, Mr. Nevrille?"

"No," he responded in utter shock. "I'm. Fine."

Rocher chimed in, "I will have the tiramisu and a cup of coffee."

Percivon smiled as he wrote, an underlying tone of laugher in his voice, "Two measures of vanilla-peppered cream and a healthy drizzle of pure honey if I remember correct."

"Your memory is nothing short of the Records of Inu."

"I appreciate your comments, Mr. Jackman. ... Very well then! I will be out with those as soon as possible. Is there anything else you require at the moment? ... Very well, then. I will be back momentarily."

*Even red tea.* Destan sighed. *And Endurance's Blush at that.*

*Your mother drank it?* Callimay responded, taken aback.

Destan nodded in a thoughtful manner as he looked out at everyone before closing his eyes: *Practically every day. It's an aroma I can smell even now.*

*It won't bother you will it?* "Per—"

*No Calli. Not at all. … Do you put sugar in it?*

*Just a little. Either a spoonful or just one cube. I only w—*

*Want it sweetened but not sweet.* He finished as he squeezed her hand. *It's meant to have an edge while enjoyed at the same time.*

He sat there, leaning his forearm on the table with his head bowed for a moment, then sat up and took a deep breath as he smiled, "I'm alright now, Calli. … I'm sure."

This situation, though a detour from what was going on, did not keep her from remembering Destan still hadn't touched his food. It befuddled her to no end and made her feel strange eating alone. Every time she tried to wait, he would tell her to go on without him. It got to the point she was worried about what happened earlier: *Are you sure everything is alright, Destan?*

*Quite.* He nodded as he glanced over. "How's the cheesecake?"

"Delicious. B—"

"Good. I'm glad." He patted her hand and then looked out again.

Not but a moment after she finished, Destan nodded to Rocher; who with a firm but gentle handle on his spoon, tapped his water glass to gain everyone's attention.

After taking another deep breath, he let go of Callimay's hand. It took a moment for him to find the small device that was buried in his pocket, but he got it out and fixed it on the inside of his lapel, saying nervous as he stood, "I apologize for having notes this year. Things weren't falling into place until the very last moment. … You can all thank my wife for it happening at all."

A round of applause rose from the crowd as he looked down to her, taking her hand and encouraging her stand to for a moment. She did and knew she was blushing the entire time — her cheeks feeling like they were on fire. As she sat back down, she looked up and saw how his eyes sparkled. Destan began reading the speech, still sounding nervous, and then at the point where he stopped the first time, he looked out. Coming as a shock to her, he finished it without hesitation or looking at the papers, yet saying exactly what Callimay wrote. This was what he'd wanted to say all these years… it just wasn't in writing. He didn't know "how" to say it; yet somehow she did.

The sound of gasps and sniffles prompted her to look out to those listening. She could see handkerchiefs in-hand and couples huddled together with heads bowed. Just as Rocher promised, she understood this was so much better than the original. It not only spoke to the heart of the one delivering it… it spoke to everyone else on a personal and heart-felt level.

When he finished, there was this overpowering emptiness in the air. Destan sat down and closed his eyes while the orchestra began playing to fill the void he inadvertently created. And yet the music was quickly drowned out by a building wave of thunderous applause and cheers. This sounded more like a rally than a formal ball!

He rose and put his hands out to calm everyone, thanking them and encouraging them to enjoy the rest of the evening. The orchestra started again, many of the tables deserted and the dancefloor filling.

Once this was all done and taken care of, he started eating. Rocher excused himself when someone waved to him, leaving Callimay to ask the direct question about his bizarre behavior. She tapped her finger on the table to get his attention, "What happened to the whole: 'I can't give a speech on an empty stomach' excuse you gave me earlier?"

"Oh… well. I guess I forgot." He put his napkin to his mouth. "I do tend to get caught up in the moment. … I don't want them to listen on empty stomachs. I guess I should have put it that way, huh?"

"That would have made more sense, but I still don't understand how 'you' of all people would forget food. You 'never' forget!"

Destan looked at her with a more serious look, "Alright, Calli. May I enjoy my meal now?"

"I'm sorry."

"I didn't mean—"

"I love you." She replied, sounding like she understood.

"I love you more, Calli."

Adding to his bizarre behavior was the fact he held her hand the entire time he ate. She wasn't exactly sure what to think of this "type" of affection out in public: *It's nothing, Rose Petal. ~ Yeah, but~ Look at him. Is he Toreon? ~ No. ~ Why is he holding your hand? ~ I— he loves me. ~ Then why are you so uncomfortable? ~ It just reminds me about him. Okay?*

*I'll stop if it'd make you feel better, Calli.* He took his hand away; his voice and face showing his concern. *I didn't mean to bring up bad memories. I really was just doing it because I wanted to. Not—*

*Oh no! You're fine.* She jerked his arm as she took his hand back.

He gave her a kiss and then smiled, *Let me know, okay?*

As always, his plate was all but licked clean when he was done. She couldn't help but laugh to herself as he picked apart the Pavlova: eating each fruit separate and saving the meringue for last.

*Hey. I've seen you eat a lemon meringue pie, Callimay Rose.* He defended as he looked at her out of the corner of his eye. *You don't have 'any' room to make fun of me for picking something apart and eating it separately.*

*I— but— you're right.*

After he finished, Destan sat there relaxed and content as he watched everyone enjoying themselves. Quite often he would rub Callimay's hand, to which she would look over and see him smile a bit more than the time before. He "felt" different as far as his emotions were; and he even "looked" different. Yes, he changed after Toreon, but even so: she could tell this wasn't something tied to that, or even the Society. She was getting to see more of who he was on the inside… and she was soaking it all in.

One guest came up and spoke with Destan for a moment, then remarked, "Since you have a partner this year, you should join everyone, Mr. Nevrille."

He shook his head, trying not to chuckle, "This is for everyone else."

"Well I'm not the only one who has been asking if you two would grace us with a dance." The man gestured to the dancefloor. "I was just nominated to ask."

Callimay remained quiet and smiled as she listened.

"We wouldn't want the nominee to be looked down upon, would we?" Destan asked as he stood and offered his hand. "Shall we give it a go, Mrs. Nevrille?"

"Whatever you would like, Mr. Nevrille." She nodded; and then shivered: *That felt wrong; us using titles and not our names.*

*I know,* he winked; there seeming to be a slight hush in the air as they came down. *Let's play along though, huh? For everyone else?*

*Wait just a second! You told me you didn't know how to dance! What are you— don't you dare think for a moment I can jump in and lead. I've never even been to a dance before!*

*I've watched for countless hours. It doesn't look difficult at all.*

*Oh dear.*

Callimay was obviously nowhere near as optimistic as her loving and trusting husband was. She knew they both were musically inclined, so there wouldn't be any issues with keeping to the rhythm of the music; but still, she had no idea what this would end up looking like.

Destan's hold on her was sure and steady, helping calm her nerves as they walked to the middle where people weren't moving much. They turned to face each other; him smiling as she slipped her train bracelet over her wrist, *I'll do everything possible to make sure I don't step on your feet, okay?*

As the first notes sounded, she was even more relieved, knowing it was a slower song: it would help her keep up with Destan. He was mindful to walk at a pace she was comfortable with; it's just — this wasn't "walking". And it also helped that the steps he was leading her in were much easier than she was expecting. In a way, it felt like he were a natural at this!

When she saw two couples bump into each other, she realized: *Sitting and watching doesn't do dancing any justice as far as the fear of bumping into someone goes. How in the world do they do it! ~ You mean 'don't' do it, right? … This seems much more like a contact sport than a soft-spoken pastime. Land sake! Now don't step on his feet.*

*Calli. Remember? Let me lead.* Destan calmed as he pulled her closer. *Just focus on me. I'll keep you safe. I promise. And don't worry about my feet. I can take it.*

*I'm sorry.*

*Hey. Look at me. … It's alright. You're just trying to watch out for others; I get it. But let me do the worrying. Deal?*

*Deal. … I love you, Destan.*

*I love you more, Calli.*

They danced around and around, her not realizing until the end, that they were the only couple doing so. Destan saw how slowly but surely everyone stopped to watch, and felt thankful they gave him the ability to lose himself in the moment with the love of his life.

Callimay jumped when applause and cheers erupted from the crowd; hiding her face the second she realized they were alone. He gently coaxed her to his side so he could take her arm, and then after bowing he escorted her to their table where Rocher was, "I must say, Sir; you are a confounding person at times. How in humanity did you muster the comprehension to achieve the feat you just did?"

"I surprise myself sometimes, Rocher. I haven't the foggiest idea. … I don't even know if I could do it again." He chuckled in a whisper as he pulled Callimay's chair out. "You kept up very well, Calli. And I'm so proud that you relaxed and didn't worry."

"It felt so good to. I— oh, I didn't mean I don't trust—"

"I never said or thought that." He smiled as he brushed the side of her face. "I'm glad you enjoyed it."

Much to her relief, they only danced that one time. And for good reason: Destan took her to those who couldn't dance so they could talk with them and do what they could to encourage them at that time. It was something he had always done, but having Callimay with him and offering her words and support was something he treasured. Uplifting and encouraging others was second nature to her, and reminded him she'd been doing this since the day they met — in fact them meeting on orientation day was due to her selflessness.

This realization brought something to the forefront of his mind again: her selflessness was a product of her willingness to submit to God's Authority. Destan knew he had a long road ahead to become the leader he needed to be, but he wasn't going to give up and was grateful to have a wife who was as understanding and patient as Callimay.

After a few more hours, couples began to trickle out, followed by larger groups. They were sure to find Callimay and Destan to give them their best wishes for their marriage and say they looked forward to seeing them next year.

It was then that she was reminded: *I get to do this again, that's right!*

Once the last guest left, Destan spoke with Graygoré, handing him a slip of paper from his wallet; doing the same with the orchestra leader. He stopped and specifically spoke to Mr. Benthvole before making his way to Callimay who was cleaning one of the tables, "Woman! What are you doing?"

"Destan!" She whipped around. "I… I was only trying—"

"Don't worry, Mrs. Nevrille." Percivon smiled as he put his hand out to take what she had in her hands. "There's not much left so please don't feel you need to help. — Do you want the flowers sent to H—"

"I already spoke with Graygoré, yes." Destan nodded as he took Callimay's hand. "It was a wonderful evening. The food and service were as I remember last year. Thank you for your help."

"It was my pleasure, Mr. Nevrille. You were sorely missed at the end of the season last year."

"I appreciate it and hope it won't happen again."

"Safe travels home."

Destan started for the door and stopped, "How was it, Calli?"

"This was the most wonderful evening I've had in so long."

"How about one last dance? It's just us. No fear of thundering rounds of applause and cheers… or people to bump into."

"I'd never turn it down. Not even if the whole world watched."

He nodded to the pianist; the same song which was playing when they first arrived rising through the air.

Not a moment later he whisked her away to their little paradise. Away from the harsh reality of their lives and the worries that went with it. The soft notes sang to them as they paraded around in the darkened room, silhouettes of them being the only thing visible.

Aside from his outburst during the winter, Callimay felt safe around Destan; but what she felt now was a safety which was at the same time liberating. There was no need to think about what was going to happen next; no distractions between them. It was just them. Nothing nor no one was fighting to pry them apart or force them into situations which could put them in harm's way. For that small slice of time the world was safe… and she wasn't alone.

As the last notes faded, the two of them clung to each other, knowing their safe world would disappear when the music was gone…

and with that, bring back the harsh reality they couldn't escape. Neither of them wanted it but they both knew it was inevitable.

Destan had Callimay pulled close against his chest, his hands so gentle but strong. Hearing his heart beat was a sound which melted her heart. It was a constant reminder there was someone who thought of her in such a way to allow her to stay close enough to them so she could hear the beating of what they promised beat because of her.

The room was almost black now; only a few candles offering light. After glancing around, Callimay looked up. And as if he knew she was looking at him, Destan opened his eyes and looked down to her. She then said in a quiet voice, "Thank you for a wonderful evening."

"It was wonderful because you were here, Calli." He sighed, sounding sad as he rubbed her back.

"Well, at least we get to keep each other; even if we can't stay here forever. Right? … Destan?"

He held onto her for a few more seconds and then let go as he admitted, "I finally know what's been missing. I don't know why it took me this long to figure it out."

"Missing? Missing from what?"

"From the balls. … It was you. It's always been you." Destan praised as he framed her face; and then asked in his well-known monotone voice, "Are you ready to head home?"

"As long as I go home with you."

"Rocher is getting the car. We can head on down and wait outside."

ℬ

As the door shut behind them, the low rumble and hum of city life greeted them. Callimay suspected everything would be quiet since it was so late — the sidewalks rolled up and the town off to bed as the ancient saying goes — but it was quite apparent this city never "slept".

Rocher wasn't there yet, so they stood and waited. Not but a few seconds later, Destan turned and said, "Calli, you're shivering."

"Oh! I completely for—"

"Excuse me," a man apologized after he ran into her. "Pardon me, I should have been watching. I'm sorry."

"You're alright." She assured as Destan jerked her to him. "W—"

"Be careful and watch where you're going." He warned in a gruff tone as the man backed away.

The man turned and staggered into the street, bumping into the car Rocher was in. After mumbling a few words and waving at him, he kept going. He even stopped and waved at them a couple times.

"Don't, Calli." Destan gripped her wrist. "Let him leave."

"But he looks like he—"

*What 'honest' homeless person would be out at this hour and just happen to bump into the only two people standing around for blocks? Don't let go of my hand.*

She obeyed, watching the man continue to stagger across the street as Rocher walked up to them.

"I took the liberty of informing the authorities just now. Was he harassing or merely passing by?"

"Did you see anyone else?" Destan asked suspicious as he hurried Callimay to the car. "They don't come out by themselves. At least no cartel I've ever heard of operates this way."

"No one, Sir. At least none I could see."

"Let's go." Destan urged as he shut the door.

"W… what's going on?" Callimay asked scared.

He opened his mouth and then paused for a few moments before he answered, "Not all people who wear worn clothes or stagger around like drunkards are homeless beggars, Calli. There are street gangs — cartel — which prowl around at night, looking for people to rob… or worse." *I've gotta say though, they don't come 'this' far downtown: the risk isn't worth what they could gain. And for it to be one, lone man?*

"Destan?" She pleaded as she grabbed his jacket lapel.

"The more I think about it…" he faded out as he rubbed his chin; and then finished after he hit a button on the door, "Rocher?"

"Yes, Sir?"

"Take the detour. I don't think he was cartel."

"Very well. Detour it is."

"I don't know for sure but I'm not willing to take the chance and risk your safety. You remember what Dakoe said about fieldwork? Well, maybe the man—" he backed off when he saw how scared she was. "You're still shivering and look exhausted, Calli."

"I… I don't— you don't— Destan?" She asked frantic as he took his jacket off and put is around her.

"Rest on the way back. It's going to be about three hours."

"How can you expect me to just go to sleep!"

"Come here," he sat back and had her sit on his lap; wrapping her in his arms. "We're safe in here. I promise you. And I said I wasn't sure. 'I' might be over-reacting." *I pray I am.* "But I'd rather keep us out an extra hour and be safer, than run back as fast as we could and risk you not having somewhere safe to be right now."

"Who could it have been?" She shuttered, fighting off a yawn.

"Don't think about it anymore." He began to rock her. "Get some rest. I'm sorry I startled you. … Calli?"

"Yes?"

"W— how would you…" he said rather nervous, trying to get his thoughts together. "Let's say a prayer. Alright? When we're worried or unsure it's what we're supposed to do. Right?"

Destan rocked her for a while, calming her inner thoughts with tender and soft words when he could. It put him at ease — in a sense — when she fell asleep, but he felt like he did when they escaped from the Society: he was infuriated they couldn't enjoy anything for any amount of time.

After all this, he noticed Callimay had a pained look. He scolded himself for letting his emotions spike; but as he worked to calm down, he realized he wasn't anywhere near as upset as he knew would cause this level of discomfort. It was then that he began to wonder if she was having a "normal" migraine flare from the huge swing in emotions.

Ever since Doctor Gerould explained what they were like, it grieved him that she had to go through so much pain so often. Granted, Destan knew the ones he was describing were due to his tie to her, but the "normal" ones couldn't be much different. It made him wish he'd done more to help her the day when she wasn't doing well and almost passed out in his arms when they were at the Society. He even recalled a couple times she would show up late for tutoring and not be herself. Looking back, he could remember seeing that same pained look in her eyes. Even though Callimay didn't say anything, he didn't take the initiative to find out if something was wrong.

ॐ

When they got back, he did his best to not wake her; being oh so quiet and careful as he got out of the car and carried her to their bedroom. He laid her down and went back to close the door, only to hear her mumble, "I don't know how Rocher does it."

"We won't see much of him for the next couple days." He chuckled as he shook his head.

"That's good." She smiled and waved to him.

"What did you say?"

"I love you too."

"But I—" he paused, realizing she was about ready to fall asleep. "Don't you wanna change into something a bit more comfortable?"

"Goodnight De…" she drifted off.

He smiled as he stroked her hair, "Goodnight my Calli."

ॐ

During the early morning hours, Destan woke from hearing Callimay mumbling and feeling her tossing and turning. He rolled over and tried to get her to wake up, but it was as if she couldn't hear him. The more he tried to calm her, the worse she got, "No. No please! Please don't!"

"Calli? Wake up. Calli, it's just a dream. Everything's alright."

"No. No don't. Please stop!"

"Calli, please! Wake up. You're fine. I'm right here."

She all of a sudden screamed herself awake and started looking around the room terrified as she tried to catch her breath, "I…"

"It's alright, Calli." He wrapped her in his arms. "You're alright. It was just a dream. It's alright."

"Oh Destan. It was horrible. I've never been so—"

"Don't think about it. Shh. It was just a dream." He cradled her head next to his and rocked her until she fell asleep.

~ 5 ~

Not but a few days later, Callimay felt like she was waking up to a dream. She could hear the beautiful sound of a piano playing as she watched the sun danced with the dust in the air. Half asleep, she sat in bed and listened to the melody that she hadn't heard in so long. Before long, she began swaying back and forth, humming along.

When a few swallows began bickering outside the window, she jumped to her feet; realizing this wasn't a dream, "Destan!"

He wasn't anywhere around.

None of this — including the music — was a dream. She grabbed her robe and rushed down, terrified.

Once she got to the foot of the stairs and came around the corner, she was left in utter shock as to who was playing… and "what" they were playing. — Destan was sitting in perfect form as his long fingers rolled over the broken cords of the piece he forbade her to play.

The further he ventured into the piece, the more he was carried away and absorbed in the memories of the instrument. He brought to life a different set of emotions that were already contained within the piece; making it sound more like a mournful cry.

Destan was about halfway through the movement he was playing, when he stopped, raised his hands away from the keys and stared at the white and black ivory; listening to the last of the notes he struck. This didn't look planned. And by the emotions she was feeling from him, Callimay wasn't sure what she should do. They weren't "dangerous" emotions, but the amount he had "could" become dangerous.

Rocher was standing by the kitchen door, looking just as shocked as she was. He encouraged her by nodding his head and motioning to

65

Destan, understanding more of what was needed in that moment: *Please, Milady. Don't be fearful.*

She took a deep breath and walked over as quiet as she could; the last notes fading when she sat beside him. He appeared oblivious to her presence: his hands quivering in midair and eyes still closed.

Biting her lip to keep it from quivering, she picked up where he left off, playing only the melody. Destan brought his hands down; but unlike what she was expecting, he took her free hand and pulled it to his chest while he played the base cleft; matching where she was.

As they continued, he never opened his eyes and kept pouring out his sorrow while she inserted her love.

The ending of this classical sonata was somber and soft regardless; this interpretation being no exception. Destan was all but doubled over as the last of these depressing notes faded. He gripped Callimay's hand tighter and tighter, prompting her to turn and see a steady stream of tears racing down his face; his entire body trembling.

It was torture to Callimay: her heart breaking for him all over again. She hated seeing him like this. But what could she do?

"How did you know?" He asked in a quiet and shaky tone, not opening his eyes. "How did… how did you know?"

What did she know?

Callimay took her handkerchief and wiped the tears from his face, then did her best to answer in her sweet and soft way that he had come to love and adore, "I love you so much."

Destan opened his eyes and looked at her smiling face. She wasn't being insensitive; in fact it never crossed his mind. The joy that was on her face was accompanied by sorrow that was hidden in her eyes; but even so, it reminded him of her love for him.

On the other hand, she saw the raw pain in his and knew none of this was easy. It was — in fact — a fight; but he managed a small sliver of a smile and got out, "I love you too, Calli. I… I'll be back in a bit."

"Alright." She whispered as she squeezed his hand one last time and then let go.

Once the door closed, Callimay heard sniffling, "Rocher?"

He was standing there, looking perfectly normal, but his nose and cheeks were flushed. — This was difficult on him too. He was there with Destan. He'd lived a different side of this. — It took a bit, but even though he was choked up, he explained, "Ma'am instructed Sir on how to perform that very piece, Milady. He was gifted with said skill and it was nothing of a chore for him to master the entire piece — all three movements — at such a tender age. I would also add this movement was his favorite since it was correspondingly Ma'am's. On the rare occasion he would forget his place, she would take up her place beside him and begin forming the melody; remaining to finish the piece with him… just as you did not but a moment ago. … The night Sir's parents were ripped from this world and his sight— it is seared into my memory as I know it is into his. He came to that culminating point when he abruptly stopped; hearing his mother's scream and her shrill voice being followed by subsequent shots. Upon hearing those bone-chilling sounds, he escaped my ill-placed grasp and searched them out. — I can, with all the confidence in the world, assure you that what you did helped and aided in so many avenues as far as healing and moving ahead from the past. It is not lost to me how I can only speak for my own person in such matters, but I am confident Sir has experienced similar closure. Now if Milady will excuse me."

"Of course, Rocher," she sympathized as he vanished from sight.

Callimay rose from her seat, looking stunned. She put the fallboard over the keys and then with a gentle hold, closed the cover. The piano never had a dust cover on it and yet it was always in pristine condition. She never recalled seeing anyone clean it but it had to for it to stay the way it was. Who did Destan trust? He hadn't let her touch it until now: *Maybe that's what he does every evening before coming to bed? ~ And he's always up well before you, so it's quite possible he does it then.*

Regardless of who kept it in this condition, she knew it was taken care of like the memory Destan had of his mother: he valued and protected everything he had left. Callimay knew exactly how he felt. Aside from her clothes, the little stuffed dog was all she had of her original life. Granted, her bond to it was different since she didn't know who Lanta was. — She "assumed" it was her mother. — It could very well have been a sibling or another relative… even a friend.

She looked at the hand-crafted instrument which meant so much to the man who meant everything to her. Its rich, marbled wood tones complemented all the other wooden pieces in the house. The finish felt like velveteen-glass — if that were even possible — and shimmered as it reflected the thin streams of sunlight.

As she came to the French doors, Callimay noticed Destan's duster coat hanging on the rack: *He… he was wearing a regular shirt, blazer, and khakis! I— how~ Something happened last night or this morning.*

ℬ

While walking outside a bit later, she expected to see him standing and looking off into the ocean surf… but he wasn't there! She was stricken with fear and ran around to the front; finding him lying on the front lawn, staring up at the crystal-clear sky. She breathed a sigh of relief and scolded herself for reacting like she did.

*You can come over, Calli. It's alright.*

She flinched and stared at him, looking confused. After a moment, she rubbed her temples and took a deep breath, walking across the lawn, "It's a good thing you have that blazer on, or your shirt would be stained… and Rocher would throw a fit I'm sure."

He sat up and offered his hand to her, but didn't say anything.

"Spring is such a wonderful time of year; everything flourishing and smelling so fresh. … Though I guess I said I love autumn because of the change in the foliage colors. — Anyway. What would you think of—"

"Calli?"

"Yes?" She looked over, the wind tossing her hair.

"About earlier," he began; uncertainty firmly seated in his deep voice as he looked away from her and down at the ground. "I don't know what came over me this morning. I woke up early and really wanted to see if I could still play it. I haven't played anything in— well, a while. I guess I've had this inkling to try ever since I stopped you. I'll be the first to admit that when I sat down I wasn't expecting much. … I'm hacking, I know. — My mother taught me that piece, Calli. I never had what most would consider 'formal training', though my mother was a professional pianist. I picked it up so easily that she kept teaching me. — Mother and I played quite a bit during the civil war. It was… well, it was what we did together. If I ever forgot where I was, she always sat beside me and began playing the melody; like you did. Half the time I was faking, but that wasn't the case this morning. … Calli? I didn't want you playing it because I wasn't ready to relive that part of my life. I wasn't ready to deal with it. I didn't want to remember the pain of death and loss. Not when I found you. I… that piece — Sonata — was the one I played the night they were murdered. And where I stopped? That was when I…"

In those few moments of silence, she flew toward him and wrapped him in her arms. It wasn't easy, but she kept from crying.

Knowing she was trying to help, Destan accepted her embrace and took a deep breath before he finished in a broken and shaky voice, "That's when I heard my mother scream and the gunshots. I rushed out and found them like I told you. … When you started playing, it felt like I had her back; for however brief a moment it was. It felt like I was four-years-old again and free from my anger and emotional baggage. I could hear her voice and see her face; even feel her hands moving mine to where they belonged. But then I realized I had something even more special than her memory. I had you — my wife — sitting beside me, supporting me, reminding me I have someone right now filling that void in my life. Ca… Calli, I— as much as I love my mother and the memory of her: I love my reality so much more… my beautiful reality. I thank God for each and every morning when I wake up and see your face. — Thank you for what you did. Thank you for being you and always trying to help; but allowing me to work through things in my own way. I know you may not think you did anything or understand why it helped, but I don't need much. Only you, Calli. Remember that."

Now she was dumbfounded. This was only the second time Destan opened up to her about his parents for any amount of time. Some of it was a repeat from what Rocher told her, but this was Destan telling her himself. He was opening up to her and trusting her more!

It was a mad-dash for her to find something to say, but when she did, Destan jumped up and lashed out, "How did you get in?"

She whipped around to see whom he was addressing when he took her by the shoulders and stood her up; all but jerking her to his chest. His emotions were spiking uncontrollably, but seeing her face and feeling her fingernails digging through his shirt reminded him that he needed to keep his cool as much as possible.

Even though his tone was cold and cruel, he repeated in a much calmer fashion, "I'll ask only one more time: how did you get in?"

"Destan," the unwanted guest requested, looking and sounding weary. "I know I am one of the last people you want to see—"

"Right now you 'are' the last."

"Destan I need your help."

"Is it impossible for you to answer a question with an honest and straightforward reply?" He gritted his teeth.

"I brought him, Destan." A second person answered as they stepped forward. "We're alone, I promise. No one else knows where we are."

"Please Destan," the first person begged. "I will explain every—"

"I'd trust a Belvedere to protect me from its Keeper more than I would your explanation. You've fed Callimay and myself too many lies for too long. — And why did you bring him here, Dakoe?"

"We ran out of options. You have—"

"Tell me what your abilities are; then I'll consider talking with you." He demanded; his eyes piercing in their gaze as his voice bottomed out.

"I am able to assume the physical appearance of practically anyone. You 'could' call it shapeshifting, but I think you know my ability as Alias." Dakoe sounded cautious as he transformed into the man who bumped into Callimay after the ball.

She gasped in horror as she jumped behind Destan, "But we were told he was found and taken into custody!"

"So they got him? Good." Dakoe sounded relieved. "After what happened when we met, he deserves what punishment they gave him."

"How do we know you are who we knew as Dakoe if you contain Alias?" Destan challenged as his emotions began to spike again.

Dakoe resumed his normal appearance, now looking dejected as he confessed, "I let Toreon hold me back that night, Callimay. You saw me didn't you? I was trying to reach you before you fell over Lookout Point. … Callimay? — And then the time you ran into the tree while riding. You were there, Destan."

*The only ones who would know about Lookout Point would be Webb, Dakoe, and Toreon.* Callimay nodded, still sounding shaken.

Destan shook his head, reaching in his pocket, "I'm not convinced. Don't make this hard."

"I don't blame you." Dakoe sighed as he kneeled and put his hands up, encouraging his companion to do the same. "I'm sorry I scared you so much, Callimay. — And I didn't mean to get you so upset, Destan."

ℬ

And just like that, their world was turned on its head… again. This monster that had been lurking, reared its cruel face and laughed at Callimay: letting her have such tender moments with Destan only to rip them away when she would find the confidence within herself to reach out and take hold of them. She wasn't allowed to enjoy time with her husband. He slipped back into his old ways.

She followed him down, but it appeared he didn't know she had. He whipped his head around and told her in a matter-of-fact way to go up to their room. Callimay refused, saying she didn't want to leave him alone with his emotions the way they were, "What makes you think me staying in our room will keep me any safer?"

"I…" Destan calmed a bit, not wanting to argue and knowing how torn she was about everything. "Calli I don't trust them. If you're at least somewhere else in the house it—"

"No one was around that day when I wrecked, you know that. And like I said: only three people in the world knew about Lookout Point."

"Toreon told Baleck so there is at least one other person. And just because he was there doesn't mean he is who he says he is." He tried to reason with her and keep his emotions under control. "That could've been a smoke screen. He's already admitted he's a Rogue."

"I know everything is screaming at me to not trust him and I know I 'don't' know his heart — I'm not God — and maybe I don't know what to look for if someone is lying, but I do know my ability is capable of sensing emotions and changes in them. — I want to believe he's repented and doing the right thing, Destan. I want to believe he's come to his senses."

He put his hands on her shoulders and sighed as he leaned his forehead against hers, "I want to believe him too. I want to know we aren't fighting alone. I'm no expert about where he was Spiritually, but I can agree about anyone turning to The Lord… especially those who were believers at one time. — But Calli? The ability he possesses is one

71

which is going to make it difficult to believe him. I'm not saying I'll 'never' trust him; I'm just not 'as' trusting as you. Not right now. — And I'm not saying that's an altogether bad thing, okay?"

"I understand."

"Just— sit here." He surrendered as he moved a chair to the window. "And stay here. I'm going in by myself."

Callimay gasped as she grabbed his wrist, "Be careful."

*You'll be with me, won't you?* Destan softened as he kneeled in front of her and ran his fingers through her hair.

*You know I always will. I love you.*

*There's my Calli. I won't be long.*

After he unlocked the door, he glanced back, seeing her face veiled with pain, "Are you alright?"

"It's just a migraine. I'll be fine."

"Migraine-migraine? Sure?" He stepped back, looking worried.

"I'm sure." She nodded as she worked to smile. "It's not you. If I get feeling really bad I'll go take something and lie down. I promise."

An ever-growing part of Destan worried about Callimay not feeling well so often, but when he looked up, he switched his focus. He double-checked the door to be sure it was locked and then walked over. With a firm grip, he pulled his chair out and sat across from the two unwanted "guests"; taking a moment to compose himself before he stared them down and began his questioning, "So… Mr. Freigh. What you say doesn't hold much weight — if any — with me, but I'll ask anyway. How did you get the information you have for the serums?"

"Oh. Well." He looked a bit shocked, but replied as he clasped his hands and bowed his head, "Baleck is the one with all that information, Destan. I was only the financial side."

"Where did you meet?" He appeared to be unfazed by the answer, though Callimay could tell he was inching his way to anger.

"At an international summit some eighteen years ago. It was called to discuss the Rogue situation. I was the representative from Gastonia and Baleck from Faberton."

*Mr. Willgun is from Faberton!* Callimay exclaimed.

"What capacity did Baleck hold within the Faberton government? Of course I'm assuming he was affiliated with them at all."

Mr. Freigh answered somewhat hesitant as he looked toward the ceiling, "He was— 'is', I believe. If memory serves me correct, his position at the time was within their military research. What it is now or if he still holds that office I have no knowledge of."

Destan didn't respond. He got up and left, baffling Mr. Freigh who called out to keep him from leaving.

He took the time to jerk on the door to be sure it was locked, but then started losing control. After a few steps he dropped to his hands and knees, slamming his fist on the floor as he mumbled under his breath. Callimay rushed to his side and put her arm around him; though part of her was frantic and terrified… remembering what he'd done just a couple months earlier to her while he was in this state.

"The snake is connected to my parents' murders. I know he is." Destan grimaced, not paying much attention to Callimay's efforts to console him. "Baleck Willgun somehow had a hand in their deaths."

*How in the world can I say anything to that! ~ Not much without him lashing out at y~ Ah! Oh that hurts. What do I do?*

Just as she started to rein him in, he started doing it himself.

While it was a much-desired victory and helped ease her already strenuous job of watching over his emotions; Callimay still had to deal with the pain while he worked through this. Right now, she wanted to break her tie to him because of the pain she was in.

Once he was in control and calmed down, Callimay hoped he would take a break. But, a few minutes later he got up and went back in, not saying a word to her.

"You said you needed my help when you arrived." Destan sat down and locked his piercing gaze on Mr. Freigh. "What did you mean by that statement… exactly?"

"This will take a while to answer… that is, if you want the full explanation so there is complete clarity."

"Take all the time you need." He took his hands off the table, sitting back so he could get comfortable.

"I had been suspicious of Baleck's behavior prior to you and Callimay leaving; recognizing the plethora of warning signs I neglected for too long: his planting operatives in the student body without my knowledge, the events surrounding Callimay's status with everyone, his neglect to alter scores to reflect what I promised you, his hesitancy to have me take back duties, the supposed miscalculation in your STM counteractant, Callimay's close brush with death—yes, I believe he had a hand in the incident at Lookout Point in some capacity. It stood to reason. That man's ability to come up with plans off the cuff like he had over the years should have hinted to me something was going on. No matter the circumstance we found ourselves in, he was always 'the man with the plan'. Granted, these incidents were not as frequent as when you arrived, but it was not uncommon for him to jump in if something went wrong. Now I see it was because he was behind every problem and knew how to sway me toward the outcome he wanted. — Looking back, I can see how he crept in; taking duties one by one and shutting me out. The sly devil did it in such a way which made it appear 'I' was giving it of my own free will." Mr. Freigh explained in a frustrated tone as he rubbed his hand over his fist. "When you two escaped, I was quite leery of leaving… concerned what Baleck would do with the rest of the students in my absence. But Willow — my wife — meant more to me. Little did I even know he was behind her death."

"Wait." Destan put his hand up and leaned forward. "So you're telling me Baleck kicked you out of the Society? That he's been after this since you opened your doors: excluding you from the very institution which bears your name?"

"Yes on all three counts."

"You know what you're claiming is dangerous, Mr. Freigh: accusing someone of being a nark isn't something to take light. That is the charge that would be brought against him if he were the one behind the whole situation with the Rogues."

"I fully understand what I am insinuating. — That is the only way I can explain the influx of Rogues after the Society opened. We— 'I' assumed it was because they were trying to keep up with what we were able to do, though I was confounded as to how they found out; we kept everything so close and screened everyone with so much scrutiny. But, I was stupid enough to think such a logical and diplomatic scenario were possible." Mr. Freigh admitted as he took a painful breath. "There were times I knew the processing equipment had been used, but Baleck said it either had to be serviced or a dry run done to keep its performance at the level we needed. I was naïve to believe this simple lie. — He would always put his vote in for certain individuals each year; all like Toreon. I dismissed them, knowing they shared so many similarities to those we were fighting. Too late, I see he was assuring they were 'free' for himself. — With all the little things that happened after I decided to go through with giving you Challenger, I believe he knew I was beginning to understand. I was attempting to go at things in the logical and diplomatic approach that I had always used; but again, I was stupid enough to assume Baleck would fall for such frivolous tactics. When he wanted me off the complex grounds and where I had no power, he snapped his finger and had my wife killed."

Destan flinched at the last remark, "He… he had your wife—"

"Murdered? Yes. When I announced on Monday that I was leaving, all I knew was she had an accident and was not expected to live…"


"Mr. Freigh, leave everything to me. We need you at your best to help guide things here since this all happened. And for you to be at your best you must see to your wife." Baleck repeated, trying to calm his livid superior. "We will find them. Trust me. The homers were tripped the moment they crossed. They can't get far. I know—"

"It is bad enough we lost them, but now the damage control!" He fumed as he shook his hand at all the students who stood there in fear of the armed faculty guarding the gate. "How in the world are we supposed to contain this? We cannot risk—"

"Mr. Freigh please! Give me a moment. I'm sure there is a way."

"All of our work— gone! In the blink of an eye: all in vain."

Baleck was deep in thought, ignoring the rant Mr. Freigh was fully engaged in; when all of a sudden he had a genius thought, "Why don't we reset everyone's memories?"

"Everyone? Every single individual? Are you mad, Baleck?"

"If I am, at least I am trying to find a way to help."

The air between these two men was so tense it felt like it could spontaneously combust at any moment. And yet Baleck was trying his best to keep things civil, "I don't blame you for neglecting your level-headed nature, Mr. Freigh. I don't. I know your number one priority has always been your wife. … Go. I will keep you updated."

They walked to the car, the older of the two stopping and speaking in a worried tone, "By the doctor's words it did not sound as if Willow was doing well at all. — If something does come up, contact me."

Baleck smiled as the door shut, "Don't worry Mr. Freigh. When you get back things will be changed and for the better."

"We were so close." He sighed as he gripped the wheel.

"Don't give up hope. — I know you will be occupied, but please let me know when you arrive and how your wife is doing."

"I will, Baleck."

Mr. Freigh's home was only an hour drive to the north, but he pushed the envelope as far as the speed limit was concerned. At this point he was willing to be "chased" by the local authorities.

What bugged him most was the fact initial details surrounding her accident were scarce. No one was around when it happened and she was only able to give bits of information since her consciousness came and went so much.

Much to his relief, he looked up only a half hour later to see his estate about a mile off. The front gate was opened, and it appeared all the medical personnel were still there. This was promising.

He slammed on the breaks, locking the tires so the car slid across the fine pebble driveway. As quick as any man his age could, he jumped out of the car and ran to the door. Some of the aides greeted him, but their attitudes were not what he was hoping for: subdued and lacking an emotional response of any kind, never looking at him as they stood a little off from the entryway.

Mortified, Mr. Freigh dashed up to his bedroom.

"Willow!" He sighed in relief, leaning on the door frame. "Oh thank the stars you are alright."

She smiled as she offered her hand, "Creigam, my love."

"I got here as soon as I could. What happened?" He asked still out of breath as he sat beside her and gave her a kiss.

"I am really not sure. I had gone for coffee with one of the faculty early Sunday afternoon and felt dreadful when I got home."

"Who was it you met with?"

"Ginger. — Speaking of which, hello, sweetie." She smiled at the young lady who walked in, and then sighed as she turned her focus to her husband, "She was such a help, Creigam. The dear has yet to leave my side this whole time."

"As requested: fresh-brewed with lemon. — It's good to see you here so soon, Mr. Freigh."

"It is good to see you as well, Ginger." He answered rather confused. "You said you two met early yesterday afternoon, Willow?"

"Yes. … What is wrong, my love? You look worried."

"Faculty was not dismissed until mid-afternoon; possibly late."

"Oh I could have my times off. You know it was never my strength."

"Even then, it is a good hour drive h—"

Just then, Mrs. Freigh started gasping for air and dropped the cup; its shattering noise so loud it shook the room like the world was coming to an end. — And for Mr. Freigh it was the beginning of just that. — He ran to the hall, seeing no one but Ginger, "Where did the doctor go?"

"He hasn't been here for over an hour. What's the matter?"

"But he was right— Willow!"

When he got back, she was already gone. He dropped to his knees and took her hand in his; jerking back because it was stiff and ice-cold. Mr. Freigh glanced at the floor and saw the cup was gone and there was no stain, "But her hand… the cup…"

"It was what you wanted to see." Ginger snapped her fingers and all of a sudden Mrs. Freigh was sitting in bed and smiling; the doctor at the other side of the bed. "She's been gone for well over an hour. And like I said earlier: the doctor's been gone for just as long. There was no need for him anymore."

"But the vehicles outside!" He started to shake his head.

She began smirking, "Didn't you 'want' to see them there?"

"What in the— who are you?"

"Your worst nightmare, it seems like."

"Nightmare! Then y… you are a…" Mr. Freigh stammered as he shook his finger at her.

"Seeing pure fear and pain in someone's eyes excites me; pardon my insensitive interruption." She laughed as a smug smile continued to grow across her lips. "You know? It's at times like this that I wonder if 'I' should be the most feared Rogue; not Origin. … Regardless of my lower status, I am glad to see my reputation has preceded me."

"Why!"

"Oh come now. You should know the answer to that. We were well aware of what you were doing, letting the two of them alone after discovering their abilities. — Your blatant defiance wasn't something Baleck anticipated, though. — But since you have such a deep and fond connection with your wife, we knew something happening to her would be a strong enough pull to get you to leave no matter what happened at the Society."

"You murdered her just to—"

"Save your breath," Ginger huffed as she rolled her eyes. "Being judgmental or sentimental about the loss of human life is something you can't possibly advocate for. You've murdered twelve young men over the past ten years: one of them being my younger brother. ... Consider this your payment in full for your past sins."

"Why not me! She did nothing to your brother."

"We couldn't afford too many questions being raised. By doing it this way, you will be stepping down due to your tragic loss; handing over all authority and operations to Baleck. It would stand to reason there would be chaos and confusion with such a sudden shift in authority, but that is exactly what we want."

"Why are you telling me this? All I have to do is—"

"Her death will be seen as a massive flare from her 'thought to have been cured' Fibromyalgia. My staying with her the whole time ensures us that protection. An autopsy won't show anything but what is found with any victim of the disease: the pain became too much for her weakened body to handle, so it shut down."

He begged, dropping to his knees, "Tell me she felt no pain."

"Really Mr. Freigh, you're not listening. She died in excruciating pain. ... Now if you will excuse me, I really do need to get back. There's a little issue of taking care of your Challenger and his Liaison so they won't undo all of our hard work. — Oh! Mr. Freigh. Thank you for giving us everything we need to operate under the radar. Ta-ta!"

Other than the dozen times a processed student would turn out to be a cliffhanger and the carnage that ensued, Mr. Freigh found himself emotionally devastated and unable to comprehend what was going on; sitting on the floor in a daze.

To no avail he tried to wake his wife; refusing to accept the reality of what happened. How could someone sit by and watch another human being go through that kind of pain for so long? … Then again, how could he sit by and watch those twelve young men drive themselves insane or give orders to have them "put out of their misery"?

"…I tried to contact him but he refused to answer. Before I even got the results back from her autopsy, all the local stations were at my door asking if the statement Baleck released was true. I was not mentally strong enough to take the badgering, so I gave in. I know that was the worst thing I could have done; but I just could not withstand it any longer. I wanted to be alone. Giving them what they wanted was the fastest way to get them to leave. — Now do you understand, Destan? Do you see why I had to come find you?"

"But why did they let you live after Ginger told you everything?" He questioned, noting a glaring hole in his elaborate and emotionally jerking story. "I don't see them as the type to openly advertise what they're doing even with what looks like a foolproof smoke screen. Baleck's no fool and doesn't strike me as one who likes loose ends. And on top of it all, I doubt you gave up completely. Maybe at that time you did, but what about the past couple weeks? There are countless news outlets that would jump on the type of story you had to offer; regardless of whether or not they thought it were true."

"The day I was scheduled to go on air with one of them was the day they posted the fallout report. Baleck somehow found out and I cannot help but believe he did it on purpose. — Surely you heard about it; the report that is. … I went into hiding as fast as possible, knowing the authorities would be— now listen for a moment, Destan. I 'do' believe in making full restitution for what wrongs I committed; do not hear what I am not saying. I only wanted to distance myself from what Baleck did in my absence and expose him before surrendering. And do not entertain the thought he sat idle."

In his own words, Dakoe finished after he returned the nod Mr. Freigh gave him, "I was the only one able to find him. He trusted me and let me feed Baleck information so I would gain his confidence and be the one eventually sent out. Yes I played both sides, but I thought it was the only way to get out of there and do what I could to save someone else. I never had any intentions of carrying out my orders. All along I planned to get him to you. — You may never believe me and I understand your reservations, but you've got to see what's at s…"

*What is this about a fallout report? Those are reserved for disastrous chemical spills resulting in massive death numbers.* "What happened to everyone at the Society, Dakoe?" Destan's eyes narrowed as he folded his arms across his chest.

He shuddered as he looked to the one-way window in the room, "It was absolute chaos after that. Baleck didn't reassign 'anyone' new memories. He had faculty corral everyone in the main lecture hall; then group by group, had them processed. He did all four-hundred and ninety-four of them that day! Toreon tried to push back, saying Gallia shouldn't be subjected to it, but Baleck was hearing none of it and took her first. — It was a massacre; the half who survived blaming Toreon, myself, Hyra, and Ingrid since we weren't taken. … Things would've been okay, but cliffhangers started crawling out of the woodwork and wanted nothing but our heads; so we were moved to the faculty portion of the complex. With their prey gone, I assumed they would calm down since everyone else was in the same situation— they tore the place apart, Destan! As if the stench of two-hundred dead bodies on the complex wasn't bad enough, there was the carnage left from their fury. They were nothing but rabid animals."

"So that's what the fallout report was issued for."

"Yes, Destan." Mr. Freigh admitted. "Baleck did not even try to cover up the fact there were that many deaths. He has no shame."

Unable to keep himself from allowing their discussion to go on; needing to let out what had been suppressed for so long, Dakoe started rambling on, "Students were turning on each other and faculty, no one knowing who to trust. If you've never been threatened with death if you didn't comply with something I doubt you can understand what happened once faculty got a foothold on the situation. There were a few who stood up, but their public and immediate execution scared everyone else into submission. Baleck was a communistic dictator to the letter. … After the dust settled, there were— oh, I don't know, close to fifty of us left? We were then moved off site to some stronghold in

Crosswall. — I'd never been to that one in particular so I really don't know much about it. — We all underwent rigorous training and what I knew good and well was brainwashing. It took me everything I had left mentally not to fall into that thinking; hearing them go on and on about how they were hungry for blood… your blood to be exact. — Once news got back about Toreon failing, someone's been sent out every week to draw the two of you out. Obviously no one's been successful yet since they've gotten side-tracked and caught every time. Apparently the brainwashing job can only go so far to curb lust and greed. Baleck's not one to tolerate such failure: he had them all killed."

*Who didn't make it!* Callimay gasped as she thought about what Dakoe said. *What about Breyan, Idela, Forest, Eerick…*

Once she was done listing those she knew, there was a short period of silence. Destan could tell how distraught she was and wanted to help give her some closure if he could, "What happened to the others you and Callimay knew?"

"No one from our home-group made it through processing except for Toreon." Dakoe replied as his shoulders and head dropped.

"You said Toreon tried to save Gallia?"

"He did. I never thought he cared much about her since he carried on with so many other girls. — The morning after he was processed he talked with me about what he was going to do to you two. The ease of him talking about murdering someone made my skin crawl… let alone 'how' he was going to do it. I can't tell you how relieved I was to know it was all bark when I saw him fly out of the dorm later that afternoon. He looked visibly shaken and only said he'd wait and surprise you. I didn't know what he meant, but then I saw you two come out together and realized: when it came down to it, he wasn't able to go through with it because of Callimay." Dakoe refused to stop until he got every single word off his chest. "When Gallia died, though, he did a one-eighty. He became pure evil, fuming constantly about you taking his 'Duchess' away from him; how it was your fault she died. Jesko and a few others said she didn't make it because she was weak. Toreon didn't tolerate the back-stabbing talk and murdered him. Willgun didn't take it too well, but for whatever reason he let it slide."

*So he 'did' care for Gallia?* Callimay asked in a stunned tone.

*As much as a snake can.* "He just showed who he truly was; there was no change in him. And I know why Baleck couldn't put a finger on him even if he wanted to… he's the Prince."

"But then why in the world did he undergo processing?" Dakoe jerked back; this eye-opening news a bombshell to him. "He said—"

"He kept feeding me the same lie; how he didn't know what they were doing and how he was a fellow victim; bullied into what he did. — That's not possible though. Callimay followed him that night he was processed. He went there on purpose. Why? I still haven't figured that out exactly. I've got a suspicion though."

"What is it! Let me help, Destan."

"I'm asking the questions here." He refused, Callimay feeling his emotions — fear in particular — spike. "How did you know where to find us? Who else knows?"

"I… I was sent with Toreon to be his bodyguard when he came to Kerogen. We surveyed the perimeter of the barrier when he figured out he couldn't transport in. Strangely enough, he cut ties with Baleck when he knew for sure this was where you were. When I'd asked why, all he kept telling me was that he wanted you and Callimay for himself to take care of as he pleased. … He didn't want Baleck or anyone else interfering. I tried to get to you — I swear I did — but even with my ability, Toreon could still see me and wouldn't have hesitated to kill me. I know I should have been willing to risk it, but…"

"But what? Quit hacking."

"I couldn't leave Hyra behind, okay!" Dakoe finished as he pounded his fist on the table. "She was too young and was the first success they had, so they wanted to play it safe. … Destan she's been at the Society as a resident ever since it opened ten years ago. They kept her there to groom her into what they wanted her to be. When I came along and was processed, they paired us for the remainder of the school year. When it was over, I was sent out even though I tried to—"

"What 'did' you do anyway when you were 'out'?" Destan sounded much more stern and direct.

"I would be given a bio for one person and sent to take their place for a certain amount of time to spy on another. Usually it was to see if they were paying taxes or working where they claimed to. It seemed more like government work, really. But, digging for that kind of information wasn't and still isn't my specialty. Why do you ask?"

"I'm just trying to figure out what you 'Rogues' are 'doing'." *That's not what I remember Mr. Freigh talking about. Which of you two are lying to me?* "So… did you get Hyra out?"

"No. She's fallen for their stupid charade. Bait, wire, 'and' weight." Dakoe all but growled as he looked at Mr. Freigh and then hung his head, now depressed, "She won't leave because she said 'they' are the ones who gave her a purpose in life. More than once she told me she was doing this so she could help her family. I've tried and tried to get her to realize t—"

"Does she know her mother is dead?"

"I— what! How do you know? Who told you?"

"You knew?"

"No! I c… I can't believe it. I was just— how did you find out?"

"Callimay and I just happened to meet her father the night we left. He explained about his view of the Society and told Callimay what happened to his daughter whom he called Hyra." Destan stated as he shifted in his chair; Callimay noticing he was tensing up. "He and his wife were sent a letter five months after she started there, stating she died in an accident. Her mother died from being grief-stricken."

"Hyra… she thinks they're fine. She's never been told otherwise."

"How sick and demented can you be?" Destan slammed the desk and leaned over, getting in Mr. Freigh's face. "Do you get 'satisfaction' out of torturing families and twisting young people's minds into s—"

"Baleck promised me it was the best way with Hyra. She was our first success, but she had family. We had not considered how to handle the fact they could not return home." *It turned out there was so much we had not considered. … We really weren't ready.* He recalled somber, remaining calm during this borderline violent outburst. "After I heard that Hyra's mother passed, I told Baleck we could not have candidates with immediate family alive; it was too risky."

Destan couldn't find words.

Dakoe looked nervous, blurting out, "Look I… I admit I did fear keeping my cover intact more than keeping Callimay safe that night. Every, single, solitary day I regret not shoving Toreon aside and saving her like I should have. I know self-abasement doesn't prove repentance but I am truly sorry for what I neglected to do. Please know that. I had no part in what he was planning to do that night. I only went with him to keep her safe."

These words fell on deaf ears; Destan so disgusted with Mr. Freigh and his twisted way of justifying what he was doing. Callimay could notice the severity of his emotions and how he wasn't paying attention, so she worked her way in and pleaded with him to take a few minutes to calm down since she was unable to open the door: *You… you're probably right, Calli. I sh—*

"I know this is not much consolation to you, Destan." Mr. Freigh took a deep breath. "'Every' life should be valued no matter the status of their family involvement or relation. Just because they do not have family does not mean they do not have others who care about them… or they have been alone their entire lives and wish to be so."

"No. No it's not." He gritted his teeth; looking over his shoulder as he finished, "What did you mean when you said you met me and knew I was going to help the world in an immense way?"

"How did you remember? We reassigned—"

"I don't know exactly." Destan shook his head and turned around. "While fighting with Toreon everything came back… 'every'thing."

"I…" Mr. Freigh hesitated, astonished at how powerful he was to overcome the STM counteractant. "I said that because I saw so much of your father in y—"

"How did you know my father?"

"I knew your parents before you were even born, Destan."

He froze with fear, his heart starting to race, "W… what!"

"Your father contacted me during his final year of studies to ask about sponsoring his final project thesis. The research he described doing instantly perked my interest. Willow had been stricken with the very condition Destry theorized was curable since her early adulthood. The amount he was asking for was not mind-blowing by my standards. In fact, I took the risk with courage rather than fear: stacked against the amount of money both of us invested in her treatment to that point, this was nothing. I shocked him by bypassing every formality and discussing terms, having a transfer slip for the full amount with me when we met. — There was a confidence in him that was infectious. I could not help but walk away from that meeting having assurance my Willow would know a better life. Even when he would give updates that sounded not so promising, I did not give up. … I believe it is needless to say his theory was correct. My wife was cured. This did not merely manage the pain or put her into temporary remission like every other treatment had. I cannot begin to tell you how overjoyed I was to see her in a truly pain-free state. She suffered for so long and this was the miracle I had been asking for since I found out she had it. — Destry knew our agreement was he would not owe me anything since it worked and met my criteria, but he told me he felt a duty to show his gratitude since I believed in him while everyone else mocked him; and gave his wife and himself the start they so desperately needed. … Your father's work ethic and concern for others was second-to-none, Destan. He was an upstanding man who was able to command a room without ever saying a word. He was the true strength you described in your essay. — Your father stayed in contact even after our business dealings were finished, which was far more than I was expecting. Time passed and I found out Lylah was expecting. I told Willow, and we decided to help in what way we knew we could. — Your father's treatment 'was' a success, but finances were still tight since he had school debts taking priority. From our conversations, I could tell Destry was not quite sure how he was going to be able to balance work and home with three mouths to feed and working so far away. I did some digging and found how much his school debt was, making arrangements to have it paid in full. Both Willow and myself attended the dinner that the University of Kerogen set up to recognize his accomplishments. — We had to see his reaction in-person. — The feeling of having the ability to give to someone who understood the worth of a gift and be appreciative— it was something I had never known. It instilled in me a desire to help others however possible… birthing the whole idea behind the Society when I found out about the Rogues."

"It sounds like in recent years that desire died." He answered cold as his eyes narrowed. "And don't sully my father's good name or dare even speak of my mother."

"Destan!" Dakoe exclaimed, shocked at his lack of gratitude.

"Now you listen to me." He bellowed as he shoved his chair to the side, it crashing into the wall. "I've stood here and let him speak his mind after I let you have free rein. All I've heard is a bunch of fluff to get me to back off. … He's saying my father — my father — is the one responsible for him desiring to help others. He's maligning what my father stood for in everything he's done: ripping families apart and showing no concern for those who do and don't have families. He's trying to play God. You should see this better than others if you are indeed who you claim to be, Dakoe. — I was right about you, Mr. Freigh. My essays were on point more than I could have ever imagined. You're weak. A coward. You hide and push others into the role you should be willing to fulfill yourself. You put Callimay — the woman I love and without a moment's hesitation would give my life for — through more torture than anyone should for five lifetimes, if that were even possible. … You talk about how you were overjoyed to see your wife pain-free. What agony do you think 'I' go through seeing Callimay in the pain and danger she's in each and every day because of what 'you' did? What I'm fighting right now so she isn't in pain. I have every right to say this. Don't call me out when I'm man enough to stand up and call him a hypocrite."

"Dakoe, he is right." Mr. Freigh calmed, trying to keep things as civil as possible so the monster inside Destan wouldn't rear its ugly head. "I was looking too much at the bigger picture. It made me neglect the individuals involved."

"You still haven't answered my question."

"I apologize. I did get caught up in the past and reminiscing. — When you were four, maybe five, I was commissioned to ask your father about doing scientific research for Gastonia. When I arrived, he informed me he had agreed to go to Faberton to help in the civil war efforts. At that point, keeping contact was not possible due to the nature of his work. I did not hear any word until almost a Homeworld's year later when I was informed your parents were murdered. … I saw you at the funeral. The mature way you held yourself — even at such a tender age — gave me assurance that no matter what came along, the training you were given by your father would carry you through, so you could rise above and conquer."

Destan didn't respond.

As if he had no strength left, he staggered across the room and picked up the chair, flopping onto it. His eyes were darting like a fly being swatted at as millions of thoughts ran through his mind… too many for him to process in the environment he was in.

Knowing Mr. Freigh didn't have the answers he needed, Destan got up and left. After checking the door again, he rushed past Callimay without even acknowledging her.

ℬ

After all she heard them discuss, Callimay was expecting Destan to go outside to his normal "cooling off" place. But much to her surprise, he stopped at the door by the piano. He gripped one side of the frame, tripping a sensor that opened a panel just to the right of the door. He punched in a code which signaled the door to slide open just like the one downstairs.

Callimay followed, trying to stay close while letting him have space so he could work through this. Though, as she came in, the door slid shut right behind her, causing her to yelp.

"What are you doing here!" He growled when he saw her.

"Destan I'm s—"

"You need to leave."

"Why? Why can't I be in here? I just want to be close so I can help. That's all. Please Destan. Please let me stay."

He opened his mouth and then hung his head and walked away.

The light in the room was so dim that it was hard for her to tell what this room was. Destan was now on the far side of the room where there were stacks of papers beside several computer screens. Her now-adjusted eyes revealed several workstations where chemical testing equipment was: *This looks like that one classroom. ~ You mean the chemistry lab? ~ Yeah.* "What is this all for?"

There was a short pause, but he finally answered in a quiet tone; not looking back at her, "You should go. I feel better now."

"What is this place? Why is it hidden? … Why didn't you tell me about it?" Callimay begged, sounding scared.

"This doesn't concern you. You should go rest. Your eyes—"

"What other secrets are you still holding onto, Destan! Please don't start this again. Just when I think everything is going fine, I find out you're not telling me everything about yourself. Stop it! Talk. To. Me! … I don't want my only way to get the truth out of you to be for me to pry your thoughts or constantly beg. Please stop this!"

No response.

Callimay dragged herself over and stood behind him. It was bad enough that Dakoe and Mr. Freigh were causing problems; but this? Half of her wanted to beg him to talk to her and the other half was fed up with everything. The only emotion worthy of this inner conundrum was dejection… and it hurt her to be torn like this.

Destan leaned on the table and stared at the papers in front of him; finally saying in a quiet and grieved tone, "I'm just trying to protect you, Calli. Everything I've ever done was because I just want you safe… I love you. I'm not deceiving you or lying. I just want to keep you out of harm's way. You not knowing—"

"How is keeping me in the dark protecting me?"

"I… I don't— it all sounds logical to me, Okay? — And I don't know everything. Saying anything about this room would only raise more questions that I don't have the answers to."

"Let me be part of the confusion you're feeling. Let me be the helper I'm supposed to be. Help me understand what you need from me so I can help you. Just let me in. Please, Destan! I… I don't care if I don't understand. There's so much of that with everything else that I doubt one more thing will do much — if any — 'damage'."

He pulled the chair out from the table and collapsed onto it; looking weary as she rushed over, "Fine. Where do you want me to start?"

"Just tell me what this place is. Why is it hidden?"

"This was my father's personal research laboratory." He sighed as he rubbed his face. "I don't know why he had one here or protected it like this. It's never made sense to me. I… I don't know, Calli."

She bit her lip, but asked after a while, seeing him finger the stack of papers, "What are those?"

"Other than Rocher's word, this is the only reason I knew my father was connected to the serums. … They're the information sheets of all the different serums; just like what ours were at the Society. — As I understand it, when things started going south in Faberton, father had Rocher send these back and stored here. When I found out about this room, I spent weeks pouring over these papers. I've tried and tried to gain access to the computers, but Rocher doesn't know the passcode and I've never been able to figure it out."

They sat there for a while and didn't say a word.

His emotions were in a better place, so Callimay took this time to rest. It wasn't something she wanted to admit to, but having that break was so well timed. But then the phone rang, catching her attention, "Oh that's right. You told me last night Rocher was going to Rayleen. It's probably him. Don't worry, I'll go answer it."

"If you're sure."

"Will you let me back in?"

Destan laughed and followed her, doing something on the panel before he finished, "There. Now it'll open when you walk over."

Callimay smiled and then left, sidestepping when she almost hit the edge of the piano. Her doing that jolted Destan's memory: *Piano! ~ Huh? ~ The Code for the computer! Why didn't I think of that!*

He flew back to where he'd been sitting and waved his hand over part of the table. The expression on his face showed he was excited and worried at the same time. And for him to look that way was quite rare! As soon as he hit the enter key he heard Callimay scream, "Destan get out here... now!"

Scared half to death, he ran out and looked around, "What!"

"It's Rocher!"

"What?"

"He said it would be too dangerous and not to worry about him."

"Callimay!" Destan grabbed her by the shoulders, trying to get her to stop spiraling out of control. "Tell me what Rocher said."

She froze from seeing his eyes flash at her; answering as her voice quivered and cracked, "Ingrid and Hyra are holding him hostage. He said not to listen to their demands. Ingrid took the phone away before he could say anything else. She said they are at the Uloy plant — I least I think that's what she said — and we both have to come within the next three hours if we wanted to see Rocher alive."

"I'd say I can't believe it, but—"

He took off and ran to the lower level. Without any hesitation he went up to Dakoe who jumped up, startled by his abrupt entrance. Destan grabbed him by the collar, "Promise me you're telling the truth. Promise me you aren't setting me and Callimay up. Promise me!"

"I have no reason to lie. I'm telling the truth. I swear. W… what's wrong? What's going on?"

"Ingrid and Hyra are holding Rocher, my gran— a very dear person to me, hostage." He trailed off as he let him go.

Mr. Freigh noted in a concerned tone as he looked over at Dakoe, "They got here sooner than you anticipated."

Destan whipped his head around, "You were expecting them!"

"It's complicated." Dakoe tried to rationalize as quick as he could. "Yes I was sent out… but I knew it wouldn't take Baleck long to figure things out. I was hoping we'd have a bit more time t—"

"You two— we need to go. Yes, I'm taking you with me."

Dakoe stood his ground, "We need to devise a plan first. Let us help. We know them. You can't run blindfolded into this. You're sure to get yourself killed if you do. You don't even know their abilities."

"Please listen to him, Destan. Please." Callimay pleaded as she put her hand on his arm, knowing he was about ready to snap. "We don't have much time Dakoe, so keep it short."

"Hyra's abilities are a bit… non-conventional. And like I said, they aren't true 'offensive' abilities." He looked over at her and then shook his head before continuing, "She has two separate ones since she was processed twice: Seer and Recoil. … Basically she can 'see' those with abilities since she said they have a certain aura, she can distinguish their strengths and weaknesses, and she has hyper-sensitive reflexes."

Callimay rubbed Destan's hand as she leaned against his side, trying to keep him calm, "What about Ingrid?"

"She's a true hybrid: Picket and Levator." Dakoe continued; using the technical terminology he knew Destan would understand. "I'm not sure how that gave her dead-on marksman skills, but hybrids are known to have some outlandish mods. … She can change vision modes at will: night, heat, monochrome, and so on. On top of that, she can fly; though only for short distances. Technically it's more like 'aggressive jumping': any sniper perch is within her range."

"This is too much, Destan." Callimay shook her head as she glanced at his face which showed a sternness she hadn't seen in quite a while. "We haven't even 'used' our abilities in a while."

"You won't need to worry. You're not leaving this house. Dakoe and I will figure it out. I'm not letting you get in the middle again."

She tried to pull away from his firm grasp without making too much of a scene, "We don't have time to squabble about this. I 'have' to go. Ingrid said you and I 'both' have to come."

"I can go as you, Callimay." Dakoe blurted out as he jumped to his feet. "Hyra won't be able to tell the difference at first, I promise she won't. If we work fast it'll be fine."

"But… I…"

Destan looked at her in a confident, yet loving way, *I'm able to control things better now.*

*I know you are. But if something—*

*It's going to be alright. Okay? I'll be up in a few minutes.* He opened the door and stepped back. *Please do this for me. … Calli?*

*Alright.* She sighed, sounding defeated.

♬

Callimay paced the floor of the entire main floor; one arm clutching the other as she stared at her feet as she crept along. Looking at a clock made her nervous… and there were several on the walls. Yes, it had only been ten minutes, but she didn't know how far it was to this plant.

The side of her that wanted to be with Destan kept her right by the lower level door. All three men's voices could be heard and were subdued… things were calm. Callimay leaned against the wall and looked up toward the chandelier, her eyes glassy and cheeks flushed: *Please tell me this is a bad dream, Heavenly Father. Please. This morning was so wonderful. I know things can change in the blink of an eye, but why isn't there any time for us to rest in between? Help me. If this is real, please give us all strength to keep going. Please keep Rocher safe. It's in Your Son's Name I pray, amen.*

After a little while, she dragged herself to the piano and sat down, running her fingers across the beautiful wood; remembering what happened just a few hours before.

Nothing could hold her attention for very long; a frustrated sigh dragging out as more of a growl while she got up and walked toward the French doors. Callimay glanced over and saw Destan's duster coat. She took it down and looked at it, a sad expression on her face as she rubbed the thick leather. She hugged it; burying her face in it as she cried: *Don't tell me this means it's back to wearing this and 'training'. … I shouldn't complain. I know. There's nothing wrong with Destan wearing this. ~ But it makes you think of Toreon and what happened. ~ Not just that, but I won't deny that's a big part. ~ You liked your 'new' Destan, didn't you? ~ More than anything else.*

By the time she stopped, her head was pounding. Part of her wanted to call out for Destan so he would come hold her and help her feel better, but was it worth trying right now? Would he even respond?

Knowing these thoughts weren't helping; she got herself off the floor and put the coat back on its hook. Callimay leaned on the wall for a bit so her eyes could adjust to the brightness of midday… but they weren't having any of it and complained even more: *Fine. I'll go upstairs and take some medicine before I~ Why not just go in here? It's dark and a whole lot closer.*

It was inviting, the opened doorway to the darkened lab. She stood there for a second and then staggered in, moaning as she held her head. Like a cool glass of water immediately washing away the sting of heat, the darkness in the room soothed her eyes like nothing else in the world could. As she looked around, she found there wasn't a sofa — let alone a bed — but the desk chair was cushioned enough for her needs.

While she got comfortable, she reached out and put her hand on the table. The darkness fled as the computer woke up, its screen shining just as bright as the sun… or at least it felt that way.

Callimay groaned as she opened her eyes to turn it off, stopping short when she saw the screen's background. It was Destan: *No. Something's different. ~ Aha! It's the eyes. ~ Is this Destan's father? … And his mother? ~ Well that sounds reasonable seeing as how that's got to be Destan sitting between them.*

This was a prime example that the back and forth with happiness not lasting was something she didn't know he was comfortable with. The picture was taken in Faberton on Jubilee. Destan was only five-years-old at the time. It was the last family picture they ever took. Seeing him so young, so handsome, and so happy, made Callimay feel better. But then she saw the clock on the corner of the screen and heard the clocks out in the other room chime. She turned her attention to the stack of papers on the desk and started skimming through them, trying to find something else to keep her distracted.

Before long, she found information about Dakoe, Ingrid, and Hyra's abilities. She hadn't gone through the entire stack, so she kept looking; expecting to find hers and Destan's. … There wasn't anything. Not so much as a mention of either serum: *That's odd.*

"Callimay? Callimay, where are you?" Destan called out.

"I'm in here." She said weakly, trying to get up as fast as she could.

The only problem was she moved too fast and collapsed. In the blink of an eye he was by her side, "Calli! Wha—"

His eyes looked half terrified, half overjoyed; and yet he wasn't looking at her. She glanced back to see what he was focused on, but even that small amount of effort made her dizzy.

"They were wonderful, Calli."

"I know they were. They raised a wonderful son."

Destan picked her up and held her for a minute before setting her down and putting her at arm's length, "Can you stand? … Good. We've got our plan ready and should be leaving in a few minutes."

He turned and walked out, completely forgetting about Callimay; only stopping to mess with the panel by the door before disappearing.

She staggered into the main room, reaching out for something to steady herself on.

"I wanted to be sure and say g—" Destan paused as he put his duster coat on, hearing her gasp.

"I'm sorry," she moaned and jerked away from the piano.

Time stood still for a minute; or so it felt like. He flew to her side and picked her up, holding her close as he rushed up to their bedroom, "Do you feel that bad, Calli?"

"I'll be fine, I promise."

He ran to the bathroom and came back with water and medicine, "Here, take this. I… I need to get ready. I'm sorry. I— I'm sorry but I've got to go."

"Oh Destan."

"Calli it's best this way. You're in no shape to travel—"

"I can't just let you go."

"Now you listen to me. Physically you can't handle anymore. Shut off your connection to me before you get worse."

"No!"

"Callimay Rose!"

"No," she cowered and jerked her hands away. "I can't— won't!"

Destan ran his fingers through his hair and slumped over, now sitting on the bed next to her, "Calli I didn't mean— I'm not going to hurt you. I won't 'ever' do that again."

She sighed and rubbed her forehead, feeling worse. When he tried to brush her hair out of her face, she flinched and smacked his hand away. Flashbacks to what happened reminded Destan he couldn't treat her with rigid formality… even in a dire situation like this. She wasn't some soldier he could order around or even another man.

"I'm sorry, Calli. I didn't mean to scare you." He said in a loving and tender way; offering his hand to her again… and waiting for her to accept it before he finished, "Please stay here. Mr. Freigh 'is' staying, but he'll be locked up. Everyone knows no one is allowed in; even our vehicle. When we're done and I'm close enough, I'll let you know so you can tell the men it's okay. … Did you catch that, Calli?"

There was a long pause, but she asked, "Destan?"

"What?" He replied concerned, feeling her hands shaking.

"I… I can't lose you." She gripped his sleeves. "I don't want t—"

"You said when I left for Rayleen you knew I'd always be with you no matter what. That hasn't changed."

"I just don't know if I—"

"I've got to get a few things, Calli." He detoured to try and get her to stop crying, himself not wanting to think about what might happen. "We don't have much time."

Destan left for a few minutes, Callimay lying there as these horrible thoughts tormented her. She couldn't bear the thought of losing him. One time was enough.

Unable to stay where she was, regardless of how she felt, Callimay got up and came out into the hall, "I'm glad you two worked out."

She jumped and whipped her head around, "Dakoe!"

He apologized as he put a hand out, "I'm sorry! I didn't mean to scare you, Callimay. Really, I didn't."

"You're fine." She assured as she tried to calm down, rubbing her face. "I wasn't paying attention."

"Let me guess — migraine?"

"Yeah."

"Try not to think too much. I remember how taxiing yourself made them worse. … You… you look like you're doing well though."

"I don't feel like it." She hung her head and interlocked her hands, trying to hold back a sob that was coming on.

"Well I meant—"

"What did you mean by what you told me before Destan and I left? How do you know so much about him and the serums?"

"My dad worked with his in Faberton during the war. There's a long story how they met, but the main thing is my dad became one of his most trusted coworkers and was one of the select few who helped with the serums when that started." Dakoe admitted, doing everything he could to avoid looking at her. "But I didn't even know Destan existed until the funeral. Ever since then, I tried to keep tabs on him; though it wasn't anything much more than making sure he was alive."

"You said you knew what the Society did. What 'did' they do? Who did Destan lose?"

"Cal—"

"Ready?" Destan asked stern as he put his arm around her and pulled her against his chest while he addressed Dakoe.

"Absolutely," he snapped to and walked ahead of them.

Destan let her go and then turned to leave, only to have her rush to his chest again and cry, "I love you."

"If things go as planned, this won't take long. Wait for me… here."

"Come back… please." She whimpered, wanting to beg him to take her with him.

❧

After a quick discussion with the other men in the house, Destan and Dakoe left. For the entire ride, neither man said anything. In their own ways, they were preparing — both for what outcome was hoped for and what had to be recognized as a possibility… no matter how grim.

Destan glanced at the clock on the dash every fifteen minutes. He was pacing himself; and it was working just as he planned.

The closer they got the more tense Dakoe became. He knew the history of that place and Destan's tie to it; he couldn't help but think it was chosen because of it: a trigger for his anger. And yet, when he would look at him there wasn't any indication that he was rattled.

Before long, Destan stopped the car where there was cover and then left for a minute to take a quick runaround of the place.

"Drains you still, doesn't it?"

He brushed off as he stood upright and took a deep breath, "Not nearly as exhausting as it used to be. I didn't see any sign of them, but that wasn't completely unexpected."

"Are you sure you're going to be alright?"

"I have to. Now let's go." He checked his watch and started off.

They walked the last two miles. Every entrance was blocked except for the western walk-in gate. The lock had been cut off but the gate was still closed. Destan growled as he looked at the condition of the hinges, "They want us to announce our arrival. I'd call them lazy, but I'll give them credit for working smart. — Get over here for cover."

"What are you planning on doing?"

"Just watch."

It felt like Destan were dragging his fingers across a chalkboard as he pulled the gate toward him, keeping sheltered by the concrete post.

They waited for quite a while, Destan tensing up when nothing happened. He looked deep in thought as he scanned the area, catching Dakoe's attention, "What are you looking for?"

"Do you know what 'fieldwork' is?" Destan scoffed as he glared at him; his hair wafting as he whipped his head around. "I'm trying to find something to distract them enough so they'll 'jump'. If nothing happens, they're either too composed to fall for it or not wanting to do us in from the get-go."

Dakoe hung his head, Destan realizing he was just trying to play his part. Callimay wouldn't know what he was doing and would, most likely, ask that exact question… and would react to his harsh comment in that exact way: *Man he's good. ~ Almost too good. He's done a kind of fieldwork I don't think he's told me about. What else are you hiding?*

He crouched down and swiped a stick nearby. After leaning back against the post for a few seconds, he peered around the corner, looking to see if there was something he could aim at and would cause even more noise.

Target was soon in sight and hit with expert precision.

Nothing? Really?

How could they miss the racket he just made? It echoed around the entire plant. Well, at least it sounded like it did. Was anyone there?

*Didn't give you enough credit again, Ingrid. And it seems Hyra has enough composure to withstand a simple distraction.* "Stay behind me." He said hushed as he turned to Dakoe, scaring him. "I get you're trying to act like Calli, but they can't see us out here."

"Sorry."

Gravel ground and crunched like baked chips as they crept along; these noises feeling like they were echoing due to the position of the buildings and the overbearing void in the air. Destan's focus was set to find any indicator of Ingrid and Hyra's whereabouts, while Dakoe took it upon himself to flinch and bump into him when nothing but a bird called out as it took off from one of the roofs: *Don't go overboard now. ~ Just let it go, Boon. A little theatrics might be what he has to do to even come close to how Callimay would be.*

"Destan!" Dakoe tried his best to have a feminine shriek; shoving him to the side right when he saw a window open in the one building.

An ear-pounding "bam" resounded within milliseconds.

He glanced over, seeing the shot was pretty much right where his feet were. Not waiting for them to have another chance, he got up and grabbed Dakoe's hand, making a run for that building.

They plastered themselves against the wall, Dakoe sounding winded as he said relieved, "Well at least we know where they are. That's—"

"At least where Ingrid is. Do you s— look out!"

Nothing appeared out of the ordinary, but the tiny green dot that was glowing beside Dakoe's forehead wasn't escaped by Destan's keen eye. Just as the shot rang out from the building across the way, he pulled Dakoe toward him and landed pretty hard on the ground.

That shot was much closer to its target. Too close.

Without waiting for him to get to his feet, he grabbed Dakoe's arm and took off for a small office building. It was at the end of the parking lot so it was a risky thing to do since Destan didn't use his ability.

Worry about how he was acting toward Dakoe started to creep in. He wouldn't have run that entire way or dragged Callimay behind him. Dakoe could've been seen as over-reacting, but Destan was under-reacting… which was worse.

"Just as I thought. Get back." He grunted as he stepped back and kicked the door a couple times until it gave way.

Once they were in, Destan kicked in every door. Part of him was hoping Rocher would be here — away from where their focus would have been — but that wasn't the case.

He was frustrated about being cornered, but what he saw didn't do anything to help his mood; him whispering so loud that he was talking in practically his normal voice, "Are you trying to get yourself killed!"

"The only reason I'm over here was to watch who was closing that window we saw open. It was Hyra. I'd never mistake that bubblegum pink hair." Dakoe jumped back while pointing; Destan now checking his firearm. "You don't think we're going to need these do you? I—"

"If you think I want to kill them you're insane. I already told you that. I've never gone into a single fight wanting to kill the other person. That's not how I operate. But at the same time don't hear what I'm 'not' saying. I'm not about to lay down and give up: let myself be killed. I've got someone who's counting on me to come home."

"H… how do you want to handle this?"

"I'd rather have you talk down Hyra. You have a good rapport with her and she sounds like someone who could come around. There's something about Ingrid though…" Destan laid out this plan with as much composure and thought as anyone could. "We'll leave out the back. I can get you to the side entrance where Hyra is, but it'll be up to you to get in and around."

"Got it."

"She might not be there now, but that window you pointed out is on the third floor. There's a staircase to your right, just inside the door that will get you up there. Hang a right when you get to that level. There'll be a long hall with a room on either side that runs the length of the building; each with multiple doors."

"If you don't mind my asking: how do you know this?"

"I do mind, actually. Just trust what I'm saying. Don't read into it."

Dakoe paused, noticing he made a disgusted expression, "What?"

"Don't. Say. A word." Destan warned as he closed his eyes and took a deep breath. "I can't run like I have been and us not be picked off by Ingrid. I know you said she likes to toy with her mark and her first shot might very well have been a scare tactic, but I've never known anyone but a Strigidae Huntress to have the confidence it takes to aim so close with the intent of missing. — And seriously, I would've been carrying Callimay this whole time. Doing this is going to tip them off at some point if it hasn't already. I can't— never mind. The only way I know for me to use my ability and this to work is to carry you. Do not! Do 'not', make this anymore awkward than it is!"

Destan got to the building with no trouble and dumped this man disguised to look like his wife on the ground.

"So… meet you at the car?" Dakoe asked unfazed as he popped up.

"Yes," he responded in a flat tone and took off.

After waiting for a little while, making sure Destan was gone, Dakoe looked toward the tree line by the gate and waved.

A few moments later, Dakoe ran from the tree line, across the short field, and to the building! He kept a low profile, but stood up and bolted when he saw Callimay crumble to the ground, "Are you alright?"

"Just… just give me a minute." Her voice quivered as she tried to control her breathing.

"I told you not to do this. You're not cut out for this, Callimay. If anything happens to you— Destan's gonna kill me if he finds out!"

"If anything happens, Destan most likely 'will' die! You know that, Dakoe." She stifled another sob as she got to her feet. "I can't bear the guilt of not doing everything I can to bring him back if he does snap. This pain right now is nothing compared to what that would be. I promise I won't do anything to mess things up. I promise."

"Come on." He surrendered as he hurried up the steps. *Looks like she used this door to get in… these aren't hers 'or' Ingrid's markings, though. It c—*

"Well?" She said impatient as she shook her hands. "We don't have any time to lose."

This building had a musky smell and shadows which looked eerie and unnatural. There was a silence in the air that felt like secrets were suppressed. Unlike what she expected, it wasn't grungy or decaying like the title "abandoned" hinted toward. Everything was in good repair; nothing looking out-of-date or worn out. The smell was simply from a lack of temperature control and ventilation in the building.

The first little bit was easy for her, but then things changed. Dakoe saw she was starting to panic and asked, "What is it?"

She yelped and jumped back from him; her eyes wild with fear.

*Callimay. Why are you so stubborn? Just go back to the car.* He sighed in anger, and then put his hand on her shoulder and finished, "Just relax. Take a deep breath. Hyra isn't the markswoman, Ingrid is."

"That doesn't make me feel better." She grimaced as she heard a single shot from the other building. "Destan!"

"Come on, Callimay. We've got to get Rocher out of here first. Then we can go help Destan."

"A… alright. I guess—"

"Can you hear Destan?" Dakoe asked in a stern whisper as he grabbed her by the shoulders to try and calm her. "Reach out. Find him. I need you to focus. Do it!"

"I… I don't— but how c— yes. Yes I can."

"Good. Now tell me where Rocher is."

"I can't, Dakoe. I can't leave Destan…" Callimay started to cry. "He's not doing well."

"Trust him. You said he can get himself out. Let him work. We don't have much time! Find Rocher."

"Wait. I… I can hear Rocher too! It… it's like when Tore—"

"Then where is he?"

"He… he's in the room with Hyra."

He grabbed her hand and took off, knowing precious seconds were ticking by and they needed to get this done as soon as possible.

They settled down beside the door Callimay pointed to. Dakoe peeked in and saw Rocher tied up, leaning against the wall near the door. Hyra was watching out the window, talking to herself out loud.

*Callimay?*

*What?*

Doing things as quiet as he could, he got to his feet while staying hunkered down; moving behind her as he motioned: *Rocher's right inside. We can't risk him making much noise, so you need to let him know we're here. Okay? … He doesn't look like he can move very well so I'll have to go in and free him.*

*What if Hyra catches you?*

Dakoe smiled as he tilted his head, *She won't shoot me if that's what you're asking. Now go on. I want him to know we're here so he won't be too shocked when he sees me.*

*Rocher? Rocher it's me, Callimay.*

*Milady?* He asked weary as he looked over.

She gasped and bit her lip, trying not to cry out. Rocher was almost beaten beyond recognition. Who could do such a thing? Surely Hyra didn't. Was Ingrid that strong? — What about Destan!

It took her every ounce of strength she had left to finish what Dakoe reminded her to do: *Rocher? A friend is with me. He's going to come in and help free you.*

Unable to even think to himself, Rocher rolled his head over to the other side. He was in no condition to be moving anywhere.

*Is she focused on the other building still?* Dakoe asked as he crept up beside her, ready to make his move.

*Umm… yes.*

*Here goes nothing,* he took a deep breath and raced in.

Without any hesitation or looking at Hyra, he untied Rocher. It was easy enough to get that done, but on the polar opposite side of things, it was just as difficult to help him to his feet. Dakoe had Callimay take his other arm as they got to the door, but Rocher was too much for her to support; he stumbled over the threshold and they tumbled into the hall.

Nothing could erase the amount of noise that now filled the air. Within seconds, booming sounds shook the air and the floor… well, it felt like the noise shook the entire building. Everything was so loud and sudden she couldn't hear and didn't know what happened until she looked up and saw the pained look on Dakoe's face. Hyra gasped as she dropped her gun and flew to him; her hands jerking back and forth as she panicked, "Wait! Dakoe? But how! But I— you're working with them? Why?"

He struggled to say as he dropped to his knees, "Please stop, Hyra."

"But I don't… I don't understand."

Out of the corner of her eye, Hyra caught something moving in the hall and grabbed her gun, jumping up and away from Dakoe, "Get in here or I 'will' shoot!"

Callimay plastered herself against the wall, hoping Hyra wouldn't come out. Her hands were quivering so much and her breathing so hard from panicking: *Destan! I— what have I done?*

"I said: get in here!"

"Callimay? Leave! Now!" Dakoe called out, sounding pained and desperate. "Don't worry about me. Just go!"

She cried as she fought within herself: *I… I can't abandon you!*

Not but a few seconds later, she tip-toed in the room, eyes darting to-and-fro; looking mortified as well as overwhelmed. Dakoe slumped and sighed in frustration, "Callimay…"

Hyra yelled as she pointed with hers, "Throw away the gun."

"A… alright." She stuttered as she tossed it in the hall.

Furious, Hyra shook her gun as she said in a shrill tone, "Why did you trick me like this?"

"Hyra I was only trying—"

"No Dakoe, I meant her. This is all her fault!"

"Hyra please." He begged as he pulled himself up.

"I came to bring you back home. I was going to fix everything. They told me you defected, but I knew I could bring you home."

"The Society isn't your home. Neither is that place we've been at for the last five months." Dakoe leaned his head against the wall. "And you can't be one of them; look at you. You're scared to death. You're not blood-thirsty like they are. Any of them would have shot me again when they saw I was alive. You didn't, Hyra."

"I'm not used to this kind of fieldwork. I'm not a Trencher."

The sound of a shot from the other building rattled its way through the air, prompting Callimay to reach out to Destan to make sure he was alright. She sighed when she realized he was; her now able to kneel beside Dakoe and tend to him since Hyra was distracted.

He wheezed as he grabbed her hand with his bloodied one, "Don't bother, Callimay. It's alright."

"You don't sound or look alright." She whispered as she grabbed him so he wouldn't fall. "Dakoe—"

More shots kept Hyra distracted; her rattled enough to contact Ingrid, "What's going on over there? ... Hey now. I've got my own problems. ... Don't remind me, missy. I know. I— Hey! Stop!"

"He needs help, Hyra." Callimay pleaded as she stepped back to appease her. "If he doesn't get some soon—"

"This is all 'your' fault, little miss 'innocent angel'!"

"You were never meant to do this." Dakoe winced and fell over. "You're meant to be with your family."

"But I'm doing this for them. Don't you see that?" She breathed hard and shifted her gaze from him to Callimay; looking like she wanted to put the gun down and help him, but didn't want Callimay to move. "I just don't understand why—"

"Your mother's dead, Hyra." He confessed, his eyes struggling to stay open as he began to wheeze more and more.

"What! What do you mean?"

"Your parents were told you died in an accident." Callimay stepped up, trying to get Dakoe to conserve his energy. "Your mother was so overcome with grief she passed away not long after. Your father's been hanging onto the hope you were alive all this time. He wants you back home, Hyra. He told me himself that he wants his little girl back."

"You're saying that to twist me into defecting." She shook her head uncontrollably as she pulled the trigger back.

Callimay yelped as she closed her eyes; too scared to move.

Dakoe yelled, summoning the last bit of strength he had, "Stand down, Hyra! Do it! I'm still your superior! Stand. Down!"

She cried as she obeyed him, "But it's all her fault."

Hyra was startled by another shot from the other building; her knee-jerk reaction to pull the trigger. Callimay was pushed to the side and out of the way just in time to save her life.

"Dakoe!" She cried out as she scrambled to her feet. "H... hang in there. Destan should be here in a bit." *He's got to!* *Destan, I need you!* "He... he'll know what to do."

He began to cough up spatters of blood, followed by a small stream running down the side of his mouth. The first shot was bad enough; but this one? He smiled as much as he could and wheezed as he rubbed her arm; barely getting out in gasps, "Tell that Destan of yours he better take good care of you… for me. Wish I would have been the one to summon the courage to ask you to marry me… but I know this is better. I wouldn't want you… you to be a widow so soon. I… I love— I'm sorry for everything I did and didn't do, Callimay. I know I did so many hurtful things. Please forgive me. I know this really doesn't make up for the past—"

"Just hang in there Dakoe. Please." She began to panic as she looked around. "Everything's alright between us. I forgive you. Just hang on."

"Godspeed Callimay." He faded out as he closed his eyes; his hand losing its grip on her and falling to the floor.

"No!" Hyra screamed as she fell across his lifeless body. "No, no, no! You can't be gone! … Dakoe!"

Callimay had never seen someone die before; she couldn't move. She'd never seen someone sacrifice themselves… to protect her.

Hysterical and in a frenzy of sorts, Hyra was trying to wake him by rubbing his face, "Dakoe. Please! Babe, don't die. I can't lose you. I can't— this is all— I— but you promised me. You said w— You! You took him from me, you hussy! No man has ever been good enough for you; have they? You threw out Toreon, toyed with Webb, and then went after Destan — and who knows who else — and now look what you did to Dakoe!"

"I… I didn't do anything!" She shook her head, still scared to death.

"Yes you did. Ingrid told you and Destan to come, not Dakoe."

"I don't— what does that have to do with—"

"Shut up already!" She screamed as she raised her gun.

"Hyra no!" Callimay heard Destan call out.

"Father?" She asked in utter bewilderment as she lowered her gun; seeing her father standing in the room. "Why are you wear—"

"Don't do this."

"She killed him, father!"

"No. 'You' killed him." He said stern as he inched his way closer, his one hand extended. "She didn't make you pull the trigger."

"She deserves to die, father! She killed the man I loved." Hyra shook her head as she turned and raised her gun yet again.

There wasn't enough air left in the room to take a breath. A single shot ripped away every last ounce of it. Callimay yelped, her facial expression matching her rigid body: frozen with fear.

Destan yelled in terror as he ran over, "No! Calli!"

He grabbed her by the arms, horror in his eyes as they screamed with tears. Her breathing skipped and stuttered as she went limp in his arms, "Calli no! I—"

"It wasn't me," she took a deep breath, gripping his arms as she gained her footing and looked up. "Destan? I— where's Justice Wan?"

The faint sounds of someone moaning caught their attention, so they looked back and saw Hyra staring at them. She let her gun fall as she pulled her other hand away from her chest. It was dripping with blood and trembling. Gasps came in fits and spurts as she stumbled, her crumbling to the floor beside Dakoe. She started crying as she mouthed something and stretched her hand out to him. After a couple more gasps, she stopped moving, her eyes having that lifeless stare in them while her hand fell to the floor; inches from Dakoe's.

"Who fired that shot!" Destan yelled, shoving Callimay behind him and pulling his gun.

"It was of my doing," a lethargic voice replied, dropping the gun they had as they stumbled and hit the doorframe. "I only found it of—"

"Rocher! … We need to get you to Doctor Gerould right now." Destan ran and caught him. "Calli? We need to go."

It was all she could do to stay standing, and yet she was so petrified that there was no way she could move. Him repeating what he said couldn't pull her eyes away from the bodies in front of her.

Seeing the look on her face kept him calm as he sighed while he helped Rocher sit down; turning back to bring her along.

"What is happening, Destan?" The fury inside her bursting open; her lashing out and beating her fists against his chest. "Why did Dakoe have to die? Why! He didn't do anything to deserve this! He was righting his wrongs. How could—"

"God is in control, Calli. We've got to trust Him. — I know it's hard, but we've got to take care of the ones left behind who are alive. … We have to leave them. They're gone. There's nothing we can do for either of them now. … I'm sorry." He tried to calm and be as understanding as possible. *If we could take down Baleck and those who know about the serums, we can end this for good. Things are bad enough and we'll keep dealing with this until they're gone — every last one.*

֍

Hearing his voice constantly reminding her to keep up with him was so much better than the gunshots still ringing in her ears, but what he was saying reminded her: this was real. Everything she kept telling herself was a bad dream actually happened, the blood on her shirt wasn't pomegranate juice… bad things happen to good people.

During this all, Destan tried to be attentive; but he couldn't lose his rough exterior: rushing around, slamming car doors, and even driving aggressively. This was who he was in these instances. There wasn't time for anything else.

But she didn't understand this; the fact that they weren't safe. By looking at her, he remembered: *She's never been through anything like this. ~ Priorities. We have to get back first. ~ I'm not saying that. I'm just saying can we tone down the curt attitude, Boon? And what about emotions? I don't think she's paying any attention right now. ~ I can't b— you're right.*

֍

There was the "small" issue of no one knowing Callimay was gone that came up when they got back. She was already cowering from him, but now she was downright terrified. The look in his eyes was much like what she remembered from when he threw her off the cliff.

Once things calmed — mainly Destan — the long wait for help to arrive started. It was evening before Doctor Gerould arrived, but once there it didn't take him long, "They gave it their best but he's one tough cookie, that's for sure. — He's fine, Callimay. Don't worry. — The dressings might need to be changed tomorrow, but other than that, he just needs rest. He doesn't need to be transferred."

"Thank goodness." She sighed; turning to ask Destan when she saw him walking past, "Where are you going?"

107

No response.

Doctor Gerould encouraged as he patted her shoulder, "You better get some food and rest."

She let out a painful breath and hung her head; nodding as she walked away. Alone and still reeling from what happened, she went out on the bedroom balcony and stood there. The day started so wonderful: Destan and her were growing closer; he was opening up about a side of him she'd been excluded from, and he seemed to be healing. Then Mr. Freigh and Dakoe showed up, followed by the phone call about Rocher: *God, I know You've made me strong, but I don't know how much more I can take. Please help me! It seems like the only assurance I have right now is that something is going to go wrong at any moment. I just— please help me, Lord! In Your Son's Name I pray, amen.*

The door opened after a few minutes; Callimay knowing from how they walked who it was. They came up and stood beside her, leaning on the railing as they sighed shaky, "Don't 'ever' do that again, Calli."

"I'm sorry."

Destan took her hand and pulled her close, "I never knew I could be so horrified, but seeing her point that gun— how did you get there? When did you switch places with Dakoe?"

"I… well I was actually… I was with you the whole time."

"You mean— you were the one who almost got shot!" He grabbed her shoulders and pushed her away.

"Yes," she cowered, turning away and gripping the railing.

"Calli!" He sighed in anguish as he stumbled back, covering his face with his hands. "Why would you do that!"

"I thought I was helping."

The muffled sounds of thunder began reverberating through the air; the wind now tossing Callimay's hair every which way. As ominous as this storm that was still over the water looked, there was another "storm" that concerned Callimay more… and he was standing right behind her.

Summoning the courage to face him, she turned only to find he was gone. She crumbled to the floor and leaned against the metal railing there on the balcony; crying, "I know I scared you. I just thought things would go better if— it all made so much sense in my mind. I was so focused on— oh what's the use! I could say, 'since I'm fine there's nothing wrong' but I know better! I know you told me to stay. And I know Dakoe was against my idea the entire time. Maybe if I would've stayed he wouldn't be dead. M… maybe I caused this all. — I'm sorry Destan! It may not mean anything but I am. … I'm sorry, Dakoe. I am. I… God, please help me!"

The storm made landfall not much later and unleashed the intense power it built up while over the churned waters. Rain came down hard and fast but Callimay didn't move while the wind rushed up the cliffside and streaked across the open area and gardens. Lightning and thunder played their duet non-stop, their melody slowly morphing into the sound of gunshots.

₨

Destan, meanwhile, went to see about having dinner brought to their room since it was getting late. The more he walked around the slower he got. Even his speech was slow. Things were starting to catch up with him. He wasn't immune to shock. This wasn't just his injuries.

As he walked up the stairs, Doctor Gerould stopped him, "Destan? Let Rocher rest. Don't force it. I know there are questions you have for him but they have to wait. 'All' of them. That's an order."

"But I— alright."

"I will head to the plant in the morning and see if the bodies are still there. If so, I'll see to it things are taken care of."

His reaction time was even slower this time, it taking a few seconds before he nodded.

The longer he looked, the more it appeared to Doctor Gerould that the young man in front of him was almost asleep standing up, "Destan? … Destan, do you need me to check your arm and leg?"

"Huh?"

He sighed as he pulled his arm to him and pushed his sleeve up; Destan grimacing, "I guess it's not 'that' bad. … Try to get some rest. At least clean these, alright? — Did you get kicked in the face? Hello?"

"I'm fine and I'll take care of it."

"Just don't wait too long." He put his hands up and backed off; waiting a little while before finishing, "I can tell you're in shock fro—

don't try telling me you're not, Destan Quinton. It's been a while since you've dealt with this. And really? It's never something you got used to because of what happened with—"

"Alright!" He snapped back.

"Rest, Destan. Now. Callimay won't be able if you don't."

"Fine." He growled; dragging himself to their bedroom.

As he looked up, he saw her on the balcony. He jerked back and shook his head, blinking a few times. Now he only saw the wall… like he should have: *You're losing it Boon. ~ After all the craziness today I'm not surprised.*

After shutting the door, he turned and saw her like he had earlier. He put the thought aside for one more upsetting. Rain was coming into the bedroom, drenching whatever it could get its merciless hands on. Destan snatched a blanket off the bed and stormed over.

"Say it and get it over with. I'm ready. You've had enough. You're done trying to be patient and deal with me. Since I'm not listening to you when you try to protect me, there's no use in you trying anymore. I'm not who you thought I was so you're going to send me a—"

"Callimay, stop!" He threw the blanket down and grabbed her by the shoulders. "Yes. I 'am' mad. I'm infuriated. But it's because I care about you. I love you. And I don't 'ever' wanna lose you. Maybe I would have reacted like that in the past, but my Calli wouldn't think me to be so shallow and careless now… would she? Calli? Calli I 'have' changed, haven't I? — Are you thinking about what you're saying? I don't think you are. I think you're in shock and terrified like I am. I think you're coping the only way you know; but you've got to stop! I need you to pull yourself together. I need my Calli back!"

Destan helped her to her feet by this time, his voice eventually sounding desperate. She stood there and stared at him; eyes glazed over and unable to focus. Nothing felt real. Him touching her wasn't even a sensation that would register. All she could see was Dakoe collapsing in front of her — and Hyra.

The sight of that carnage was horrifying in its ability to hypnotize, and it reveled in torturing her. No matter what she tried, she couldn't erase those memories which were now burned into her.

"Calli! Calli come back to me."

Not but a moment later her eyes rolled back and she collapsed into his arms. He scooped her up and ran inside, slamming the doors behind him. She was soaked to the bone, her skin pale and ice-cold.

"Calli? Calli wake up." He continued to plead while he rang the buzzer, realizing Rocher couldn't help; this causing him no shortage of frustration and desperation. "Calli I can't have you both— fight! Come on. I know you can. I'm not giving up. You're worth too much to me for me to give up. I've given you so many reasons and opportunities to give up on me, but you never have. Please don't give up. Not now."

What upset him so much just a minute earlier didn't matter anymore. It felt as if what happened about a month prior was repeating itself. But this wasn't that serious… was it? She was just in shock. Why was he reacting like this: telling her to fight?

Time passed painful and slow. Or was it gut-wrenching and fast? Possibly a combination of both? Whatever the case was, it was too long. He held her in his arms; trying to keep her warm while at the same time trying to find comfort and rest for his exhausted body and mind… working through the shock he now admitted he was in.

A cold hand eventually brushed the side of his face while a soft voice whispered, "I'm here, Destan. I… I'm sorry I—"

"We'll talk about it later. Just… rest."

"You're hurt!" She gasped, seeming to finally realize the condition of his face and arm. "What happened?"

"I'm fine. It's nothing. Lance said it just needs a good cleaning. I'll do that before dinner. It should be up soon. … And then we both need a good night's rest."

# ~ 6 ~

Even though rain tapped on the windows in a repetitive manner, Destan knew good and well it stopped one hour, seven minutes, and thirty-one seconds ago. He did get some sleep, but he couldn't put to bed all the inconsistencies from the day before: *She had me dead to rights and knew I couldn't pull the trigger. I couldn't pull it even for Calli. I just couldn't do it. Ingrid had no reason 'not' to pull the trigger. … But then why did she vanish when she had the chance to carry out what she was being paid for?*

The sun started streaming through the window, landing on the peaceful and resting face of his wife. Unfortunately, this wonderful sight did nothing to calm his irritation and questions. He rolled over and looked at the clock, then let a rough sigh drag out as he got up.

Ƌ

Once he was in the hall, he poked his head in Rocher's room, finding him asleep. This helped some, but he still wasn't his normal self.

When he got downstairs, he could hear a couple of the men in the kitchen starting breakfast. Their chatter was hushed; but if you put your ear to the door, chances were you'd hear what they were saying. The topic being discussed wasn't one he needed to hear, so Destan went to his father's laboratory until it was time to eat.

As he sat at the computer, he saw the papers Callimay pulled out of the stack. He groaned as he spread them out, seeing what they were: *This is all my fault. I should've listened to Calli. Maybe—*

"Destan, don't ever blame yourself." She looked timid and afraid as she spoke.

He jumped up from his seat, saying worried, "Calli! Calli it's still really early. You should be resting."

"You got up and I couldn't bear being alone after everything that happened yesterday."

"I'm sorry I woke you."

"I…" she hesitated as she looked at the floor. "I've been awake. … I really didn't get any sleep last night."

"You didn't have another nightmare, did you?"

"Not exactly."

"Oh Calli." He sighed as he motioned to her; letting her curl up on his lap. "I wish I had a better handle on things… catching my spikes sooner or preventing them altogether. If I could change things, I'd—"

"You have a better hold on things, Destan. You do. Yes, you have your moments, but you're also noticing them quicker and even taking care of it yourself when you can. Like yesterday afternoon. Remember? When Mr. Freigh told you about Baleck? … Destan? I… I know I've made things harder for you as of late and I'm sorry—"

"You were doing what you thought was best. … Just remember: under stress, people can react very different than you would assume from knowing them under normal circumstances. Ingrid and Hyra aren't your roommates anymore. … And I think you know that's true because of me. Right? … Don't start blaming yourself."

There was a striking pause. He almost didn't want to, but he looked down. After sighing, he leaned his head back and closed his eyes, "I know, I know. You told me that very same thing not but a minute ago."

"No. That's not what I was going to say. I'm not saying it's not true, but— how's Mr. Freigh doing? Did you check on him last night?"

The look on his face was more than an answer. It scared her so much she leaped off his lap and pinned herself against the wall. Callimay heard his footsteps thunder down the stairs after the lower level door slammed against the wall.

When she started down the stairs herself, she heard Destan's deep voice growling and grumbling. A small part of her didn't want to get anywhere near him in this state; and yet the bigger part of her that loved him won out. As she came around the corner, she saw the door to the room wide open. It was empty!

"I should've stayed. I'm sorry. This is all my—"

"Callimay stop it!" He snapped; flashing his green eyes at her.

She jumped behind the corner — scared he might grab her and do who knows what — but he whipped back around and didn't pay any attention… or even care to ask why she was so scared.

It took a bit, but she gathered herself and stayed. She skirted the edge of the room and sat where she did the day before. The only thing was: she had to pick the chair up off the floor. Why was it on its side?

Something wasn't right. The more she looked around where they were, the more she wondered. Destan was standing by the opened door, having the fingerprint reader opened and its "guts" hanging out. He was engrossed in it for some reason and kept bickering with himself as he worked.

Callimay crept over and peeked in the room where Mr. Freigh should have been. There were scuff marks on the floor from the desk that was now on its side; dents peppering the walls. What an effort he made to escape!

Or was that wat happened?

The table was bent and twisted in the middle of the one side; blood drops here and there: *What in the world happened!* "Destan?"

"What?" He replied, an edge still in his tone.

"Umm… did you do that to the reader thing?"

He tugged on the wires sticking out of the wall, "This? No. … What is it? Why are you down here?"

"I… I don't think Mr. Freigh left of his own accord."

"And 'why' would you think that?"

"Well excuse me 'Mr. Nevrille' for apparently being the only one paying attention to how this place looks compared to when we left — or at least when 'I' left." She clenched her fists; tired of fighting the pain she was feeling. "Have you abandoned all logic and just jumped to the conclusion Mr. Freigh used us? How did he get out? There's no way to open the door from inside. And by what you've said, it looks like someone destroyed the reader. — And what about the lies he would've needed to keep straight that whole time?"

Destan didn't answer. He looked around the room and then to her, his eyes now staring at her in a confused and questioning way.

"Look at the blood. Look at how everything here has been pushed and tossed around: as if Mr. Freigh were fighting someone who broke in. — 'Look', Destan! Why can't you see it? I'm no sleuth and yet I can. Someone came and he didn't want to go with them. … I know you think this was made to look like there was a confrontation, but I have a harder time believing that than this. — Destan at least listen to me. Come back!"

He disappeared up the stairs for a while and then plodded back down in a haphazard way. The expression on his face pretty much said what he uttered in a shocked voice, "But who could've known how—"

"Mr. Nevrille?" They heard someone call down the stairs. "Rocher is awake and asking for you."

"We're coming." Callimay answered as she looked back at Destan who was standing there, oblivious to everything.

🕉

The journey up the stairs was long, painful, and lonely. She gripped the railing as she went, trying to keep her balance. It felt like the staircase was a never-ending ascent; as if the lower level were holding her hostage. But this was because of her migraine and the "fog" she would have from it: time perception and distance becoming skewed.

When she got to the main floor, Callimay took a deep breath and attempted to smile, "Did you take his breakfast up?"

"Yes'm." The young man nodded as he bowed his head. "That was why I came for you. — Your breakfast is ready as well."

She glanced back but there was no sign of Destan. Her face melted into a look of depression as she nodded him on and dragged herself up to Rocher's room.

What in the world? Destan was already there when she opened the door: *How did y—*

*I don't know.* He shook his head, sounding shocked and worried.

"It is an endless source of comfort to lay eyes on you both and be secure in knowing you are both well." Rocher grunted as he started to sit up.

Destan jumped up and stopped him, "Lance said you need to rest as much as possible."

"Pay this light affliction of mine no special affection, Sir. There have been many a time in the past that would rival it for title of being my worst experience with pain. And by your appearance, you tick all the boxes of dealing with a similar situation… and I would in fact be so bold as to suggest you would not think it as such a horrid situation for yourself. Plus, I would not hesitate to guess you wish to have nothing short of a debriefing on the situation to know what transpired."

"I…" he paused; remembering Doctor Gerould's warning. "You need to rest for now. When you're better we can talk."

"But Sir—"

"Please rest, Rocher." Callimay agreed as she walked over. "You getting better is much more important. — Right Destan?"

"As you wish. … Might I at least have the brief audience to request if you did indeed apprehend all three culprits?"

Destan asked unsure, seeing Callimay's expression change, "Three?"

"The young man and two young ladies. Were they all still present at the time of your arrival and subsequent recovery?"

There was an awkward moment of silence. Well; fearful would be a bit more accurate in describing how the air "felt". Not wanting to upset him while answering his question, Callimay wrung her hands as she looked at Destan, "Not all of them."

Rocher nodded, sounding sad and tired, "I see."

"We'll be in later to check on you." She replied in a soft tone as she laid her hand on Destan's shoulder. "Just rest for now."

❧

Though they didn't run out, Destan and Callimay left so they could talk as soon as possible. There was another person they needed to account for: a young man who had free rein to watch their every move and report that information to whomever… even the Syndicate.

Not wasting any time, Destan ran down and talked with one of the men. Callimay then saw him and a few men dash out the front door followed by several voices outside being raised before dead silence.

After quite a while he came back up, wide-eyed and unsure, "Are you positive Ingrid said it was 'just' her and Hyra? I'm not saying she wouldn't lie; I just want to know exactly what she told you."

116

She nodded quickly as he took her hands, "Yes. Yes I'm positive. Who could the young man be? You don't think Toreon got—"

"He's in Ferdinan, Calli. — Do you think it could've been Dakoe?"

"How did he get back here to get Mr. Freigh? There wasn't enough time. And then with security the way it was— if he were the third, why did Hyra shoot him? I've watched movies where things go wrong during 'spy missions', but shooting one of your own? That doesn't make any sense."

Destan leaned against the railing and tapped it in a methodical manner as he listened; then answered as he shook his head, "That's running off of the assumption the third person is also the one who took Mr. Freigh. We don't know that, Calli."

"I… I guess I knew all along there was someone else. Rocher was too injured for even Ingrid 'and' Hyra to have done it. … But the way downstairs— how could it be Dakoe?"

"Now this is all hypotheticals, but. Do you think Willgun already knew Dakoe would bring Mr. Freigh to us? That he was going to have not only the perfect opportunity to destroy the only person who could uncover the despicable acts being done at the Society; but the two who were evading his relentless grasp?"

"It almost worked, didn't it?" She leaned against his chest, her voice quivering as much as her arms.

There was a moment's pause, but then Destan replied in a reluctant and confused manner as he leaned his head on hers, "Almost."

"What's wrong?"

"Ingrid. Everything you said makes sense, but what happened between her and myself doesn't fit this 'assassination' idea."

"What 'did' happen?"

"I'm sorry I dumped you on the ground, Calli. I—"

"I almost laughed, knowing what you were thinking. I was alright."

He rubbed his face a bit and then continued, "When I got inside, I dashed to a spot where I knew I would have cover; though I barely made it there — she 'is' a good markswoman."

"Destan!" Callimay shrieked as she grabbed his arm.

"Shh. Don't get too worked up, I know your head's bothering you. … Her doing that helped me find her faster; but when I got up on the catwalks, she already moved. — I'll say this much: she can't fly for long distances, but she's extremely quick and quiet about it. And the way that building was laid out was perfect for her…"

"So. You got me, huh?" Ingrid laughed as she lowered her rifle.

"Not by accident."

"Well, it'll be more fun for me this way. Callimay would've been 'way' too easy of a target." She snickered as they heard a shot from the other building. "Well I didn't think she'd be 'that' easy."

Destan snapped and lunged at her. By the slimmest of margins she evaded his grasp; sending him tumbling down the metal stairs and slamming into the brick wall. When he came to himself — able to resist the urge to lose complete control — he took off. If not, he would have been a sitting duck.

Feeling comfortable and in control of the situation — his quick response not making her worried — Ingrid stepped out of the shaded corner she found. As she took her rifle out and switched to her heat-seeker vision, she complemented, "You're quite a bit faster than before. You only topped out at 60 when y—"

Right at that moment she could sense someone nearby. But before she could react, he stripped the rifle out of her hand; making her jump up and whip her head around to see where he went.

*Just keep on talking, that's it. I'm not about to complain about you making enough noise for even a bat to find you.* He rolled his eyes as he ducked back in his safe spot and hid the rifle. *Now to finish this. … She was able to see me. ~ Her vision modes. ~ Right. ~ By what she said, she can see you when you're running; but then she can't. ~ Let's use that against her.*

At first she didn't know why he would stay out in the open, but before long she realized he was trying to draw her out. And to add to her frustration, her heat-seeking vision only showed the trail of disturbance he left. But, for as much as she was frustrated, she was equally impressed. She flipped through her vision modes for a while until she found one better suited for her situation.

In the meantime, Destan found himself another hiding spot and waited for a while. She wasn't taking the bait like he was hoping, but that wasn't his concern: *Come on Boon. You haven't done much of anything. Don't lose it. Remember Callimay. Remember how scared she looked and how her hands trembled when you let her go. Remember. Remember her voice and how she begged you to come home.*

When he opened his eyes and took a deep breath, a couple shots ricocheted through the catwalk and landed right beside him. Destan hunkered down a bit more but didn't panic. Were those warning shots? Was she still toying with him?

For as much of a professional as she was, it struck him to hear her, "I'm working. What do you want? … Oh come on, Hyra. This is what we trained for. What's going on with Callimay? … Hyra? Hyra, w—"

In those few seconds, Destan was able to get behind her and knock her down.

To be frank, she was livid that she only had to let her guard down for a few seconds to get in this predicament; so the kid gloves came off. Ingrid wasn't about to let him hold her down.

Knowing she wasn't going to pull punches or toy with him any longer, Destan took off. In the moment's glance he got, he noticed the lone earring she was wearing: *Strigidae Huntress. I should've known: what Dakoe said about her shooting abilities coupled with her stone cold attitude, cadence, and 'fashion'… it all makes sense now. Though that's not much consolation. ~ True. She works with the Syndicate… just on 'her' terms.*

Meanwhile, Ingrid shot at what was now nothing, leaving her infuriated and mumbling a few choice words under her breath. She holstered her pistol with an equal amount of anger and got to another perch so she could regroup.

He was extremely quiet on a normal basis, but, when he tapped his ability he lost that veil. And yet, for as much as she heard, Ingrid still couldn't tell where he was. Had she relied totally on her abilities she would have never gotten anywhere; but she was one who was trained to use all their senses — similar to assassins and mercenaries of the Homeworld. Her nature was to study her prey and adapt so she could take them out.

Nestled in her reclusive corner, Ingrid "listened" to the path he made; her fingers making subtle movements as if she were tracking him without even watching. And then at one point she opened her eyes and came out. Her steady hold on her weapon didn't falter and her breathing was calm. She'd calmed so much that a smile started to spread across her face as she calculated her jump.

Ingrid dropped from her perch onto the catwalk right as he headed toward her.

Destan stopped and drew his gun in one fluid motion.

They stared at each other; looking like they were waiting for the other to fire first, "Don't make me do this, Ingrid."

"The first time is hard, but it'll get easier. Trust me." She chuckled and then narrowed her eyes to match her fiendish smile; fingering her pistol when she saw him eyeing it, "You noticed my baby, did you? I have to say it was a surprise graduation present from my chief sponsor; he really shouldn't have, but I couldn't say no. — Of course for 'you' of all people to recognize it shouldn't surprise me. You loath our code which is a shame, really."

"Who hired you, Strigidae?" Destan demanded; and then asked startled: *Calli?*

She laughed as she threw her head back, "We don't go by that 'title'… Doyen. We affectionately refer to each other as 'sisters'. And you know good and well it's not best practice nor is it financially permitted for any of us to declassify such details."

Destan started to panic, but not by what Ingrid said — Callimay was there! His hands began shaking. She was there! Why was she there? How did she get there? Where was she, exactly? Was she safe?

"This is pathetic." She fumed and rolled her eyes; rubbing the barrel of her gun against her temple before spitting in his direction. "'You're' pathetic. You can't take someone else's life even though it'd be in self-defense and would save others… even your wife."

"There's been enough death, Ingrid. Just put your weapon down."

"There's only two ways out of this, Destan: fight or die." She shook her head and pulled the trigger without any forewarning.

Shattering glass beside him was accompanied by the piercing sound of a shot from the other building. He looked in that direction; Ingrid seizing her opportunity. After a few flamboyant somersaults, she landed a clean, unhindered kick to his face.

She stood over him, snickering as she leaned her stiletto heel into his side, "There's no hiding or taking prisoners in real life, Destan. That barrier won't keep everyone out and you know it. So be a good little coward and run back to your hole where all you Shadows live. It is referred to as Bulwark, right? That's the only safe place on Quidoria you have left. — Take my advice: if you don't kill those in your way without hesitating, then they 'will' kill you. … The Purge will happen. You won't stop it. Not acting like this, anyway. Man up or die."

Destan was down but not out… and she knew it. Ingrid laughed as he tried to knock her feet out from under her, kicking him in the face again, "You're a horrible actor and I highly doubt you would be able to lie if it would save your life. … I hope Callimay's funeral drains your bank account. It seems it's drained your will to live."

Once he came to, Destan staggered to his feet and looked out the window. Ingrid was long gone. He raked his hands through his hair and yelled as he slammed his hands and kicked the catwalk railing; it quivering and rattling from the impact. As aggravating as it was that she outsmarted him, there was an unsettling truth she revealed about him. He'd stared death in the face before and walked away without being shaken or worried about the altercation; but he'd never known the fear of having the woman he loves nearby while going through this kind of situation: *Why in Heaven's name are you here, Calli!*

"…when I was about halfway there, I saw Dakoe lying on the floor and— well you know the rest." He finished; the fear he felt still fresh. "See why I'm confused? Ingrid's a trained assassin-for-hire. She's not the type to take what's called a 'branding job'. There's no money in those. At least not that I've ever heard of."

"I— what's going on, Destan!"

"I wish I had all the answers." He said in anguish as he wrapped her in his arms and rocked her. "I wish I knew, Calli."

"I want this to be over." She gripped his shirt; her voice strained and cracking. "I want a normal life. I don't want to run and hide or look over my shoulder constantly to make sure I'm not being followed, or have to fight to stay alive. We already have a hard life as it is being left-handed! … I don't want to deal with this all as far as Mr. Freigh,

Toreon, and the Society goes. Please make it stop. Please! I want my life with you back! We were just starting to get it and it feels like it's gone now."

As much as he tried to, Destan knew he couldn't find words to appease her. He knew he couldn't let his guard down or make light of the situation. Part of him wanted to, begging him to; but his head knew it was suicidal.

Destan "felt" the same, though: it frustrated him to no end that their life together had been turned on its head. Yes, it was "normal" for him to live like this, but he didn't want it for her. It tore at his heart to see her like this; and even more so to know what danger she was in being with him. Some things started to become clear in his mind as far as why he'd never gotten married… and part of him regretted what he'd done. It wasn't a selfish regret, but the sorrowful type concerning Callimay's safety. What had he done!

He tried not to, but Destan felt he was failing. Failing to keep his Calli safe and give her the life she deserved… and he wanted for her.

## ~ 7 ~

In the blink of an eye, the day was over and the time for rest and relaxation in sleep came. That sounded wonderful, but for Destan it was time for brewing about things he couldn't change or explain. Aside from Ingrid and the young man who were somewhere lurking, there were several other things which concerned him… in a way. How was he able to hear Callimay over the past week when each time she said she made sure he couldn't? How could he see real things through solid objects or jump from place to place? And what about him looking like someone else? How was that possible? Yes, those were known abilities, but they weren't ones he possessed.

The more he thought, the more he became restless. He tossed and turned; trying everything to turn his mind off, "Destan?"

"I— don't worry Calli. Just go to sleep." He brushed the side of her face which was veiled with worry.

"Are you sure?"

"Positive," he let out that small smile. "Just go back to sleep."

He waited until he was sure she was asleep, then got up and went down to walk around outside. It occurred to him as he passed the laboratory door that he had access to the computer now: *I wonder.*

Sure enough, there was a drive overflowing with information about different serums. One stood out. It had the name "Unknown".

It didn't seem "complete" since it only had two documents in it. The name given to both documents made it quite clear though… this was intentional. He opened the first one and began reading what turned out to be the "official" information compilation his father wrote for the Challenger serum. This document was what he remembered reading from his file at the Society — word for word: *Willgun stole my father's work. That murderer~ Why are you surprised a murderer is a thief?*

Destan went back and opened the second document which was hand written. In it, his father summarized how things in Faberton were getting out of hand… to the point that he felt he had to leave out the information concerning what he referred to as "the catalyst" for Challenger: what made it the most powerful serum.

But this document — part of his personal journal — was his safe place where his deepest secrets were kept. He was free to describe what he left out without fear of it being stolen or abused. It was extremely technical at some points, but he did give "layman's explanations"… well, most of the time.

In reality, Challenger was the ability to mimic others by cloning them. There was a contingency though: Challenger had to be in its pure form and given to a person who had the natural ability to learn new skills by observation alone. On top of that, the new abilities could only be gained through physical contact. This contact only had to take place once — a handshake would suffice — but there had to be an instance where the two individuals' skin touched each other's. Destry went on to state that contact time and mimic ability were directly related: more contact equaled more complete mimicking and control. He cautioned it was merely a theory, but finished by saying it was very possible for the person with Challenger — if given enough time — to gain full control of the ability the other individual had.

At the end of this lengthy entry was something that rocked Destan deep. His father's writing style changed… it was personal now.

*…I never meant for this to be used in real life; the serums. It was just something I had always been fascinated with: the stories of old where superheroes rose to fight the ever-elusive villains who always seemed to hold the power to put every individual into subjection through various means. I dreamed of creating a "superhero" who could defeat anyone who stood against them without needing to sacrifice themselves. It was an intriguing thought to explore, but more dangerous than I could have ever imagined.*

*Things were simple for a long time and no one at U of K was bothered by my lack of commitment to duties I had been assigned to… at first that is. I hit a wall in trying to find how someone could mimic other abilities. It was then and there that I should have stopped and burned everything; the stopgap God was giving me. But as a scientist, I merely saw it as an obstacle needing to be overcome for the "good of mankind".*

*I look back and want to take myself behind the fuel cabin and give myself a good once-over. Maybe even two. I was stupid enough to believe this was something worthwhile.*

*There were other red flags I ignored that were "bigger", but this was the first and it should have been the last.*

*It was such a lucrative desire that I pushed my own family aside; being obsessed to the point that I missed out on enjoying moments for what they were. I was missing my only child growing up. Case in point: the first time Destan played the piano. I wasn't seeing it as a magnificent milestone like my Jewel did. No. I saw it as the fix I needed for my addiction.*

*My marriage was even on a decline and yet it didn't bother me. I had to "fix" this problem first; then I could take care of "it". I was losing sight of my marriage as being a bond between two humans instead of an employee/employer contract.*

*I've been able to piece together what I can remember of Destan first playing for the most part; but I know I've lost so much of that event I'll never get back:*

*I'd been written up for missing an important deadline with an experimental treatment for migraines, so I spent most of the evening sulking in my armchair. My stubborn self wouldn't dare tell my Jewel what happened, but she knew something was wrong. I remember how she tried in her sweet way to talk with me earlier, but I snapped at her and stormed out of the room. — I was such an idiot.*

*My Jewel did what she has always done when I'm "in a mood" and had my "treatment" prepared following supper. Destan loved these times when, "Mother's going to entertain you, Father." — The innocence of children. — Those graceful and familiar melodies did their best to pry me away from my secret addiction, but I refused to accept the help being offered.*

*She never showed Destan how to play; he only sat beside her on the bench as her constant companion. He would clap, praise, and then give her a kiss after each piece concluded. — That I do remember. — My Jewel enjoyed her little audience being so close; one smitten and captivated by her ability to make such beauty and emotion come from such a strange piece of furniture. It seemed as if my company alone weren't enough anymore. — I'd say this is in jest, but there is truth to it. She was lonely. I was nothing short of a hopeless reprobate in my role as husband "and" father.*

*Destan got so mad when I went to get him ready for bed. He pushed me back, "I haven't finished yet," and planted himself in my Jewel's lap — making her stop playing. And then the most extraordinary thing happened. He began playing what she had been. Some chords he just couldn't reach because of the size of his hands, but there was no denying the melody.*

*Seeing Destan's natural aptitude to mimic a skill by simply watching was seen by me through my addictive eyes. This gave me the piece I was missing: it wasn't something I could formulate but rather a quality within the person which had to be present for it to activate. I raced out of the room and down to my office. — I didn't even wait for him to finish. I just left.*

*I can formulate so many things, but what I want most can't be: you can't turn back time. There is only one end no matter what people may say when it comes to time. God has set it, and so what we lose in this life is forever gone.*

*This should have been earlier, but I'm afraid my wandering mind isn't able to think in a straight line right now. Perhaps this entire entry is nothing but my endless ramblings of regret, but it is at least something I have Godly sorrow over.*

*If I am to do this confession justice I have to come clean: I formulated Challenger tailored to Destan. He was always so*

*attentive to the stories I would tell about superheroes, that his mutual interest cemented my desire to fulfill this addiction. He always said so determined how he wanted to, "be a superhero when I grow up," but I see my error in justifying my addiction by his immature and skewed reaction to stories "I" created…*

"You made Challenger for me?" Destan said under his breath as he read that small portion again. "It was always meant… for me?"

*…I know at the root of everything Destan only wants to keep everyone safe; and I couldn't be any prouder of my son for that. But the reality of life is: you can only do so much. Sometimes your best one day isn't your best on another. It's not that what was done was wrong, but it wasn't what you knew was possible. No matter how much you know or how much you are capable of, you can't protect those you love from the unknown. You can only prepare them for it and support them when it comes. Life happens and evil is ever present. You don't have to be a superhero to do this. I realize that now.*

*God let me have this idea for a reason, though I fully believe I failed that test; and in a miserable way. But I still have time and Faith that an opportunity will arise to "make this right".*

*This makes me think of when I told my father I was going to marry Lylah. He gave me such sound advice I wish I'd applied to more areas of my life, "We can either choose to see the bad or choose to see the good from things that happen. And then we can either run and ignore it or put the work in and amend the wrongs if there are any we are told of, or find ourselves."*

*The only problem is: time is my enemy right now…*

All along, Destan knew there were important things stored on this computer, but he had no idea just how important! There were so many questions he had, but he only had what was written.

*… When I returned to Faberton to help with the Civil War efforts, I was hopeful to get human trials started within three*

*months. My team consisted of fifteen fully dedicated scientists who were just as enthralled as I'd been.*

*There's not a day that goes by I don't regret letting my pride get the best of me: allowing their lies to feed my addiction. My Jewel warned me the moment I told her about going back, but I chose to ignore the wisdom she was offering me and continue with what "I" wanted...*

"Like you've done for me so many times, Calli." Destan grieved as he thought back. "I really am my father's son."

He kept reading through the document; listening to what he knew was the anger and regret in his father's words. What he said was truly a confession. It was raw; and it was painful... not just for Destry.

When he read the list of the first group of men to undergo processing, Destan shook his head and rubbed his eyes: *Yorick? Abril? Ashte's father? Why would he be in Faberton; they're from Kerogen?*

The rest of the list wasn't something that struck Destan the first time through. He read it again after the shock of seeing the familiar name wore off.

*... Abril Yorick, Kenn Griswold, Joel Purdon, Zeek Vern, Uli Barge, and Len Berchoff...*

"Berchoff!" He exclaimed aloud as he jumped up. "Callimay's— oh please don't tell me this is how he died."

*... They were enthusiastic and eager to get started; as were we all. After explaining what they were being given and how everything would proceed, they were put into processing at the same time.*

*We lost all six at almost the exact same point...*

"Oh, father." Destan cringed as he put his head in his hands.

At this point he had to stop reading. He sat there in the dark and musky room in a daze. Nothing felt real... that was until he heard Callimay scream out.

He darted out of the room and met her at the head of the stairs. Her face was as white as her nightgown and she was screeching and wailing as she clung to the banister.

The second his hand touched hers and she was able to calm enough to notice he was there — locking eyes with him — she collapsed.

☙

Destan was cautious as he walked into their bedroom… but nothing looked out of place. The curtains were pulled and the doors locked. What happened?

By the time he started to lay her down, Callimay had come to and refused to let go, "Easy. What's wrong?"

"They were going to kill me!" She wailed, grasping his duster.

"It was just a nightmare, Calli." He tried to soothe as he stroked her soft, glossy hair. "It's alright. I'm right here."

"It was real, Destan!"

"Calm down, Calli. It was just a dream. Don't think about it."

"Please don't rock me."

"Calli are y—" he paused when he saw the ever-familiar pained look in her eyes. "Do you need me to get you something?"

"Please."

"I'll be right back," he rubbed her arms; trying to convince her to let him go. "It's alright. No one is going to hurt you."

After she took the medicine, Destan held her until she drifted off. His mind was still running laps with all the bombshell news he found out from his father's writings; but then this?

*If I had to guess, it was probably a nightmare about what happened at the plant. She's still torn up about it. Maybe it's going to be similar to how it was after I threw her off White Cove. … At least I don't know what else it could be.*

$$\sim 8 \sim$$

Come morning, Destan woke up and looked down to Callimay who was still safe in his arms. Her face was pale, and she looked like she was in pain. He brushed her hair away from her eyes and kissed her on the forehead before he got up.

Sleeping in the position he did left him sore and stiff, but after a bit he shook it off and got ready so he could head downstairs.

When he shut the door, he saw it wasn't much brighter in the hall than it was in their room. Destan checked the clock against his pocket watch and then looked outside again. Another storm was rolling in: *That could be why she's not doing so w—*

"How are you this morning, Sir?"

"What in— what are you doing out of bed!"

"I purposed myself to venture and see how you and Milady were. Was it her who screamed out during the night?" Rocher asked as Destan put his arm around him for support.

"It was."

"Is she quite alright? The noise which jolted me was quite striking."

"I think she is."

"I am unmistakably convinced she is more than overwhelmed by the events which transpired yesterday. … As I am sure you are, albeit maybe not as severe."

"That pretty much sums it up. It's been a while." Destan sighed as he stopped at the side of the bed.

"If you find there is anything you desire to inquire of me regarding yesterday I am more than willing to—"

"Not right now, Rocher. I— not yet."

"As you request," he nodded; though he looked a bit confused. But he came to understand, since Destan kept staring at the wall, he was worried about Callimay.

Once Rocher was comfortable, Destan left; stopping at the door as he looked back, "I'll get with Lance so he can check on you."

"Thank you, Sir. I do appreciate everything you are doing with regards to my weakened state."

"It's the least I can do. You've done so much for me over the years." He replied thoughtfully as he fiddled with the doorframe.

"It has been of my utmost pleasure, Sir. Truly."

ℬ

After a short phone call with Doctor Gerould, Destan went down to the lower level. But, while down there, he could feel his emotions creeping up. So, he took a walk around the first floor for a while. When he knew he was alright, he went back down; focusing on the fingerprint reader. Much to his surprise, when he put his thumb to it, it responded like it always had. Now he was suspicious and kneeled down to have a closer look. He kept mumbling as he twisted the wires: *That's odd. How could it— what in the world is going on here?*

From what he was seeing, it occurred to him that he might be able to use any finger.

It worked: *Whoever did this knows their way around technology.*

The small box swung back and forth as he let go and stared at it; but he sighed and went in the room. Destan looked where Mr. Freigh had been, agreeing with what Callimay said: a struggle had occurred. Beside the fact things were askew, there was an issue with the cuffs… the set used on Dakoe was intact but Mr. Freigh's was ripped out! There weren't any marks to suggest it was pried off. It were as if someone ripped the clasp and plate straight out. These were soldered into the table! He pulled on the remaining clasp with everything he had: *I'm no wimp and I can't even get it to budge. ~ They must have an ability, look at how the table's bent where they would have grabbed it. ~ Who from the Society could it be and how did they get in without being noticed? ~ What about~ Toreon's in Ferdinan. I called to make sure. You know that. ~ But how else could someone get in and out without being seen?*

133

Destan walked out of the room and stared at the fingerprint reader again; becoming disturbed with what he was concluding: *Unless they never came up the drive. If they were able to hack this… the barrier is nothing but an over-glorified technology screen. ~ But they'd have to hack it from the source. You've never been able to find it. Maybe—*

"Destan?" A weak voice called out from the head of the stairs.

"Coming, Calli." He switched his focus and ran up to her. "Did you get enough rest?"

She grabbed his hand as he walked past, "Some."

"What's wrong? Is your migraine still—"

"Yes," she whispered as she steadied herself.

"Is it the weather?" He asked in almost a whisper as he kneeled in front of her and rubbed her cheek.

"No. Well. I— I know I've had nightmares before, even you know that, but I've never had one like that. I could really feel the pain. I kept running into things as I tried to get away from the person chasing me. My arm and side that I hit are bruised, Destan." She shivered as she pulled her sleeve up. "I don't remember hitting my head, but maybe I did. I… I don't remember."

"Who was it chasing you?"

"I… I don't know. I never saw anyone and I didn't recognize the voice." Callimay sighed as she leaned on him harder.

ℬ

Doctor Gerould showed up shortly after they finished breakfast and checked on Rocher. He was doing much better than expected, but was kept on bedrest for another two days. Destan wanted him to look at Callimay, but she said she was feeling better.

As he got into his car, he heard someone walking over followed by the question, "What did you find when you went to the plant, Lance?"

"I actually didn't get in." He shook his head as Destan leaned on the car door.

"Why not?"

"The walk-in gate was chained like it has been since they closed. I walked around to see about that broken window… it was intact."

"That's impossible!"

"If they 'are' Syndicate, or 'employed' by them, then they're going to do everything they can to cover up a botched job. You know that. — But there might still be residual blood stains that can be picked up… though I wouldn't be too optimistic. And I know you hid the rifle, but we both know Strigidae keep chips on their 'babies'. I doubt I'd find it."

Frustrated and fed up with everything, Destan rubbed his face and groaned. Doctor Gerould wanted to help, but didn't want to set him off again… not when he caught the sight of Callimay looking out one of the upstairs windows, "How are you doing?"

"Calli's having a really hard time." He sighed as he shoved his hands in his pockets and slumped. "She had that nightmare last night and now this migraine…"

"I'm sure it is going to be rough for her, but I asked how 'you' were doing." Doctor Gerould corrected as he raised his eyebrow.

"I'll be fine. I'm starting to remember how it feels."

"Remember. For you to take care of Callimay, you've got to take care of yourself. … If you need me, call."

♉

He stood in the drive and watched his dear friend leave; part of him left wanting. Wanting to talk about what he found out about his father and the serums. Destan knew he'd understand and listen without turning it into a dialogue. Rocher would, but he still needed rest. And Callimay? She didn't need to be concerned with this.

The wind started kicking up, so instead of going for a walk like he planned, Destan headed inside.

As he shut the door, he saw movement in the living area. Curled up on the sofa by the fireplace, fiddling with the chess pieces on the table in front of her was Callimay, "Why don't you go lie down?"

"I've been cooped up in that room for so lo— I'm sorry!"

"It's okay. I know it's hard." He smiled as he kneeled beside her. "I just want you to feel better. How is your arm?"

"Better," she nodded as he took her hand and pushed her sleeve up. "My side is sore, but it's better too."

*I don't want to ignore the fact something bizarre 'did' happen last night, but I want her to rest. She's been through enough. ~ Just ask her,*

*Boon. Get it off your chest.* "C… Calli? Do you… do you need to talk about what happened?"

"No." She said rushed and started fiddling with the chess pieces again, avoiding looking at him.

"Calli if you need to, I'm right here."

She softened as he framed her face with his hands, "I probably just flailed around last night and hurt myself. I mean it's not like there is an ability that could allow someone to do that when I'm asleep. … Right?"

"None that I know of." Destan replied a bit worried; but finished on a better note, "If you do stay here, I'd prefer you cover up. It's going to be chilly and damp today with the storms rolling through."

"Does it do this all the time? Storm, I mean."

"No," he laughed as he opened a small chest on the far wall and started digging around in it. "Technically, pinwheel season is over, but we've had a strange winter with the 'heavy' snow and frost, so things are a bit off. … Here. Try this."

The plush throw felt like his warm embrace as he draped it over her. Callimay looked up and smiled as he leaned over the back of the sofa and gave her a kiss, "I love you Destan."

# ~ 9 ~

Destan waited that night for Callimay to fall asleep and then went down to finish reading what he was almost done with the night prior. His mind was ready this time for whatever shocking news there was in the last part of this document… and he wasn't disappointed.

*…I was devastated — I'd failed these six men and their families — but it didn't faze any of the others. The next day was the same.*

*And the next.*

*And the next.*

*Two weeks and no survivors.*

*This blood bath "had" to stop. I requested an immediate hearing with leadership and found it to be promising; things beginning to improve. And yet, their interpretation of this improvement was far more optimistic than my view. In medical research, a progression from zero to five percent in a treatment's survival rate was in no way "improvement".*

*After a couple weeks of this dismal result, I requested to speak with leadership again. The request was denied and operations return to normal. I tried to detour candidates, but my attempts were met with horrible backlash: I was no longer allowed access to the processing room during its use. At that point, I realized they had no intentions of listening to me. They got what they needed: used me like Lylah warned. My part was done. All they needed were those willing to take part in this lethal experiment that stemmed from my toxic addiction.*

*From the start, they wanted to manipulate and mix serums to "potentially" amplify and compound abilities, but I did all I could to keep them from it. The process for basic abilities was volatile enough; mixing them was asking for nothing but outright mayhem.*

*But with the Civil War reaching its breaking point — the rebels are on the brink of capturing Quaverly at this very moment — the government is looking for quite literally anything to help turn the tide in their favor no matter the collateral damage it may cause.*

*I found proof of their twisting of my work and went to the head of leadership without even stopping to let his secretary know I was there. He tried to calm me; saying the compounds, as he called them, were much more effective and stable than the original serums. Harmon was bold enough to tell me they mixed two of the strongest serums with success — Origin and Dreamer. From the paperwork, Origin was altered in the fusion; but he told me it would serve its purpose nonetheless. The traitor decided that adding insult to injury was fitting; telling me the government wanted to express their gratitude for my help. Perhaps I deserved that "complement" for the wrong I'd done.*

*I rushed home and told Lylah we would be leaving late tonight. Something doesn't feel right. I just hope I'm getting her and Destan out in time; that is if what my gut is telling me is right. Rail transport south is going to be tricky…*

*You mean this was written the day you were—*Destan said in shock as he double-checked the date stamp. *This was the last thing you—*

He pushed as much of his emotions aside as he could; finding the other files for Origin and Dreamer. There wasn't much paperwork on them, but he did discover that Origin was the ability of complete invisibility while Dreamer could manipulate what other people saw: letting them see everything they wanted and loved or everything they feared and dreaded. Destry made notes stating these two were extremely dangerous and could be easily manipulated for evil, so he wasn't going to continue work on them in an effort to keep people safe from what they could turn into.

While he was looking, he saw one he didn't recognize: Liaison. He was rocked hard again when he saw what it was: *Calli!*

*In her true essence, Liaison isn't an offensive ability. She is an aid similar to Seer.*

*Unlike Seer, though, she's much more malleable. Reach and effectiveness are based purely on the person who has her. The individual can receive multiple channels to maximize "reach", but she will lose her effectiveness. — These qualities being inversely related. — If things are kept to an absolute minimum, they can communicate with a single individual from virtually any distance — including both incoming and outgoing aspects.*

*Even though she is malleable, emotions play a huge role in her effectiveness and do limit her.*

*I stated earlier that she has no offensive ability, but there do appear to be indications that some type of offensive capability is hidden within her. I have yet to be able to unlock what it is or how it would impact her. With things so out of control here, I've had little time to work out this "loose end", let alone find why Liaison is one of the most unstable serums being used.*

*Since she is cemented directly into the subject's brain, sharing that characteristic with Dreamer and Grappler, there are so many things that can go wrong. — Neither has been tried, so I am not even sure if they will have the same outcome.*

*I've become more and more concerned about her staying in the lineup, but cannot give up my hope in seeing the potential Liaison may have. Hopefully, once leadership listens to me and things calm down, I will be able to get with Ray and a couple others to dig into this more.*

"When did you send this?" He mumbled as he started looking. "Jubilee Night. That would make it a couple months prior to what you wrote for Challenger." *Calli has an ability she doesn't even know about... and maybe never will? And she could have very easily died!*

Once the shock wore off… again, he happened to glance at the clock and his body instantly remembered how tired it was; him yawning nonstop: *I guess I should try to get some rest at least.*

He pushed his chair back from the desk and then jumped when he turned around, "What are you doing here!"

"I woke up and saw you were gone," the exhausted voice of the woman he loved said in a timid way as she bowed her head; hands clasped in front of her. "I just wanted to see if you were alright."

"Oh. I'm fine, Calli. H… how long have you been standing there?"

"I just got here."

"Are you feeling any better?"

"Much. Are you sure you're alright?"

Destan smiled as he hugged her, "Let's go to bed, huh?"

# ~ 10 ~

Rocher was up and about by the end of the following week, but needed reminders from both Destan and Callimay: he needed to take his time and make sure to ask for help if he was getting tired. They were kind in how they said it, but still firm with making sure he didn't add insult to injury.

During that week, Destan would stay up late and research what abilities he had been mimicking, trying to find the solution to how he was triggering them… and hopefully how he could control them. He wanted to tell Callimay, but things just calmed down — it had been almost a week since her last nightmare, and she hadn't spoken a word about what happened at the plant for just about the same amount of time. More than anything, he wanted to spare her any undue stress; and he knew this would be more than she could handle.

Whether it was intended or accidental, Destan forgot about asking Rocher for his side of things, or looking into what happened to Mr. Freigh. Or had he? Even though things seemed peaceful for the next week, Callimay could tell he saw it as the calm before the storm. She tried in her own little ways to get him to relax, but it wasn't helping.

Desperate to get him "back", she commandeered the kitchen one evening. As she worked, she kept wondering: *Is he going to be alright with 'just' this for dinner? Do I need to fix something else? A dessert maybe? Rocher never said his mother fixed anything else with it.*

"When she fixed what?"

"Oh! Destan! … This was supposed to be a surprise."

"Oh, I'm surprised," he chuckled as he pushed off the wall and walked over. "What are you doing in here?"

She said rushed and worried, "Rocher said he didn't see anything wrong with me fixing dinner for us. Though he did say he didn't know what your wish—"

"I'm not upset. I was just wondering what you were up to. I've been looking for you everywhere. Didn't you hear me calling?"

"I'm sorry. I guess I got so tied up trying to keep from making a mess or dropping something, that I zoned out. — This is the only other thing I could think of to help you since you've 'felt' so unsettled." She looked dejected as she turned back to watch what was on the stove.

"Oh, Calli." Destan sighed as he put his arm around her. "You didn't have to do all this just because of that."

"But I wanted to." *I just want you back. I miss—*

"Wait. Is this—" he started to ask; his eyes wide as he jerked back. "Is this soft lasagna?"

"It's alright isn't it? Rocher said it was a favorite of yours. If it's bringing up bad memories I'll stop— Destan?"

He stood there and looked like he stopped breathing. It scared her, but before Callimay could say anything, he started smiling and his eyes became so soft and tender in their gaze. He pulled her close and rocked her as he struggled to get out: *I love you.*

*I love you too. It… it's okay then?*

A longer than usual pause filled the air before he took a deep breath and smiled; him now making a face, "Well I haven't tried it yet. And to answer your earlier question: oyster crackers. Better yet, that 'and' buttered bread. It can be our dessert."

"Alright then!" Callimay smiled as he tapped her nose; leaving to look in the pantry: *I saw it when Barton showed me w— aha! Here it is.*

When she came back, he was standing beside the stove with a bowl and spoon in hand, "Destan Quinton Nevrille! What are y—"

"What, Callimay Rose Nevrille?" He swallowed what he was able to sneak a bite of; exaggerating practically every word he said. "I'm just doing quality control. Remember, I said I couldn't say it was alright until I tried it. — Woman? You may have to make another batch. What in the world did you put in it?"

Without paying attention, she ran over and started fretting, "Oh no. What did I do wrong! I tried so hard to follow what Rocher gave me."

Destan laughed as he set the bowl down and wrapped her in a bear hug; burying his face in her hair, "Nothing. I was just kidding."

"You…" Callimay fussed, trying to be upset as he took hold of her wrists and "fought" with her. "I…"

"I love you too. Now where's the butter?"

"Really? … Ugh! It's over here."

"Good." He winked at her; and then paused when he saw how her eyes sparkled, "Thank you, Calli. This really did help."

ß

They enjoyed their dinner and then cleaned up the kitchen together. It was awkward to her — having help around the kitchen — but as far as Destan was concerned, he was comfortable helping in whatever capacity she needed him… and knew exactly where everything was. He even rolled up his sleeves and washed the dishes!

Callimay wouldn't have thought him to ever step foot in this room, let alone work in it. But then again, she was thinking of rich young men like Toreon — and her Destan was nothing like that.

She was hoping since he felt more relaxed that he wouldn't be restless and stay up; doing whatever it was he was doing so late at night. Anxious and cautiously optimistic, she lay there with her eyes closed… only to be crushed with grief.

The door made a painful sound as it closed; her clutching the bedspread: *Nothing lasts with you, does it? Oh, Destan. Why! Why am I not enough to make you stay!*

ß

It was well over two hours later while Destan was pouring over all the notes he had when he heard Callimay scream for him. He reached into his boot and grabbed a knife, rushing out to the vestibule. Her screeching and desperate voice that echoed through the main floor felt like nails on a chalkboard. And yet, as cringe-worthy as it was, it scared him so much more.

"I'm here, Calli." He called out as he got to the foot of the stairs.

Like last time, she collapsed into his arms and started to wake up as he got in their bedroom.

143

He held her and didn't try to lie her down, hoping it would help her calm down faster. She was breathing heavily and had a pain-ridden look on her face. He wondered if it could be from a migraine, but it looked like she had a black eye! Destan thought back, but he was sure he caught her before she hit anything. It was then that he noticed she had bruises all over her forearms.

*What in Heaven's name is happening, Calli?* He set his knife on the nightstand and barely touched her eye, causing her to moan.

She woke up a bit startled and clung to Destan as tight as she could while she cried, "Please don't leave me again."

"I…" he paused; hit hard with what she was implying. "I'm here. I won't go anywhere. Just… try to relax. Whoever it was won't hurt you. — Do… do you have a migraine?"

"Yes."

"Would you let me go so I could get you some medicine?"

"Please don't."

"It's okay." Destan soothed, letting her cling to him as he got up. "It's okay. I'm not leaving."

What in the world would cause her to panic that badly; her not letting him walk twenty feet from her where she could see him… and for nothing more than two minutes?

Some might think she was begging for lost attention, hurting herself on purpose, but Destan knew Callimay wouldn't do that. He saw this as nothing less than his "red flag"… the warning God was giving him that he was falling back.

In short: he was slipping down the slope of becoming addicted. He couldn't deny it. His focus was on finding his "fix" and pushing the woman he loved away. … He was becoming more like his father in a dangerous way.

# ~ 11 ~

*I* *don't understand, Calli. What's causing this? 'Who' is causing this?* Destan said in a frustrated tone as he sat there and looked at her bruised arms and face. *How can a nightmare do physical harm? I can understand mental, but this makes no sense.*

He was entertaining the thought, more and more, that someone with an ability did this. It was now the only logical conclusion in his mind. And in a logical extension of this thought, he realized something else: could this someone be the third person Rocher mentioned?

The sun made sure to remind him that he left his knife on the nightstand; him squinting after the burst of light flashed in his eyes. He put it back and then called for Rocher.

Destan explained that he wanted to be sure breakfast was ready as soon as possible and was something on the bland and soft side.

"Certainly, Sir. I will s—"

"Rocher, one more thing." Destan said in a hushed tone as he motioned and followed him out; but left the door opened. "I should've asked this long before— do you know the name of the young man you talked about when you were held hostage?"

"Well let me reflect for a moment. … I fear that information has escaped me. I am at a loss as to the recollection of that detail. … The more I ponder the thought as well as the event in its entirety; I do not have any memory of him making a declaration of his given name nor hearing the two young women address him by such a style of name."

"What do you mean?"

"The Miss Ingrid, if I am recalling her name correctly, referred to him as Dodge." Rocher explained in his usual, long-winded way as he stroked his mustache. "I'm inclined to believe he holds some higher office within the ranks of Syndicate Falconers by such a demarcation in title being given to him. That of course bears all of its weight upon the contingency of what I overheard indeed being that exact word and its intended purpose being for such a recognition."

Destan let out a heavy sigh and asked more desperate, "Can you describe him? I 'need' you to remember."

"Well, Sir. They did have me bound in such a way that my vision was obstructed during the vast duration of said incarceration. His voice by no means was remarkable. I cannot even recall an accent in his voice. … Though 'none' could be an indication in and of itself."

"Anything, Rocher. Please. Try to remember."

There was a moment of apprehensive silence; Destan on the edge of his seat, so to say. His eyes widened with hopeful anticipation as the older man he'd respected for almost his entire life opened his mouth, "I'm sorry, Sir. I fear my aide in this situation is nonexistent."

That was it; things looked hopeless. It would be easier to track down what year it truly was on the Homeworld compared to finding the person Destan theorized being responsible for this.

"Bear with me. I do remember why I became suspicious of the name being used as the title of a Falconer. His apparel bore the resemblance to what the Prince wore, though it was much more… 'scarce', shall we say? His stance with the fairer sex must be unstable since he finds such 'exhibition' necessary. And to add to that far-fetched ambience, he had longer white hair which was spiked. A tad flamboyant if you inquire of me. He did not strike me as any Falconer we've yet to—"

"Webb." Destan fumed under his breath. "The filth bag."

"You are capable of a positive identification from those details alone! How is that possible?"

"He had to be from the Society, which narrowed my suspects. There was only one guy there with white spiked hair. Webb Whyte. He was the other one who aided and abetted Toreon when he tormented Calli; which would explain his high standing with the Syndicate. And he had the aura about him in regards to— was he the one who beat you?"

"I wouldn't hesitate to say the young lady with me most of the time didn't have enough strength to discipline a duck; let alone the power and skill needed to do what was done to me. And then the other young lady was a breed of Strigidae that makes me fear for your generation and Gathering Night as a whole: she could not have been any more cold, methodical, or secluded. She didn't see it as her 'job' as she said, to get involved with me."

*So she was just there for me? And for only a warning? Who paid her to do that!* "If it 'is' him causing Callimay these nightmares," Destan continued to theorize in a furious tone as he looked back to her. "I swear Rocher: I will find him and he 'will' regret he ever did this."

"I did not mean to cause any undue stress. Please forgive me."

"It's fine, Rocher. Really. I was the one who asked." He, with some force, spread his hand out and laid it on the doorframe while he sighed.

ℬ

By the time he got back to her, Callimay's eye had swollen shut. In a panic, he called Doctor Gerould who tried to keep him calm, "You said you don't see any blood from her eye or nose, so that's a good thing. If she does have a migraine, it's a good chance that the inflammation is from that. — But, go ahead and give her a low dose of pain medication as soon as she can handle it. And then keep cold compresses on her eye it if she can stand it."

"Are you sure, Lance? Doesn't she need—"

"Destan take a deep breath. I wish I could drop everything and come out there, but I can't. … I'm sure she's alright." He continued in his fatherly tone. "Call me if you think something's wrong, or she says she doesn't feel right and asks for me. Okay?"

"O… kay."

Each time got more difficult for Destan; the whole situation with her migraines. He hated seeing her in pain, which in turn made him mad; so then he had to watch himself so he didn't cause her more pain!

She soon began rocking her head back and forth as she worked to wake herself; him keeping her still since she moaned and winced. Even though she was extremely sore — complaining that her arms ached and she felt miserable — she "was" coherent. What a relief!

ℬ

Destan carried her around so she didn't have to walk, even taking her outside for some fresh air. The weather was now kind enough to make up its mind and turn the corner for consistently warmer temperatures, so he wanted her to get as much sunshine and fresh air as she could.

Callimay did enjoy being carried, but it hurt to be held for too long. He was skittish when she yelped and would all but fall at her feet to apologize. She wanted to ask why he was acting so strange, but let it go and enjoyed their time together that was only dotted with interruptions when someone would bring her a new compress.

Yes, he was normally the type to walk with purpose — no deviation from the goal — but today was different. His only "goal" for this walk was to stand beside her; and so, they wandered aimlessly wherever Callimay wanted to go.

❦

After dinner was enjoyed and their evening over, Callimay's attitude flipped… she refused to go to bed, "I know I sound like a silly child, but I don't want to— I 'can't' go through that again, Destan."

"I don't want you to either." He tried to give her a hug without hurting her. "But you can't stop sleeping. You've got to at some point."

She cried as she gripped his shirt, "I'm terrified to even try!"

"It's my fault for leaving. Whenever I'm here nothing happens."

"Y… you'll stay?"

"I should've never left."

He kept at this negotiation of sorts; talking to her in a loving and concerned way while convincing her he would keep her safe. Destan stayed up and watched over her, thinking somehow he was going to keep whatever — or whomever — away by doing so.

Under normal circumstances it wasn't an issue for him to stay awake, but with all the emotions he "endured" that day, he passed out.

Not long after this, Callimay opened her eyes. She looked terrified, but bit her lip and kept herself from screaming. — the poor thing! — She then tried to slip out of Destan's arms without waking him.

Once freed, she tip-toed to the balcony and pulled the curtain aside. The moon was almost full and was so bright that it looked like the early morning hours outside.

She leaned against the doorframe for a while, her head beginning to bob. At one point her knees started to give way, scaring her awake. Callimay jerked herself upright and crept to the door. While opening it, she kept an eye on Destan to make sure she didn't disturb him. So she wouldn't have to worry about it when she came back, Callimay left the door cracked. Then, after waiting a few moments, she scurried down and around to the veranda.

Not having any purpose but to stay awake, she moseyed up the stone path to the cliff and stood there. She was ginger as she folded her arms across her chest; taking a stuttering, deep breath when she did.

The stones on the path caught the moon's rays in certain places and reflected them back, just like the sun. Though the orb in the sky was bright enough to scare the stars away and change the "fabric" of the night sky; the moon was soft in such a way it calmed the waves that normally crashed against the cliffs.

As she glanced around at the sleepy landscape which curled up and went to sleep long ago, her weary eyes cried out for something to help her stay awake. The roses answered her, showing how they were wide awake and enjoying the stillness of the night.

Callimay was so tired, but she couldn't bear the thought of going through what she had just been through the night before. Destan was with her, but somehow that didn't feel like enough protection… or the right kind.

It was quite obvious her mental faculties were moving at an inchworm's pace, and in no beneficial direction: she was standing right at the edge of the cliff. The soft breeze that rushed up from the water's edge, accompanied by the glistening light which flickered off the water, began its deadly serenade; knowing it wouldn't meet much — if any — resistance from its prey.

ॐ

Destan woke up and rolled over, only to find Callimay's side of the bed empty and the curtains pulled back from the balcony doors. Not but a second later, he gasped as he jumped up and looked around. Seeing their door ajar, he yelled out, "Calli!"

He grabbed his knife and bolted into the hall, calling for her.

No answer.

Not caring if he woke everyone, he darted downstairs and searched everywhere… even the lower level.

Still no sign of her and no answer to his repeated calls.

The only place left was outside. Destan made as much sound as a herd of thundering, wild Mustangs as he ran through the main floor and out the front door; his eyes darting as he started yelling out.

When he came to the back of the mansion, he panicked, "Calli, no! Don't— Calli!"

She flinched when she heard his boisterous voice, but was so tired that it was all the reaction she could muster.

In less than a second, he scooped her into his arms and held onto her as tight as he dared; cradling her head against his, "Calli please don't. This isn't going to fix it. I'll find out what's going on, I promise. Please just… just don't do this."

"Huh? I… oh. I wasn't going to jump." She answered groggy as she blinked slowly. "I was just trying to stay awake."

"Why didn't you wake me up?"

"You were resting. I didn't want to disturb you."

Destan took a shaky breath and leaned his cheek against hers. His heart was still pounding from the horror he felt of not knowing and then seeing where she was; but at the same time, he was calm because he had her in his arms and she was alright. — His emotions were working overtime tonight.

As he began walking back, she drifted off. He whispered as he kissed her forehead, "Just rest, my Calli. I'll figure out what's going on and do whatever I can to fix this."

# ~ 12 ~

The next morning felt like a different world; Callimay woke and saw Destan sitting next to her. He looked relieved and happy to see her, was holding her hand, and she felt him fiddling with her hair. Without him even saying a word, she knew by the way he smiled and sighed… things were alright, "Good morning Destan."

"Good morning Calli. Are you feeling any better?"

She nodded while she rubbed her arms and sat up, "Some. At least I don't have a migraine. — Did you get any rest last night?"

"Enough."

$

After breakfast, he let her join him while he started investigating what ability Webb had. He had a sofa put in the room so she could relax, but Callimay preferred to curl up on his lap. Destan didn't object to having her close; though he was concerned he might hurt her.

It wasn't long before she fell asleep, but even before that, she never asked what he was doing; her mind too sleep-deprived to care since her body was still trying to recover.

Destan first scoured through the serum names to find something that "sounded" like a mental ability. His father's naming method was similar to two other naming systems he was familiar with, so there were several he "tossed out" without even opening them.

The "possible" list was still long, and he often became cross-eyed from reading one promising description after another. In those moments, he would rub his face and mess with his hair, then look down at Callimay, and remember why he was looking. Hearing her

151

moan or mumble in her sleep would make him forget about everything and hold her close. He wasn't about to lose sight of who was important to him. … Not again. He was going to learn from his father's mistakes and make this change in his life last.

♫

A few days passed with no leads. He was discouraged but wasn't about to give up.

Buried at the bottom, so to speak, was something which sounded exactly like what Webb could utilize… and then another. Fixated with this victory, he flew through the last few and found these two contenders were all that stood the second test.

The only problem was: Destan needed something to prove which one it was. And what that something was wasn't what he wanted: *She has to get into the nightmare so she can figure out if she's able to see anything around her. It's the only way to distinguish them from each other. ~ But that's the last thing I want her to go through! Especially if this 'is' the ability Webb is using! — Why can't it fall on me? Why does Calli have to go through this? … Why did you do this, father? Why did you make these? Why!*

He again looked down at Callimay who was fast asleep on his lap. Her black eye was about gone and her arms were clear of any bruises… she was healing. — Both emotionally and physically. — Destan still had no idea what Webb did and didn't want to put her through the emotional experience again by asking. And yet, by telling her she had to put herself in that situation again, he knew good and well that would uproot and destroy any progress they made.

Was it worth it?

Was it?

Then something else dawned on him: no matter which ability it was, Webb was the one who controlled if she was put in that nightmare: *I can't protect you from his mental connection to you. The only way is to break the connection. … And the only way to break it is to… to kill him. There's just no way from what I've read to suppress his ability or break the connection he has to you. But I don't know if I can do it, Calli. I just don't— Lord? Please. Help me!*

# ~ 13 ~

It had been just over a week and nothing happened that entire time. Part of Destan was relieved and hoped if he stayed with her, Webb would leave her alone. He kept praying this would end without things escalating like last time. Though, he had to be up front and admit the other part of him that was small, but very influential it seemed, was waiting to wake up in the middle of the night from hearing her scream.

He kept working and working to stop those thoughts from lingering, but his gut feeling wouldn't go away. And sure enough, a couple nights later his fears were founded. He almost felt like he was shaken awake by the way she was thrashing as she writhed in pain.

"Calli? Calli wake up. I'm right here. Calli? — Webb, you demon! Leave her alone!"

The next second she stopped moving and fell limp in his arms. She was barely breathing, and her skin's color drained more and more with each passing moment. Bruises started showing on her arms and then her left side started bleeding. He was in utter disbelief as he looked at Callimay's body beginning to show signs of a physical fight without moving an inch. And now her nose was bleeding!

Destan was thrown into a fit of hysteria: he now lost control to protect his wife. He had nothing to fight with. Sure, he'd done what research he could, but what good was it? There wasn't a "physical" person anywhere within reach for him to fight.

Just when despair was about to deal a devastating blow to him, the strangest thing happened: she sat up and screamed while gasping for air; arms flailing and eyes darting everywhere.

"Calli! I'm here."

She fixed her wild eyes on him and reached out with a shaking hand, then passed out. Destan caught and pulled her close, trying to calm himself more than anything. He wasn't ashamed to say he was trembling as much as she was at this point.

The faint sounds of the clocks downstairs announcing the new hour rang out; their distinct sounds snapping him back to reality. He laid her down and took her hand in his. With how fast she was breathing, he could tell she was petrified. After managing himself to take a deep breath, he stroked the side of her face: *I'm here Calli.*

She squeezed his hand as tears began to fall from her closed eyes: *He even did it when you were here.*

"I'm so sorry, Calli." He grieved as he gathered her in his arms. "I—wait. You said 'he'? Who was it?"

"I… I don't know. I just heard a man's voice the whole time."

"Could you see anything? What was he saying?"

"He kept saying he wasn't going to let me go so easily and that I'd have to fight harder than I was. But I couldn't do anything, Destan! It was like when you're dreaming and can't run fast enough or scream or do anything to help yourself. I couldn't—"

"Shh." He cut her off, noticing she was becoming hysterical. "Take a deep breath, Calli."

"But—"

"I know you can do it. Your migraine's going to be worse if you don't. Please Calli. In. Out. Deep breath. … There."

"Oh, Destan." She sobbed as she leaned her cheek against his. "He scared me so much; jumping out of nowhere and disappearing just as fast. It felt just like what Toreon did! But I know it wasn't him. This guy was so much skinnier. And his hair was white. To—"

"Was it spiked?" He gasped as his eyes got wide.

"Uh— yes."

"Could you tell where he was?" He pushed her back so he could see her face. "Was there anything around you?"

"I— there wasn't anything around us. It was like a void that was either really dark or bright."

He caught himself and stopped for a moment; sighing as he replied, "Alright. Now try to rest. I'm here. I've got you."

She would sob in fits and spurts; causing her to moan from the pain of her cut side. He held and calmed her as much as he could; relieved when she drifted off.

Anger burned inside Destan as he stood in the bathroom and stared at the running water. Webb was the one doing this. He wanted to go after him right then, but he had no idea where to go. Frustrated, he wrung the wet cloth until it ripped. Hearing the horrendous sound of that thick cloth being shredded, Destan jumped back and realized he was out of breath. — He was on the brink of falling into frenzy mode!

Before he went to bed, he called Doctor Gerould; but realized after the third ring: *He's not on call. ~ That's not a bad thing—*"Lance? Calli had another nightmare. She has a nasty gash on her side and I can tell she has a migraine. I've… I've tried to do what I can, but you need to check it. Please come first thing. Please, Lance."

He did all he could by calling and begging Doctor Gerould to come, but Destan didn't feel it was enough. It did nothing right then. But what could he do? Well, what could he do except sit, stand, and pace while worrying for the rest of the night?

Ѧ

His alarm went off at its usual time, but Destan was upset he dozed off. In an instant, he ripped his phone off the nightstand and checked it: *No call? This isn't good. It's already five thirty.*

As he started dialing, someone rang the doorbell. He leaped up and flew down, beating Rocher who was much closer to the door.

There stood a man who looked calm in every way except for his eyes which were full of worry, "I'm sorry I didn't reply. I left the second I got your message so I could get ahead of peak hour. How is she?"

"Still asleep," Destan sighed in relief as he shut the door and followed him up. "At least she was when I was up there."

The room was dark and cool, but the cheerful sound of the birds made things less dreary. Callimay was fast asleep, though she looked less than comfortable by the expression on her face.

"It's best she's asleep. — I know you said some, but what happen?"

"Calli started thrashing out and wincing in her sleep—and then she stopped. She turned into a ragdoll in my arms and just about stopped breathing." Destan said concerned as he rubbed her hand. "Bruises started appearing on her arms and then not too much later I noticed her side and nose were bleeding."

"When she wasn't breathing much, how long did it last?"

"I… I don't know. Maybe five minutes?"

"Anything else?"

"Out of the blue — when she was just lying there — she jumped up and screamed; trying to catch her breath. And then after she realized I was there she passed out like before. … How is she, Lance?"

"These treatments are meant for migraines of 'natural' origins." He said a bit unsure as he worked with the small machine. "With her constant connection to you, I don't know how long this will keep working. She's not in any danger I know of — having them on a routine basis — but at the same time I don't know how long this will hold. You may need to think about seeing a specialist."

Destan mumbled as he looked away; ignoring what was said as he gripped a handful of bedspread, "I've gotta find Webb."

"Excuse me?"

"It's nothing, Lance."

He frowned as he stood up and glared, "Seriously, Destan?"

"Fine. I know who's doing this. He's a guy we knew to a certain extent at the Society. He's using one of father's serums to get to her."

"How? I thought you said the last time we talked you didn't."

"She saw him last night."

"I'm sure that was a frightening experience to recognize him."

"Well… she didn't."

"Then how do you know it's him?"

"She described him to a tee. So did Rocher."

"Wait." Doctor Gerould looked up and waved his hands. "You're saying the person who beat Rocher is the same person doing this?"

"Yes."

"Rocher told me you were hanging your hat on a wafer-thin piece of evidence. What is so prominent about his hair color and its style that would make you positive it was him?"

"There's only one person from the Society who had white, spiked hair. Only one. And—"

"Hold up there. You only know the person doing this to Callimay is someone with abilities."

"I… well it's—"

"You're jumping to conclusions, Destan. How do you know he was there the same time as you two? This could be another Rogue who's twice this young man's age for all you know."

"Webb's just as twisted as Toreon. And by what Rocher said, he 'is' a Falconer who has an official title. You know good and well that makes him close to Toreon on a 'business level' if you will."

"Just because someone is 'twisted' or even a Haut Monde does not automatically make them the opponent you're up against at that point and time. — What's happened to you, Destan? You're not the type to fly after whims."

"I… I don't know, Lance. I just…" he fumbled to say.

"Yes you do," he smiled and nodded; sounding more supportive as he kept working. "You just won't admit it to yourself yet."

ß

They had a long discussion over breakfast after Callimay was tended to and resting. The similarity in their appearance was uncanny; though the closer you looked the more differences you saw. Still, they were mistaken for father and son when seen together.

Once he saw him off, Destan wandered inside to the laboratory door; but hesitated when he reached for the panel. He stood there for a moment before turning away and jogging upstairs.

When he got up to the bedroom door, he cracked it open.

She was still asleep.

He came in and closed it, his hand against the door as he tried to muffle the sound of it closing. But, as he turned, he heard her crying, "Why does this keep happening?"

"I… I don't know, Calli. — Just take it easy. Lance said those stitches need some time to set."

"You asked me where he was. Why?"

"I've gotten it down to two different serums that Webb could h—"

"Webb! That's who it is? … What ability does he have? How do you make him stop? You can, right? Please make him stop!"

He paused for a while, realizing the gravity of what he knew and had pushed away, "I…"

"Destan?" Callimay pulled away, the bruise on her face amplifying the fear in her eyes. "What's wrong?"

"There's only one way. I… I'd have to— I'd have to kill him. It's the only way to break the link."

A frightened pause hindered a response. Did she hear him right?

"There's got to be another way!" She said distraught while she clamored for him to hold her. "It can't be—"

"It's the only way regardless of which ability it is." He closed his eyes; taking the obvious hint. "I spent days scouring through those papers, trying to find another way. There just isn't, Calli. But I don't want to do it."

He caught himself and jerked back as he opened his eyes and saw her face, "I didn't mean it that way, Calli! I swear I…"

The painful fear in her eyes burned a hole in his heart. He was trying to find words, but what could he say at that point? He'd already dug himself into a ginormous hole. Any excuse or explanation he said would do nothing but bury him.

If the term dead silence was ever to be used, this would be the perfect scene for it. They were in the same, self-inflicted void and yet they weren't looking to each other for help to free themselves… even though they were physically touching each other.

Words hold so much power, and yet a wearied mind isn't strong enough so many times to endure anything which might "suggest" a negative outcome… even if that was never intended. He didn't finish his sentence and yet it appeared both of them took the initiative to draw the bleakest, cruelest, and most devastating meaning.

A few minutes passed before a third party — unknowingly — entered this bleak realm. Callimay bowed her head and let Destan go as a soft knock came to their door, knowing he would leave regardless of whether or not she tried to get him to stay. He began to reach out and say something, but there was another knock.

Outside stood Rocher.

As the door cracked open, he could feel the overwhelming pull of this void. Of course he didn't know what was causing it, but he knew enough to use tact… being brief and quiet in his comments, "Breakfast is served, Sir. Is Milady faring well?"

"She… she's fine, Rocher." He answered without making eye contact while he continued to close the door. "We'll be down in a bit."

⌘

Neither of them said a word during breakfast and they never looked at each other. They didn't even come down at the same time. This was only a simple misunderstanding that could be fixed with a relatively short conversation; why would they treat each other like this? They had outgrown the evasion and seclusion phase of their relationship… right?

All she heard was her fork against the plate and the clock on the wall. She couldn't stand it. Callimay got up and marched up to Destan. His head was bowed and hands gripped the armrests of his chair.

Fed up with his cut off persona and cold attitude, she left.

Destan wasn't ignoring her, though. He was so focused that he didn't know she was standing beside him. What he said about killing Webb and his inability to, it rattled him.

And then his thoughts wandered back to the incident at the plant. Destan had a gun. He saw Hyra: ready to pull the trigger… murder Callimay. There was no doubt that would've been in self-defense; but what did he do? *I stood there like a helpless fool when Toreon had Callimay in his filthy grasp. — I'm capable of more than what I'm doing; I know I am! What's wrong with me! I haven't choked when lives have been on the line before. … Ah!*

He shoved his chair back and looked across the table to apologize when he heard a gasp, only to find Callimay gone. Destan jumped to his feet and called out, but only the strained echo of his voice answered him. Regret, sorrow, anger, frustration, and worry were becoming a toxic cocktail about ready to explode inside him.

As he turned, he jumped; his emotions toppling from this ticking time bomb into an endless pit of self-blame. Callimay was standing directly behind his chair. He hung his head and slumped his shoulders when he saw how she looked: hair falling down, right arm grasping her side, left one quivering as it was outstretched to him, and tear streams as clear as day on her drawn and battered face.

Destan crept up and took her hand, scared if he walked up too fast she'd run. He slipped his arm around her to pull her close. His stinging eyes didn't care how strong he wanted to be. Seeing her cry was contagious; and so his emerald green ones poured out their sympathy as they looked at the deep brown ones that took the time and had the patience to teach them to not be afraid of appearing weak if they needed to show how they felt. Destan rested his chin on top of her head and closed his eyes as he mourned, "I said that because I remembered what happened at the plant. I was so focused on Ingrid, but then realized you were there. … When I jumped from the parking lot into the building and apparently looked like Justice Wan— I didn't know what was going on or what to do. My emotions were so out of control I didn't even know what I saw was real until I heard the shot. I'm sorry, Calli. … I love you. I love you so much. I don't want to know the pain of losing you because I wasn't willing to protect you like I am supposed to. … I promise you I won't hesitate again."

After nodding and taking a shaky breath, she stepped back and turned to leave — not looking up. He was still holding her hand, but Callimay assumed he would let go like he always had.

Both of their arms were stretched out at this point and Destan had no intentions of letting go. She turned back as he begged, "Stay with me. D… don't go. I need you. Please stay, Calli. Please?"

His immediate answer was an empty stare since she didn't know what to say. He'd never begged for anything before… at least she'd never known him to.

Before long, she let her head fall against his chest as she sobbed.

৪৩

Once he felt composed and knew Callimay was as well, Destan walked over and opened the door to the laboratory. Seeing her clutching her side reminded him what the early morning hours were like. He changed his gait so it was slow and almost jerky as they crossed the floor of the darkened room; him watching over her every breath, step, body language cue, and sound.

At one point he rubbed her hand — his little way of asking if she was alright when she had a migraine — her looking up and nodding.

He relaxed and closed his eyes, the air in the room much lighter and easier to breathe.

"What's this?" Callimay asked while she looked at a workstation on the far wall; letting go of his hand.

As she moved and pushed things out of the way, he turned, "Huh?"

The table was wide enough that she was straining herself to reach a small box. Destan reached out but was too slow.

This little box was a dusky brown color, but the fingerprints on it suggested this color was only due to the dust that had accumulated for over twenty years.

She looked around, and then without saying a word, left. Destan was in a daze, standing like a statue until she came back with something to wipe off her treasure.

As she began to unveil the true hue of this wooden box, her smile vanished as she sneezed. It caused her side to hurt so much that she dropped to her knees; startling him so he dropped to his, "Calli!"

"I'm okay. I— ah! I just—"

Destan reached out to her as she sneezed a few more times in rapid succession, "Calli how c— what do you—"

"Help me to the other side of the room."

While he tried to do what she asked, he stopped when she hissed through her teeth and grabbed her side. This painful and slow process was repeated several times; but before too long she came to her resting place on the sofa, which was more of a relief to him than her.

When the pain subsided, she finished wiping the box. It was plain but beautiful; made of the same chestnut wood found throughout the mansion. And yet there was something odd about it. Somehow it looked "broken". The wood's grain didn't ebb and flow the full length like it should, and there were strange burn marks here and there. Last but not least, she noticed one of the top corners was missing: a perfect square.

Callimay looked up to him and saw his eyes were wide-opened and focused on the box, "Do you know what this is?"

There was no response; well, verbal response. He took the box and began sliding his fingers across the top. As it turned out, there were wooden panels on it that moved. Callimay was mesmerized as she watched him work on the puzzle as if he'd done it a million times.

A few seconds later, the corner of the box popped up followed by the side of the box closest to her opening, "Oh! It's a puzzle box!"

After emptying the compartment, he handed it back. The burned sections made the seal of the University of Kerogen. She pushed the side back in and the top shuffled itself back to what it looked like when she first picked it up. It startled her, but Callimay nestled against Destan and started playing with her little treasure.

Somehow this little box jolted her memory; her gripping her necklace: *My music box! I— how could I have forgotten about it? ~ If we could go to the ball, surely we could make a quick trip—*

"Calli, look at this."

She looked over at the computer screen and saw a list of names. At first it didn't strike her, but then she saw it — "Cliffhanger".

"Was this on the computer this whole time?"

"No. There was a portable drive in the box. This is what's on it."

In this file was a lonely document. He recognized its format, but this was the first time she saw one of his father's hand-written entries.

*Over the past two weeks, I have observed several successful subjects beginning to show excessive aggression; which still might be making light of the situation. Each of my colleagues says it is due to the grim reports from Quaverly, but I have my doubts. Each subject was under pressure from their superiors to undergo processing, exhibiting — for whatever reason — what I refer to as toxic emotions: rage, anger, frustration, and hate to name a few "big ticket" types.*

*I'm wondering if my serums draw from one's emotional state rather than physical. No one cares to listen, but I've been noticing correlations to the emotional state of the person just prior to processing matching what is present when they tap into their abilities.*

*The toxic ones appear to allow the ability itself to consume the subject; them not showing any type of restraint or control over their ability — unlike those who successfully make it through under other emotional circumstances. Some "thing" should not be able to overpower a human like this.*

*For those who have these toxic emotions, things have escalated to the point that we're having to restrain them like animals and administer powerful sedatives in an attempt to keep them from harming staff or themselves. With each consecutive episode, they have to be administered almost a double dosage than the previous time.*

*We have already lost a couple because of the amount of sedative needed to curb their emotional and mental state was lethal to their physical bodies. We've tried communicating with them during these times to negotiate and prevent injury, but so far, the subjects zone out and/or refuse to respond.*

*A good friend and fellow comrade of one was brought in to see if someone close to the subject could break through, but it ended with deadly outcomes for both individuals.*

*I feel like I'm the one trying to save someone whom "I" pushed off a cliff and they are now caught in the brambles, screaming to be freed. I never imagined a near-death experience in my childhood would come back and manifest itself in such a way — Cliffhanger.*

*I've only witnessed the actions of a rabid animal on a few occasions, but the sight is something no one soon forgets. The sight of a man acting this way: lethargic to reality but easily irritated, blind to surroundings but able to see obstacles of any kind, and viewing anyone as an enemy — someone trying to kill them — all while they're more than willing to end their own life... how can anyone here believe what is being done is right? How can "I" allow this to keep going? Something that is right and good shouldn't cause problems like this.*

*Since Harmon won't stop, I have to keep searching for answers. I've got to stay as long as I can and do whatever I can to fix this — or stop it if necessary.*

*As hopeless as it may seem, I still want to believe Liaison will work. There's got to be a way to help these Cliffhangers live. Right now they last — at most — a week before they drive themselves insane and commit suicide; providing the sedative hasn't killed them by this point. There are a few I've convinced about using her, but it's nearly impossible to work out the issues we're still having with her. It's bad enough I'm working double overtime.*

*I know my Jewel is lonely even though she never says anything. I am too. Ever since the wake-up call Lance gave me when I was studying at U of K, I realized more and more I was feeling the same way. The only difference was: I was shoving it aside and seeing it as emotional "irritations" due to vastly different reasons. Remembering this past reality, I feel like I'm putting her through all that heartache again. Maybe she was right: maybe I shouldn't have agreed to this at all.*

*Destan though, he isn't afraid to speak his mind. No matter what it is that he takes issue with, he speaks up and makes sure he's understood. I hate to say it, but he's got almost "too" much spunk and openness. Though, for him to be the opposite way would be worse. I can see so much of myself in him: stubborn, unwilling to tolerate others who don't care, hard-headed, and determined. If he can keep those within healthy boundaries, he's going to become a fine young man. I only wish…*

She only glossed over what was written since Destan was scrolling at his pace — mister speed reader. When she saw where he stopped wasn't at the end of the document, she turned and saw he was rubbing his face and shaking his head. Callimay bit her lip and reached out; she knew anything attached to his father was difficult for him to handle.

But then he said in regretful repentance out of the blue, "I'm sorry I'm doing the same thing Calli. I… I'm not meaning to abandon you. I guess I— I forget too easy now. I know it and I haven't done a thing to try and change it. I've built a barrier in my mind and around my heart over the years to keep me from going insane. Pretty much all of my memories are full of pain and grief; so I've 'taught' myself to forget. But now I've forgotten how it felt when you were practically in a coma. I forgot the promises I made; what this ring is supposed to be a constant reminder of. I forgot you vowed to stand beside me through whatever comes. Maybe this doesn't mean much if anything but: I 'am' trying to change. With what is now going on with Webb— I've realized if I don't do something about him I won't remember until it's too late. I'd never be able to forget it or have an opportunity to fix it. … I already have enough of those memories. I don't want an— I 'will' protect you. If it comes down to it: I'd give myself up to the Monarch themselves and go to death row if it'd keep you safe."

Destan never lifted his head to look at her. With his emotions right then, he knew he couldn't bear to see the pain in her eyes. Deep down he knew he couldn't survive that emotional torment again; and yet he was demanding she suffer through it time and time again. How cruel could he be?

Without any hesitation, she put her small, delicate hand atop his trembling, large one and leaned over; kissing him before embracing him. He breathed a heavy sigh and melted in her arms.

"Please forgive me, Calli." He pleaded; anguish stealing his voice away. "I don't know—"

"Oh Destan," her glassy eyes and loving voice tried to comfort him as she stroked the side of his face. "I love you. — And about earlier… I jumped to some horrible conclusions again. I know that's not what you meant. — Destan? Destan as long as your heart and my heart continue to beat, I will 'always' forgive you. … Will you forgive me?"

He hesitated for a moment and then sobbed, "I love you, Calli."

She could hear and feel his heart pounding, reminding her that she needed to keep watch over him; something was frightening him.

Unsure if it would help, but knowing it wouldn't hurt any, she laid her hand over his heart and cradled his head next to hers, "I'll always be here. There's nothing you could do to make me leave my home."

They held each other for a while, after which they heard a knock: *Rocher? I swear…*

If that one knock would have been it he would have stayed. But it appeared the person at the door was persistent. Begrudgingly, Destan got up and stomped to the door.

Sure enough, big as day, bright-eyed and bushy-mushed, Rocher was standing there as formal as ever, "A relay from Fidus."

Destan tensed up as he turned, his eyes flashing as he smiled, "I'll be right back, Calli. Just stay here. I won't be long."

"Alright," she answered cheerfully and nodded; though he could tell she had a pained look on her face.

Once the door was closed, he growled in a hushed voice, storming to the other side of the room, "Why in the world did you say that so loud, Rocher? Calli was right there! And I thought I told Fi—"

"Is it too much of a burden to request that you remember my holding the highest of levels in regards to respect and devotion toward your wishes in such things? I was not aware Milady was in your company, Sir." He said stern; almost gritting his teeth. "I never would have ventured to utter such a statement as I did if I would have held the knowledge I do now. — And allow me to be bold and bring to memory I 'did' inform Fidus of your wishes. I kept him at bay outside for that very reason when I discovered he had arrived unannounced."

"Why is he being so pushy? I just checked yesterday and nothing's happening that warrants this rude and intentional invasion. The extension was granted, so why is he getting—"

"Fidus implied this information only surfaced today and he came directly because of its urgent nature." Rocher explained as he offered the envelope again. "By his comments, it appears only you are affected by the news contained within; and so, any needed steps to resolve the situation created by said relay would rest firmly on your shoulders."

He brooded for a minute and then ripped the black paper out of his hand and read this so-called urgent message.

Before long, Destan's hands gripped the paper tighter as his face became paler… as if the paper were sucking all the life and color out of him. In a frivolous effort to stop it, he crumpled it in his hands and threw it in the fire. His eyes darted back and forth as he slammed his hands against the mantle, "I take it the message was urgent, Sir?"

"The Syndicate has Freigh. — Freeze everything; and don't argue with me, Rocher. I mean 'everything'. Lock it all down." He ordered, his voice sounding just as stern as his chiseled chin and slanted brows looked. "Start moving everything you can to the Nest. Send everything you can't to Bulwark. Let everyone know right now."

"Did he release any sensitive—"

"Apparently Canary couldn't get much information out, so no one knows for sure. Even if he hasn't, it's only a matter of time." *Either we have a Nark or Webb compromised the barrier; which means I was right, he 'is' a Falconer: Dodge. I don't reca—*

"What about Milady? Do you plan on relocating 'her' to the Nest? I wouldn't think you would take her to Bulwark. That in no way would be wise… would it? I only perceive it serving as t—"

"I—just let me worry about that." Destan stopped and put his hand out. "I'll… I'll figure something out."

"Very well. Do I need to transmit a relay of confirmation back to Fidus directly?"

Destan whipped his head around, "Where is he?"

"I sent him away and assured him I would confirm any necessary items with him before the shadows rose."

"Tell him… tell him I got his relay and the encounter will go as planned. I… I can't— tell him the encounter isn't changing. Tell him what Canary said but make 'sure' he understands I'll take care of it."

He raced to the panel and then caught himself; taking a deep breath before he walked in: *Calli doesn't need to know about this. I've got it under control. She'll be fine. … 'We'll' be fine.*

"Warn me when Rocher makes you upset." She scolded as she rubbed her temple. "What was wrong?"

"Ugh! I'm sorry. Everything's alright now."

"I was reading this section again and— who's Liaison? Why did he refer to a serum as a person? And 'she' at that?"

"The last two I'm not sure about, but I do know 'who' Liaison is. She's you, Calli." Destan stroked her hair as he sat down. "Yes. I found all of my father's notes on yours 'and' my abilities; even the ones Mr. Freigh called Nightmare and Origin."

"Would you let me read them?"

"Why don't you sit here and read what you want while I—"

"No." She kept hold of his arm as he got up. "Please stay. … Unless you have something you need—"

"No. No I don't have anything to do right now. Come here."

❦

Callimay read through everything and was left stunned, to say the least. She got up and began pacing; still speechless and confused. Her arms were cinched around her stomach as if she were trying to keep herself from hyperventilating, "I… I may have another ability?"

"That's what it sounds like."

She whipped around, her eyes looking terrified, "He said you could only last a week b—"

"I have you." Destan calmed as he got up and gave her a kiss. "My father was right about Liaison in more ways than one. 'She' is the answer the 'Cliffhanger' needed."

"I… I never realized 'how' you would die if you lost control. I—"

"Calli?" Destan soothed as he got down on a knee and rubbed the side of her neck. "Calli look at me. … It's alright. I knew it wasn't something you truly understood, but I didn't— I should've told you myself, I'm sorry. … But think about it, Calli. I've made it— wow. It's been seven months! Lord-willing, I'll make it another seven decades. I mean, I've been alive over thirty times longer than what my father even said was possible. There's no reason I can't keep going like this. Right?"

"I guess so," she rubbed her arm and look to the side.

"Guess? I think we can do a bit better than that. Where's my ray of sunshine? … Smile. Please?"

This situation wasn't one that struck Callimay as fitting of such light emotion. She sighed and slumped her shoulders, but did as he asked. And then it struck her, "Y… you can gain abilities!"

"From father's notes on cliffhangers, I may have found the secret to how I tap into them. I'm trying and recall the emotions I was feeling when I made first contact with each person I'm mimicking. If I can figure out which emotion it is, then I'll be able to use them knowingly."

"It says the longer you're in contact with the person the better your mimicking ability is."

Destan dragged out as he raised his eyebrow, "Yeah."

"So you should be able to mimic mine the best."

He laughed loud and clear, "That's true."

This thought obviously made her think of something else. She hesitated as she looked at him, a half determined, half fearful look on her face, "What if… there are so many variables it might not work."

He put his hand under her chin, "Just tell me."

"What if you tap into my ability and guide me like I guide you?"

"Why?"

"To find Webb. I… I know he can do it whether or not I 'invite' him. But if I have you with me, maybe I'll be able to fend him off."

"But I don't know when I first made contact with you after I knew you had your ability, Calli. Well I do…" he scratched his head as his face began to flush. "But I don't know if I had to know I had Challenger or not for it to work. If so, I— smells like lunch is ready."

"Seriously?" She rolled her eyes as she shoved his arm.

"Wait…" he held up a hand, sounding serious as he showed the number of fingers he was counting. "Five, four, three, two, one, and…"

Just then there was a knock on the door as Destan pointed to it.

"Now I know how you felt earlier." She pursed her lips and crossed her arms across her chest.

"Come on." Destan laughed as he picked her up and carried her to the door. "We need a break from this, anyway."

ℬ

The thought of "turning off" her ability scared Callimay. But Destan reminded her doing that would be the only proof-positive way to see what emotion he now had tied to her ability. He assured her this wasn't going to be something dangerous.

How was she supposed to "turn it off" if she didn't know if it were actually possible? And then what if something happened? She didn't want to "leave him" and risk losing him.

"I'll be fine, Calli. I can't think of anything that'd make me upset. Go ahead and try again."

"Oh… fine. … I… I think I got it."

"I know you have."

She tilted her head and wrinkled her forehead, "How?"

"Your eyes." He mourned as he sighed. "They're clear like they were the first time we met; before you were forced to carry my emotional baggage. — And don't argue with me. You can't tell me you're not always in some level of pain while you're synced with me. I can see it plain as day since you stopped."

170

"I… I take this… this—"

"Burden."

"Role. I was going to say role." She shook his hands; trying to be supportive while correcting him. "I take it on gladly. You didn't and still don't make me. I make the choice to do this every single day. Just like you chose to protect me and stay up those three days. Remember? … You're my protector and I'm your helper. … Destan? … I'm alright. I promise. I've had migraines my whole life. At least now I have a reason and purpose for the pain. It makes it more bearable, believe it or not. I'd go through the worst migraine I can remember having if I knew it'd save you. I love you just as much as you love me, 'mister competitive'. … Ready?"

"Yeah," he nodded as he looked back up.

Several times toward the beginning, he caught her closing her eyes and raising her face toward the sun. He knew she enjoyed the break; but from what his father's notes said, he'd always need Callimay to a certain extent. She'd always have to be willing to endure the pain associated with keeping him in check — keeping him alive. But he didn't want her to. Destan wanted her to stay like she was in this moment forever. He loved seeing her eyes sparkle like they were… the sparkle of being pain free.

Laughter and clapping was later, and unknowingly, traded for grunts and clinched fists. They were walking on the front lawn when Callimay began to notice this change; but it was his tone she noticed more than anything else. Not but a second later, she was flooded with the influx of emotional pain. She let out a screech as she clutched her chest and temple, gasping for air as she collapsed onto the grass.

Destan caught her, realizing what was happening and working to calm himself as fast as he could, "Calli! Calli wake up."

In this moment of panic and hysterics, something worrisome caught his attention. He whipped his head around toward the entrance and saw a man standing there. Though he was far away, it was easy to tell he looked like the huskier version of Destan — same length black hair, black shirt and pants… and duster coat.

Disgusted, Destan shook his head and jerked Callimay to his chest. Without a moment's thought, he jumped her inside. The way he was acting, it were as if he knew who this man was and wanted to keep her away from him. But why? Who was he? How did he know where to find them? Was this the same man Destan was furious about showing up to the mansion?

Taking a brief moment to act civil, he laid her on the sofa; then switching back to his former attitude, stormed over to the window which faced the drive. He grimaced as he gripped the curtains and threw them across the window: *Leave. Us. Be!*

✿

This was a failed attempt on every level as far as Destan was concerned. He didn't figure out which emotion was tied to Callimay's ability and she was in even more pain than before.

When she woke up, she kept telling him she felt better, the dagger-like pain nothing but a dull pressure at this point, but she didn't have any strength to object to his suggestion about going to bed early.

He followed her up, ignoring and refuting her pleas for him to go eat dinner; him lying beside her as she became more and more groggy.

"Just be my rock, Destan." She smiled as she glanced over and took his hand. "He may not bother me tonight… or ever again."

# ~ 14 ~

Destan sat up that night; cold sweat rolling off his brow. His heart was pounding in his ears and his fists were clinched. It actually hurt for him to pry his fingers apart: *This is the second time this has happened. ~ It wasn't this bad last time. Ah! Geez! ~ What did you do, Boon? ~ How should I know? Quit making me more upset, alright?*

After taking a quick look around, he sighed and flopped back on his pillow. His fingers still felt like they were being grated with the quills of a porcupine, but at least he could move them. He then looked over and saw how peaceful Callimay was sleeping; making the pain vanish.

*I love you.* He smiled as he brushed her hair out of her face.

While he sat there, he noticed she started to smile. That's when it clicked for him: *Love. It's love, isn't it? Why didn't I think of it before?*

She smiled more, confirming what he was thinking; but it was stolen away as she started to moan.

*Calli? Is he coming?*

No response.

*Calli I— what do you need me to do? Is this even working?* Destan began to panic as he took her hands in his. *Can't you just wake up?*

He tried everything he could, but the fact she couldn't use her ability or he couldn't reach her while she was asleep couldn't be changed. It wasn't something they considered.

"Callimay!" He yelled as he felt her leave, though he didn't truly understand what this feeling was. "Callimay where are you? I'm not— how am I supposed to feel love when I'm terrified!"

His opportunity came to use what his father intended to help people, and he failed. He wasn't able to do what he was supposed to. … Again.

The clock now showed it had been nine and a half minutes since she was ripped away. Destan became more and more worried, seeing her breathe less and less. Unlike the other times, though, Callimay wasn't having cuts and bruises show up. As much as he was grateful she wasn't being beaten, he was terrified what "was" happening.

Out of the blue, he felt something moving faster than anything he'd known. It wasn't the strangest feeling in the world, but it was right up there at the top. Right when it felt like it was going to hit him, Callimay jumped up and screamed.

"Calli I'm here." He begged for forgiveness as he pulled her close. "I'm so sorry I couldn't s—"

"It's Webb." She gasped for air as she grabbed his hair and yanked his head toward hers. "He hasn't changed."

"Are you alright?"

She quivered as she continued to hold onto him with a death-like grip, "I am now. … I saw where he was."

"Where?"

"Where I used to call home. The exact house."

"Faberton? Berchshire? You're kidding me!"

"No, I'm not, D…" she faded out as she went limp in his arms.

What! How was that possible? Callimay's old home in Faberton was over twelve-hundred — yes, hundred — miles away as the crow flies!

Regardless of this wild statement she made, one thing was sure: he needed to go now if he was going to have any chance of catching him.

♗

It didn't take him but a few moments to make up his mind; hitting the buzzer and gathering Callimay in his arms. He met Rocher at the base of the stairs and told him in the same stern tone as the day before, "Get in touch with Grounder. We're flying to Faberton."

Rocher sounded confused and very tired, "As you wish. First thing come m—"

"No. Tonight. We're leaving now. I don't care if the moon's full."

"A… alright, then. I will see to arrangements straight away."

A few other things were said before they went their own ways. The moment they were finished, Destan carried Callimay back upstairs while he gathered a couple things. He didn't know when she would come to, but knew she would be hysterical if he wasn't right with her.

Once he finished his initial task, Rocher went directly to get the car and didn't move an inch from his seat when Destan came out. The speed he was driving at suggested the small discussion they had made him fully aware of the gravity of the situation.

With nothing else to occupy him, Destan looked out at the blur of scenery around them. His jaw was set and his eyes intent on making sure he was focused on his "mission". Seeing the moon bathing the ground with its light made him narrow his eyes, looking furious and scolding it for thinking it could dare have cheerful thoughts at the time.

ℬ

When they pulled into the parking lot at the airstrip, all the pre-flight checks were complete and the jet was idling. Rocher went ahead and got ready while Destan grabbed his bag and kept Callimay close.

"It is going to be a two and a half-hour flight, Sir." Rocher broke his usual flamboyant style of speaking. "From what Grounder gathered from Confederate, conditions will be decaying rapidly right as we are scheduled to arrive."

"Let's not waste any more time so we can hopefully miss it." He answered impatient as he carried Callimay up the stairs and into the jet. "We're landing in Downing then?"

"Yes." Rocher continued as he looked up from the papers. "This is most likely something you were planning on doing anyway, but please stay with Milady. If I require your assistance I will inform you."

"Alright." Destan walked back to his seat; finishing in a tone that couldn't have been more opposite the one he just used with Rocher: *Calli? Calli can you hear me? Please say something. Y… you've never been out this long. … Calli?*

ℬ

There was no pause between taxiing and takeoff, and Rocher's pilot capabilities were second to none: a seamless takeoff. Once he felt the jet level off, Destan checked his watch. His eyes were still focused and narrow, his lips moving ever so slightly as he talked with himself.

175

This all was interrupted by him feeling Callimay moving. It made him feel better she wasn't scaring herself awake; and not too much later she opened her eyes.

Even though it was dark, she could still see Destan's green eyes and was so relieved that she smiled; though he could tell she was worried, "There you are. You were out quite a bit longer than the other times. — Here. Take this. I figured your head would be bothering you."

She sighed as she reached out with her trembling hand, still sounding groggy and disoriented, "Thank you."

It if weren't for the fact she felt the leather seat as she put her arms around Destan's neck, Callimay wouldn't have known they weren't home. She pulled back from him and looked suspicious as she focused as much as she could on what was around them. It was so dark that nothing "jumped out". Maybe he was just in a chair? No. There was a constant low hum she'd never heard before and a repetitive light flashing from somewhere outside the room, "How did we get here?"

"Don't worry. Everything's alright."

"But— where are we going? 'Why' are we going?"

"Faberton. I'm not letting Webb slip out of my grasp. Just rest."

"Destan you can't be serious! What if he has another ability? You barely made it out of that fight with Toreon. I… I can't help watch over you right now."

He pulled her close and gave her a kiss, "We've got a way to go yet. Get some rest in the meantime. I'll let you know when we get there."

"But—"

"Calli please," he said stern, his face looking intense.

Her nod almost looked more like her cowering from him; her keeping her distance. Destan picked up on this and calmed; offering her to nestle close to him. She was reluctant but eventually did.

The moment she was settled, he flipped back and stared out at the black night; returning to the thoughts he was entertaining before. If he hesitated it could very well be the last time he would. If that happened, Callimay was going to be defenseless. He glanced at the duffle bag and let his head flop against the headrest: *Is there any possible way to get him to see what he's doing is wrong? … Who am I kidding? It would take a miracle for him to change.*

*Miracles are possible. You know that.*

He sighed as he stroked her hair and leaned his head against hers: *I know, Calli. … I know. — Try to sleep. Everything's alright.*

Quite late in the flight, after Callimay went back to sleep, there was enough turbulence to prompt Rocher to get on the com, "Storms are closing in on the area. It may not feel anything close to it, but I am faring well alone. I'll keep Raven as steady as possible, but with the rugged terrain it will be unsteady to some extent the rest of the way. Touchdown should be in fifteen, just ahead of the storm system."

❧

It was usually noises that woke Callimay, but this time it was the absence of it. As she opened her eyes, she saw Destan standing just across the hall. She rubbed her eyes as she sat up, "We landed?"

"Yeah." He said monotone as he finished pulling his shirt on.

"Where?"

"Just outside Downing, so we're really close." He helped her up and handed her some clothes. "You'll need to change."

"Downing? There's no airstrip—"

"This one isn't used very much."

"What do you have in there?" She asked when she heard metal clanking coming from the duffle bag he was messing in.

"There's a room in the back where you can change." He looked up at her with a dead serious expression and pointed. "I'll be outside."

"I— I'll be out as fast as I can." She said scared as she stepped back from him; and then asked timid, "Destan?"

"What?" He sounded perturbed as he sighed and looked up.

"I… is everything okay?"

He took a deep breath and closed his eyes for a moment, then calmed down and replied in a soft tone, "Everything's okay. I'm just— everything's okay. I promise."

❧

What he brought for her to wear was an awkward combination; but, knowing she needed to get out as fast as she could, Callimay dressed rather than pondered these tiny details that didn't matter.

As she came to the door, she hopped along, trying to get her other shoe on. She lost her balance and tumbled into one of the chairs but was quick to her feet. When she looked out, she saw Destan standing a little off, talking with a few others, "It is good to see you up and about."

"Rocher! What are you doing here!"

"I beg your forgiveness, Milady. I did not intend in any way to startle you. … Sir has yet to complete his pilot courses, so the said duty fell to me for this occasion."

"Oh." She took a deep breath in relief as she closed her eyes and tried to catch her breath. "Destan said we're in Downing?"

"A more accurate description would be the southwest side of the hamlet, Milady." Rocher clarified as he helped her down the steps.

"We're much closer to my house this way."

"What?" Destan asked as he put his hand on her shoulder.

She flinched, scaring him too; and then stepped to the side and pointed, "You see that peak up there?"

"Yes."

"Well just on the other side of it is where my home is— I mean was! I'm sorry. I'm trying to r—"

"Don't worry about it. Let's go."

"Wait." She grabbed his arm, the wind picking up and tossing her hair everywhere as she tried to corral it. "What is this place Destan? I never remember seeing an airstrip down here and I've been playing on these hills my entire life."

"This is a newer one. And like I said: it's not used much."

It wasn't the answer she was hoping for, but she knew that was all she was going to get. The more she thought, the more it seemed less confusing: if it were new then there was a good possibility she wouldn't know about it. Private airstrips weren't advertised, and it was a fact she hadn't been down this way in a couple years. And then if it indeed weren't used much, that would explain the lack of her seeing planes.

She started to follow and then heard Destan comment: *It's too windy for me to talk out loud. Are you well enough to do this?*

*You mean talk like this and walk up there?*

He nodded as he stopped, handing her something small after he took her hand.

*Oh! Thank you for thinking of that. — It's not necessarily the easiest thing to do with the weather added on top of everything, but I can manage for now.* She smiled as she finished tying her hair back with the band he gave her.

*Let me know if you need a break, okay? — Why don't you take the lead? Then I can see you easier.*

Something felt wrong about walking around the hills she grew up around during the middle of the night. Well, maybe wrong is a bit too strong. She'd walked around at night many times before, but doing it this way didn't feel right somehow.

The cloud cover couldn't be thicker, the moon's light unable to penetrate and drive the blackness away. She could see distant lightning flashes to the east: *It's going to get really bad here in a bit, Destan. That's a—*

*A howler, I know.* He replied, sounding a bit frustrated. *If you can keep this pace we should make it there before it hits.*

Callimay glanced back to see where he was and accidentally slapped his face: *I'm sorry! I couldn't see you.*

*Don't worry about it. I'm right here.* He looked up, his face the only thing she could see. *What's wrong?*

*I was just making sure you were there. I can't see you since it's so dark and you're wearing all black.*

When they were still about a half mile off, Destan took her hand: *Easy! It's me. … We're not gonna make it in time and I don't want you getting hit by something that gets kicked up. Is there somewhere close you can hide? — I guess I should've left you at the jet.*

*There's a cellar not too far from here. It's right across the road if I remember right.*

*Let's go.*

When she got to where she thought it was, she started second-guessing herself. It was so overgrown that she couldn't find the door latch. She gasped as she looked up, feeling the wind die down and the ground beginning to tremble: *I'm sorry, Destan! It's been eighteen, maybe nineteen years since it's been used. I'm trying to find it.*

*Don't panic. It's okay.* He kneeled and started feeling around. *We've got a couple minutes still. Wait. I think— yeah, I've got it. …

The ladder is still in good shape and the supports don't look worn. Just watch out for the dust catchers when you get down. I know spiders aren't your favorite.*

*How can you see?*

He shook his head, *I must've tapped Ingrid's ability.*

Callimay shivered as she clung to his arm, *Destan?*

*Just stay here.* He rubbed the side of her face and then helped her down: *I'll be back.*

*Wait!* She grabbed his wrist. *I…*

*Stay safe.* Destan replied much softer as he kneeled and gave her a kiss. *I'll be back soon.*

ℬ

After she got down the ladder she yelped. These deadly straight winds had the reputation of a piercing sound that could be heard as a low and rumbling roar up to fifty miles away; as well as packing the power to uproot a hundred-year-old tree and carry it five miles before throwing it into whatever was in the way. She'd seen this power personally when she was young. Ever since that day she got lost in the hills, she only knew them to cause death and was petrified of them.

Wait. Destan stayed out! Even after he said he knew what they were! She hurried to climb back up and open the door latch. It was heavy and the direction the wind was coming from wasn't helping any. She panicked: *Destan!*

*What!* He gasped, stopping in his tracks and hunkering down.

*Come back. Wait for the howler to leave.*

*I'm alright.* He smiled and chuckled as he got up and kept going. *It takes more than this ground-level wind to knock me down.*

*You don't know these winds like I do. They—*

*Yes I do, Calli.* He corrected, trying to calm her nerves while not brushing her off. *And I'm okay. I'm talking to you, right?*

*I… I guess so.*

*Oh Calli. Please don't cry. I'm right beside the house, so I'm out of the wind. Does that make you feel any better?*

*You're there already?*

*Yes. Can I get into the basement without breaking the bulkhead?*

180

*Y… yes.*

Destan snuck over and checked around before opening it: *He's here. With it being so confined in there, I'm not going to be able to use my ability, so you can turn o—*

*You can still fall into frenzy mode without tapping your ability. You know that.*

He sighed as he shut the door behind him, *I know. How are you?*

*Better. Thank you for the medicine. — Oh! I forgot to tell you there's a drain in the middle of the basement. It's not huge but I've tripped over it I don't know how many times.* Callimay paced the floor, unsure what to do.

*Alright.* Destan replied rather jovial; and then cutoff to a serious tone: *Something's off. He's sitting in the living room like he's waiting. The lights are all on.*

*Come back. Don't do it. It's not worth it. Please, Destan! Please.*

Part of him wanted to comfort her, but Destan knew he needed to focus: *I have to do this, Calli. It's the only way to get him to stop. I'll be back as fast as I can. Do 'not' leave the cellar.*

He got up the stairs and cracked the door. There on the sofa with his muddied boots on the coffee table sat Webb. His eyes were closed and his nose was in the air like any arrogant person's would be. A grin came across his face as he snickered, still not bothering to open his eyes and look, "Older houses don't let people sneak around; doesn't matter if a howler is screaming or not. That's the most endearing quality of them. … Well are you gonna kneel there and sulk or come in and get your pound of flesh?"

A moment later he kicked the door open and stormed in the room, looking infuriated yet in control, "Thanks for keeping the lights on."

"I could turn them off if you'd like," Webb reached over to the lamp; eyeing him as he laughed, "But, I don't think your 'delicate' eyes would appreciate the light show outside, would they?"

"You know why I'm here."

"Yep. Sure do. Pull the trigger. … I'm sure you've been on pins and needles the whole time for this and I wouldn't wanna let you down."

This was way too easy. Not even Webb would leave himself out in the open like this. Someone else had to be around.

"Ingrid's right, you are a coward. No guts to pull the trigger." Webb shook his head and slowly rose from his lounging place. "Why do you have that thing then? Think you'll scare me into 'being a good boy'?"

"Valuing life isn't being a coward. You know we don't shoot first and ask questions later."

"Even when you know what they've done?" He looked out of the corner of his eye as he turned away and walked across the room.

"Why Callimay?" Destan gritted his teeth.

"You know exactly why."

"Pervert, what did you do to her this last time?"

"That's the 'only' name you could think of? Oh come now, Destan. — Though I guess for your 'clean' language that'd be all you 'could' say, Huh? — And why be worried about the past?" Webb scoffed as he looked out at the lightning. "She's alive isn't she?"

"I swear. If you—"

"You know? Letting Toreon live was probably the dumbest thing you've 'ever' done. Wait. Let me think about that a bit more. … No, yeah. Dumbest for sure. It didn't take the Syndicate any time to get him out. Thanks to me of course. Haven't met a lock, computer, or even a 'barrier' that could keep me out. But, I guess even the great Doyen is prone to mistakes, right?"

He flinched when he saw Toreon appear beside Webb.

"You should see the look on your face." Toreon slapped his leg; laughing so much he started coughing. "Oh. … This is priceless. — Excuse me. Sorry about that. — I am so glad I agreed to do this your way, ole chum. This is so much better."

"Prince." Destan hissed under his breath as he glared at him; moving so he had a better position.

"I must say, Webb was right, Destan. I mean, you 'should' have killed me." Toreon smiled; that fiendish gleam in his eye. "Now? Now you are a duck with no pond to return to, a shadow with no light to let it exist. You and Callimay both. But… like my ole chum Dodge said: even 'the great Doyen' is prone to making mistakes."

Destan didn't respond, verbally that is. His eyes got wide and he shifted his grip on the gun. Both of their comments hit him wrong. They knew something they shouldn't. … But what was it?

"I would 'love' to stay... but I do have more important things to tend to at the moment." Toreon commented as he glanced at his watch and nodded to Webb. "You 'can' take care of this, right?"

"What is more important, you Syndicate scumbag? Tell me or so help me you w—" Destan demanded as glass shattered.

"I have to inform the Monarch I have the confession of one Destan Quinton Nevrille that he is Doyen: leader of the Shadows. That and I can give them the exact location of his personal residence where he's hiding his lovely, 'precious' little wife who could pose a threat to the Syndicate if allowed to live. — Such a waste of beauty."

Destan fell against the mantel and grabbed his right shoulder; a sudden shock of disorientation and immense pain taking him over. He glanced at his shoulder to see blood oozing around his fingers. Not but a second later he staggered as he tried to reach for the gun he dropped.

"Ingrid is a perfect shot. Knows just about every weak spot any man has. Huh Dodge?" Toreon approved as he leaned on Destan's shoulder, causing him to fall to the floor.

"Killing me won't prove a thing." He grimaced, writhing in pain.

"Oh you won't die here." Toreon assured as he laughed and slapped his arm. "I wouldn't get any money if you did. — I know, I know. I changed my mind. I'm entitled to change it every once in a while. — And we wouldn't want the Monarch getting mad, would we? They wouldn't appreciate their dear, devoted Prince coming home empty-handed. ... Let's put it this way: I need you in a state that is easier to transport and less likely to fight back seeing as how you have extraordinary abilities. Or would you like it if I put you in feelers?"

Toreon took this opportunity and had his payback for what Destan did last time; not stopping until Webb pulled him back, "He won't be alive if you keep this up. Let him go. You told me to take care of this."

"Leave me be." Toreon pushed him back; but then fixed his hair and switched his demeanor when he saw a picture on the wall, "I just thought of something. Your precious wife won't be home. You'd never leave her for this long or go that far away. Which means — she's not that far away. And with all you've gone through she can't be able to defend herself. It has been a while since I've seen her..."

*Don't you dare touch her!*

Callimay had been trying to lift the latch this entire time. She knew who was there and the trap Destan walked in to. After the shot, though she didn't hear it, she screamed and fell down the steps. As fast as she could, she got back up and pushed through the pain and weariness to lift the door just enough so she could slip out.

The howler had set in with full force at this point; the lightning dancing and snapping as it sliced through the air. She was terrified… but of what was going on with Destan. There wasn't one thought that ran through her mind about the storm around her. It was difficult to stay upright with the pain she was in; the wind pressing hard against her as she stumbled back.

Thankfully before long she made it to where the house acted as a windbreak. She fell; feeling utterly exhausted. In a moment of strange silence, she heard what sounded like glass shattering. Callimay picked herself up and took off.

As she pulled herself up the stairs, she saw Destan lying on the floor, facing her. His face was bloodied and his eyes closed. After she got up the last couple steps, she saw he was in a puddle of blood, his gun just out of his reach, "Destan? Destan wake up. Please wake up. Destan!"

She heard quick footsteps on the porch and ran to see who it was, not thinking of the danger she would be in if she did catch up with them. Callimay ran out into the yard, but the wind was causing so much noise she couldn't hear anything and the lightning was never around long enough to help her see.

Not but a moment later, Callimay ran back inside. Destan was still breathing — thank goodness — but she didn't know how much longer he had. There was a constant stream of blood running down the front of his coat and onto the floor, it pulsing every couple seconds.

Ingrid landed a perfect shot through the back of Destan's shoulder: missing every bone and blowing out his axillary artery. It was a death sentence, but the type that dragged out for a few minutes so the person could "experience" bleeding out. With every heartbeat, his chances of survival dwindled. Callimay pushed him so he would be on his back; he looked so uncomfortable crumpled up on his side. He moaned, the blood flowing faster and causing her to panic, "What do I do Destan! I… I don't know—"

*Sit me up, Calli.* He sounded hoarse.

"Destan!" She cried out as she pushed his hair away from his cut and bruised face.

*Get me off the floor. I can't lie flat.*

She struggled to, but pulled him toward her and leaned him against the wall. It worked; kinda. The bleeding at least slowed. Callimay bit her lip as she pealed back his coat to look at the wound. Anyone would know it needed something to stop the bleeding. Glancing around the room proved unfruitful, causing her to become more frantic and cry, "I… I don't know what to do, Destan."

No response.

*Destan?* She started to become hysterical.

Still nothing.

Rational thought flew out the window; the hysteria she was in knew no bounds. Callimay looked at her sleeve and without any prompting or consideration, tugged on it.

It wouldn't give.

The closest scissors were in her mother's sewing room, so she ran and grabbed them. Because of the state of mind she was in, she ended up stabbing herself with the scissors… but thankfully it wasn't deep. Once the fabric had a hole, it was much easier to get off. She folded it and pushed it against and into the wound; mumbling a desperate prayer this whole time.

When she was satisfied the blood flow was slowed enough, she ran outside. Exhausted and in pain, she forged ahead and ran down to the closest house. Their gate was bolted because of the storm, so she ran to the back and beat on the kitchen window, "Trever! Trever get up. Trever please! I need your help! Trever!"

Her begging and pleading seemed to be drowned out by the wind, but it didn't stop her from pounding and screaming. She was even willing to break the glass if it would get his attention. Precious moments were slipping by; her husband's life at stake!

Finally! She saw a light down the hall come on. Then she had the painful and long time to wait for the one in the kitchen to come on.

Trever stopped buttoning his shirt and stared at her as he yawned, "Ca… Callimay? Wh—"

"Open the window!"

"What's going on?"

"I need your help right now. Please drive us to the hospital."

Seeing the amount of blood on her hands and clothes, as well as the fear in her eyes made him snap to, "Alright Callimay. I'm coming."

He ran out to the garage and unbolted the door, then jumped in his car and let Callimay in before taking off.

When he got inside, he saw the pool of blood in the living room and Destan who looked almost gray. Not bothering to take the time to ask questions, Trever dashed over and picked him up.

Poor Callimay was frantic and didn't know what to do as they got to the car, "If he's gonna have any shot of making it there alive you have 'got' to keep his head and shoulder up as high as you can."

"A… alright." She answered terrified as she took Destan into her arms. "He's gonna make it… isn't he?"

Trever sighed as he shut her door and jumped in his seat. He just didn't have the heart to tell her. How could he? He threw the car in drive and flew to town; it taking him every ounce of strength he had to keep the car on the road.

*Destan? Destan please answer me.*

The next second made Callimay's heart jump into her throat: she felt like she did when she turned off her ability. She couldn't "feel" Destan: the pain he felt from the beating he took nor the pain from his gunshot wound. In short, she knew he was dying, "No, no. Destan? Please don't give up! You've got to fight! Please. Don't leave me alone. — Trever help me! Please! I'm begging you! He can't die!"

It was still dark, but the lights in the parking lot showed it was as empty as a landing strip. Trever carried Destan, telling Callimay to go ahead and get someone to help. She didn't want to, but the look on Trever's face scared her.

Again, the hysteria that gripped Callimay made her lose all sense; the way she yelled as she ran in being enough to wake someone in a coma. Needless to say, all the night staff out front were quick to their feet. Even those who were clocking out ran back and jumped in to help.

They took him from Trever and, as quick as a lightning flash, took him into another room.

Trever stood there heaving, trying to process everything. Callimay was pulling on the door to the room where Destan was; calling out for him the entire time. One person ran over and pulled the curtains so she couldn't see, making her that much more hysterical as she jerked on the door, "No! No, please! Let me in. Please! He's my husband!"

He had enough and stormed up, grabbing her by the shoulders and pulling her away. Trever's outburst scared her so much she fought him… to the point she scratched his face. He corralled her flailing arms and wrapped her in a bear hug while she kept crying out, bellowing as he scolded her, "Callimay Rose Berchoff! You've got to let them work!"

"Destan." She cried in a calmer voice, turning into a ragdoll as she sobbed, "You've got to be alright. Please Destan." *God please. Please don't call him Home. Not yet. I still need him. Please don't let this be all we get. Please God. Keep him safe. In Christ's Name I pray, amen.*

A minute later they pulled him out of the room and rushed him down the hall, talking with each other about things Callimay didn't understand, "Where are you taking him? How is he? Where are you going? Wait! — Let go of me, Trever!"

"Snap out of this!" He grabbed her again and shook her. "You can't help so just stop it! Alright? … They got him stabilized enough so they can take him back to do what they can to save him."

"How…" she asked shocked, noticing he wasn't the same joking boy she knew less than a year ago.

"I got a job here while you were gone. It's stressful but better pay than a carrier gets." He said in his normal tone as he let her go. "What happened anyway? Who is Destan? When did you get back?"

"I— someone broke into the house so he went to investigate. I wasn't in the room when it happened so I don't know exactly what did. Destan's my husband, Trever."

*I never would have guessed you to marry, Callimay. Let alone to the likes of him!* "You're married?"

"Yes," she cried as she looked at her blood-stained hands.

"H… how long have you been—"

"Five and a half months."

"I know I'm not clocked in right now, but I'll get you in a room so you can wash up." Trever offered as he looked around. "Come on. There should be one open down here. And you need some new clothes. … I'll see if there's anything I can find."

Callimay followed, but it was a delayed response. As she passed the room where Destan was, she gasped in horror when she saw the blood tracks on the floor. Trever came back and put his arm around her, trying to comfort her.

"He's got to be alright," her voice quivered.

"He'll pull through if he knows what's good for him. With a girl like you, he'd be an idiot to give up and leave you behind. Come on."

⌗

It took every ounce of energy she had left to stand upright. And then she had to scrounge together enough emotion to put up with looking at herself in the mirror and seeing how much of her husband's blood was caked in her rings and splattered on her skin and clothes. Her pants hid what was on them, but she could "feel" it… and this sensation made her skin crawl.

Not only the sound but the feel of the warm water against her skin helped so much; but she sobbed more and more as the blood ran off and circled the drain before vanishing. To her, it felt like she were dying; as if she were circling the drain and had no hope to win against the current washing her away.

Trever returned with nothing but his own jacket to show for his efforts. When he came around the corner, he paused when he was going to knock. The sight of this poor young woman he'd known for so long being so disoriented and utterly exhausted hurt him. Her skin was practically white and she looked half dead, almost.

He jumped forward when she started to faint, "Callimay!"

The sudden jerk from him catching her startled her awake. She jumped away from him and yelped, looking horrified and scared. He calmed her as much as he could, offering her the jacket since she was shivering, and then helped her out to the waiting room.

"I…" Callimay hesitated as she stared at the floor, not sure what to say. "I know I probably wasn't the best of a friend the past—"

"Your best friend is usually the one you marry." He nudged her arm, trying to be light-hearted while not cruel. "But on a more serious note, I… I'm glad you came to me when you needed help. Kinda makes me feel like you 'have' trusted me all these years. Guess you were never in a bad enough bind to need me before; but I'm not complaining. — Have to say I was more than shocked to see you standing outside my kitchen at four in the morning; during a howler of all things."

They were sitting right next to the front doors, so when they opened she glanced over to see who came in, "Fairove!"

"Callimay?" He replied confused as he braced for her hug. "W… when did you get back? And of all places what are you doing here?"

"The young man who was with me, do you remember him?"

"Extremely tall, lean build, black hair, green eyes?"

"He's my husband. Someone broke into the house—"

Just then a nurse came up and greeted, "Good morning, doctor."

"Good morning, Jessica. Callimay said her husband came in? What's his status?"

She checked her watch and shook her head, "There hasn't been a recent update. All I know was he presented with a gunshot wound through the shoulder that severed his axillary artery: catastrophic blood loss. He was rushed to surgery after being given three units."

Fairove turned to Callimay and tried to be positive, "Well, if he only got three units it means he still had some blood in him. As long as there are no patients to see right now I'll go check on him."

Jessica shook her head without hesitation, so he patted Callimay on the arm and smiled, "High time I find out more about this young man you brought back with you. I'll be back when I have news, okay?"

## ~ 15 ~

It was now a quarter of six and the sky was just beginning to show signs of the sun's rays; the howler now gone. Callimay sat down and curled up, terrified of what she might be told. She was seeing what Fairove and Trever were telling her as hopeful and optimistic white lies — which she hated just about more than anything. Why would they do that? She wasn't "that" naïve. She knew what the house looked like — she had his blood still on her. And the room?

*How could he have survived that? Am I stupid to think he could make it? ~ Calm down, Rose Petal. ~ I can't! I hate this place. I hate this town and this country. I hate it all and everyone here!*

But she didn't mean that. She didn't feel that way about Trever. Callimay appreciated it more than anything that he hadn't left her side this whole time. Her emotions were just so out of whack that she wasn't thinking clearly.

He was doing his best to comfort and calm her, but every person who walked by would startle her enough that she would jump out of her seat, "Easy Callimay."

"Why is it taking so long? What are they doing? Why isn't Fairove back?" She started to panic as she pulled away. "Why won't anyone tell me anything?"

"It's only been ten minutes. Fairove might've stayed to help. He is a surgeon in his own right. 'Please' try to relax. You're gonna throw yourself into a nervous breakdown. I know it's not easy, but please try."

Part of her didn't want to, but what he said was right. It hadn't been that long… and if it came down to helping save Destan or keep her informed; she knew what Fairove would do.

She sat down, wrapping her arms around her legs. Not but a few seconds later she began crying.

The air circulation turned on in the room, fanning ice-cold air on them like they were known to do. — No amount of technological advancements changed that fact about hospitals in over five-hundred years. — She pulled the jacket close to her neck, getting out between sobs, "Thank you for the jacket, Trever."

"It's not a problem. Why don't you try to sleep?"

"C… could I ask another favor? I'll pay you back."

"What is it?"

"Could you get me a tea? Red tea?"

"Sure! Not a problem. I'll see what I can find. And no need to pay me back." He smiled as he popped up from his seat; looking happy that he had something he could do to help her feel better.

By the time he got back, her body won the fight of mind over emotions. After all she'd been through, she couldn't fight against the power of sleep. Trever sighed in relief: *That's it. Just sleep, Callimay. Everything will be alright. … It's got to be.* — *Pull through this, Doyen.*

☙

When she woke up some six hours later, Rocher was sitting next to her, "When did you get here?"

"I just now arrived, Milady. When you didn't return after the timeframe Sir gave, I took it upon myself to investigate the delay."

"Oh," she nodded as she turned her attention to someone walking toward them. "Fairove! How is—"

"Come with me." He ordered; his voice and face looking furious.

"A… alright."

"I'll wait here, Milady."

The second she got to his side, Callimay knew this wasn't just him venting from some other problem. No. No, something was wrong in regards to Destan. She tried a couple times to say something, but he wouldn't answer her.

Callimay's heart began racing as he opened the door of a darkened room, "Is this Destan's room?"

Again, no answer.

She crept in and looked around. The room felt empty and lifeless; a curtain pulled around where the bed was. Callimay began trembling as she stepped toward the curtain. Was Fairove too shaken to tell her he was gone? Was he upset because he couldn't help save him?

He marched over and picked up something long and dark off of a chair in the room, offering it to her, "Is he alright?"

"So it 'is' his."

"Of course it's Destan's." She grabbed the coat and held it close. "Fairove what's wrong? Why are you acting like this? How is Destan?"

"You need to leave here. 'Now'." He ordered as he opened the door. "I shouldn't be doing this, but I promised Carla I'd—"

"What are you talking about? What has Destan's coat got to do with anything? Where is my husband!"

"I have that same question." Fairove slammed the door shut and threw back the curtain to show a freshly made, empty bed. "I know who wears those 'coats'."

"What are you talking about? I've seen these coats for sale in shops everywhere." She started arguing as she showed the coat tag to him.

"With the sleeves gone?" Fairove asked suspicious as he grabbed that part of the coat and shook it.

"So he doesn't like them. What of it? There are worse things in life than ripping perfectly good sleeves out of an expensive leather coat."

"You don't know, do you?" He asked a bit shocked; and then sighed as he rubbed his face, "Callimay Rose? You've gotten yourself into a heap of trouble; marrying this man. … Tell me so I can get you out of this; don't protect him. What name does he go by— and don't say Destan. I mean his 'professional' name. It would be exotic and—"

"You think he's some outlaw or cartel member, don't you? Well let me tell you: there are many things Destan is — especially to me — but for him to be someone who would be hunted like a criminal? I can't believe you'd even think such a thing of someone you don't actually know, Fairove! Do you not trust my judgement of character?"

"Then why is my patient gone?" He glared at her as he bellowed. "Why has the room been wiped down and cleared?"

"I… I don't know." She became flustered, clinging to the coat. "I— if this 'is' something so incriminating, why would he leave it behind?"

They continued back and forth for a bit, and then the door opened. Callimay jumped while Fairove glared at who was coming in. — They were both left in for a shock. — A nurse was speaking softly as she came in with Destan who was hunched over, a firm hold on the IV pole that he was, in a way, attached to.

It took her a moment, but she started crying, "Destan!"

"Calli." He sighed as he welcomed her warm and loving embrace.

"Y… you're alright." She brushed his hair aside so she could touch his forehead, then framed his face with her hands and leaned her cheek against his. "You are alright, right? — Oh thank you, God! Thank you so much. Thank you. — I love you so much. I…"

"He was getting impatient, so I took him for a short walk while they came in to clean the bed." The nurse told Fairove as Callimay helped Destan to bed. "I know it was earlier than discussed and walking is not with protocol—"

"It… it's fine Anneque." Fairove brushed off; his face plastered with a look of shock.

"How long do I have to stay for observation?" Destan asked as he got comfortable. "I'm assuming things went alright— doctor?"

"Four hours. We'll do a scan to make sure the repair was successful — which will be able to be read as it's taken. If it comes back clear, you're free to go at that point. With restrictions that is."

"And if not?" Callimay asked worried.

"Thank you," Destan sighed as he closed his eyes.

"Don't think about that, Callimay." Fairove comforted.

She sighed as she trotted over and gave him a hug, "Take care and don't work too hard. I don't think I've ever argued with you."

He smiled and patted her arm, "We haven't and I'm sorry. You're right. I wasn't thinking and jumped to conclusions. … If I can get back before you leave I will be sure to."

"If not, it was good seeing you."

"Leaving?"

"We live in Kerogen now. When he's well, I'm sure we'll be heading back. In fact, I think I'll have rosebushes waiting on me."

"Don't want to keep them waiting." He laughed; his face and voice sounding like the Fairove she'd known for her whole life. "Take care,

Callimay. Tell Destan I said the same for him. Don't worry about the house; I'll look after it until you decide what you want to do with it."

"Thank you. I will be sure to on both counts."

She closed her eyes and sighed; letting all of her emotions relax as they needed. This flood of fear, despair, joy, peace, and even a bit of anger came together in her eyes and screamed out in their own ways as tears drenched her face. She was usually good about knowing her breaking point and when it was "safe" to fall apart; this being one of those times. Things were safe, the danger was past. Destan was alright.

Callimay took a deep breath and walked back, dragging his coat by her side. Destan tapped the bed beside him and smiled as much as he could; her returning the gesture and curling close to his side.

In no time at all she found the bullet hole in the coat. It went through the back 'and' front; blood splattered, smeared, and streaked all over it... much like her own clothes. She put her finger through both holes, her voice quivering as she asked, "Ingrid?"

Destan nodded, sounding groggy, "Yeah."

"Why did they leave, Toreon and Webb?"

"I don't know, Calli." He shook his head and sighed in a painful way. "The last thing I remember was reaching for my gun as Toreon walked toward the door."

"It doesn't matter. I'm sorry I asked." She set his coat down and put her arms around him. "Destan? I... I love you."

He pushed her hair aside and rubbed her neck, sounding content and happy that she was there, "I love you too, Calli."

The silence seemed to be teary-eyed as well; happy to see the two of them back in each other's arms. And then there came soft sobs from Callimay that started getting louder as she felt his warm breath on her skin, "I don't know what I w—"

"Easy. It's alright. I'm okay. I—" Destan interrupted himself when he saw the oversized black leather jacket she had on. "Where did you get this?"

"Trever. He's the one who drove us here."

"Oh. — Just calm down, Calli. Everything's gonna be alright." He began to yawn. "I... I want to talk but I can't keep my eyes open. It must be that medicine the nurse gave me. I... I'm sorry."

"It's okay." She said choked up as she ran her fingers through his hair to brush it out. "Just rest, Destan. Just rest."

They both were startled awake due to the sound of clanking metal. Callimay jumped up but at least realized what was going on before she said anything. It was the same nurse from earlier; she was moving Destan's IV bags to a pole on a wheelchair. Taking a moment to calm herself, Callimay sat back down as Destan worked to gain his bearings; disoriented and sounding lethargic, "W… what's going on? How am I— oh. Has it been four hours?"

"It has." Anneque smiled; and then warned as she stopped him from sitting up, "You can't put 'any' weight on your right shoulder. They 'should' have put this sling on when you were in recovery, but, we can do it now. No worries."

"Here, I'll help." Callimay offered as she got up.

"Splendid! I'll show you now and you'll be ready to help him with it at home." She nodded as she opened the box, her realizing as she laughed, "Well it would help if I would've picked up the right size. You'll lose a bit of muscle tone in that arm, but I don't think 'that' much. I'll be right back. — If you want to, you can help him sit up. Just make sure he doesn't put any weight on that shoulder. None. What. So. Ever. Okay? … Good."

A few minutes and dizzy spells later, Destan was upright and fitted with his new clothing accessory.

"We'll be gone… oh about an hour I'd say." Anneque commented while she double-checked to make sure Destan's IV wouldn't be tugged on or his arm disturbed.

*Why can't they do it here like they did for me at the Society?* Callimay grieved, and then finished while making the effort to sound positive, "Is it alright if I wait here?"

She smiled as she went and opened the door, "Of course."

"I'll make sure to come back here." Destan reassured as he took her hand and squeezed it. "I promise, Calli."

When they did get back, it was a quick succession of events to get Destan ready for discharge. Anneque was so good at putting them at ease and explaining what she was doing or what his discharge papers were discussing. So many little things she said were not things Destan nor Callimay considered asking. She stayed until there wasn't another question they could think of and then gave her well wishes and left.

Before they left, Callimay looked back once more to make sure nothing of theirs was in the room. She tilted her head and walked over, seeing a note on the clipboard Anneque left.

"I 'guess' it could be Destan." She jokingly turned the envelope upside down and crossed her eyes. "Looks more like Doyen to me."

"Oh?" He laughed from seeing her face as he took the note and she started pushing the wheelchair. "It does, doesn't it."

Rocher jumped to his feet when he saw Destan; rushing over, "It is such a relief to see you, Sir. I am not ashamed to say I was becoming overwhelmed with concern regarding how much time had elapsed since Milady departed."

Callimay gasped, "I'm so sorry, Rocher. I totally forgot to—"

"Everything is as it should be, Milady. Have no fear."

❦

It was a slight detour, but Callimay asked Rocher to go back by the house… and yet had him stop at a house down the road from it. Destan was confused, but understood when she reminded him Trever let her borrow his jacket. She wanted to be sure to return it and thank him.

She stood on the porch and waited, knocking a couple times, but he never came. Accepting the fact she wasn't going to see him, she set the jacket on a chair. A moment later she ran and asked Rocher for some paper; using the hood of the car to write on before she ran back and tucked it in one of the pockets where he would see it.

"This road goes to Downing, doesn't it?" Destan asked as she got in.

"Huh? … Oh! Yeah. But not the side we're going to. Why?"

"Your house is right there."

"B… but you look so tired. We don't need to stop."

"I don't want that house to be nothing but bad memories for you. And you need to change. We're going. I'm doing okay, alright? — Hey Rocher? Go to Calli's house. I don't think waiting a few more minutes will kill anyone."

❦

Rocher helped him out when they arrived; disagreeing the entire time with his decision. Destan was in pain and had a short dizzy spell, but he was firm in saying he wanted to make something good out of all the bad that happened.

He got the gate for her and then hurried to the front door so he could watch her come up. She paused and looked around at the flowers and trees which were still being tended to; though some of them looked worse for wear from the storm. Seeing them like they were tempted her to stop and tend to them, but she knew they would be fine — they were just plants.

Callimay looked up and smiled, the lingering wind from the storm blowing her hair around while the warm sunrays grabbed hold of some of them, making them appear blonder. Her eyes were tired and worn, but she was happy; and more importantly, she was safe.

Destan returned the smile, grateful to have this opportunity to see her like this. He knew how close he was to dying and making her a widow. And seeing her outfit made him realize some of what she went through during those few, frightening hours.

She walked up and reached above the porch awning for the key, but gripped her side and hunched over as she grunted.

"Here Calli." He reached up with his good hand and took it down. "Are you alright? I'm sorry t—"

"Thank you Destan. I'm alright. I… I guess I aggravated it when I was trying to move you— but don't worry! I'll be alright."

🕉

As they walked in, he happened to look back and saw — off in the distance — the same man he saw at the mansion. His eyes widened and his heart began racing. Destan glanced back and was relieved Callimay didn't notice. He turned and followed her, but made sure to lock the door behind them… as if that would help.

Who was this man and how did he know where they were… again? And why doesn't Destan do something about him?

Unlike what she was expecting to find when she walked in, Callimay found a house where everything was clean and put back in its place. She could even smell fresh paint!

As she looked around, trying to make sense of everything, she saw a note on the floor where Destan had been. She opened it and tried her best to not cry.

*Callimay? Consider this your wedding gift. Hope to see you and Destan soon! Maybe a double date to go dancing?*
*Trever*

She sighed as she wiped her eyes, "Oh Trever."

"Who 'is' this Trever, anyway?"

"Oh. He's an old friend." She sounded very casual as she smiled.

Destan asked with a raised eyebrow as he turned, "Friend?"

"He's the kind of friend who I believe is content to be a lady's man for his entire life. If the girl he asked to go dancing with was taken or busy, he just went down the list. — Rest assured, my answer was always no. I really don't know why he kept asking."

"Oh! … That type. — What brought him to mind again?"

"He cleaned everything on top of everything else he did. … I wish I could've thanked him." Callimay explained as she showed him the note. "But, he probably had to get to work."

"He's that sure he can get a date at any time?"

"There are enough girls around who will go with him without notice. They know he'll pay and make the evening enjoyable for them."

"To each their own." Destan shook his head and walked over to the fireplace. "Calli? Is this your mother?"

"Yes." She sighed as she took the picture down. "This was taken at my graduation. … Destan?"

"Hum?"

"Do I smile? I mean— do I smile like I'm smiling in this picture?"

"Calli." He comforted as he pushed her bangs out of her face. "You have the sweetest smile I've ever seen… and that goes back to the first day I met you."

"You're not just saying that?"

"You know I wouldn't lie to you, Calli." He said a bit worried.

"It's j— after she passed, I don't think I ever smiled. Not like this. I just didn't know if—"

"You do, Calli. You do." Destan assured after he kissed her

One tear jumped off her eyelash and that was it. Destan held her for a while and let her calm herself. He didn't want to force anything. She needed time to process everything. In a way, he did too.

"Since we're here," she got out in between sobs. "Could I bring a couple things home with me?"

Destan chuckled as he rested his hand on her neck, "It's your home too, Calli. Just remember we need to be able to fit it into the car."

Without needing to be coaxed any further, she started smiling. Once she'd soaked in the moment as much as she wanted to, she rushed off to her room.

After a bit, he strolled in, catching her off guard, "It's just me."

Callimay calmed as she went back to packing her bag, "It's okay. I'm just not used to others being in this house with me. — I know. It's girly with all the frills and sparkle. ... Destan?"

"Huh?"

"What's wrong? Are you not feeling well?"

"I'm fine. I was just looking at what your life was like before I came along… and thinking. Is it alright if I wander around?"

"Of course. I can't lose you in here."

"Don't forget to change."

"I won't."

Even though the time spent freshening up and going through some of her belongings was relaxing, Callimay didn't want to be separated from Destan too long. She poked her head out of the bedroom and then came out, glancing at the front porch before walking back toward the kitchen: *Now where could he have gone? ~ I thought you said you couldn't lose him? ~ Oh shush.* "Destan? Destan where are you?"

"In here," she heard him call out.

"Where is 'here'?" She laughed.

As she walked back into the living room, she saw the door to Mrs. Berchoff's bedroom opened. It was the only place he could be other than the basement. She glanced at the picture and then closed her eyes, pulling herself down the hall.

He was looking at the framed photographs that occupied an entire wall of the bedroom; all of them having Callimay and her mother in them. Destan was enthralled by them; so touched to see his wife at different points in her life and how she loved living regardless of what limits had been placed on her: *Her mother was a strong woman. She let Calli be who she was and gave her the chance to have more freedom than most do. … I remember how father t—* "Calli? What's wrong?"

"It's nothing. I… I'll be fine." She backed out of the doorway, fiddling with the hem of her shirt.

Destan took off after her; having to work extra hard to keep his breathing and voice normal as she squirmed and cried out while he worked to keep her flailing arms still, "Calli. Calli, please. It's okay. It's just me. What's wrong? … Calli? … Please don't be quiet. I don't want something to happen like last time. — Calli I can't bear you not talking to me when something's bothering you. Please tell me. I'm alright. I can handle it. Okay?"

"I almost lost you like I lost her." She blurted out as she gripped his shirt; her whole body trembling at this point. "You might not think it's the same but it is to me. Being alone is the same. I was almost a wid—"

"I know what you're saying. It was 'too' close; I can only imagine what you went through. I'm so sorry you had to stay so strong through so much without me. Calli please don't tear yourself up about this. … I know the last day has been hard for you, but… but I don't want to lose you because of what 'could' have happened. Please." Destan explained in his tender voice as he leaned his head on hers and rocked her.

She managed a nod; her grip on him slowly fading.

He waited for a little while and then asked, "Did you get what you wanted to bring?"

"They're on the coffee table."

"I love you, Calli." He said grieved as he wiped her cheek; her leaning her face into his hand. "I'm right here. I always will be."

"I love you too Destan. — Let me go get the key so we can lock up. I think I left it in my room."

"Alright." He encouraged as he let her go.

Callimay searched her room for a while and then the living room; eventually throwing her hands in the air and rubbing her face. Sadly, though not entirely surprising, she couldn't find the key. And it now appeared Destan disappeared with it. So, the room-to-room hunt began; culminating in the kitchen: *Why am I surprised to find you here?* "There's no food in here. At least there shouldn't be any that can be eaten right now."

He jumped; shoving a paper in his pocket, "Oh!"

"What's that?"

"That note from the hospital you made weird faces at. Ready?"

"Do you have the key?"

"Yeah, why?"

"Ugh! Nothing."

ᛞ

When she got to the car, Callimay looked back. Everything looked like she'd never left… even though it was a different season. The smell of lilacs was so strong it made her — for a split second — wait for Mrs. Berchoff to come out onto the porch and wave goodbye.

"Are you alright? Calli?" Destan asked as she hung her head and folded her arms across her chest. "Are you cold?"

"D… do you think we might be able to come back sometime?"

"I don't see why not."

She closed her eyes and took a deep breath, then turned and smiled, "I don't know if you'll ever understand how glad I am to have you back. Let's get you home."

ᛞ

As she walked over to the jet, Destan excused himself to talk with the small group of men it appeared he had when they arrived. She wandered around the rows of seats, looking at everything with curious eyes when she overheard him talking with Rocher. A moment later, he ducked his head as he walked in.

"Is this 'your' jet?"

"Yeah." He half-chuckled. "Why?"

"I just… wondered. It looked so much like the car."

"Are you okay?"

"Yeah." She muttered as she sat down.

By reflex, Destan sat in his normal seat which was a row behind and across the aisle from where Callimay planted herself. He leaned forward and could see she had her hands stuffed in the bag she brought, "What did you bring?"

No answer.

When the jet started taxiing, she yelped as she jumped. The next second she looked like an armadillo; curled up on the seat as tight as humanly possible. Destan got up and walked across the hall, kneeling next to her, "Calli? … There you are. Do you wanna sit with me?"

"Am I allowed?"

"That's how you rode out here."

Without saying a word, she scrambled to her feet and took his hand to help steady her. It was quite apparent he'd done this several times since he knew how to shift his weight with the movement of the jet.

He flopped down when they got back to his seat, taking a deep and labored breath; alarming Callimay. She stood there for a second, Destan tilting his head as he looked up, "Wha— oh. I'm fine, Calli. Just tired. … Okay. No more mister tough guy: the pain meds are starting to wear off. But I'll be fine until we get home, alright? You can sit on my lap. Just put your bag here. … Better?"

She closed her eyes and held onto him, "Yes."

Once airborne, Destan repeated, "So. What did you bring?"

"A couple little trinkets and some clothes."

"Am I not allowed to see them?" He asked in a shocked tone; she always shared information. "Not even the trinkets?"

"They're just little things that have meaning to me."

"Like…" Destan egged on.

"It's the picture you saw, a music box, a stuffed a—"

"Music box? How did you get a music box?"

"I… I don't know. It was a birthday present my mother never got to give me."

There was what felt like a painful pause from Callimay; such a switch from her flustered response. Destan wanted to ask, but knew if she could she would finish, "The morning of my eighteenth birthday I woke up… and she wasn't in the kitchen, so I… I f… found her…"

"I'm sorry Calli." He put his arm around her and let her cry.

Destan didn't like that he'd caused her to relive another horrible part of her life, but at the same time he was hoping she could let everything out right then and be able to let it rest like it needed to. She was harboring emotions and suppressing memories, just like he was.

As soon as she could, she continued; trying to forget about those painful memories in the way she always had: diverting attention, "It plays the song we danced to before we left the ball. I don't know where she found it; let alone how she afforded it."

The little box was soon prepped with tender care and ready for its performance. It wasn't capable of what Mr. Benthvole did, but the melody was clear. Destan even started humming the tune with her when he recalled how it went.

"The ball was fun. And the next one is in… about a month."

"Really!" Callimay asked as the sparkle came back to her eye.

"I'll have to check with Rocher to be exactly sure, but I don't think my brain was jostled so much that I forgot the right date."

"You mean we can go?"

"Why not?"

"But Toreon and W—"

"They won't ever bother us again, Calli." Destan comforted as he pushed her bangs back behind her ear.

"But I thought you said you didn't know what happened?"

"I… I found out…"

"They're dead?"

"Yes Calli. They're gone. Forever."

"How?"

Destan answered what he knew was her next question; purposefully ignoring what she actually asked, "Now this doesn't mean we can come out of hiding, I hope you understand."

"Toreon and Webb are really dead?"

"Yeah."

"I… I want to be happy, but I can't help but feel sad." She admitted as the music box stopped playing. "It… it's hard to—"

"They weren't saved. There's nothing wrong with mourning that loss. But they kept making choices to lead lives which couldn't have any other ending than this."

Out of the blue, Callimay chuckled, "I can't believe Fairove thought you got up and left the hospital in the condition you were."

"Huh?"

"He brought me back while you were out and tried to make you out to be some outlaw since you wear that coat. He even made a point about it not having sleeves."

"Maybe he meant it was illegal fashion." He laughed as he looked at the garment that was in the seat next to them.

"I don't think so." She shook her head as she picked it up. "He even asked me what name you went by and said I didn't know who you really were. I haven't any clue what he meant by that, but he wanted me to tell him so he could save me f—"

"What did you tell him?" Destan asked concerned.

"I said you weren't an outlaw and if this coat were incriminating you wouldn't leave it. And then of course I told him you don't have any other name than Destan Quinton Nevrille. — Well, other than Rocher calling you Sir. — We kept going back and forth, arguing about you and this dumb coat… and then the door opened and there you were." She said light-hearted as she looked up to him and then snuggled close. "I don't know why he made such a fuss over something so trivial. There's no band of people running around with coats like these, breaking the law or anything like what he was accusing you of. Surely you'd tell me if you were, right?"

Destan put his arm around her and gave her a kiss, "I couldn't pick up and leave. I had to come back for the one person I can't live without. … I'd give up everything if it meant I got to keep you, Calli. I wouldn't do anything to put you in danger. I promise. I love you, and everything I do is to protect you."

~ 16 ~

Rocher observed when he saw Destan coming down the next morning, "Do you think it wise to be up and about, Sir. I know you may wish to fulfill your duties which are exponentially heightened for the time being, but you are not in any condition to be exerting yourself so much. Do not think of yourself so high to give me such sage advice while being capable of ignoring it for your personal situation."

"How much longer before we're ready?"

"A day or two yet, Sir. Possibly longer. It is difficult with Milady around to move things without inquiries being made. — Are you quite sure you are still wanting to endeavor this? … Does Milady know yet?"

"No." Destan sighed heavy; his breathing labored as he leaned on the banister. "How can I uproot her like this, Rocher? She's just gotten used to everything. And then it has only been a day since—"

"Have you attempted to sit down and lay everything out to her?"

"How do I explain it! She's already got so much to deal with."

"It is your choice — let me reaffirm I am aware of such a reality — but neglecting to inform her about what your life's mission is, will do nothing but make things more precarious, Sir." Rocher warned as Destan began rambling. "Sir, I may be stretching beyond my bounds… but I believe you are focusing on issues too far in the future; neglecting the now. What is the most pressing matter right now?"

"Rogues or Syndicate. Whichever moves first. And I'm starting to get the impression they're one and the same… for some reason. Call it a gut feeling since I never got any solid information on—"

"I believe Sir is wrong on both counts."

He flashed his eyes and grimaced, "Excuse me?"

"It very well could be the less than optimal way in which I worded my inquiry which muddled your understanding of my goal. … 'Who' is most important?" Rocher clarified, not backing down.

"Right now? Who?" Destan questioned; still on edge. "Just spit it out already, Rocher!"

"Who did you just previously say you loved and would protect?"

If he wasn't in pain already, he was now. This metaphoric slap of cold water in the face was more like a dagger to the heart. He hung his head and groaned, "Callimay. Second only to The Lord. … Whatever she needs or wants that I know He would allow me to give and I know I am able to. — She said something about rosebushes?"

"Oh! Even I allowed my memory to lapse concerning the prickly beauties. Orange ones, Sir. She came to me and inquired about the likelihood of having some ordered to mingle with the ones she has devoted herself to accumulating. They arrived midday yesterday."

"Then I guess I'll need to wear something that won't cause an uproar if it gets soiled." Destan laughed; his mood doing a complete turnaround. *You know Barron and Ted are gone, right? ~ 'No'. I had no idea. I just said that because I want to get muddy— of course I do. I can't see her letting them sit until those two get back tomorrow; which means 'I'll' be working. She'll argue with me in her little way, but I'm not going to let her do it by herself.*

Ƀ

And sure enough, Callimay wasn't about to leave them in their happy packaging until the next day. She was adamant he sit and relax, but Destan wasn't having any of it and started carrying them over. She fussed at him time and time again; jumping to grab the plant out of his raised hand, "You're going to hurt yourself, Destan. They're not heavy at all and my side doesn't hurt."

His timing was perfect, catching her in the split second during her jump while she was closest to his face so he could kiss her, "You're right, they're not heavy… which is why I'm carrying them, woman."

"Oh," she complained as she put her hands on her hips.

They both laughed for a bit before continuing to work. Destan's mind was still running in circles, trying to figure out how to approach the issue he had been putting off. But then again, he knew better than to think too long: Callimay would catch on, "How would you like to go on a… well, a trip that vaguely resembles a vacation?"

"Vacation? What kind of vacation?"

"There are kinds?"

"You know what I mean."

"I know." He handed her the bush and wiped the sweat off his face. "It would be spending some time in Rayleen."

Callimay asked a little concerned, "'In' Rayleen?"

"Well, more like on the edge."

"Why the sudden change? Yesterday you said no, w— ouch!"

Destan dropped what he had and ran to her, "Are you alright?"

"I just grabbed the base where there was a thorn." She scolded herself as she shook her hand and then started sucking on it.

"How about we take a break? I pay people to do this sort of thing."

"I know," she sighed as she got up; immediately noticing his sweaty brow streaked with dirt, his shirt and pants soiled by his hand prints on them. "Don't you look a sight!"

He glanced down and then back up, laughing, "I only had one hand, too. Just imagine how it would've looked if I had both!"

"I meant your face, silly." Callimay smiled as she rolled her eyes, taking her handkerchief and standing on her tiptoes. "You're, so, tall."

"Better?" Destan chuckled as he leaned over and gave her a kiss.

"Much."

She wiped his face and then stepped back, smiling. Destan smiled back and asked, "Do I look presentable now, 'Milady'?"

"I can now see myself being proud to stand beside you in public. — You never answered my question."

"Which one?"

"Why can we leave now?"

"It's not really a permanent thing, and it's secluded where we'd be. Not as much as here, but we still wouldn't be out in the open."

After she thought for a bit, she asked excited as she hopped a couple times while they strolled back to the mansion, "When do we leave?"

"A few days would be best. Monday sound good?"

That hit her wrong. She stopped dead in her tracks, "Days?"

Destan replied nonchalant, "Yeah."

"But— 'days'? Not weeks or months… Monday!"

"You won't need to pack much."

"But we just got home. And then w— you need your rest."

He slumped his shoulders and sighed… he feared this was going to be her "excuse". But he knew she was right. Yet, the protective and logical part of him knew they needed to get away to make sure they were indeed safe. He loved that she thought of him, but aside from the dull pain in his shoulder and where he was bruised from the once-over Toreon gave him, he felt fine. As strange as it may sound, he was accustomed to dealing with physical pain while moving at a normal pace. This wasn't anything special.

The only thing was: Callimay didn't know that. She was worried about him. Deep down she wanted rest for herself, but she knew he needed it more.

Seeing her face reminded Destan she was still processing everything that happened the past two days. But this could be something that would help with her recovery. They just had to get there, "Vacations are for rest, right?"

"Yeah." She surrendered. "A… alright. If you really want to."

"I only want to if you do." He rubbed her arm, shaking his head. "I'll be fine wherever we are. … One thing this would help with is give you a nice change right now. Be somewhere new for a bit."

"It would be nice to get out and see new things… new people. But, then again, I 'am' comfortable with everything here. And you need rest… lots of it."

"I promise you I'm alright."

She looked away and bobbed her head as she thought to herself, finally turning around, "I don't k— let's go."

"Are you sure?"

"Y… yes. Yes, I'm sure."

Now relieved, he rested his chin on top of her head, "I'll let Rocher know we'll be leaving on Monday."

<h1 style="text-align:center">~ 17 ~</h1>

At different moments over the next couple days, it would dawn on Destan as to what happened. And then seeing Callimay and how she acted… he was astounded how well she was taking it all; but, from how her eyes looked he knew she was struggling.

Sure enough, it began to show. There were times he would look over and she would burst into tears or beg him to hold her.

The more he thought, the more Destan remembered it hadn't been that long since their whole ordeal at the plant with Hyra and Ingrid. He felt guilty; uprooting her with no warning and asking her to adjust yet again… this innocent plan seemed so cruel now.

On the day before they were going to leave, Destan asked her if she wanted to wait. He knew it would be extremely dangerous to, but he couldn't stand the guilt that was burning him up inside. More than anything, he wanted to show Callimay he did care and understood it was going to be a rough change for her, "If we need to hold off—"

"Oh don't worry about it. Like you said — and I did too — a change of scenery and pace would be nice; even if it is just for a little while." She assured while she opened their bags; and then stood up and said sweetly, "Destan? I'm looking forward to this. I'm alright with going. You'll be with me, right? And we'll be safe where we're going? … That's all that matters. — It's been a long day. Go finish what you were working on so we can get to bed early."

"You're something, you know that?" He smiled as he ran his fingers through her hair. "Somethi— some 'one' very special."

ॐ

While she finished packing, he went down and finished moving his father's work from the computer to several backup drives; wiping the computer clean when he was finished. It was a relief to finally know what was on there; but now there was the added bonus of what the puzzle box held.

As Destan worked along, he came across what his father wrote on cliffhangers and remembered he never finished reading it.

*…There is one subject who has shown promise. I can't recall his name right now and wish I had it so I could include it. Regardless, I was able to obtain a waiver to test one subject with my theory on the relation of their emotional state and it being the trigger. It wasn't a test I instigated; I would have to be nothing short of a madman to "want" this to happen. — Though if I voiced my personal experience and predictions, I wouldn't put it past a few I work with. Lenön would be prime suspect number one. — I knew the grim reality a Cliffhanger would present itself again. I just had to be patient and ready.*

*He was extremely angry just prior to the inhalant portion of the serum being administered. After it was given, the process was stopped. The subject was monitored and allowed to "sleep it off". For the first week they were observed: no manifestations of the ability which had been — in part — administered, nor excessive emotional swings present.*

*He was released last week and appears to be doing extremely well. I'm hoping a second waiver will be granted so I can see if this is indeed our "quick fix" so we can avoid Cliffhangers altogether.*

While waiting on the wipe to complete, Destan played with the puzzle box. He already had a few of these and enjoyed the challenge they presented… even though he had to buy a new one every so often since it would become too easy after a few tries. There was one box in particular he recalled not being able to solve, no matter how hard he tried. When the drawer on the box he was holding at the time popped open, he smiled and shook his head: *I remember accusing father of giving me a fake puzzle box. ~ That sure worked out well, didn't it? ~ Pfft. One touch and 'bam' it opened! It's almost like he just had to 'bless' it. … I wonder where that box went. I don't remember taking it to Faberton. ~ Why was that one in here, hidden like it was? ~ That's a good question. ~ Should we look?*

This escapade only ended with a clean room. The dust which hadn't been touched in over twenty years was camouflaged, but when he started moving things it "woke up". As bad as that was, he just couldn't stand how "messy" things started looking the more things were moved.

As he came to the table Callimay "disturbed", he saw her handprint in the dust. He reached out and left an imprint of his own atop hers. His handprint covered and protected her delicate one, but was placed with love so hers wouldn't be erased. That "picture" made his heart melt as he stood there and stared at it.

"What in the world are you doing?" Callimay asked as she walked in and saw all the tables emptied; beakers, test tubes, burners, scopes, and other items all over the floor.

"Well… it started out as me looking for more boxes like the one you found earlier." He laughed at himself; looking around at the chaos.

"Need some help?"

"I thought you were packing?"

"You said two bags per each of us, so I did four total and no more. I must confess: it wasn't easy."

He said under his breath, "It's good to see you listen to me now."

"Excuse me?"

"Nothing, Calli." Destan deflected as he looked wide-eyed at her; her expression showing she already knew what he said. "I… I said it was good to see you listening to me now."

"Oh really?" She said perturbed.

"Really." He exaggerated as he went back to cleaning the table; accidently wiping the handprints away. "Ugh! — W… well, are you gonna stand there and look all prune-like or are you gonna help?"

She turned her nose up and scoffed, "I haven't decided."

"Well, just let me know if you do." Destan laughed as he continued.

# ~ 18 ~

Move day was odd. At least it started off that way for Callimay. She couldn't help but feel like something was off. Breakfast was very simple and somewhat rushed… and "they" did the dishes! Where was everyone else?

Callimay kept bugging herself to ask; and won when she heard Destan say he was going to get the car, "W… where's Rocher at?"

"He's off running errands." He put his briefcase down and shut the front door; looking confused when he saw her face, "What?"

"I thought he's the one who drove."

"I'm not completely helpless," he leaned back and laughed. "Even if I do only have one usable arm right now. — I have my license and am fully capable of driving us there. — Are the bags still in our room?"

"I can get them. I don't want you to—"

"Hey, listen to me." Destan calmed as he stopped and stroked her hair. "I can carry them. It'll just take me a couple trips. Okay? … I'm not telling you to not think about me. I love that you do. I—"

"But I do." She sniffled as she laid her hand over his sling.

He smiled and gave her a kiss, "Rest assured: I know you do."

She tilted her head as she gazed in his eyes, "What's changed?"

"What do you mean?"

"Why are you so… so—"

"Present? … I was reminded by Rocher where my priorities need to be, and how I was neglecting someone very important. I'm not slipping back again and messing things up. Not again."

℔

214

When they arrived, Callimay was left dumbfounded. It wasn't anything like what she was expecting; the house, that is. Destan chuckled while he reached for his car door handle, hearing what she was saying to herself, "It is smaller, isn't it? Now I'll get your door. Just wait, woman. I'm coming. It's not gonna disappear if you don't get in it in the next two seconds. ... Once we get t— oh! I completely forgot to tell you!"

"What!" She flew to his chest, too afraid to look around.

Destan calmed as he rubbed her arm, looking past her and down the block, "Nothing's wrong, Calli. Just relax. I just remembered— oh I'll let her introduce herself. She should come out here any moment. ... I knew it. The little nark was waiting this entire time. Here she comes."

"She?"

"There you are, young man," an elderly voice called out.

She turned and saw an elderly lady who couldn't have been more than five-feet tall, waving her lacy handkerchief at them from the house next to the one Destan parked in front of. Her rich, steel gray hair was braided and wound into a bun; a perfect complement to her slate-blue blouse and skirt. And her smile? It was as cheerful as the sunshine itself.

Callimay glanced at Destan and saw a bright smile on his face as he looked over and then back to her, "She's gonna love you, I just know it. Come on. — Good morning, Mrs. Manning."

"High time you got here. I was beginning to wonder if you would be coming at all." She chastised as she leaned her cane against the iron fence and took his hand. "What in the world did you do?"

He glanced at his arm and then back to her, saying light-hearted, "Oh don't worry. It's nothing time won't heal."

"Men!" She fussed as she slapped his hand, and then paused with a profound look and a glimmer of anticipation in her eyes, "And who might this beautiful young lady be? ... Young man?"

"This is Callimay Rose… Nevrille."

"Oh, bless The Lord for answered prayers!" She clapped her hands and clamored to take Callimay's. "Where did he find you, my child?"

"We met at school last fall."

"I just am at a loss…" she brought her handkerchief to her mouth, her eyes watering as she did her best to contain her emotions; and then turned to Destan and wagged her finger, "Young man? You see to it you treat her well."

"I'm trying my best."

"Oh you two will need to come for tea this afternoon."

"I'm afraid I'm going to be gone for most of the afternoon." Destan apologized; and then hesitated as he looked over, "Calli may want to rest. It was a long trip and the last few days have been rough with me getting injured."

"I could come by later this afternoon after I rest some."

Mrs. Manning waited for a moment and then smiled, "That would be delightful, my child. I'll expect you at two sharp then."

He whispered as he leaned over the fence, sounding stern while at the same time laughter danced in his eyes, "Be sure to serve red tea."

"Young man you know that is the only tea I serve!" She rebutted in a normal tone. "How can— you leave for half the year and forget—"

"Apologies, Mrs. Manning." He winked at Callimay; flinching when he was slapped yet again, "What did I do this time? And why would you strike an injured person?"

"Serves you right, what damage 'I' did. Goodness! I do n— oh, why fuss? — I will see you a bit later, my child."

ℬ

This was more of a shock than she was expecting. He held a perfect and "healthy" banter with an elderly, sweet, while somewhat formal lady. In fact, she did it just as much as he did! The more she thought of it, the more Callimay smiled, "She's sweet."

"She's like the grandmother I wish I had. … But, she's happy to be one to anyone who wants her in their life as such. I'm nothing 'special' as you can plainly tell."

"You're not special at all, huh?" She chuckled as she started to walk inside; only to have him stop her. "What is it?"

Destan smiled as he took off his sling, "Just stay there."

"What are you doing! You'll hurt your—"

"You all but carried me across the threshold back at the mansion when we got there… I do remember that. I'm not about to let it happen again. 'I'm' supposed to be the one carrying my wife through the door

216

when I bring her home for the first time." He huffed and exaggerated to hide his grimaces as he swept her off her feet.

"Destan please, don't—"

He didn't want this moment spoiled by her well-meant worry, so he kissed her as he walked in.

After a moment of staring at each other, he felt his arm give way. He let her down and quickly flipped the sling strap over his neck, beating her to the punch, "I'm fine, Calli."

"I just—"

"You want me to take care of myself, I know. If I felt bad I wouldn't have done it. And I stopped when I did. Okay?"

She sighed, taking a moment to appreciate why he carried her: *Such a softy. ~ Makes my heart skip a beat every time.* "I love you. — So… you stay here alone? No Rocher? Or is this special for us?"

"I do occasionally live the life of a normal bachelor." He laughed as he walked ahead of her.

"You do 'everything'? Like the shopping, cooking, cleaning, dis— you do your own laundry?" She listed as she moseyed across the hall; gasping when she saw almost every kitchen cabinet opened.

"Calli, I wasn't raised with a golden spoon in my hand and a dozen nurse maids to bring me whatever my finger's snap demanded. Believe it or not, I grew up dressing myself." *I don't know how in the world Toreon survived at the Society.* "I 'can' take care of myself. I like doing this for the summer when most of the balls are. It keeps me close to Rayleen so Rocher isn't driving nonstop. … The added benefit is I'm not alone this year." He grinned as he tilted his head; his face flushing. "Are 'you' alright? … You look tired, Calli."

"I'm fine. I was just thinking."

Destan was concerned about her entranced expression and soft voice, but he started to understand she was happy. It's not to say she never was before, but she was changing because he was. Seeing her like this made him even more excited about their stay. It had the potential to be everything he was praying it would be. He gave her a hug and then went back to what he was doing.

"What are you doing?" Callimay asked as she snapped to, seeing him disappear behind the counter.

"Making a grocery list."

"Oh."

Destan stopped again; noticing her sad tone, "What is it Calli?"

"That's where you're going for the afternoon, isn't it?"

"I promise you: this won't be the only time I go to the store." He almost laughed; trying to be understanding while keeping everything light-hearted. "Is there anything you'd like me to get, specifically?"

"I can't think of anything right now; though by the look of things you may want to get a little of everything."

He smiled as he reached for his pen and paper, "Why don't you go get some rest? I'll get our bags here in a bit."

"I'll go look around, first."

This was what felt like "home" to her from the moment they walked in. Them being here felt real; making everything in the past almost like a dream… both good and bad. Nothing about this house was odd, and yet the way it was laid out was so unique. It was a closet compared to the mansion and yet everything "felt" huge. Was it the height of the ceilings? What about the way the staircase led to the second floor and split the level of the living area? Maybe it was all the windows and the color of the paint. — Whatever the case, this oversized concept didn't apply outside: no amount of architectural arranging could make this postage stamp of grass by comparison to the mansion look big. — She shook her head and sighed; not really surprised with the bareness. There were well-established shade trees out back, but nothing "pretty".

As she glanced toward Mrs. Manning's, Callimay saw the most beautiful rainbow of colors. There looked to be every flower she knew in addition to ones she'd never see. The staircase that spiraled up from the backyard deck to the second-story porch whispered that it offered a better view of the garden… and she couldn't resist.

It was a sight to behold. Callimay leaned on the railing, reminiscing about her home in Faberton. There were some similarities; though Mrs. Manning didn't seem partial to trees. Perhaps it was since she took advantage of the shade of the ones in Destan's yard that made it so she didn't "need" any.

While she looked around, Callimay saw this offered her much more than just a view of the garden next door. She could see parts of downtown Rayleen itself: *Now 'this' is a view. ~ Tell me about it. ~ And he's had this… how many years? ~ It's not a peaceful, country view; but you know? I think I could get used to this.*

Callimay wandered around to see how far this partially covered porch went, seeing a door at the end as she turned the corner. The window's curtains were pulled so she couldn't tell what room it was, but it didn't matter since it was locked: *And you were expecting it to be unlocked 'why'? ~ Oh hush.*

Once she was satisfied with taking in the view, she came in. She went to the kitchen through the dining room to check on Destan, but found all the cabinets closed. Callimay looked around then headed up the stairs, asking in a normal tone, "Destan. Where are you?"

He wasn't anywhere on the second floor. She began to get a bad feeling and flew downstairs; calling out as she ran from room to room, "Destan? Destan!"

By this time she was back upstairs, standing in the hall. She was beginning to panic. Where could he have gone! He wouldn't leave without saying something. Right?

Just as she decided to see if the car was still there, she screamed when the front door shut.

"Sorry!" Destan called out, sounding perfectly fine. "I didn't mean to kick the door that hard. I just—"

"Where were you!"

The impact of her running into him caused Destan to lose his balance. He winced from his shoulder jamming into the door, but didn't say anything when he felt her shaking as she clamored to get her hands around his neck: she was crying and hyperventilating.

"I guess you were still outside when I went out." He stroked her hair as he worked to regain his footing. "It's alright Calli. I'm right here. Everything's fine. Just calm down."

"I came in and everything was closed like you'd never been there. I looked everywhere and called for you. I didn't know where y—"

"Callimay. It's alright. I just went to the car to get the bags like I said I would. — You're safe here and I'm fine. Please calm down. I know you're thinking we're out in the open, but trust me: we're safe. I wouldn't take you anywhere I thought was dangerous. Okay?"

She stifled her sobs as best she could; working to calm her hysterical thoughts as her startled eyes darted to-and-fro. It took some doing, but she let go and took a step back; nodding when she felt calm.

*Guess she needs this vacation more than you thought. ~ I didn't know, Calli.* Destan said frustrated as he pulled her close. *What needs to change so we talk to each other more? Wha—*

"I'll take these if you want to get the others."

"Don't worry. I can— you know what? That sounds like a good idea. … Are you sure you've got them? Here, just take the one."

"I've got it."

"You're sure?"

"Yep." She smiled and sighed; a lingering sob interjecting itself and giving her the hiccups.

"My poor Calli. … I'll be right back. Put them in the bedroom that's on the left at the head of the stairs. I've got some clothes already up there, but we'll get that all rearranged later." Destan gestured after he opened the door.

When he got up to the bedroom and set the rest of the bags down, Callimay was passed out. He sat next to her and sighed, that small smile growing more and more as he kept watch over her. Before he left, he leaned over and whispered as he gave her a kiss, "Love you."

ᚼ

Callimay's eyelids felt like lead weights as she worked to open them. A few seconds later she leaped up, worried what time it was. She ran to the hall and eventually found a clock, "One-thirty." Breathing a sigh of relief, she walked back in the bedroom and let herself wake up before she began unpacking; after which she made the bed and freshened up.

As she stepped outside and the door closed, she froze. She tried to open it but it was locked: *First day and I've already locked myself out. ~ You're getting better at this. Usually it takes you a week or so. Nothing says 'I'm comfortable and not worried about a single, doggone thing' like locking yourself out of your 'own' house. ~ Please stop. I know I'm forgetful when it comes to that. … I'm sorry, Destan.*

She stared at the handle, thinking she could open it by sheer thought, but surrendered and dragged herself down the steps.

When she shut the gate, Callimay looked around and couldn't help but recall how this neighborhood reminded her of a place Mrs. Berchoff and her visited in Reeg one spring. It was only a brief visit to see relatives, but that stuck in her mind because it was the first "city" she remembered being in. She also recalled how, for the longest time, it was hard for her to understand why people lived so close together.

This area was pleasant and quiet for being "in" a city… and the principal city at that. There was hardly any traffic and she could hear several children laughing as they played a game which required at least one of them to be blindfolded. Callimay remembered when she heard, "I'm coming for you," that Destan wasn't with her. This realization scared her enough that she ran to Mrs. Manning's door and knocked; trying her best to keep calm: *He wouldn't leave me if he thought I'd be in danger. It's okay. It's okay…*

A little greeter sat next to the door on its perch and did its best to calm her. The giant petals of this flowering plant burst from their white centers into vibrant red and deep orange marbling tips; it's leaves bobbing to-and-fro as if to say "there, there".

"Oh, I am so glad you made it. Do come in." Mrs. Manning praised as she opened the door. "They are beautiful, are they not?"

"They're stunning. I saw some you had in the back from our deck."

"Then I shall need to send you home with one to start your own garden. That house and its grounds are begging for a woman's touch. Men have no appreciation for these 'finer details'. — Come."

Callimay smiled as she walked into the sun-filled parlor, "Thank you for being so inviting, Mrs. Manning."

She chuckled and winked, "Flattery will get you everywhere with me. Just do not tell your young man that. Please have a seat wherever you would like. I will only be a moment."

The smaller room was drenched with the deep-seated aroma of potting soil and herbs. One wall was nothing but lacy, ivory curtains which didn't even try to impede the sunshine. Floral wallpaper camouflaged the plants in the room, serving as another reminder of Mrs. Berchoff to Callimay.

Mrs. Manning came in a minute later with what sounded like bells on her heels. But, it was a fluffy, lilac-gray, long-haired cat that pranced alongside her. She set the tea tray down and sat directly across from Callimay; the cat taking its place on her lap.

After a moment, she took hold of a cup and sighed, sounding content, "So. Remind me of your name, my child."

"Callimay. Callimay Rose Berc— I mean Nevrille."

"New names are difficult to remember. — Sugar?"

"Umm, I… I hate to be a nuisance, but…"

She looked up, a hint of fear in her voice since her guest abruptly stopped; not answering her question, "What is it, my child?"

"Well you see, I'm allergic to cats— not horribly, though!" Callimay was quick to clarify.

"Oh I am so sorry, my child! Come, Sasha." She set the cup down and shooed the cat away. "Should we retire to the garden?"

"If it wouldn't be too much trouble. I don't want to have a sneezing fit that would cut our visit short." She sounded ashamed as she looked away; but popped up and finished, "I can take this if you would like."

"I do not want you to work, my child. And it is no trouble. Come."

"Oh, this isn't work." She smiled as she picked up the tray.

Once they were settled outside, it was plain to see this was a much better idea. The rich and vastly different fragrances in the air were perfect accompaniment for the tea.

Before long, their conversation picked up where it left off, "Where are you from, my child? Your accent is quite different than ours here in Kerogen. It is quite charming though."

"I'm from northern Faberton."

"That would explain it." She nodded, sounding well-informed and pleased with the short reply. "I was torn between that and Reeg."

"My mother was from Reeg; I know it's often confused. Though I don't know why people say I have one. I don't think I do. But everyone has some form of an accent, wouldn't you agree? … If you don't mind my asking, your last name is very familiar. Are there any members of the Manning family in northern Faberton?"

"I would assume you heard the name from your history studies. My husband's family as well as mine — Hemingway — were founding families of Kerogen. That was… my word, almost three-hundred years ago! Of course to be clear, that is by our years; not the Homeworld's."

"Oh! I remember now."

She smiled and sat back, looking relaxed and happy as the birds sang to them, "Now let me get what could be seen as a bold question out in the open: are you religious at all, my child?"

*Goodness. She had me going there for a bit.* "I really like you, Mrs. Manning. Thank you for letting that be your first 'true' question. That gives me comfort. — I've attended at Christ's Church for as long as I can remember and was immersed into Christ nineteen years ago for the forgiveness of my sins and the gift of The indwelling Holy Spirit."

"Bless The Lord above. I knew you had to be out there somewhere." She replied choked up, but refused to stop smiling as she dabbed her eyes. "Praise God for answering my prayers in such a way. … Oh, my child, I almost feel like no other conversation needs take place now."

"Was that why you asked me over so soon?"

"I cannot allow myself to conceal such a purpose: yes. Now it is not to say that I do not trust my young man, but I take it upon myself to do my part in caring for those I love."

"Thank you."

The two women sat and enjoyed the blissful silence for a while; Mrs. Manning finally asking, "Tell me how you met my young man."

A look came over Callimay as she revisited that memory. She looked lost in thought, but in a good way. The way she smiled warmed Mrs. Manning's heart, "It was orientation day last September. Destan was the last person to arrive, so I offered to let him be in my group. They had it set up where you were supposed to have a home-group to work within to build your social status. — It took me no time to notice he was different from all the other young men. His eyes and height, not to mention his attire, stood out to me; but even so, it was how he acted that was the biggest difference. — He has a rough exterior that I've had to work my way through, but I found over time that he has the softest heart of gold… even though it is so strong." *So very strong.* "Anyway! When we first met, he didn't shake my hand when I offered it to him. He did bow in respect so he wasn't completely ignoring me, but I'll never forget how awkward I felt in that moment. — We didn't spend much time together after that; maybe an hour at the beginning, but then he was gone."

"What school was this again?" Mrs. Manning asked as she picked up her teacup and added a bit of milk.

There was a tense-filled pause: *Destan never said telling someone this was 'off limits'. ~ I know. But my ability? His? I—*

"Are you alright, my child?"

"I'm sorry. I'm fine. I'll get talking with myself sometimes and space out. — It was Creigam Freigh Society."

Now there was a profound pause from Mrs. Manning as she took a hard swallow; followed by a slow and baffled response, "My gracious. I would have 'never' imagined my young man to apply to such a place. Will wonders never cease. … When did you see each other next?"

"It was the first day of class; a week later. I don't think it started too well for either of us: we were both running late. Things happened and I ran right into him. It was my fault and I was so embarrassed." Callimay blushed as she continued to think back. "He didn't look upset and didn't say much in response. But when we looked at each other, it was as if his eyes were trying to talk with me. Something inside him had something to say. But, first bell rang; so, that all went by the wayside and we went our own ways for a while."

"When did he start showing interest?"

"That's something I'm not quite sure of. For all I know, he could've been smitten from the first day… though I highly doubt that. — I didn't know for sure he was 'interested' until he proposed. We had been friends and shared some moments that were, in my eyes, special; but marriage wasn't something we talked about."

"When did he propose?" Mrs. Manning continued to ask, her voice sounding so soft and her eyes beginning to sparkle.

"The twenty-third of December."

"Oh, let me see them." She set her teacup down and reached out with glee when she saw the glimmer and sparkle of the rings Callimay was looking at. "Oh, they are beautiful! And a trinity. I wondered if he would opt for such a style. — How long was the betrothal?"

"Well. … Two and a half days."

She chuckled as she patted her hands, "I told him time and time again that when he found you he would not be able to help himself. — You loved him all along, did you not?"

"It took me a while to figure it out, but you are right. I think I was scared to since he was so distant. … My mother told me about how it would 'feel' so often, but I never understood. — We still have our moments of, well… growing pains, I guess you could call them; but it's been such a wonderful journey."

"It is a rare thing indeed, my child. One that is only trumped by our devotion of love of God. … Treasure those growing pains. With this kind of love, those pains will reap a deeper and truer love. Be strong in those times. The Lord knows, as do I, how hard-headed men are. He made them that way for good reason — and that is not to say we women cannot be at times — but in my experience, the men hold on to their lone-wolf mentality stronger and longer."

"It's been rough at times, I won't deny it. But the joy and happiness I have in those times gives me strength to keep fighting. And I know Destan's working through things with me as well."

"It warms my heart to see that you have such a strong heart and willingness to — what some may say — 'suffer' through hard times. Take courage and do not lose that will."

Callimay now remembered how she craved this deep, Spiritual type of conversation. She sat there for a while; part of her trying not to cry. More and more, she saw her mother in Mrs. Manning. Part of it had to be their generational ties, but there was something else that tied the two of them together: their faith in God.

Still overflowing with questions and not wasting any time, Mrs. Manning asked, "How large was the wedding? Where was it at?"

"I… it was done in the justice of the peace's home. Just us three."

"Oh. — What about your dress, what did it look like?"

"Well I… I wasn't wearing a dress. Just a blouse and skirt. I don't even think they were white."

Mrs. Manning huffed, sounding more and more upset, "Well I hope he at least took you somewhere for a honeymoon."

"We took a train ride that lasted a couple days and then there was the late night car ride we took through northern Kerogen that was very beautiful and relaxing."

"I need to have a talk with that young man; tomorrow at two. No excuses. The nerve of his— I am so sorry, my child."

Callimay replied timid, shocked at the uproar her answers caused, "I'm fine with how everything was. Really. I'm not upset."

They continued to speak for a while longer, covering just about every topic under the sun. Oddly enough, Mrs. Manning never pried much into details if Callimay didn't offer them. It was refreshing, but her contentment with "basics" was almost foreign to Callimay.

Before she knew it, Callimay caught a glimpse of Mrs. Manning's watch and gasped, "Oh my goodness gracious! I didn't mean to overstay my welcome like this."

"Oh, think nothing of it, my child. I am happy to have the company. Things get lonely when there is no one else around. — My stubborn Bartholomew was not as bad as he was at other times when I think about it in such a light. — There are not many of your generation left who would take it upon themselves to do such a kind and seemingly small gesture for someone like myself. Your mother was an admirable woman. I applaud her attention to your upbringing and your tenderness of heart to accept it. — Oh! I promised you something to start your garden." She remembered as she opened the front door. "I have just the thing. Take the hibiscus. It appreciated the attention you gave it. And before you ask, I am sure. Enjoy its beauty. It feeds off yours. Remember: flowers are God's perfume, and they remind woman to appreciate and properly showcase her beauty."

❦

Callimay wandered back and sat on the front step since Destan wasn't back… which also meant the door was still locked. But it wasn't a total loss; this gave her time to admire the flowers she now owned… her getting a chance to figure out where their new home would be.

Her fear of being separated and alone had disappeared; knowing she had a safe place she could go if needed. But before long she felt someone watching her. Callimay whipped her head around and saw a little girl standing at the gate, staring her down, "Hi there."

At first the little girl refused to budge; saying in a tone that sounded like she was mad, "Who awe you?"

"Oh! My name is Callimay." She smiled; though she was a bit shocked that the little girl unlocked the gate and came right up to her.

She continued her grilling as she stared at Callimay — more like glare, "Why awe you hear?"

"I live here. Where do y—"

"No. You doan wiv hear. You wong! My—" she stopped and ran over. "Wook at duh spawkles! Dey so pwetty. I wuv dem."

The little girl squirmed in place and giggled as she, without asking or being concerned about this stranger, reached out and grabbed Callimay's ring finger. Callimay noticed she reached out with her left hand and began to grieve: *How could anyone think this beautiful and innocent child could do anything as evil and heinous as what this world thinks?* "They are sparkly, aren't they?"

Hearing her voice startled the little girl. She ran behind the brick gate post and peaked around the edge; now eyeing the flowers. Callimay glanced down, smiling as she picked one, "He was asking if I would let you have him. I don't see anything wrong with it. Do you?"

It was hard for her to resist such an invitation; the little girl slowly emerging from her hiding place. Her eyes were full of joy and wonder as she gazed at the flower.

Callimay reached to open the gate, only to see the child scurry to the corner fencepost. She sighed and kneeled, putting her hands through the gate and setting the flower where she knew the little girl could see it, "He would be so sad if you left without him. And I understand a stranger isn't someone you'd want to be around. I'll go."

"Rose? Where are you, Sweetheart?" They heard a man call out.

This voice caught the little girl's attention. She perked up and ran past Callimay, down the sidewalk, and toward the house on the other side of Destan's. A middle-aged man stood in its front yard, his hands cupped around his mouth as he called. Callimay could hear the girl giggle and call back to him as she mimicked what he was doing.

His face lit up when he heard that precious voice; him running to the sidewalk and bending over so he could snatch her into his arms. He wrapped her up so tight she complained about him "squishing" her. A few seconds later he threw her in the air, making her squeal in delight.

Callimay's eyes were glazed over, but like they were when she was talking with Destan: entranced. As she turned, she saw the flower on the ground: *Should I? ~ Why not? Maybe this is another friend of*

*Destan's. Surely he knows him. The little girl felt comfortable and knew how to open the gate.*

A few seconds later, Callimay found herself standing in front of the man. She flinched a bit but waved, "Hello."

"Well hi there," he smiled; looking a little confused as he glanced around. "Can I help you?"

"If you don't want her to have this, I understand; but I'd offered this flower to her and would like her to have it. She loved looking at it, so I thought it would be alright."

"It's fine. Thanks for asking first. — What do you say, Rose?" He asked as she slowly reached out and then snatched it close to her.

"Tank you." She said quiet as she nodded; and then giggled and buried her face in her father's shoulder.

"You're welcome. — I guess I should introduce myself. I'm Callimay Nevrille. My—"

"So Destan finally put a wedding band on that rebellious finger of his, did he? It's great to meet you. Callimay, right?" He had a broad and joyous smile spread across his face as he shook her hand. "I'm Redje. Redje Hemingway. You've met my daughter Rose it looks like."

"Mama stiwl in bed. She tyward fwum being siwk."

"Mama's alright. — I'll admit she'll be upset she wasn't out here to meet you. — Rose? I'm sorry, but Destan's found someone else."

She stopped playing with the flower and started looking around, her head darting in every direction, ponytails smacking Redje in the face.

Once her survey was complete, she tilted her head as much as humanly possible, looking confused as she puffed her cheeks, "Desan is in hear, Papa. How you no dat? Did he cawl! Did he! Why you no—"

"He didn't call, okay? Callimay is who Destan found. She told me." Redje laughed as he calmed his little bundle of energy.

"Dat make no sense, Papa."

"Is your wife doing alright?" Callimay interrupted.

"Oh she's fine. Of course I say that with tongue in cheek. Tabby's got a bad case of morning sickness that won't let her go today."

They all looked to see who it was when they heard a car horn; Rose instantly beginning to wiggle and twist, "Papa, wet me go! Is Desan! Put me down, Papa!"

Destan called out as he opened his arm and kneeled, "Rose!"

She shrieked as Redje set her down and she took off, "Desan!"

He grunted as he scooped her up, "Geez you're heavy! You've gotta hold on tight, got it? — Since when did you have bangs?"

"You wike dem? Iza cuts dem mysewf aftur I wash mama do hurs!" She petted her jagged hair. "Dat was just wast week!"

"I take it Tabitha didn't know? Huh Rej?"

"Not in the least. She came to me wailing and carrying on, holding locks of Rose's hair in her hands. But it's not like there was anything we could do. I'm just glad she didn't poke an eye out. — It's good to see you. Congratulations on finally 'seeing the light'. I told you that someday you'd get sick and tired of being miserable and alone. And on the subject of being random, what did you do this time? Fall out of a tree? Misjudge the distance in a jump?"

"Either would have been much better than what did happen. Had a 'run-in' with someone who didn't like me or want me around."

"There's quite a few out there. Glad you're alive. It'd be nothing short of an insult if you kicked the bucket right after coming to your senses and settling down."

"Wear you bean, Desan! I wait four 'so' wong! I cwy evewy day when I wook out duh window and no see you caw." Rose continued to smother him with kisses. "Papa and Mama keep saying dey doan no when you come back."

Redje smiled as he gestured to Callimay, "I was trying to explain you found someone else, but I don't think she quite got the memo."

"Wook Desan!" Rose exclaimed as she stuck her flower in his face, doing everything she knew to keep his attention on her.

"I see." He turned his head away for a moment. "It's very pretty."

"Is fwum hur." She pointed to Callimay with the flower.

"Well that was very nice of her, wasn't it? — Thank you, Calli." He leaned over and gave her a kiss. "Thank y—"

"Des-an!" Rose lashed out and slapped his face.

"Roselyn, you know better." Redje intervened as he took her back. "What do you say?"

After she took a moment to calm she pursed her lips and puffed out her cheeks, refusing to do what she was told. And then she fixed her gaze on Destan; her expression changing to betrayal. Not but a moment later she started screaming and crying as she reached for him; huge tears jumping off of her eyelashes.

Destan sighed as he scratched his head, "I'm sorry, Rej. It's my f—"

"Roselyn? What do you say?" Redje ignored his friend's apology; repeating his command in a firm tone as he set his daughter on her feet and kneeled to her level. "I know Mama's not feeling well, but that doesn't give you any right to act like this. Now what do you say?"

"But he no wuv me. How tan I say sawry?" She rubbed her eyes; sobs jumping out as she whimpered, "Desan! Doan weave me. Pweeze! … If I say sawry wiwl you wuv me again?"

He sighed as he kneeled down and took her small, out-stretched hand in his, "I never said I stopped."

She wailed as she clung to his shirt, "I sawry! I bad four swapping you. Pweeze no be mad and tewl God to sen me to hewl. Pweeze!"

Redje picked her up and leaned over the fence, setting her down on the lawn. She didn't want to be separated from Destan, but she knew she was being reminded to mind; so she sat… and pouted.

"Well. Now that she's burned some energy off, hopefully she'll be a bit quieter. Thanks for taking one for the team. — I'm glad to see you're putting roots down. I know it's going to come as a shock to the Ve—"

"Where's Tabitha?" Destan blurted out.

"She's got a bad case of morning sickness. I think it's gonna be the same this time around as it was with Rose."

"Well congratulations! If you guys need anything, let us know."

"But you— I'll let her know. Thanks. … Well. It looks like you've got groceries to get in so I won't keep you. It's good to see you, Destan. Don't be a stranger. We'll have you over sometime for dinner when Tabby is feeling up to it. I was telling Callimay earlier that she's going to be upset she didn't get to see you first thing, but she's not in any shape to be seen by anyone… so she says."

"Thanks for the invite. I'll go ahead and accept it right now. We're looking forward to it. — I'll see you later, okay." He kneeled down and got close to the fence, tapping his cheek.

Rose stopped crying — though she'd have a sudden sob every now and again — and ran over, giving him a kiss, "Otay."

"See?" He looked to Callimay and then to her. "It's alright. Callimay loves you too."

She stared her down for a few seconds and then her eyes lit up. She ran over to her flower and picked it up, staring at it and then looking over at Callimay; this back and forth going on for a few seconds as she looked deep in thought.

"Ca… Caw… Cow… Cowi… Cowi-may. Cowimay." Rose struggled to find a way to say, but jumped with joy when she did, "Cowimay!"

The three of them laughed as she danced around the yard, singing to her flower and chanting Callimay's now butchered name, "Pfft! Now mine sounds normal. … And I didn't think that was possible. Oh my poor Calli."

"It's fine. I'm just glad she's not crying and screaming."

"Oh, she'll probably find something in a bit." Redje sighed as he rubbed his neck. "Terrible twos? It's the flighty fives that's testing me."

"Your last name is Hemingway, right? That was random, I know." Callimay grinned as the thought dawned on her.

"I'm used to conversations flipping faster than wind-blown pages. Rose keeps me on my toes in that area, don't you Sweetheart? — Yes, I'm a Hemingway. … And let me guess: you've met Destan's other girlfriend down the street. Mrs. Manning is my great aunt."

Callimay grabbed Destan's arm as he turned to leave; trying to be sneaky about it, "Other?"

Redje clapped his hand over his mouth, "Did I let that slip?"

Destan scolded, failing at trying to look furious, "Redje Ar—"

"Are there any 'other' girlfriends on this block you have yet to tell me about?" Callimay crossed her arms and tapped her foot.

"Well… I— fine. You got me. Other than Rose and Mrs. Manning, there 'was' Victoria; but she's passed. Dalilah and Olara are another two, but they're older and in school now. And—"

"Alright," she put her hand over his mouth and rolled her eyes. "I get it. Little girls and elderly ladies."

"It's amazing he found someone who would put up with him. Well, someone his age, that is." Redje backed away as he spoke. "Tabby thought he was a jerk."

"Redje Archibald H—!"

"Alright, you two. That's enough for right now."

"Papa en wubble! An so ez Desan!" Rose giggled as she bunny-hopped; then ran to the door, "Mama! Mama! Mama!"

"I better go explain things before I have to un-explain and then re-explain." *And before my sweetheart throws Tabby into another weak episode… if she hasn't already.* Redje made a face as he turned to leave. "It's good to see you two! Thanks for being a good sport and letting us poke fun at each other, Callimay."

"It was good to meet you. And you're welcome."

"That guy. He's such a character." Destan sighed as he shook his head; putting his arm around her. "So! How was this afternoon?"

"It went really well; although I do have some bad news. … Your 'other girlfriend' demanded you go see her tomorrow."

"Oh dear. Sounds like she wants to whoop me. What is it this time?"

"She was 'extremely' put off about our wedding and honeymoon."

Destan sighed as he closed his eyes and put his hand over his face, "Oh no. I'm in for it now. I'm sorry Calli. I—"

"I found it rather amusing," she grinned to try and cover the fact she was about to burst out laughing.

He looked through his fingers, "I'm not in trouble with you, am I?"

"As long as you have keys to get in the house, no."

"What kind of question is that?"

"I…" she avoided his gaze, tapping her fingers together. "I 'may' have locked myself out of the house when I left."

"Oh, Calli. You poor thing."

"You can laugh. I'm not a bit surprised I did. I'm horrible about that. That's the reason the basement door in Faberton doesn't have a lock. Me putting the key outside wasn't enough. And apparently I still don't bother to think about it."

"Makes sense now. I was wondering why it was like that. … Well, you'll be with me practically the whole time — sorry to inform you — so in theory you shouldn't ever get locked out. I'm good with keys."

She gasped and planted her hands on the sides of her face in an exaggerated way, "I'm not going to have 'any' alone time?"

"Nope."

"You mean that?"

Destan paused for a moment, realizing she wasn't joking with him anymore, "I've been waiting for this… bringing you here. I know I never said anything, but I'd been hoping things would calm down enough so I could bring you here. I never got to take you anywhere when we first got married, and I know this isn't a true honeym—"

"It's perfect." She threw her arms around him and laid her head against his chest. "Just perfect. Thank you."

ℬ

After putting everything in its place, Destan began fixing dinner. Callimay tried to help, but he insisted he wanted to do it alone. With the look in his eyes, she couldn't help but let him: *You've changed so much. ~ That's bad? ~ No! Not at all. I was just— I'm just happy.*

Without anything else to do, she sat and watched. It made Destan a bit uncomfortable to have someone see him fumble and mess up so often while doing the simplest things; but then he would look and see her worried smile and remember when he was learning to control his ability; how she was so patient and encouraging, "What?"

"Nothing." She spread her hands out on the counter like she was cleaning it. "I just didn't know you liked to bake and cook."

"Who do you think made the Lord's Supper bread when we were at the mansion? It doesn't grow on trees, and it most certainly didn't make itself. — Now that 'would' be a miracle, wouldn't it? Ha! — And there's no way I'd buy those cardboard Chiclets with who knows what in it."

"You know what Chiclets are!"

"Who doesn't?" He chuckled as he went back to his tedious work.

"Obviously yellow is the best."

"Never. It's green or nothing, woman."

Once the laughter subsided, there was a feeling of blissful calm in the air. She didn't want to distract him or cause a problem, but he'd been gone all afternoon. Her best chance came when he was watching the pasta cook — a watched pot never boiled, "Destan?"

"Yes Calli?"

"Is… is Redje left-handed?"

She could feel an unsettling change in his emotions, but she wasn't exactly sure what it was. Regardless, he didn't answer her for a few

233

minutes. Callimay was ready to ask something completely different right as he sighed, "Yes."

*Well he didn't sound upset about answering it. ~ I wonder if I— well. Maybe...* she kept going back and forth; finally finding the courage to finish, "Did you know Rose is?"

"She was pretty grabby with that little left hand of hers, wasn't she? — It's easy to spot when no one does it, isn't it? — I figured she would be. She was so indecisive last year, but since she's in a lefty home it made sense she'd follow suite."

"Isn't Redje worried?"

"We always have that concern in the back of our minds." Destan sighed, his shoulders dropping and voice becoming sad. "But we've worked hard to build this part of Rayleen as a Safe Haven fo—"

"Wait! You helped 'build' this part of Rayleen?"

"It was a bad part of Rayleen... 'Really' bad. And it feels like forever ago that Redje and I started working. It's not complete, but we're close."

"But how?"

"This is our vacat— honeymoon, right?" Destan looked back and smiled. "Let's not make things stressful or complicated, huh?"

"You're right," she leaned her elbows on the countertop, sighing.

"Good. ... Would you like to set the table? It's almost done."

𝕾

Once dinner was over they took a stroll. There were some people who were out and about; them always stopping to say hi to Destan and welcome Callimay when they found out who she was. They were so nice; and yet she could tell they were shocked. The more this happened, the more she became unsettled: *Why is it so strange that Destan got married? I mean, I was just as surprised as any of these people that he asked, but that was completely different.*

"How would you like to go for a drive?" He asked as they stopped to cross the street.

"Now? ... I guess so. Do you feel like it?"

"Of course I do. Come on."

She kept trying to think of where Destan would want to take her so late in the evening, but what else was there to do?

234

"So… where are we going?"

"Nowhere," he shrugged his shoulders as he pulled out of the drive. "Do you 'want' to go somewhere? I don't know 'every' coffee shop and museum, but I c—"

"No. I was just wondering." *Is everything alright? ~ Maybe he's tired. He 'did' have a long day: driving here and then leaving to get all those groceries. And what about fixing dinner and going for a walk? ~ If that's the case we shouldn't be—*

"I'm fine, Calli. I just felt like going for a drive. It's a thing to do around here on nice days like this: just pick a road and go. Nowhere for no reason. … Maybe I am being a little over ambitious about doing everything right out of the gate. It's just that I've really looked forward to this. And— it's still hard for me to believe you're here, in Rayleen, meeting everyone."

It touched her to see he was so vocal about being emotionally tied to this surprise he'd had waiting. She didn't see him as the type to "get excited" over something like this. She would, but him? — How sweet!

⅌

As they drove through the countryside, something caught Callimay's eye, "Can you stop?"

"Sure." Destan smiled; knowing what she was saying to herself.

The sun began to slide down to the horizon that wasn't blocked in any way. It was so flat! For all intents and purposes, it was the exact same sun she'd seen her entire life; and a sunset like all the ones before it. And yet this was so different.

Just beneath the sun she could see a cluster of clouds that looked ablaze; a pool of fire. This was the perfect place for it to land. And it didn't disappoint: splashing red and orange hues across the sky.

A few waning rays reached out and tickled her necklace as she got out of the car; the burst of light reminding Callimay she had it on. Taking it in her hand, she looked over at Destan's content expression: *You were right. You knew. I don't know how, but you did, Mother. I 'have' found someone who is overfilling this heart of mine. It's been hard, but we're finally heading forward… together. With that in mind, I wouldn't want it any other way.*

Destan stood there, leaning against the car as he listened. He knew things were far from what was safe for Callimay, but he couldn't help but have this feeling of freedom; similar to when they were at the ball. It felt lasting, strong… true. Something clicked. He felt in control and confident: knowing what his responsibilities to Callimay were and that he had the ability to fulfill them. Destan was now free to enjoy life — the life he now shared with his wife. Yes, there was an ever-lurking danger, but he wasn't consumed by it. And the anger and fear of the past weren't haunting him like before. He had his heart back and was able to love and care for others the way he knew he needed to. It wasn't forced or segmented. It was freely given and done in a joyful attitude.

"Are you alright?" He asked, the sun's last rays now fading.

Callimay smiled as she locked eyes with him, "I'm doing wonderful. How are you?"

"I'm doing great. Ready to head— wait!" He pushed off the car and snapped his fingers.

"What?"

"Why don't 'you' drive back!"

"But… I don't know h—"

"I know you don't but it's okay. I'll help. Most people go to the lake on the north side during this time of year so there won't be much, if any, traffic. The road is flat and wide so that'll help too."

She hesitated as he laid the key in her hand, "I… I don't know, Destan. Am I even allowed?"

"Me plus license sitting in the car and instructing you equals legal. Don't worry. I— you don't have to. I'm sorry, Calli. I just thought—"

"Why not?" She closed her hand, smiling now. "What's the worst that can happen if I go slow? … Never mind. Don't answer that."

They hopped in their seats and Destan started giving a quick lesson on the different bells and whistles in the car that had to be pressed, moved, or watched at any given moment. The amount of information he was giving was overwhelming; her mind wandering back to their early morning "dates" at the Society when this first happened.

"The pressure of sixty-three point seven grams of chlorine gas is eight point three atmospheres at three-hundred seventy-five Kelvin. What is the volume of the gas?" Callimay read aloud and then took a deep yet shaky breath as she tapped her pencil on the paper. "So, this is…"

Destan waited for a few moments, seeing her eyes darting across her notes and the book page to find what she was looking for. He always allowed her a minute before helping, "General gas law."

"Gas law," she said with him as he said it. Though a bit repetitive, she wrote the equation while saying it out loud to make sure she was doing it right, "P V equals n R T. … Okay. I know what the temperature is: three-hundred seventy-five. I know the pressure: sixty-three point seven. Umm… oh! That chart. It shows what the number of moles would be. Hum. Hum. So! It would be… well it's gotta be here somewhere— aha! Thirty-five point four five."

"Not quite. The subscript with chlorine — two — doubles it."

"Oh. Yeah. So— oh for the love of everything orange and sparkly. I should have changed the equation first!"

"Well, just do it now. It's okay." Destan encouraged as he turned more toward her and rested one hand on the back of her chair; doing an amazing job of not laughing at her comment that he'd heard only a couple times before.

"I'm looking for volume. — No. I have to find R, first. … Right?"

He shook his head slowly as she bit her lip from worry.

"But it's not listed in the problem!" She began looking frazzled. "How do I know I'm not looking for it? What is this even for!"

"Remember that R is your constant of proportionality: point zero eight two one. Right now you have three completely different units of measure that won't cancel each other out when you work the number side of the equation. You need a value that will remove your moles, Kelvin, 'and' atmospheres so you're left with a measure of volume: liters." Destan showed; speaking in a calm and patient tone.

"I'm doing miserable. I don't know if I'll ever understand this." She let her pencil roll out of her hand and off the desk as she face planted on her work. "This makes no sense. Why measure this anyway?"

"You're being too hard on yourself. You're trying to learn three subjects at once: physics, chemistry, 'and' algebra. Just give it time, Callimay. You're doing really well, considering your background."

"But Destan, it's been four and a half 'weeks' since we start—"

"Not even a short-month. It usually takes a school year for pretty much anyone to have a good grip on advanced algebra and formulas so they can be used like this." He let his small smile escape as he put his hand on her shoulder. "You're doing fine, Callimay."

"…you'll do fine, Calli. Ready?" He let go of her shoulder.

"Huh?"

Destan pushed her bangs back, his face looking exactly as it did in the memory she was reliving, "Thinking about other things?"

She blushed and turned away, "I'm sorry."

"Don't be. We can do this another time."

"I… I was so overwhelmed during class. I think a few in my group understood, but they weren't concerned about it. And then when everything fell apart I was desperate. I'll admit I was terrified to ask for your help. But you proved me wrong; taking the time to help me understand something that I admit still doesn't make a whole lot of sense. — I didn't mean to ignore you right now. I… I was reminiscing. And about something you already know. I'm sorry that I w—"

"I like listening to you retell 'our story'. It's good to remember the past and see how far we've come. — You're the best first student I could have 'ever' asked for, Calli." Destan leaned over and gave her a kiss. "We'll do this another time, okay?"

"I can do it. Just give me a quick rundown of the main points: what makes it go and stop? That's about all I need right now, right?"

"Are you sure?"

Callimay nestled into her seat, paying close attention now, "Yep!"

"The pedal on the left makes it stop. The pedal on the right makes it go. Don't slam either of them to the floor. Well, you can if you want to get us pulled over or give yourself a bad case of whiplash. … Just ease them in or out and don't push them at the same time. Then, when the computer on the dash tells you, push in the button on the clutch and move it to the next number up or down — whichever it tells you. All while you keep your eyes on the road."

"Right go, left stop, don't do them at the same time, and don't ignore the computer-screen-arrow-thingies or the road. … Wait. You only have the one hand. How d—"

"You can do it from the steering wheel; the up and down arrows. It's up to you which way you want to do it. I personally prefer the clutch, but it's easier t—"

"Oh. Okay then. Ready?"

"If you need me to take over, just tell me. Got it?"

"Umm, how do I reach the petals? I can barely reach the wheel."

"Pfft!" Destan laughed as he reached across. "How's that, shorty?"

"Do you 'want' to sleep on the sofa tonight?"

It didn't take long for Callimay to become frazzled. And the fact that it was dark outside wasn't the issue, "I can't keep track of the computer 'and' road 'and' which slot I'm putting the clutch into at the same time. I only have two eyes… and it's hard enough to keep them off you."

*Well at least I'm not the only one.* "You're doing fine. If you want to try one more time, you can use the arrows on the wheel."

"But it's not how you like to do it."

"You don't 'have' to do it exactly the way I do."

"But I want to. I— I'm doing terrible. I wouldn't be surprised if this thing didn't start again." Callimay closed her eyes and leaned her head on the steering wheel, just about at her wits' end.

*This is just like how it was teaching her Physics. ~ Some things never change. And it's okay.* "No, you're not." Destan said soft yet firm; rubbing her shoulder. "You're being too hard on yourself. This is your first time driving. I can't tell you how many times I killed Wo—the car, when I first started. … Do you want me to drive? Calli?"

There was a long pause, but he could sense she didn't want to give up, "I… I'll get it. I just need to keep trying. — Is there any other way for me to know when to shift?"

"Let me turn the computer off so you'll be able to hear the engine." He grunted as he reached over and hit a button on the dash, "There are a few 'old ways', but this one should be the easiest for you… I hope. Listen to the car. It'll tell you when you need to shift."

Callimay rolled her eyes, "Listen to the car? The car can't 'talk'."

"In its own way it actually can. Just start going and I'll show you."

"Oh, alright."

She looked to make sure it was clear as she turned the engine on and hit the gas; the car lunging forward and dying again.

"What did I do now!"

"You just forgot to put it in first. It's alright."

"How are you so patient with me?" Callimay asked depressed as she put the clutch in the right position.

"I know I'm not like this all the time like I should be. — That's on me. — But I'm doing better remembering what it's like."

"Huh?"

"Believe it or not: I don't know everything, Calli. I learn things just like you do. And like I said: I know I still am. … I know what it's like to start out and have no idea what's going on, and I want to make sure you feel comfortable and don't go it alone. — Whether you know it or not, you're being patient with me. I'm learning too. Learning to teach. You make it easy; maybe 'too' easy. You pick things up so fast."

"I do?"

"I was running out of things 'I' knew to teach you when it came to the mathematics of physics and where we were in class. You picked everything up so fast after the first month that— it was like you were turning into this math guru in front of me. You even corrected me."

"What!"

"You sure did that one time. I 'knew' you were wrong, but man if you didn't lay it on me hard; stabbing the page with your pen where the right answer was." He chuckled as he sat back, looking thoughtful as he stared out at the night. "But back to what I was saying: don't worry about not knowing everything; especially now. Don't worry about running into issues. This is something physical, so they 'will' come; but they'll work themselves out as long as you don't give up. Learn to learn as you go. We're going to stay the entire summer and hopefully some of the autumn, so there's plenty of time."

Callimay smiled as she sighed, looking more relaxed, "Thank you Destan. One more try for tonight and then you can take us home?"

"I can work with that."

"Wait. Some of the autumn? Where are we going after that?"

He looked like he was backed into a corner; but replied as he closed his eyes and grinned, "I'm entitled to keep a few surprises of my own."

The car did die after a couple miles, but she was pleased with how well she did. They switched places — and in the nick of time. Callimay nodded off not but a few minutes after Destan got back on the road. It was a quiet drive, but fulfilling nonetheless. His wife was beside him and safe… and they were miles away from everyone.

As he pulled in, she woke up. He offered to help her, but she refused and dragged herself in the house. Callimay spoke slowly and mumbled, but Destan somehow understood she was going to go ahead of him to get ready for bed. He nodded and said he would be up in a bit after double-checking on a few things.

While he watched her head up the stairs, he started thinking… the house felt so different. Especially now that it was night. The mansion felt like being in a museum after hours. This? He had a flashback to his childhood and how his home felt: *We're home now, Calli. We're home.*

# ~ 19 ~

Surprise was the word of the day as Destan opened his eyes. It was an hour earlier than normal, but he wanted to make breakfast "before" Callimay woke up. That wouldn't be any fun and would throw out the whole "surprise" idea.

His plan was to get right downstairs, but he couldn't help but linger. After all the comments yesterday, and what Callimay even mentioned, he sat there and thought about the amazing reality he was living out. He was married to the most perfect, precious, beautiful woman. She was with him in the house he'd always envisioned being his "bachelor pad": *Thank you Lord for giving me her.*

ℛ

While gathering what he needed in the kitchen, he saw something flash by the front window. He wasn't concerned — it was most likely a bird — but not a minute later the same thing happened. Now alarmed, Destan jogged over and looked around. There wasn't anything there. He turned around and leaned against the bay window, sighing: *You're in Safe Haven, so quit jumping. ~ But what if they 'have' found us? I know it's possible since what happened at the mansion. ~ You can't fly off the handle at every little thing. It could've been a number of harmless things. Have faith, Boon. Trust God to take care of you and her. You're imagining things and making something out of nothing.*

As he started back, he heard something tapping on the window. He whipped around and saw dark auburn hair flash by: *You've gotta be— it was you all along? Little one, you're gonna give your 'Desan' a heart attack. ~ Told you. … So, Boon, what do we do? Ignore her? ~*

*Maybe— oh! How about scaring her? ~ Are you crazy? Why not just do a one-handed pushup on your injured arm? ~ True. — I know!*

Now with his plan sealed, Destan went back and started fixing breakfast. It took him every ounce of self-control to make sure he kept a straight face; knowing Rose was at the window. This was no easy task since she had her face pressed against the glass and her tiny hands cupped around her eyes so she could see. He could even hear her muffled voice repeating his name over and over… and over.

Whenever he stopped and turned to look, she would scurry to the side. After waiting for a little while and checking to make sure it was safe, she would poke her head around the corner and come back.

The second everything was done, Destan got her to hide and then hurried to the dining room; making sure to stop the swinging door so she wouldn't know where he went. He snuck down the main hall and kneeled beside the window. The morning sun cast Rose's shadow on the kitchen floor as she moved back and forth: she was searching for him.

Destan shook the curtain and saw her shadow disappear.

He slowly peeked around the corner, catching Rose off-guard as she began to creep back. She jumped and shrieked as he returned to his hiding place so they could continue the game.

Not but a moment later, he saw her shadow, so he whipped around, causing her to jump again. Rose giggled and tossed the doll she had all around. She ran back to her hiding place and waited while Destan went back to his.

This was so comical, part of him finding a new source of joy in this game he'd played with her so many times. A few seconds lapsed before he poked his head around, "No Rose? Now where could she—"

Without warning, she jumped out, unable to keep from giggling and laughing; the brightest smile on her face as she screeched, "Boo!"

Regardless of how his shoulder felt, he played along as he always had and fell over, looking shocked and surprised. Rose jumped around for a bit and then pressed her face up against the window. He laughed and came over, doing the same, "Can you see me, Desan?"

"Yes."

"May I comes en?"

"Callimay's still asleep. Maybe later."

Rose thought for a moment, squinting as she looked up and talked to her doll, "Cowimay ez my new fwend. — Ez she siwk wike Mama?"

"No. She's just asleep. She had a busy day yesterday." He chuckled as he sat on the window seat; realizing why he didn't feel so great: *Medicine only works if you take it, Boon. ~ Yeah, yeah. I hear ya. I'll quit complaining. ~ So you aren't going to take it? ~ I'm not a moron. Stupid at times, yes; but not a moron. I'll take it after breakfast.*

For as curious as she was this morning, she babbled on with her doll quite a bit before getting to the point. When she was ready to get right down to it, she stood on her tip-toes and offered, "Desan? I kood hewp! I wiwl go wake hur up! I vewy good at dat. Mama say so."

"No. She needs her rest."

Feeling hurt, Rose stepped back and let her lower lip quiver.

Unable to resist, Destan opened the window, motioning for her to come to him, "I'll give you a hug, how about that?"

"Otay!"

It didn't take but a moment for her to notice his other hand was in a sling; her poking and prodding, "Awe you huwrt, Desan?"

"A little," he nodded as her inquisitive hands started to tug and undo the strap. "Now let's leave that be, little one."

"You no my name ez Woze. I not 'widdle won'."

He leaned back and laughed at how she still couldn't pronounce her own name, "I'm beg your pardon… Rose; but I need it to stay put so I get better."

"So you tan whoa me wike Papa?"

"Ex-actly."

Undeterred, she found something else to entertain herself with; exclaiming as she grabbed his ring finger, "You newver wear dis be four. Dis wook wike Papa's!"

"That's because it is."

"You taked away Papa's wing and marweed Mama? Why?"

"No!" He laughed even louder: having to calm himself as he glanced up to where Callimay was. "No Rose. I'm married to Callimay. The ring just 'looks' like Redje's. It just serves the same purpose as his does."

"Oh! — Cowimay's ez shiny. I wike hurs bedder."

"I'm sure you do. Now you best be getting back home."

"Otay." Rose hugged his arm and then ran off.

♂

Destan closed the window, still chuckling to himself about the "deep" conversation he had as he finished getting everything ready.

Once satisfied, he went upstairs to see how Callimay was doing and reveal his surprise. He cracked the door and saw her lying there: *That drive wore her out, poor thing. ... I guess yesterday as a whole did.*

He crept over and kneeled next to her as he whispered, "Good morning, Calli. Time to wake up, my beautiful sleepyhead. ... Come on. It's time to eat! Up, up!"

She groaned as she rolled over, not saying anything.

"What's wrong, woman? Come on. Daylight's burning."

His optimistic voice helped her open her eyes; her hearing what he was saying so she could answer, "I feel miserable."

"Is it a migraine?" Destan asked worried as he put his hand on her cheek. "Calli! You're burning up!"

"Please don't touch my face." She begged as she pushed his hand away; her voice fading as she finished, "My head is pounding—"

"I'm going to call Lance right now."

♂

The next hour felt like torture to Destan as he paced the floor in the kitchen. Thoughts raced through his mind as to what was wrong, but they were interrupted by the entry chime ringing and then some fifty minutes later when he looked up and saw Doctor Gerould standing in the hall after taking care of Callimay.

Doctor Gerould saw the wild fear in his eyes, so he put his hands on his shoulders, "Slow down and take a breath. ... Her body is healing. I know it doesn't sound like it makes any sense but listen: her system is being flooded with toxins she's been holding in from stress, most likely. It's overloaded, irritated, and exhausted. In short? There's not much I can do. I gave her a treatment for her migraine, but the fever needs to run its course. Once it breaks, try to get her cooled down — but don't let her get chilled. Make sure she gets plenty to drink and some soft food. I know she'll say she doesn't feel like eating, but here's the doctor 'ordering' she get at least two, small, soft meals a day until she feels well. … Do you think you can handle that, Destan?"

He ran his trembling fingers through his hair, "She's okay?"

"She'll feel miserable for the rest of today, but don't be alarmed. She will be alright. I wouldn't be the least bit surprised if she feels bad tomorrow as well. Just keep doing what you're doing by being there for her. — I'd watch yourself, Destan." Doctor Gerould warned as he gestured to his arm. "Remember: if you don't take care of yourself you won't be able to help Callimay. I know this time of year gets busy, but you've got to take things slow."

"I know. I wasn't trying to neglect— I'll take care of it."

"Destan… enjoy this before you go back to Bulwark. I'll be in Vock for the next week — board convention — so just know if you call me, don't expect me to come. I'll do what I can to help, but you may have to take her to the hospital if something comes up or if 'you' need it."

ℬ

After closing the door, he leaned on the handle and closed his eyes. It felt like every little thing was a life or death situation — even a simple thing like dealing with stress: *This is the second time today 'alone', Boon. Don't let this control you. Fight the fear and doubt. Everything's falling into place. Don't ruin it. Be the rock Callimay said you are for her. ~ Heavenly Father? I… I need Your help and guidance. And Calli needs Your healing hand. Please help me lean on You and rely on Your Spirit; not only when I'm in hard times but 'all' the time. I know only then can I lead Calli the way You have laid out in Your Word. God, please give my Calli strength. Help her body heal so she can enjoy this time we have here. I pray this in Your Son's Name, amen.*

Breakfast was now cold, but it wasn't something she could eat. He packaged it for later and quickly fixed something that would work.

Then came the problem of getting it upstairs… he only had the one hand. He dug around and found what turned out to be an actual breakfast tray. The look on his face was rather comical: utter shock and disbelief at what he was holding. Did he "not" know he had one?

It was a trick to carry it, let alone open the door, but Destan was bound and determined to figure it out.

"Calli?" He whispered as he came in the darkened room.

There were soft rustling sounds of the bedspread followed by an exhausted moan, "Yes?"

"Do you think you can eat? Lance said it would be best."

"I… I'm not sure. — No. No, I don't think so."

"Well how about some water? It's got bubble ice in it."

Callimay struggled for a minute, but eventually sat up and said in a surrendering tone, "Alright. … I think it's needless to say I can't go with you to see Mrs. Manning."

"Don't worry about it."

"You're still going, right?"

Instead of answering right away, he spent a little time helping her get comfortable. He then replied, "I'll make you a deal: you eat a few bites and finish the water… and I'll go see Mrs. Manning."

How could he load a proposition like that? It wasn't fair, "Destan. I— ugh! Give me the tray."

℞

Callimay fulfilled her promise and then had him help her settle back down to rest. Destan took the tray down and saw the same little figure in the window. He almost stomped over; opening the window as he huffed, "Don't you have a home?"

She begged as she clasped her hands beside her face, "Oh 'pweeze', Desan? I has en seed you in four ever! Pweeze!"

"You've got to be very quiet." He said firm as he lifted her into the kitchen. "Callimay isn't feeling good."

"I hewp!"

"Rose! Rose, come back. Rose!"

By the time he caught up with her, she was curled up next to Callimay; playing with her ring finger and talking with her in a sweet and quiet tone about something to the effect of how diamonds are God's glitter. She looked over and waved, then went back to babbling.

He sighed in a frustrated and hushed tone, "I'm sorry, Calli. — Rose, we need to go. She needs her rest."

"No!" She whispered loud and threw her arms around Callimay's neck; glaring at him. "I hewping hur."

Callimay winced and moaned as she tried to get free, irritating Destan so much that he grabbed the innocent child and pulled her away, "Roselyn Twilight! Stop hurting my wife!"

She gasped as she looked back, "I sawry, Cowimay! I dinuh mean two huwrt you. I sawry!"

Destan was furious with her lack of attention; but then Callimay yelped and moaned again. The pained look she had was quite different from earlier. He knew he'd spiked and was doing just as much harm as Rose had… more, really.

Rose hid by throwing herself against Destan's chest and sobbing.

This would make it overreaction number three for the day. — Who said this was a competition, again?

After taking a deep breath, Destan took Rose out into the hall, asking in a calm tone, "Will you forgive me, Rose? I didn't— I know you didn't mean to hurt Callimay."

"I dinnuh, Desan. I pwomise. I no twy to huwrt no body. I vewy sawry dat happen." She looked up at the giant of a man who towered over her. "I wiwl awlways wuvs you and Cowimay, Desan."

"I know you will." He sighed as he closed his eyes and rubbed his face; knowing that was her way of accepting his apology. "Would it make you feel better if we looked for something to help cheer her up?"

"Yes," Rose nodded as she wiped her nose with her skirt.

He kneeled down and spoke with her for a few moments, telling her to go to the kitchen and wait. She nodded and hopped off, looking much happier.

"I'm so sorry, Calli." Destan crept over and kneeled next to her. "I should've made s—"

The feel of her soft fingers against his lips instantly hushed him, "It's alright. I'm just glad you're calm again."

"Calli? What can I do to help? I… I wish I could do something to take it away." He reached to touch her face but stopped short. "I don't like seeing you like this."

"Go enjoy some time with Rose. She hasn't seen you in so long."

"But I want to be with you."

At first she laughed, but then winced, "I'm not dying, Destan. … I want to be with you too, but I'm not going to be much of a companion right now. Just don't wear yourself out and leave me waiting for you, okay? Which means: take your medication."

"Alright. I... I wasn't thinking earlier w—"

"Destan. Please!" She said irritated and then softened, "I'm just weary. I'll be alright, I promise. Don't worry. Please don't. You said we were going to relax while we're here. Well, in a strange way I am. I need you to. For me?"

"I promise. ... Let me know if you need anything."

He gave her a kiss and then left after making sure she was as comfortable as possible. He turned to say he loved her when he opened the door, but she was fast asleep.

ℬ

When he got to the kitchen, Rose was sitting on the window seat, swinging her legs back and forth as she watched the birds. Her red sundress had white polka dots all over it and matched her buckle shoes perfectly... and her rosy cheeks she now had.

As soon as she saw Destan, she jumped down. He put his finger to his lips and shook his head, so she tip-toed and took his hand.

They took what looked to be their "usual" places on the front step: him on the lowest, her on the highest when they came out.

"How tan I hewp, Desan? Cowimay no mad, ez she?"

"She's just in pain, Rose." He took a deep breath and sighed. "She's not mad. And I'm not mad anymore. Alright? — Now. How can you help? Well, let me think. ... How about— did Redje do your hair?"

She tugged on one of her ponytails, "Mama's stiwl siwk, so Papa hewp. He hads to weave for wuk so he was wushed. He apawageyes dat it wook funny, but I stiwl wike it!"

"Well I can't stand it. Turn around."

"Yay!" She bounced as she began pulling on the hair ties and moved so she was sitting with her back to him. "Desan, he do my hair!"

If only Callimay could've seen this. It was more entertainment than any comedy act this side of the Bright!

Not but a couple seconds into it, Destan knew he'd bitten off more than he could chew: *Boon, you dummy. ~ I couldn't leave it... it looked terrible. If I explain~ She'll have your hide if you don't finish.*

"Desan?"

"Yes Rose?" He said preoccupied; taxiing his brain to figure out how in the world he was going to make this work.

"Wha tan I do to hewp Cowimay?"

"Hum? — Oh! Well. … She loves flowers. Do you think we could go see Mrs. Manning and ask her for some?"

"Wike deez?" She pointed to the hibiscus, pulling her hair out of his fragile grasp.

"Rose I just got— ugh!"

It took her a bit, but she figured out why he was upset, "Is otay, Desan. Is otay. I sawry I move. Mammy tan fix it. Come, come!"

They were quite the pair: the tiny Rose running and skipping along to keep up with her Destan's steady gate, while he hunched over so she could hold his hand. He helped her up to ring the doorbell and then set her down while they waited. Standing still wasn't her strong suit, so she bunny hopped while they waited. When she heard Mrs. Manning's sweet voice as she came down the hall, Rose tugged on his pants leg and giggled; her eyes sparkling as she waited for the door to open.

"Why my Sweet Flower, how are you this morning?"

"Mammy!" She exclaimed as she ran to her; abandoning Destan.

He began to apologize, seeing the shocked look Mrs. Manning had on her face, "I know it's not two—"

"Oh think nothing of it, young man. Why… where is Callimay?"

"She's not feeling well."

"What seems to be ailing the child? She looked well yesterday?"

"She woke up feeling horrible, so she's staying home and resting."

"Oh really?" Mrs. Manning asked with an eyebrow raised as she shooed Rose on down the hall.

"She's not— she's worn out." Destan quickly responded as he shook his head and waved his hands; hearing what she said to herself. "We've had a rough few months, so she needed some extra rest. It's not— no."

Mrs. Manning huffed as she walked into the kitchen where Rose was, standing on her stool and eyeing a certain container, "It would do you a world of good to have deeper roots than just a wife. You are stubborn enough that it might take two or three of Rose running around the house to keep you in line. Maybe another Quinton?"

"I…"

The profound pause in his voice made her turn and immediately begin chuckling; poking at him with her cane, "Oh my, Destan! Do not look at me as if I am speaking Yeronich. And even if I were — if my memory serves me correct — you would still understand me. … I shudder to think that such a thing was not on your mind at all. It was part of the reason why you married, is it not? And you are so good with little ones. Is he not, my Sweet Flower?"

"I 'wuv' my Desan, Mammy." She gloated as she looked over her shoulder and smiled at him.

"See. — Oh my. I completely neglected to ask why you came early!"

"We wood wike some fwowers for Cowimay." Rose answered as she took a bite of shortbread. "She siwk."

"Well we can fix that. — Come along. I must have something the child would fancy."

"Yay! We go tawk which de fwowers!"

Mrs. Manning's back yard may have been on the smaller side, but what it lacked in space it made up for in appearance. Countless types of flowers clung to the trellis for support as they raced to be the tallest. Others crawled over the rocks and grass, spreading out like lazy rugs. And yet others bunched together like a group of chattering friends, allowing visiting birds to rest during their journeys.

She glanced around as she stepped off the deck, asking, "What is the child's favorite color, young man? Surely you know that?"

"Orange, ma'am." He answered without hesitation; a warm smile covering his face. "Bright orange to be exact."

He stood there, gazing at the plot of land he'd seen so many times as he let Mrs. Manning search out the perfect flower for his ailing wife. Magazines from around Quidoria came to take pictures and interview Mrs. Manning because of her exotic and flourishing floral collection. It never stood out to him as something so noteworthy, but now since Callimay was around, he found a new appreciation for it and began to understand why others saw it as such an amazing place.

"What is it, young man?" Mrs. Manning, who had Rose by the hand as she looked at the butterflies, asked when she noticed him looking around. "Is something wrong?"

"Oh, nothing. I was just looking."

"Out with it, young man."

Destan obeyed, though he sounded embarrassed and looked away, "I smelled a certain flower I know Callimay likes."

"And here I thought you were all but a lost cause when it came to my delicate beauties! It appears your bride is working wonders beyond human comprehension. What flower would that be?"

"Red roses."

"Aha!" She nodded in approval as she raised her hand and started walking toward the edge of the yard closest to the deck. "They are 'quite' distinct in their fragrance. By far one of my favorites. — Rose? Could you fetch your mammy her gloves and shears? Remember to be quite slow and careful."

"Yes, Mammy." She bounced over to the small table on the deck.

"Young man? There are vases in the kitchen under the sink. Fill one with hot water and bring it." She instructed as she leaned over the bush and began combing through the blossoms.

Once all her tools were assembled, it only took a few snips and pats later to create a beautifully manicured bouquet of a dozen red roses with a few flocks of orange lily of the Incas and pure white baby's breath, "Oh Mammy! Ez so bootefal!"

"Now, now. You will get yours later. Stay and help me get things ready while your young man takes these to his bride."

"Otay, Mammy. I wiwl." Rose said satisfied as she quieted down, immediately becoming distracted by a butterfly.

Mrs. Manning warned as she opened the door, "I expect you back."

"I will. Two, sharp. And thank you."

She smiled as she patted his arm, "Tell the child I hope she recovers quickly from whatever is ailing her. — One thing before you go: how long will you need that uncomfortable harness?"

He glanced at his arm that was tucked and strapped tight against his chest, "About a month. It was just my shoulder."

"'Just' your shoulder. You young men nowadays! No wonder the poor child is doing poorly. You need to take better care of yourself." She wagged her finger at him; her eyes narrowed as she waved him on and shut the door.

Before she knew it, Mrs. Manning looked up at the clock when her doorbell rang again: *Punctual. Good.* "I must say it is a comfort to be able to depend on you."

"I was in fear of my life after I was five minutes late the one time! I wasn't about to let that happen again!" Destan exaggerated as he walked in, chuckling a bit.

"Now see here!" She reprimanded as she poked his side so he'd keep moving down the hall. "If you make a commitment to a certain time then you best keep it. Five minutes could determine a hot or cold cup of tea! — Well! It is getting ready to storm. I will go fetch Rose first and send her home. I will only be a few minutes."

"Take your time." Destin calmed as he sat down and relaxed in the armchair; finishing as the cat pranced in and hopped up on his lap, announcing her presence with her nose turned up, "Hello to you too, Sasha. Oh yes, please, your majesty. Make yourself at home."

It took her a bit to get Rose sent on her way, but Destan kept himself occupied with the little creature that made its home on his lap. He heard the door shut and Mrs. Manning squabble with herself as she made her way down the hall and into the kitchen. A few moments later he looked up and saw her at the doorway, "Let me help."

"With only your one hand available, I am afraid you will not be of much help to me as you are, young man." She said in almost a laugh, but smiled as she finished, "Thank you for your kind offer."

He tried to help her arrange things, but she kept slapping his hand and bickering with him. But he wasn't about to be denied.

After he was satisfied, Destan sat back and asked, "So. What's changed since I've been gone?"

"You heard from Redje about Tabitha, I assume."

"How far along is she?"

"Three weeks was it?" She paused as she tilted her head and looked up. "No. No I think it is eight. — Quite a difference! — Rose, poor dear, does not understand. She just told me today how Tabitha wanted her to know what it was like when she was born. Oh, the mind of a young one. — But to further answer your question: there are a few changes to the area. The Jenkins did end up moving in November. They are the ones who moved here four years ago right before she had their son who has Downs. ... Then Mr. Pickling was moved to a rest home in January. — Horrible time to have moved him in my opinion, but what does my opinion matter? ... A couple young men who said they knew you from your travels moved in on Sexton Avenue earlier last month. And… well it seemed there was something else."

"The Jenkins moved to Pheafoul, isn't that correct?"

"Yes. Her mother was doing poorly and she wanted to be closer."

"No update?"

"I am afraid there was. Last week. The last treatment was of no help and she passed not but a day after. I would say the blessing was she had the chance to be with her the entire time. The poor dear. She is going to be grieving this loss for a long time to come."

"Her father never tried to get in contact?"

She almost growled as she gripped her saucer, "That vagabond could not have cared any less than he did. As I understand it, toward the end, Flossy asked for him… begged was the word Yannabelle used. It took her every ounce of self-discipline to reach out to him. And he had the gall to flat out refuse. If I have 'ever' known evil to dwell in a man it would be him. Such a disgrace."

There was a prolonged time of silence; it seeming Destan was taking a moment to grieve before he continued. His latter thoughts hinted otherwise: *…since he's an active Falconer it's no surprise he would not value life.* "What is this about Mr. Pickling?"

"You remember how after Victoria passed his health turned; and not for the better? They should have moved him that week, but with his daughter and son not wishing to be involved— he had a half dozen falls before they consented to him being moved!" Mrs. Manning scolded as she shook her head. "And to have him moved in the middle of the winter we had? Inhumane."

"Is he doing alright?"

"He seems quite content when Redje took me to see him. I know he is forever saddened his Victoria is gone, but he is in good spirits."

"I'll need to make sure to pay him a visit soon. Did the young men who moved in take his residence? You said Sexton Avenue."

"They did. Though they've let Victoria's garden go by the wayside."

"I'm sure you let them know."

"Of course I did! It would be a travesty to be silent. They were kind enough, but are typical bachelors and have yet to salvage anything."

Destan chuckled a bit, now understanding what she meant, then continued, "What about you?"

"Me? Oh my, young man. There is never anything newsworthy concerning me." Mrs. Manning laughed as she rocked back in her chair. "But you! Now there lies a treasure trove that I 'must' know more about. I have heard your dear Callimay's account of everything, and I am more eager than I can tell you to hear yours."

"I'd just say the same things." He made a face and then slurped his tea on purpose.

She sat there and fumed; making just as much of a face as he had.

He grinned as he put his cup down; taking a deep breath before he began addressing what she wanted to hear, "Before we get started, I think the air needs to be cleared. I heard you have an issue with me?"

She set her teacup on its saucer with quite a bit of force, "I 'do', as a matter of fact. What do you mean by only having a small ceremony? I know money is not everything, but the poor child deserved more than what it sounds like she was given."

"It was— it was rushed. And it wasn't what either of us had in mind I don't think." Destan sighed, sounding sorrowful. "I 'wanted' to give her so much more than I could at the time. Things just didn't work out like I was hoping they would."

Seeing the look on his face prompted her to not pry, "Has she been with you to one of your balls? I would think her to enjoy those."

"She has." He nodded, a smile slowly appearing on his face. "And she's completely fallen in love with the whole idea."

"Your next one is soon, is it not?"

"In about a month, which will be perfect because that's when I'll be rid of this. It makes me feel like a prisoner."

"If you are going to continue this childish complaining; best you find a new set of ears. — Which one is this next one?"

"Vienna's Ball. It's the inaugural."

"Oh yes. I remember." Mrs. Manning recalled as she sat her teacup down to refill his. "It is in honor of Mrs. Jackman: Vienna. She was a big supporter of your work and quite the stickler for etiquette. — This

is the white tie ball you asked me about before you left, correct? …
That is what I thought. — Has Callimay chosen her gown yet?”

“I haven’t taken her yet, no.”

She asked with a raised eyebrow, “You are going ‘with’ her?”

“And why not?”

“I just did not see you as being one interested in such ‘frivolous’
things.” She answered rather coy.

“I admit it’s not my area of expertise, but I enjoy seeing Calli happy.
I know she doesn’t require anything fancy to make her happy; but they
don’t repulse her either.”

Mrs. Manning sat there for a moment; soaking in every word he
was saying before she switched topics, “So tell me how you two met.”

“It was September third. I’d been rushing to get things for the
Gregorian Ball finalized before leaving, but I still ended up late. I did,
however, take the time to forewarn Mr. Freigh of that possibility, and
he was kind enough to accommodate.” Destan explained; repulsed at
using the word kind to describe Mr. Freigh. “It was a warm day, which
made me regret wearing the wool suit I chose.”

“Wool is the choice for any formal event, regardless of weather.”

*You have no idea how wrong you are.* “When I got there, Mr.
Freigh told me a young lady named Callimay Berchoff volunteered her
home-group until I found my own. When I looked over, I saw…”

There was a moment of pause, Destan sitting there and staring; but
he wasn’t looking “at” Mrs. Manning. It was more like he was staring
“through” her. This all made her concerned, “Saw what?”

“I saw ‘her’. My focus was on a million other things, but I forgot
them when I saw her. It kinda scared me; I wasn’t sure how to react to
the emotions I was feeling. I know I was cold and detached at first; but
as she talked to me— I don’t know how to explain it, Mrs. Manning. I
admit she caught my eye by her appearance at first; but who she was
on the inside kept pouring out and shining so bright: what ‘kept’ me
interested. At every turn she was ticking all those boxes: when she
stopped at lunchtime on orientation day to wish me well, how she acted
when we met the first day of classes, the way she looked at me when
Toreon was mistreating her, how she greeted me each morning—even
after I pushed her away… she still came back. She didn’t change.”

He looked like he was trying to catch his breath. Mrs. Manning only saw this happen twice before; and each of them was tied to a bad situation. What a relief to know he could experience this tongue-tying emotion in the healthy manner it was meant to be experienced! She reached over and patted his hand; sounding like a grandmother who was more than willing to let her questions take second fiddle to the heart-felt memory being told to her, "Speak your heart, Destan."

"I went there with no intentions like she did, and yet Calli knew I could be — to myself — who I knew I needed to be to everyone I loved. She gave me the hope and strength to believe things would heal. That there was something better than 'existing' in life after heartbreak. Even if our world crashes down around us, we still have the love of those who left; and we can choose to stay tied up in the past or enjoy what we have to look forward to. — There were so many tiny ways she showed that. So many words she would say or smiles she would give to demonstrate it to everyone… not just me. You just had to be paying attention to appreciate it. I admit I didn't catch it at first, even though I was drawn to it. And there are some things I still don't catch, but she somehow finds it in her to put up with me. Even when things are at their hardest, she powers through."

"You are describing her reliance on God, Destan. And it appears she's encouraged you to grow in that area as well."

"I know I have. She showed me how to find that zeal I had when I was first immersed… and I'm ashamed to say I didn't see I was losing."

Mrs. Manning was stunned to hear Destan's detailed account; but at the same time it warmed her heart to see how deep his feelings were and the Spiritual bond he had with Callimay.

There was this shroud of secrecy she could sense concerning what happened while he was at the Society, but she knew there was a side of Destan which had always been hidden. She found out quite early to leave him be when it came to certain things.

"Did I hear you correct that someone mistreated her?"

Destan tried to stay calm, but was unable to keep his frustration hidden, "Toreon. Toreon Philpod. He saw her as a trophy, a thing to be shown off and tossed around. When she stood up to him and told him to stop, he threw her out and treated her like dirt."

“Oh, the poor child! I… I had no idea. She never said a word concerning any of this when we spoke. — The nerve of that— his 'family' knows no shame. … Was he held accountable? I pray his name did not save him.”

“He got his due… eventually.”

“Is the child alright? He did not hurt her did he?”

“Each time I asked she said he didn’t.” Destan stared at the floor. “I… I don’t know though.”

Nothing was said for a while. She was sickened and appalled such a thing could happen at that institution. It spoke nothing but ill to her of those who conducted the Society… and she obviously didn’t know the half of what was reality.

Seeing how he reacted, she knew better than to discuss it further. He wasn’t unruly, but she could sense there were strong and hard emotions tied to what happened. She didn’t want to be someone who constantly inflamed things just to know details.

Destan sat there and continued to stare at the floor. He was working to keep his emotions in check, but thoughts began circling in his mind: *How is Calli doing? Is she alright? Maybe I—*

“I dare say that storm is just about here.” Mrs. Manning looked at the trees which bent and swayed from the strong winds.

“Would you be offended if I went to check on Calli?”

“I would not at all. We will have other times to discuss things. … Are you alright? I am so sorry I allowed such things to surface.”

He took a deep breath, trying to smile, “I’ll be alright. Thank you.”

♬

The wind pressed hard against him as he raced home; the gate not wanting to stay closed when he got to it. After fussing and fighting with it, he shut the door just as the rain let loose. Destan flew up the stairs, stopping short of the bedroom door to calm down.

When he came in, he saw Callimay tossing and moaning… about to fall off the bed. He ran over and caught her, “Calli. You’re drenched!”

After knocking all the towels off the rack and leaving a river of water from the sink to the bedside, he leaned over her and patted her face with the soaked cloth.

For whatever reason, she was thrashing out, reminding him the times Webb would fight with her, "Calli! Calli, wake up! This can't—" *There's no way! He's dead!* "Calli! Wake up!"

She was now mumbling and crying, using every ounce of strength she had to fight him; but he knew she wasn't fighting him: *If I could only understand what she's—* *Calli? Come on. Listen to me. Calli it's alright. I'm right here. No one is going to hurt you. … Can you hear me? Calli?*

He stayed there next to her as the sounds of thunder caused the air to quiver and tremble. Rain strengthened within minutes to a numbing roar as it pounded on the metal roof and windows. Occasional flashes of lightning would cause Callimay to moan, but other than these moments she was now still.

Seeing her like this still worried him; Destan having his head bowed and rubbing her hand in his: *You're going to be alright, Calli. I know you are. At times like this I need to be reminded of that. Knowing what happened in the past scares me. … I miss your smiling face and glistening eyes. I do. I start to get lonely even though you're right next to me. It's hard when you're not feeling well. … I hate seeing you in pain. I want to take it away and bear it myself.*

"I hate seeing you in pain too, Destan." She reached over and ran her fingers through his wind-tossed hair. "I'm not one-hundred percent but I feel 'so' much better now. It's amazing what rest can do. … What's this?"

"Rose felt horrible — me more, though — so we thought we'd get you this to apologize and make you happy."

"She is so sweet. And she loves you dearly."

"I don't mean to be rude by changing the subject, but are you doing alright? You were crying in your sleep and fighting me."

"I… I don't remember w— I didn't hit you, did I?"

"No. No I'm fine. I'm just glad you are."

<h1 style="text-align:center">~ 20 ~</h1>

Bit by bit, Callimay regained her strength. By the end of the week she was better than ever. Redje would come over and talk with Destan from time to time during the week, while Rose made her daily "rounds"; helping when she could.

One evening, Callimay could hear the two men talking in raised voices; Destan yelling out Redje's name, "What's wrong?"

"Nothing," Tabitha laughed as she stopped Rose from spinning the swivel chair next to the kitchen counter. "You need to be still."

"Otay, Mama." She obeyed; quickly finding something else to entertain herself with: stretching her arms out on the counter toward Callimay. "What aw you wooking four?"

"I'm not quite sure why, but when you get the two of them together, they progressively talk louder and louder 'and louder' until it sounds like they're yelling at each other. I swear it's some 'Kerogen gene' in them. They both do it. It took me a while to get used to it. I was so worried at first and ran in, begging them to stop. You should have seen the look on Redje's face. ... They have no idea they're doing it!"

"Well thank goodness for that." Callimay rolled her eyes as she kept searching. "I'm just trying to find something I need for dessert, Rose."

"Dezert? I wuv dezert!"

"I do want to thank you for having us over. It's nice to get out and around without being worried. — I can never find anything when Redje puts things away, either. The mind of a man is so…"

"Illogical? ... There has 'got' to be a method to his madness!" She sighed in frustration as she looked around the room. "And there has got to be flour here somewhere!"

"It's in that lower cabinet," he poked his head in.

"Destan!" Callimay gasped as she jumped.

Rose exclaimed as she started to climb down, "Desan!"

Tabitha took her hand, "No, Sweetheart. You're staying with me."

"Why in the world do you put flour in a bottom cabinet?" Callimay asked puzzled as she threw her hands in the air.

"Because that's where I always put it, woman." He stuck out his tongue and then left.

"And that is why men would starve without us." Tabitha laughed.

꿈

Callimay was thrilled to have company over. It was refreshing to talk with others close to her age who had a moral compass they followed and weren't swayed by what other's thought — instilling this in their child. But with as happy as she was, she was nervous. It had been a while since she fixed such a large meal. Destan jumped in with pleasure and helped finish things up.

Their visitors were carefree; none of them the least bit concerned about using their left hands. This openness was foreign to Callimay… a tad frightening, actually. Mrs. Berchoff never "made" her, but she would ask her to use her right hand… just in case.

This concern though was drowned out by the laugher of watching poor Destan, again and again, being interrupted by Rose. She started at the opposite end of the table, but transplanted herself to his side the first chance she got. He was at least able to keep her at bay enough so he could finish his meal without cluing her into his scheme.

As soon as they were done, Rose became fussy and irritated with even Destan, "And that would be our cue. — Ready, Tabby? — She fights sleep like none other."

"Thank you for having us over." Tabitha smiled as she shook Callimay's left hand. "I really do appreciate it."

"You're… welcome."

"It's alright Callimay. You're safe here. We all are."

"I'm sorry. I'm just not used to this."

She smiled as Redje put his arm around her, "It'll come back. I'm just so glad you're here; that Destan— I just can't find words!"

"It's been so nice to spend the evening with you." Callimay nodded while Destan came up to her. "I hope it's not the last."

"It better not be!" Tabitha made a face at Destan.

"I didn't say anything! Geez!"

"I'm sure Rose will make sure you're in no short supply of having company from our family. — Do you guys need any help cleaning up?"

"Thank you Redje, but I think we can handle it."

"Speak for yourself, Calli. He's leaving a huge mess. You're still on the mend and I've only got one arm."

"Destan!" She scolded in a hushed tone.

Tabitha warned as she turned and pulled on Redje's arm, "Now don't you two start."

Destan rolled his eyes, "I'll behave." *You're no fun now, Tabitha.*

❦

Once they left, Destan came back and helped Callimay clear the table. Usually they chatted the entire time, but she was distracted and distant as they washed the dishes, "Is everything alright?"

She said timid as she continued, trying not to cry, "I'm scared. I've never been where I wouldn't be called out as a Derelict and carried away to death row for using my left hand. I… I'm just not sure how to fit in with 'my own' anymore. I can't relax and enjoy it. I guess I've become so numb that even 'I' think it's a sin to use my left hand."

"Just give it a little time," he encouraged as he reached over and shut the water off. "Look at me, Calli. … I know things are different here, but don't let it scare you."

"But you told me a Falconer could be anywhere!"

"I… I know I did, Calli." He sighed as he leaned back against the counter, rubbing his neck. "It's hard to explain, but this area of Rayleen is protected from them. Redje and I still haven't gotten the last part finished, but we're close. So close."

"What is it?"

"I… I can't say."

*Why not?*

"It's not that, Calli. I just— let's not worry about it. Huh?" He did everything he knew to avoid the answer he knew he'd have to give.

She closed her eyes and hung her head, sad he wouldn't explain.

This silence continued for a while; Callimay finally asking, "This may seem out-of-the-blue, but how long have you been flying?"

"Let me guess: Rocher told you when we were in Faberton? … I started last spring." He picked up a plate and started drying it. "I'd been meaning to do it for a few years, but just couldn't fit it in. — Rocher's been a great help; he's like a living pilot/aeronautic thesaurus. He says it all comes with time, but I feel like I've been doing it long enough that I should be farther along. — You know? I only need… was it ten or fifteen hours? Maybe I should ask if he wouldn't mind starting up again."

"C… could I go?" She asked in a quiet voice as she handed him another plate. "Is it allowed?"

"Sure! I could teach you to drive on the way there and back — when you feel like it — and then you can sit and watch me sweat. … Calli? Just give this all some time. It's hard adjusting back to something considered illegal in man's eyes when we know good and well it's not wrong in God's. I get it. You're bombarded with it every day that it starts to sound 'right'. Just… don't worry. And remember: this is our special time with each other. It's our ho—"

"Honeymoon." She finished, looking up to his loving eyes.

"There's my Calli. … Oh! I forgot to mention— Redje and Tabitha showed up and I forgot. I got a call from my overseer today."

"It's going to be nice to 'go' somewhere for Assembly." She said relieved as she turned back to the sink. "What is his name?"

"Asdum Utree. He came to the mansion several times, but it was—"

"Destan?"

"Yes, Calli?"

"Would you be alright if I called 'my' overseer and let him know how I'm doing? I'm sure he's worried. It's been around eight months since I've spoken with him. I know Fairove probably told him—"

"I can finish this if you want to call him right now."

"Thank you," she smiled as she took her gloves off and gave him a hug. "I'll try not to be too long."

"Take as much time as you need, Calli. I'll be fine. — And if I need you, I'll call for you. Okay? Now go on."

<h1 align="center">~ 21 ~</h1>

"Ready?" Destan asked as he checked his watch and knocked on the bedroom door. "That was just Rocher wanting to talk about times for my flight training. ... Calli?"

"Just a minute," she replied frightened.

"Calli? Calli what's wrong?" He jiggled the door handle and then continued to knock. "Calli unlock the door."

There wasn't any response for a while.

He was getting ready to body slam the door when it finally opened. Callimay jerked back from seeing his wild expression and then calmed, "I was startled by you knocking so loud. I didn't hear you come up."

"Are you sure you're alright? Why didn't you say anything?"

"I'll be alright." She assured as he stopped her. "Destan, I'm fine."

"Okay. — You look really nice this morning." *So beautiful. ~ When did you get her that dress? ~ Huh? Oh.* "I don't remember seeing that dress before."

"I grabbed it when we were in Faberton. It's one of my old ones." She smiled as she looked at her floral sundress and swished the free-flowing skirt. "You look very handsome yourself."

No response or reaction other than the fact he kept staring at her.

"Are you alright? Destan?" She asked worried as she laid her one hand on his chest and rubbed his cheek with the other. "Did you take your medication yet?"

"I'm perfectly fine and yes, I did. Ready?"

"Yep! Who was it that called? Was it Mrs. Manning?"

"No. It was Rocher. She called late last night. She's going with us, but said she would ride back with the Retoys so we can stay and visit."

The pitter-patter of rain on the windows was a relaxing sound to hear as they traveled; but even so, it worried her how fast they were going: *I've driven in much worse, Calli. This is nothing.*

*Maybe for you, but I've never been in one of these contraptions during a storm.*

They drove to the southeast side of Rayleen which was just over a half hour drive. It looked like they were in a business district, but nestled in it was what they were looking for. Destan pulled up to the door and helped them out before leaving to park the car.

Mrs. Manning did her best to keep Callimay secluded until he got back; noticing she looked very nervous being away from him and in a large crowd. She didn't take her eyes off where he was and kept wringing her handkerchief.

"Mammy!" Rose called out as she waved her hands and looked up to Tabitha who nodded.

"There you are, my Sweet Flower."

"Cowimay! … Wear ez Desan? Ez he siwk wike you wur?"

"Why I'm right here!" He chimed in as he patted her head.

She spun around and hugged his leg, "Desan! May I pweeze sit necks to you an Cowimay waiter?"

"Well… I—"

"Rose," they heard Redje call out. "Come on, Sweetheart."

"I coming, Papa!"

"Well hello," someone greeted as Destan took Callimay's hand and whispered to her. "I thought I heard Rose call out your name."

"I will see you two inside." Mrs. Manning patted Callimay's hand and then turned to leave. "It is good to see you, Mr. Utree."

"You as well, Zelpha."

"Mr. Utree." Destan acknowledged as he turned around.

This gentleman reminded Callimay of Trever, almost. They were but a shadow of their former luster, but the freckles on his face reminded the world that Mr. Utree was a red-head. His voice wasn't very deep, but it had a certain quality to it that made up for that, "It's good to see that you're back. — And this beautiful young woman is Callimay."

"It's good to be back." Destan sighed and then turned his smiling face to her, "Calli? This is Mr. Utree."

"Welcome. It's wonderful to meet you under… well I guess you could say: 'better circumstances'. — I hope you are not 'too' overwhelmed with everyone's greetings that I know they'll be giving. Destan's news came as a surprise to so many once he let me make it public. Pricilla, my wife, couldn't contain herself last evening and made me promise I'd do my best to be the first to extend an invitation to you for lunch at our home this afternoon. I know you have things to tend to later, but we were hoping you two could come so we could enjoy your company and give you a warm welcome home."

He had prepared for this, but Destan recalled the fact that: even though Callimay was doing much better, she just got better. He didn't want her to overdo it or put her in a position where she would be: *Would you feel up to it?*

*Unless something drastic happens, I'd love to.*

*You're sure.* He double-checked; his focus completely on her as he rubbed her hand.

*I'm sure.*

*Alright then.* "I'm not sure 'when' we'll get free, but we'd be delighted to join you."

"Perfect. I will let Pricilla know… wherever she is." Mr. Utree chuckled as he looked around.

Once they were alone again, Destan held Callimay for a moment and then started walking as he whispered: *Let's see if we can get—*

*Why are you whispering? I'm the only one who can hear y—*

"Destan Nevrille! It's been forever. How are you!" A lady called out; grabbing the attention of those who heard.

"Did she say Destan Nevrille?" "Is he back?" "I thought he off on some extended-stay trip and wouldn't be back for almost a half a year?" "Oh my goodness it 'is' him!" "Who is the young lady?" "Remember what we heard last week about him getting married?" "You don't think!" "Land's sakes. What did he do to himself this time?" were the comments and questions that filled the air within seconds.

"Oh dear." He sighed, sounding defeated as he stopped walking. "Looks like 'the fans' found us."

"Oh Destan. It's fine. I was expecting this."

He spent a moment introducing her to those who came over and then let them begin to ask their questions. Callimay deferred to him most of the time, not sure what information he wanted to offer.

When he noticed she moved closer to him, her grip on his hand quite tight, he asked, *Calli? Are you alright?*

*I… I'm just having a hard time. I'll be—*

"I hate to cut this off," he gave her a quick hug and smiled to the group. "But Callimay isn't used to all of this attention; and—"

"Oh, of course, Destan." One of the men acknowledged as he took a step back. "We'll talk with you later."

"It was wonderful to meet you, Callimay." This gentleman's wife smiled as she stepped back to her husband's side.

"Do you have your afternoon free?" Another gentleman asked.

"The Utrees beat you to it," Destan shook his head as he smiled.

"Well, they'll be other times. It's not like you're going to run off into the night… right?"

"It's never my intention to 'run off'." He put his arm around Callimay. "I try to make sure things are planned."

ℬ

Destan took her in, the occasional person stopping them to say a rushed and quiet hello or welcome. He looked around and took a deep breath, smiling. One of the gentlemen they spoke with earlier passed by and waved, the two of them returning the gesture.

"Where do you want to sit, Calli?"

"Well, where do you usually sit?" She replied timid, turning away.

"Calli? Are you okay?" Destan stroked the side of her face.

Without any warning, she jerked to the side and almost bumped into someone, "I'm just trying to take this all in."

"Y… you're sure nothing's wrong?"

"I…" she grabbed her right arm and looked down as some of the people who talked to them earlier walked by.

*Calli please tell me.* Destan wiped the few tears off her cheek.

She started walking; still gripping his hand: *Let's find a seat.*

*Cal— alright.*

He got closer to the front with every short stride he took; her grip on his hand getting tighter and tighter. Was she nervous… or was she scared? And if so, of what? Destan hoped she would calm if they sat down, so he stopped short of where he usually sat and ushered her to the middle of the row: *Maybe she's just nervous about not being seated before the reading started. ~ I hope so.*

That would have been wonderful, but she looked up to him as he sat down with the most terrified expression on her face, and then scooted over so she was all but sitting "on" his lap; plastering herself against his side. Destan leaned his head on hers while they prayed; then asked when they were done: *What's wrong?*

She didn't reply.

*Tell me if you need some space from everyone… Calli?*

There were a few moments of silence, but she at least nodded.

Hearing her sniffling prompted him to reach in his jacket and take his handkerchief out. She was trying to hide her overflowing emotions from everyone, so she didn't look up as she took it.

By the time everyone got up to greet each other during a short break, she was back to her normal self. Destan wanted to be at ease since she was better, but it bugged him that she was acting like this: *I'll tell you when we get home. Is that alright?*

"I just want you to be alright, Calli." He sighed as he began fiddling with her wedding band.

"Cowimay!" Rose called out as she shook her paper in the air and ran over. "Wook! Dis ez Ehud fwum duh Bible. I dwew him. He weft-handed wike Mama, Papa, you, 'and' me! And he was duh hewow!"

"Wow." Destan tried to look at the paper she kept shaking.

*Destan! Should she be talking about—*

*Do you remember where we are?* He reminded in a calming voice as he turned to her and smiled.

*But there may be visitors— Falconers!* Her eyes darted around.

*It's alright. Okay?*

"He was wike a spy, did you no dat, Cowimay?" Rose began to crawl over Destan's lap to her.

"I did," she nodded as she lifted her up and set her on her lap; talking in a hushed tone. "He was a very strong and brave man."

"Wike Papa and Desan!" Rose beamed as she leaned her head back and laughed; cupping her hand to look like the letter c. "White?"

"Sure." He smiled as he did the same thing, touching his fingers to hers so they made the letter s.

"May I say which you now? 'Pweeze'? I behave. I pwomise."

Destan raised his eyebrow, "What did Redje say?"

Rose opened her mouth and then closed it a couple times. She then bowed her head and admitted, "I dinu ask Papa 'or' Mama."

"Well, I think you need to do that first." He nodded in the direction of where Redje and Tabitha were.

"Otay," she nodded in an exaggerated way as she crawled off of Callimay's lap and ran to her parents.

Before long, Redje looked over and shrugged his shoulders.

"What do you want to do, Calli?"

"I don't mind if she sits with us. It's up to you."

"Alright." He took her hand and nodded to Redje.

"Oh, tank you Desan. Tank you Cowimay." She exclaimed out of breath as she crawled up on the chair and threw her arms around Callimay's neck.

"You're welcome, Rose." She smiled as she hugged her back; though it was a bit longer than what she wanted.

"I dun now, Cowimay. … May I sit in du middle?"

"How about you sit 'by' Callimay, huh?" Destan suggested as he scooted closer. "You sit by me all the time."

She nodded as she turned and plopped down right next to her, fixing both hers and Callimay's skirts so they looked nice, "Otay."

"You look very pretty this morning, Rose."

"Tank you, Desan." She grinned and giggled; her eyes closed tight as she petted the overskirt of her lavender sundress. Then out of the blue she held up her fingers, "Mama got dis for my burfday since I turn five. — Why you no dare, Desan? You forget?"

"I was busy, I'm sorry." He apologized as he glanced up to the front. "It's time to be quiet now."

She put her finger to her lips, "I be stiwl. I pwomise, Desan."

ℬ

"Now I'm not complaining, but I never thought we were going to get out of there. I haven't been in the situation where I've had to tell the same story what— ten times?" Callimay laughed as Destan pulled out of the parking lot. "So where are we going to meet your overseer… what was his name again?"

"Utree. Asdum and Pricilla Utree. We'll stay for a couple hours before I need to leave."

"Oh yes. I rem— need to leave? You? 'Just' you?"

Destan groaned, "And I forgot to tell you this. It's nothing bad, Calli. I just don't want to exhaust you. I know this morning had its breaking point so I'll go by my—"

"Well I need to know what's going on first. I might be able to go. I'm feeling much better now."

"I guess so. Redje and I work at the boys' institute here in Rayleen… it's an orphanage. Every Sunday afternoon one of us — though it's been on him since I've been gone — will bring the group that wants to come to accord and evening session."

"I knew you didn't sit around all day. What 'is' your job?"

"Technically I'm a volunteer. The money the institute has is better spent elsewhere." Destan clarified as he bobbed his head back and forth between her and the road. "I mainly help council the teenage boys; trying to help them get ready for adult life whether or not a family comes along. I got the trouble cases so often that it's kinda my 'job' now. — It teaches me just as much as it teaches them. — I used to have a different boy over for a couple days each week during the spring and give him different duties and such to help him learn how to take care of himself and be responsible. Then when summer would come, I'd have a 'boy' who is just about to turn eighteen stay the entire summer, find a job, and work out what he wanted in life. But with you around I don't—"

"Oh please don't stop it because of me." She begged; the sweetest smile on her face as she grabbed his wrist. "It sounds like such a wonderful thing you're doing. I'll be fine."

"Now let me finish. When I say they are 'trouble cases' it is a variety of different issues they're dealing with. Mainly it's how they deal with authority, but there are those— I'll just have to see. Okay? … And as far as this summer goes, I don't know if there will be a graduating boy this year: which would be a blessing on several fronts."

❧

Their time spent with the Utrees was relaxing, enjoyable, and most importantly: encouraging. Part of Callimay didn't want to go, but the other part of her wanted to meet the boys Destan worked with. Mr. Utree reminded her they would have many other times to talk, so that helped her not feel guilty.

By their discussion on the way home, Destan's appreciation for the security and support which came with being around other like-minded people became even more convicting. — The Society provided nothing like this. — And it wasn't hard to tell Callimay was thinking the exact same thing, "I love our talks like this, Destan. I don't know if I ever said anything before; but I do. It makes me excited to know I have someone to talk to about these things whenever I want. And to have a man my age— I… I've never had that before and didn't think I ever would. … It's very special to me. 'You' are very special to me."

"I do too, and you'll forever and always be the most precious person in the world to me. — Are you sure you're going to feel like going to the institute? I don't want to push things. I'm sure Redje would be willing to let you tag along with t—"

"You're the one doing all the driving. I'm just along for the ride. If I need to rest I can on the way there."

❧

After talking with Redje and the on-duty staff at the institute, Destan came up to their room and found Callimay out on the porch. He looked concerned; fiddling with the identification card he had in his hand as his eyes darted back and forth.

As if she could feel this uncertainty in the breeze that was fingering its way through her hair, Callimay said in a melancholy tone, "I… I was just a bundle of messed up emotions this morning. I'm sorry I acted the way I did. I didn't mean to—"

"There's no need for you to be sorry. I just wanted to make sure you were alright. I hadn't seen you like that since our last Sunday at the

273

Society. … Are you alright?" He rushed to her, catching her off guard as he wrapped her in his arms.

"Yes. Yes I am, Destan. I promise."

"You're sure you want to go?"

"Why wouldn't I?" She leaned her face into his hand. "Oh. Do I need to change?"

"Not unless you 'want' to. You're perfect the way you are. Perfect and complete, lacking in nothing as James said."

She frowned, "That's 'not' what that verse means."

He grinned as he tugged on her arm, "I know. Come on."

❦

Where they ended up wasn't where Callimay was expecting. The boys' institute was almost downtown where they'd been for the ball. She felt bad that the boys were so "confined", but Destan assured her they had plenty of room. And they did. The grounds occupied a few blocks; one being nothing but a green area for them to "run free" and play.

The rain stopped and a beautiful rainbow painted the sky as they pulled into the parking lot. After getting her door, Destan swiped his identification card and let Callimay in ahead of him.

They walked up to the front desk, greeted by a man she guessed to be in his late thirties… though his hair made her wonder if maybe she was wrong.

*He's from Zervonith, Calli.* Destan tried so hard to keep a straight face. *And he's actually in his mid-forties, believe it or not.*

*Oh! That would expl— are you 'sure' about his age?*

"Well, well, well. It's about time you showed up. … I'm just kidding. It's good to see you." The man stood and smiled; shaking his hand.

"Trouble, Izon?" Destan replied, seeing a couple teenage boys sitting to the side of the office — black eyes, busted lips, and torn clothes.

"Just the usual." He sighed as he shook his head; and then took a double-take when he saw Callimay, "Umm… who's this?"

"This is my wife. Callimay. — Calli, this is Izon Groombold, one of the head—"

His jaw about hit the floor. He didn't shake Callimay's hand, even though he offered it to her. Parts of words kept coming from his gaping mouth, but nothing that made sense. Destan tried his best, but he couldn't hold his laughter in, "I had to see your face when you found out. I couldn't tell you on the phone."

Not but a second later, his loud and boisterous laugh reverberating through the building, a few doors opened down the hall and several young boys started running toward them.

"Mr. Nevrille!" "Uncle Destan!" "Destan!" they all heard the small crowd shout as they gathered around, asking him a million questions at the same time.

"Hold on there," he reached out and brought Callimay back to him. "I know you're all excited to see me, but don't push my wife away."

"What!" They all gasped in unison.

"You heard me. I'm married now."

"So— you won't come see us now?" One of the younger boys began to bawl. "You came to say goodbye?"

"Oh no!" Callimay dropped to her knees and hugged the boy. "Not at all! I'm going to help too!"

They stared at her, not one of them saying a word. The little boy she hugged was as stiff as a board. She wasn't sure what to make of all the attention, but Destan smiled: *They're not around women very much, Calli. … Let alone the most beautiful one in the world.*

*Why not?*

*I… I'll explain later. Deal?*

*Okay,* she nodded as he helped her stand; the phone ringing.

"Rayleen-South Institute for Boys. This is Izon; how can I be of assistance? … I see. … And where did you say you were? … Okay. Do you know how to get here? … Alright. … No, everything will be ready. I appreciate you reaching out to us. We will see you in a bit. … You're very welcome. Goodbye. — Destan? We've got a tyke coming. Do you have time to help out? I know you're not technically on the clock—"

"Sure. But do I need to clock in so it's 'official'?" He replied as he took Callimay and opened the door to the office.

"Probably would be best if you did. You know those custody lawyers and judges. Makes you sick sometimes when t— oh never mind. As far as the paperwork goes, Yana and Phylip have been running things for the past couple weeks. I just got back from vacation yesterday." Izon warned as he walked over to a shelf and took down a binder. "I've already had a time of it; hunting some things down."

"Duly noted. — Hey Orville?"

One of the roughed up teenage boys jumped to his feet, "Yes sir?"

"Could you wait at the front and tell me when a car arrives?"

"Absolutely, sir!"

"Oh! Take Tand with you."

The boy stopped and opened his mouth, looking disgusted with what he heard, "But— seriously? Him? He's useless."

"Is that so…" Destan stopped working and leaned his face against his hand he had propped on the desk. "Well, you can't very well watch both directions by yourself at the same time, can you? Or have you developed some superpower since I've been gone?"

"But 'him'?"

"Just give it a try, okay?"

Orville huffed as he frowned; sneering, "Fine. — Come on."

A few moments later, Destan went back into another part of the office. He dug around for a bit, and then turned to Callimay, "Would you hold t— there's a baby being surrendered. Tyke is code for baby. I'm not sure why they use it since everyone knows what it means."

"A baby?"

"Calli?" He started in a hushed tone as he pushed her bangs behind her ear. "Babies aren't surrendered very often, thankfully; but they require quite a bit of work that is done in rapid succession since we don't have the facilities necessary for extended care. With that said, these little ones never stay more than five hours. Why? There's a waitlist for adoption of infants. Izon's contacting the next couple on the list right now. While it's great to see there are people willing to fill the void, at the same time it's sad to see those who have been here three or four years — sometimes more — passed by just because of their age."

They came back out, her looking at the boys and then Destan: *You do this because you didn't have anyone, don't you?*

He smiled as he wiped the tears from her cheek: *Yes. There were so many things the staff wanted to do, but since they're a state institution they had to have clearance. Redje and I both had pull in that area, so things are much better than they were even five years ago.*

"I think they're here, sir." Orville called out.

"Would you be willing to be custodian until the couple arrives? Callimay, right?" Izon asked as he turned around.

"Cust—"

"Would you be willing to hold them until their new parents arrive is what he said. — She doesn't understand your ill-conceived, coded language, Izon." Destan rolled his eyes.

"Oh. Of course I can."

There were a couple medical staff along with a security patroller who was holding the wailing baby. Destan escorted them inside and had to confirm everything before he or Callimay could touch the child.

It was hard to hear how the child ended up like this. His fiery-red cheeks were drenched with tears that only existed because he wasn't happy… not because of what happened. And his little arms and chubby fingers were thrashing, reaching for the mother and father who he knew loved him… and were taken from him in such a tragic way.

Before long, all the paperwork was signed and the security patroller handed the baby to her. She was scared to death, but the second she had him in her arms he quieted down; looking at her with his big, green eyes.

Destan even noticed the lack of noise; but more known to him was how Callimay changed. She spoke in a soft and tender tone, her voice sounding rather high as she rocked him, "Hi there. Oh! Such a big yawn. My goodness. You've had a long and hard couple days, haven't you? I know. Shh."

The response by this baby was priceless and tugged at Callimay's heart. He began to giggle and reach out with his slobber-coated hand, grabbing her earring, "Oops! Let's not play with that. — It's a good thing I wear clip-ons, isn't it? That would've hurt if they weren't."

Having his "toy" taken away made him fussy, but then he saw her hair moving and put it in his mouth instead. She chuckled to herself and let him keep it for the time being since she felt it was safe.

Destan had gone to see the staff and patroller off, making sure to thank them for their efforts during this ordeal. When he came back, he found her sitting exactly where he left her. The baby was content and happy as he cooed; nestled close to her. She had a look about her

Destan had never seen, "The couple will be here in about an hour. There's a nursery with a rocker if you want."

She replied in the same tone as earlier, "Okay."

After a few seconds and her not moving, he kneeled beside her and put his hand on hers, "Calli? Do you want to stay here?"

"Huh?" She asked dazed as she looked over to him.

"Do you want to stay here or would you like to go to the nursery?"

"Oh. Okay. Sure. That's fine."

"Are you alright?"

"Of course I am. Why would you ask?"

"I— let's go."

He had to keep his arm around her and guide her because it was quite apparent she was somewhere else, mentally. If he didn't know better, he would have guessed the baby hypnotized her. He'd been a custodians several times before and never had this happen.

A group of the boys followed and asked if it would be alright if they stayed. He nodded and turned his focus as he kneeled, "Calli, look at me. … I'll be back in a bit."

It was apparent she wasn't paying much attention as she nodded, but he left anyway.

Destan came back and found a small group of teenagers around the nursery door. Not but a moment later he heard Callimay's sweet voice. The boys stepped back so he could get in, but begged him in whispers to let them stay.

When he saw her, he felt something he never had before. She was slowly rocking the chair as she sang a Faberton lullaby he remembered his mother singing to him after he would have a nightmare. Her eyes were fixed on the baby, them so soft and loving as was her gentle hold on him. He held her finger in his tight grasp, his eyes glued on her shining and loving face.

*Night has come to bid sweet dreams*
*Watch now my love the moon it beams*
*Sleep my baby, sleep.*

*There is nothing left to fear my love*

She'd collected all but a handful of the older boys; them sitting on the floor around her while the stragglers were in the "standing room only" section by the door. Some of the younger ones had fallen asleep while others began looking groggy as they leaned their chins on their knees or against the wall if they were close enough.

Now that she was quiet, Destan's presence caught their attention. He motioned for them to leave, even though the looks on their faces suggested what he'd heard from the others, "let us stay." But they respected his authority and started filing out.

The ones close to those who were asleep shoved them as a "sibling courtesy". Of course, not all of them felt that was necessary, but they held their comments until they were out of Destan's hearing... unaware he was still able to hear them.

He kneeled next to Callimay, now understanding what was going on: he'd had no reason to want a family before, so he didn't understand — truly — what it meant to hold a child. To be blunt, he didn't even have the thought in his mind of being married, so it made sense that thought wouldn't register either.

But now? Now he did. And he knew deep down she had all along.

# ~ 22 ~

Monday morning dawned warm and beautiful. After a quick and delicious breakfast, Callimay and Destan headed south for their high-flying adventure. With all her constant questions and laughter, Destan began to worry she was nervous. Was this going to be fun?

As they pulled into the parking spot, Rocher stood there in awe and amazement; causing Destan to laugh, "You may be out of a job. Sorry."

"I dare say that would be a blessed gift, Sir." He toyed with him as he came over. "It is a treat to see your radiant face again, Milady."

"It's good to see you, Rocher." She smiled as she popped up out of the driver's seat and gave him a hug. "How have you been?"

"Enjoying a bit of downtime. — Your necessary paperwork is laid out and awaiting your completion in the office, Sir."

"Thanks, Rocher. — I'll be back in a bit, Calli."

After brushing up on how to fill out his flight plan and complete the ground check, he waved to Rocher and Callimay. At first he didn't see it, but when they got closer, he could tell she was lagging behind.

He was right. Rocher noticed as well and encouraged, "She will be in your presence for the duration of the flight. It may be differing circumstances, but I have confidence in her reliance and comfort in seeing you being ample enough to compel her to stay. And if it would become of necessity, I would be present to assume your duties."

Destan sighed as he let the paperwork fall back onto the clipboard. As nice as it was for him to say that, he could hear what Callimay was saying to herself. Was it enough to help her through; her seeing him? He closed his eyes and took a deep breath, finishing in a shaky tone, "Rocher? Remind me I need to get with Wilmont."

"I will," he nodded as he helped Callimay up the stairs; turning back to encourage, "You 'are' a good pilot. Have faith in your abilities."

He looked to the sky and mouthed something before climbing the stairs into the jet, "Ready Calli?"

"As much as I can be." She answered as she rubbed her arm, trying to sound positive. "Can I sit anywhere back here?"

"Well… I thought you'd like to be with me." He sounded confused as he motioned to the cockpit. "At least I'd like you t—"

"I can?"

"Of course." Destan comforted as she ran to him.

"Welcome to Raven's glass cockpit, Milady."

"Oh. My. … W… where do I sit?"

"Either back seat. Your choice." Destan hugged her from behind and then scooted by.

His light-hearted comment fell on deaf ears.

"Might I offer the suggestion of sitting opposite Sir? It would afford you the ability of seeing him instead of myself. And I wouldn't hesitate to think you would enjoy such a view better — nor take any offence whatsoever if that be the case."

"Don't worry, Calli. You won't turn anything off or make us crash. Those buttons and such are by Rocher and myself."

She tried to smile as she got comfortable in her seat, "A… alright."

"You will want to wear this if you wish to talk with us or hear what we do, Milady." Rocher handed her a rather bulky headset. "I suppose your choice of hairstyle is not quite compatible, is it?"

"Oh, it's alright." She rushed to take her hair down.

"That's my fault." Destan took the headset so Rocher could get himself ready; kneeling beside her and helping calm her shaking hands and fumbling attempts to loosen her hair. *I'll be sitting right here the entire time. … Are you sure you want to do this?*

Callimay smiled as she let out a nervous sigh, *I'm sure.*

*You still look beautiful.* He smiled as he helped her adjust the headset; leaning in to give her a kiss. *Love you.*

*I… love you too.*

Destan put his forehead against hers for a moment and closed his eyes, then squeezed her hand and took his seat.

Next on his never-ending to-do list was checking everything he had three times already one last time. It seemed so monotonous to him, but he knew it was necessary. He glanced out the windows and then to the clipboard so much; it was enough to make anyone dizzy.

Once everything was done, he began to unfasten the strap for his sling, "I'm just going to use it a little. I promise I'll put it on when we get back. Hold onto it so I'm sure to remember, alright? And don't forget your seatbelt."

"O… kay," she begrudgingly consented; her voice coated with hesitation and her forehead wrinkled with worry.

"It's alright Calli." He assured when he felt her shaking hand touch his. "I barely have to use this hand, but I 'do' need it. Okay?"

She folded it with care and then reached for her seatbelt while Destan put his headset on and looked back, giving her a thumbs up. In fact, Destan grinned so big he closed his eyes! He looked excited and nervous at the same time. It wasn't "him", but this uncharacteristic display of emotion made her smile and return the gesture with more excitement and less fear. He then turned back to the control panel, "Let's see if I can keep Raven from stalling."

"Have faith in yourself. — Oh! Did you record your payload?"

"Payload? … Quit messing with me. This is my first time back."

Rocher whispered after he flipped a switch, "Milady."

"Really?" Destan asked perturbed as he looked down at the papers.

"Any 'unnecessary' weight is strictly defined as—"

"Well she isn't to me." He grumbled as he snatched up the pen. "But, I get why it's 'necessary'. — Umm… what do I put?"

"I wouldn't have the foggiest!" Rocher did his best to suppress his laughter. "Ask her."

"I'm not gonna ask Calli that!"

"I seem to recall certain personal information of which no one would know that you held about Milady at an earlier date."

"T… that was different and I really don't know how it stuck with me. I wasn't 'looking' for it."

"Well if you contain some other form of deducing such knowledge, please divulge to me its secrets. — How else are you going to do so with any amount of accuracy otherwise? And I wouldn't think it would be

something so precarious for you to ask if you explained its intent. She 'is' your beloved."

"I… I'll just put a rough estimate. Even soaking wet she's still not enough to change anything as far as fuel goes." Destan shook his head as he rushed to write down a number. "I can bench four— maybe even five times her weight and barely break a sweat."

Rocher flipped the switch again, letting Callimay hear only the trailing portion of his laughter. It obviously stunned her that the first thing she heard on the headset was such a light-hearted and joyful voice, but at the same time it helped calm her.

After clearing his throat, Destan got on the com and said he was heading out. Callimay answered without thinking and quickly clapped her hand over her mouth when she heard another man answer. He smiled as he looked back, the other man still talking, "Who was that?"

"It's my wife, Kendal. I forgot to tell her."

"Pfft!" He snorted; the muffled sound of a hand slapping a table audible. "Does this mean she can take over ordering you around?"

"Not quite yet, as far as this goes. But who knows! Maybe she will."

As the private jet woke up and began "walking" along the apron, the sudden movement caused her to jump so much that Destan saw her out of his peripheral as clear as day, "I did punch it a little. Sorry Calli."

"You're fine," she assured, though her voice was extremely shaky.

Destan talked with Kendal up until the point they were sitting at the end of the runway.

Callimay's heart couldn't stop pounding. It was almost to the point it hurt; it causing her ears and head to pound. She knew everything was going to be alright, but she started to contemplate every single "what if" scenario which came with a bad ending.

"You are cleared for takeoff. Clear skies and tailwinds, Destan. You too Rocher, Callimay."

That ripped her back to reality faster than anything could. The poor thing was breathing so heavy and fast. Callimay wanted Destan to hold her, she wanted to have that extra reminder it was going to be alright.

"Roger that, Kendal. Ten-four." He nodded to Rocher and put his hand on the throttle lever; turning to her one last time: *Close your eyes if you want; and take a deep, 'slow' breath, Calli. Everything's alright.*

All of a sudden she felt like she was being pushed against the seat as the jet rushed across the runway. She knew the runway wasn't very long, and as fast as they were moving— they had to be close to driving right off it into the grass! Flying was a different world that she didn't know much about, but driving a jet into the grass?

But as any normal takeoff went, the sleek, black jet jumped from the ground and upward into the sky at the same point it always had. Right after this, Callimay could hear Destan: *Don't stall on me Raven, come on girl. Work with me. I want Calli to enjoy this. Please.*

Usually when you jumped you came back down right away; but not with this. Nope. It'd be quite a while before this "jump" would land them back on the ground, "Alright, Calli. We're up!" *You can let go of the armrests. ... Calli?*

It wasn't easy for her, but she let go. Things were going well and felt normal until the plane "slid" to the side. — Back to square one.

"Make sure you compensate for the crosswind."

Destan nodded as he turned the flight stick, looking like he'd received his first red mark. He glanced back and saw Callimay as stiff as a statue; reminding him he needed to keep her as a priority and remind her he was there. This was actually going to be a good exercise for him in that way: *Calli? Calli, open your eyes for me. I'm right here. Come on. You can do it. ... There's my ray of sunshine.*

What a comfort it was for the first thing she saw to be Destan's smile! He gave her his handkerchief and then looked back to the skies, discussing a couple things with Rocher.

Feeling his skin against hers was comfort in and of itself, but him being within arm's reach and keeping her in his thoughts… she began to feel confident enough to look around at the different knobs, levers, gauges, lights, and screens which, to her, "littered" the cockpit. Everything looked different while at the same time it looked the same. This helped her understand why he was feeling overwhelmed: * How does he know what to pay attention to and when?*

*Hours and hours of practice, Calli. ... Are you doing better?*

*Yeah.*

"Love you," he responded loud and clear as she saw him smile and look at her out of the corner of his eye.

"I… I love you too." She curled up on the seat, feeling warm and fuzzy now. *He doesn't say it often without you saying it first, let alone so loud in front of others. ~ No. No, he doesn't. I'm glad he did, though.*

"It's not any easier flying than it is when driving."

No response.

"Woman? I was talking to you." Destan started becoming sarcastic as he turned his head and glanced at her.

"What?"

"You make it hard to focus on the road — or the sky. I wouldn't change a thing though. Well, I'd rather have you in my arms, but…"

"I understand." Callimay smiled, touched yet again by him taking the time to talk to her. "It's okay. I know you're not ignoring me."

She could relax now, knowing it was sticking this time. Something about moving to Rayleen changed Destan. He wasn't afraid to tell her how he felt and wasn't worried who heard it.

Destan always had his left hand around what looked like the clutch from the car; occasionally typing on the keyboard in front of him as he glanced around at the numerous screens. She saw him move his right hand to type and then shake it before resting it on his knee: *Destan.*

*I'm being careful, Calli. I promise I am. It's just stiff because I haven't used it. Therapy's gonna be rough, I think. But maybe not! We'll see. … I guess we don't need the headsets, do we?*

*Not really.*

*Well, why don't we use them so Rocher doesn't feel left out?* "See the rails? It's easy here since there aren't any major roads near them." Destan pointed out the window. "They're known as iron compasses to some airmen even today. It's a really old term dating back to the Homeworld when planes were first introduced. These 'landmarks' were used for navigation purposes. — See the one headed straight in front of us? That was the one we came in on back in December."

Callimay nodded as she peaked around Rocher's chair… and then looked right back at Destan. Saying she was frightened was the understatement of the century. She plastered herself against the seat, a wild look of terror in her eyes.

It took a while for her to calm to the point she would even think of looking out again; but when she did, she was stunned. Between the green that stretched out in front of them as far as the edge of the world or the coastline which was just now becoming visible on their left; everything looked unreal! There were jagged, white strips and streaks that stuck up here and there to the north — mountains — while near-black painter's brush marks indicated where rivers were all around them; "drips" being lakes. Dense forests looked like carpets thrown across a floor to cover all the toys underneath; far off clouds looking like stuffing or what Callimay heard described as spun sugar. The shadows they cast baffled her. How could something so loose and fluffy block the sunlight the way it did? There were these tiny little clumps of gray scattered on the ground, some larger than others — most of them tiny. One spot in particular reflected the sunrays more than others, perking Callimay's curiosity, "What is that, Rocher?"

After looking where she pointed, he smiled and replied, "That would be Rayleen, Milady."

"Rayleen! But it's so small!"

"We're just up that high, Calli." Destan interjected. "If you keep looking out that window, you should be able to see Arable. At least where the Oasis Valley is. And then in front of us where all those mountains are would be Prig… maybe as far as the boarder to Indalla."

The conversation died out; Callimay now focused on watching Destan. He was nervous and flustered when Rocher made a comment. It was then she remembered he was in training. But the reality was: Rocher offered advice only on occasion… most of what he said was praise. So, regardless of what either of them through, Destan was doing great after having such a long break.

This larger-than-life trip continued, the overall feeling of the air becoming more and more relaxed. Callimay loved it when she would catch his gaze every now and again; him flashing a smile at her before looking back.

At one point, about an hour or so later, Destan began to fidget. She could feel him becoming tense and couldn't help but wonder what was wrong. Rocher wasn't concerned, though. What was going on! She wouldn't be held in suspense for long because he announced over the com, "Tower control? This is Sierra Romeo two fife checking in. Over."

"Sierra Romeo, this is tower control. Over," a man responded.

"Requesting permission for six touch-and-go sequences." Destan stated in his professional tone as he scanned the area and messed with a few switches.

After a moment, the man replied, "That's a five by five, Sierra Romeo. You have a green light for all six."

"Wilco." Destan nodded as he looked at Rocher who also nodded.

"Who's your Pilot in Command today, Sierra Romeo?" The man asked, sounding casual.

"You have Destan, Vernon." Rocher answered with the same tone.

"I thought that was his voice. Glad to see you back in the skies, Destan." He voiced his approval; poking fun as he finished, "Well what do you know. Apparently miracles 'are' possible. You're riding the beam for once."

"Well thanks." He laughed as he glanced back at Callimay. *We're gonna start heading down now. Hang tight.*

"A touch-and-go is a maneuver where Sir will land the jet and then immediately take back to the skies. He will repeat this six times prior to our return to Rayleen." Rocher explained as he flipped a few switches. "We will be rising and falling quite a bit during this exercise, Milady."

"Okay." She nodded; and then yelped as she felt the floor drop out from underneath her, "Ah!"

*Calli? Calli, look at me.* Destan sounded concerned, though he tried to stay calm. *This first time is probably going to be pretty rough, but I promise you the others will be better. Everything's fine. I'll do my best to let you know what's going on so you know what I'm doing. Deep breath, Calli. It's alright.*

No response.

He whipped around, looking scared, "Calli?"

"Yes?"

"I— just checking to make sure you're alright."

"I'm okay." She closed her eyes and tried to keep calm: *I wonder— where are we? I'd ask, but I don't want to bother Destan 'or' Rocher right now. ... I really just w—*

*We're right on the Kerogen, Prig boarder, Calli.*

*I'm sorry!*

*For what?*

*I'm bothering you. You're trying to focus.* She curled up on her seat, facing away from him. *I'll be quiet. I'm sorry.*

*Calli. You're not bothering me. I'm not 'so' bad at this that I can't talk to you and focus on this at the same time. This isn't—I… I'm sorry if I sound like I'm upset. I'm not. … I just want you to know this hasn't changed anything: I'm still here. Alright? If I don't respond right away, I'm just finishing something. But I 'will' answer you. I always will, Calli. I promise.*

She closed her eyes and clung to his sling. He wanted to hear her voice, but Destan could tell she was feeling better… somehow: *Well this feels odd. ~ Her ability? ~ I can't think of anything else.*

Unexpected, Rocher scolded as he typed on the keyboard, "I should have taken it upon myself to request your presence to land us in Faberton. It would have been a prime proving ground for your skills."

Knowing what gauge he was checking, Destan could tell why that came up, "I'm still learning. No crosswind is good. — And how could I? I had my hands full, quite literally."

"You've been quite capable of accomplishing a number of various 'strenuous' tasks with Milady in your arms." Rocher pointed out point blank, his mustache even looking perturbed as he stared at him. "That refute you put forth will not withstand even the minuscule weight of tissue paper, Sir."

"Okay. You got me. — Alright Calli. Here we go! And… we… are… down!" He announced as the tires gripped the runway; the engine revving as he finished, "And now it's back up."

Once airborne, Callimay gasped from the feeling of having the ground taken out from under her.

"You remembered to flare this time. Very good. Very good." Rocher praised as he continued to record things on the computer.

"I'm gonna make four quarter turns to the left and then do the same thing again, Calli. Since we're closer to the ground, you won't feel like you're falling or getting pushed back as long until we head home."

Rocher quickly cautioned, "Now don't skid as you come around."

"Or slide," Destan said nervous as he backed off of his turn.

"Good job."

"These touch-and-goes will go pretty q— Calli?"

"Alright." She answered without looking up. "Just— I'm alright."

Within the next half hour they were on their way back to Rayleen. Destan hadn't heard a word from her since the first touch-and-go, so he motioned for Rocher to take over so he could check on her, "Calli?"

She jumped when she felt his hand touch her shoulder, her jerking away as she whipped her head around.

"Easy. It's alright." He put his hands out to calm her; and then rubbed her arms, "I thought you fell asleep on me, so I came back to check on you."

"Destan." She let out a shiver of a sigh and threw her arms around his neck. "Are we back?"

"Not yet. It won't be much longer though." He promised, seeing how worn she looked. "I'm sorry it's not what you thought it would be. I… I didn't think it'd be this bad."

"Don't worry. I'm okay. I just… I just need to get used to it is all."

Before long, Callimay heard a similar conversation take place between Destan and Kendal. It wasn't as bad this time since she knew what was going on; but the feeling of falling without any end in sight wasn't something she was comfortable with.

After a few seconds of a deep rumbling noise, the jet came to a halt, "Very well done, Sir. Smoothest landing you have accomplished to date. You'll be soloing in a very short time, I have no doubt."

He sighed as he shook his head, "Maybe in optimal conditions. And this airstrip is nicer than the one up by Prig. … There's no way I'd make it through a high-level howler like you did in Faberton."

"If the need arose, I know for a fact you would be up for the task; regardless of the circumstances. Do not put your knowledge or skill base in such low regard." Rocher encouraged as he got up to open the door. "Confidence goes quite far in such endeavors as this."

As if relieved to be free, he took his headset off and messed with his hair for a second, then took a deep breath and started his final checks while going through the paperwork.

Feeling like something bit him, Destan grimaced and shook his right hand before moving it to different positions until he found what would alleviate the pain. His hand being tucked against him reminded him that he needed his sling. Rolling his eyes and shaking his head, he turned around to ask for it; but stopped when he saw something much more concerning.

"Calli?" *I should have…* he grumbled as he threw the clipboard down and unfastened his seatbelt so he could get to her. "We're on the ground, Calli. We made it."

She was like a figurine doll that always had its eyes open. He took her headset off; her not responding to his questions or touch. Her eyes did eventually widen as she came to; her asking rather dazed, "What?"

A wearied and shaky breath came out of Destan, "There you are."

"We're back?"

"Yep. I still have some paperwork to finish, but we're on old 'terra firma'." He nodded as he unfastened her seatbelt, smiling as he kept talking, "We can go sit in the back where it's more comfortable while I finish it. Sound good?"

Callimay grabbed the seat in front of her as she stood. She was pale and looked disoriented as she turned to follow him; Destan catching her before she hit the ground, "Ca— Rocher! Come here. Now!"

"Yes, Sir? — Oh my!"

"Get her some water." He grimaced as he picked her up.

"Right away."

Rocher came back and found Destan kneeling beside Callimay who was passed out in his chair. They exchanged only a few words before he excused himself.

Destan looked at Callimay and felt this pang in his heart: *You're rushing everything, Boon. Calli thinks so much of others — you — that she forgets about herself. This wasn't enjoyable at all for her. ~ I get it, Okay? ~ You're supposed to watch over her, value her; yet you're still neglecting to think about her. ~ Stop it!*

He looked at his hands and saw they were clinched and shaking; then whipped his head up to see if Callimay was in pain. … What a relief! That would've added insult to injury like none other.

After a little while, Callimay said in a sweet, calm tone, "Someone I love with all of my heart once told me while they were teaching me something that was very hard: 'you're being too hard on yourself'. They reminded me it was my first time and issues were bound to come. But they encouraged me that in the end, everything would work out as long as I didn't give up. That I needed to push ahead when things got hard. … Sound familiar?"

Destan buried his face in her hair and held her close; recalling what he told her just a week earlier.

"Remember how you told me we both needed to have patience with each other?" She asked as she sat up and fixed his hair.

Once he thought about it for a moment, he nodded.

"Well… this is a big test for us. I need to be patient with you while you learn to be patient with yourself. — This is our first time, Destan. Neither of us has ever been married before. My goodness, neither of us have been in any type of serious relationship before! We didn't have our parents to turn to if we had questions, and I think we sometimes are too scared to ask each other because we don't want to bother the other, or we're not sure what to ask. — At least I know I find myself doing that from time to time. — We've had help while growing up to prepare us, but in the end we didn't have the luxury Rose and so many others do… what you're trying to give the young boys at the institute."

"But I should have a better handle on things by now."

Callimay reassured as she leaned her cheek against his, "You do. Each day you do. … I told Mrs. Manning we've had rough times — growing pains — but we're working through them. She reminded me how those hard times make love stronger and deeper. It's true Destan. It really is. Don't blame yourself for what 'I' should've better prepared myself for. You didn't make me do anything. 'I' chose to come. 'I' chose to be with you in the cockpit. I 'chose', Destan. I did this of my own free-will. Whatever I do, I do of my own free-will. No one can ever 'make' me do anything I don't, deep down, want to do. I don't care who it is or what they threaten me with."

He pulled her close and rocked her for a while; part of him trying to forget the emotional pain he was in. As he started to get up, Callimay tapped her fingers together, "Destan?"

"What?"

"The ball is in about three weeks, right?"

"Umm… oh! Three weeks from today, actually. What is it?"

"It never occurred to me to pack my evening gown. Maybe we could take a nice relaxing drive b—"

"You won't be able to wear that gown to this ball."

"Why not? It's a ball gown… of sorts. Granted it's not the traditional ball gown skirt type, but so many aren't anymore."

"It's because this is a ball based off of the Homeworld Vienna White Tie Ball. It's extremely particular about what can and can't be worn." Destan explained as he fiddled with her hair. "There was a lady who was very supportive of these balls, Mrs. Vienna Jackman, passed a few years ago. I'd wanted to do something to honor her memory and finally found this."

*Such a softy.* "Was she by chance another one of your 'girlfriends'?"

Destan shook his head as he let a deep, loud laugh out, "No. She was a very pomp and regal lady. Emphasis on very. Social callings and visits were something she called 'shenanigans'. — Laugh all you want to at how I butcher that word, I don't care. Rose can't say it either and you'd probably say she was cute for saying it that way. — She was still very kind, but she held everyone to the highest of standards. That's the reason I chose this type of ball. It embodies who she was. So! To answer your question: we don't need to go back for your gown. Instead, we need to go to the tailor to get your dress made."

"Made!" Callimay jumped up, hoping she heard what she thought she did. "Like 'made just for me' made?"

"That's how your other dress was made."

"How did you k—"

"Your application." Destan shrugged his shoulders.

"Out of everything on there you remembered 'that'?"

"It wasn't hard to. — And it wasn't the only thing I remembered nor was it what I intentionally looked for!" He rolled his eyes. "Geez, Calli!"

"It's no fun that you can read my mind. — Where's your sling?" She stifled her laughter as she complained, seeing him holding his arm close to his side.

"Umm…" he went back to the cockpit to look. "That's strange."

"Wait. I have it. … You promised me you'd put it back on."

"And I told you to keep track of it to remind me, woman." Destan made a face as he tapped her nose. "Good job."

"'Thank you'. Goodness. — So! What type of dress do I have to wear? How specific are these details? Does this mean I have to wear a certain color or style? And why do you have to go? What would you need? You have a tuxedo."

"So. Many. Questions!" He chuckled as he leaned against the table at the front of the seating section so she could reach to help him put the sling on. "The only requirement I've been able to find concerning your dress is it must be a white ball gown that's easy for you to dance in with a pair of matching opera-length gloves. As far as the finer details, I'm pretty sure you get to decide all of them. Then when it comes to me: I don't own a tailcoat. And then there are a few other 'mandatory' pieces I don't have; one being a bow tie."

"White?" She stopped, gazing into his eyes with excitement and wonder. "You mean—"

"I thought the exact same thing when I was talking with Mrs. Manning last week." He put his hand under her chin. "You'll get the wedding dress you've always deserved and I've wanted you to have. And you'll have a reception — of sorts — to wear it at."

"Whatever I want?"

"Whatever you want, Calli." *Whatever you want.*

**~ 23 ~**

The next three weeks felt more like a few days; each being packed to the ceiling. Callimay's excitement, though, kept her going and allowed her to overlook so much of the stress and lack of sleep. She was getting to do all of these amazing things "with" Destan. Who could ask for more!

She kept what her dress looked like a secret from him, hiding it under their bed and holding Destan to his word not to peek… she wanted it so be a special surprise for him that day.

On the other hand, he tried his coattail tuxedo on the minute he got it home. It was a process, making sure all the tiny details were met… this was a good idea: having a "dress rehearsal". Destan took a step back for her to see it and then turned to see himself in the mirror. It took her everything she had to not bust out laughing; him contorting his face as he complained about first one thing and then another. He'd done this already at the tailor's, but this was the first time she heard it. The bow tie was something he was in no way thrilled with, and then the long coattails and top hat were awkward in every way possible.

Callimay did go with him a few times when he flew, but she would be exhausted when they got back; so, she preferred to stay at the office or in the private hanger. On those rare occasions she went, he was thrilled beyond anything when he would come around the nose of the jet and see her standing by the stairs, waiting for him to get his ground check done. Part of him wished it happened more, but he knew it was hard for her… no matter how much she was "progressing".

Things worked out so Destan did have a couple boys stay, but he didn't feel comfortable having a teenager roaming around the house with Callimay there. She truly believed it was helpful for them to have the added lesson of learning how to treat women in a controlled environment. It made sense, but he wasn't fully convinced since some of them were the type of trouble cases he didn't want anywhere near her, even with him around. For that reason, he was strict about whom he would accept and still was overly cautious: locking their bedroom door every night and not leaving her alone.

And then nestled in between everything else were the days when they sat around and did nothing. There weren't many of these, but Destan made a point to do what he intended during this trip: give Callimay and himself time to heal, rest, and bond.

Sometimes these days came as a necessity when she would have a migraine. They had nothing to do with Destan — which made him feel better — but he still felt bad, finding her in the dark bedroom with soft rain noises playing; crippled by a pain he knew he'd never understand. She felt horrible for being useless for an entire day — sometimes a couple in a row — but Destan reminded her: he was glad to "spoil" her when she felt bad.

Rose came by every morning, but smiled and said she understood when she wasn't allowed in. That didn't keep her from asking why, but she truly was a sweetheart about it all.

Callimay loved to watch Destan with her. It made her heart skip a beat… reminding her of the little baby boy she'd been blessed to hold for a short time. But how could they think of having a family? There were still things they didn't know about their abilities. What if they would cause problems for the child? Did this make it so they couldn't? They could adopt right then with no problem, but there was another issue: Origin and Nightmare. They were safe enough for the two of them, but they both made the painful decision there wasn't any chance in the foreseeable future for them to think about a family… not until this danger was taken care of — for good.

Destan knew this decision grieved Callimay. He could see the well-hidden pain in her eyes and hear the subtle agony in her voice at times. It pained him too. He loved Rose and enjoyed his time with her, but it never clicked until Mrs. Manning mentioned children. That desire now bloomed in his heart: he wanted a family. But how? Their reality couldn't allow such a precious, innocent, and dependent human to be thrown into the mix. It wouldn't be fair or safe.

To help push that sorrow and hurt out, Destan dedicated himself to his physical therapy; that physical pain he endured drowning out the mental and emotional pain he still didn't know how to handle.

Callimay wanted to help, but he would politely thank her and say he would let her know if he needed any. It saddened her since she now knew partially why he was doing it, but she didn't want to make matters worse by bringing it up.

As much as Destan's change was sticking, there were some areas where he needed to keep working.

🕉

"I… I can't believe it," he heard Callimay cry; making him lean even more against the door. "I never thought—"

"I am so happy for you, my child." Mrs. Manning replied in her soft voice as muffled rustling noises were heard. "I told you to stop leaning on the door, young man! She will be out when she is ready."

Upset he was found out — yet again — but unable to do a thing to change his circumstances, Destan began pacing the floor.

Late that morning, Callimay locked herself in the bedroom and refused to come out or let him in; asking him to get Mrs. Manning not long after. She came right away about an hour ago and hadn't come out since. He would hear phrases and sentences similar to those he just heard every now and again; making it that much harder to wait.

Mrs. Manning soon came out and shut the door with a delicate touch, winking as she whispered, "I'll leave you two alone. … You look quite dashing, young man."

"Thank you for coming over."

"Enjoy yourselves."

"We will."

After Destan saw her to the door, he heard the bedroom door close. He whipped around and looked up, seeing Callimay standing at the head of the stairs. She looked as radiant and beautiful as ever.

The second she began to walk, the fabric of her dress made a soft and hushed brushing sound as it moved according to her command.

She fingered the banister with her gloved hand as she floated down the steps; the air around her overflowing with the fragrance of roses.

"You. Look. So beautiful, Callimay." Destan said breathless as he stopped her a few steps from the bottom so she was eye-level with him.

Her dress glistened in the sunlight, feeling like the softest of velvets. The lush satin caressed her shoulders in such a way to cover the scar from Toreon's Sai; hugging her figure down to her fingertips where it let loose and flowed in billowing folds to the floor.

"Why did you choose this one, Calli?" He took her simple, yet familiar diamond necklace in his hand.

"I went through what you gave me, and it was just the right amount of added sparkle. I didn't want too much since the dress has so much already. — Why? Did you want me to wear something else?"

"No. I was just wondering. … This piece was my mother's."

"I hope I didn't ruin it!"

"What do you mean?"

"I added my heart locket to the back part so I could keep it with me." Callimay said a bit frantic as she turned so he could see what she altered. "I didn't want to leave it, but I can go—"

"It's fine," he said in the same soft tone as he slipped his arms around her and laid his cheek on hers. "It's perfect. … You're perfect."

Unable to contain his joy, he picked her up and twirled her around. Bright bursts of color and light emanated from the dress when the sunlight would catch it at just the right moment.

Destan set her down and gazed at her in almost the same way he did right after he proposed. A tear ran down his face, but she caught it before it jumped to his shirt. He kissed her and wrapped her in his arms as he did his best to not cry: *It's so good to hold you and it not hurt. …* "I love you, Calli. I'm not just saying that. I truly mean it."

"I know you do." She cradled his head; herself trying not to cry. "I love you too, Destan."

"I wish things would've been different. You deserved better than I gave you at first. I want to go back and—"

"It's alright. Everything is alright. The past is done and gone."

Why such moments as these were spoiled is something to ponder and yet expected. Someone rang the entry chime and knocked.

Destan growled under his breath as he loosened his hold on her, "I swear. If it's you Rocher, I'll—"

"Here, I'll get it. — Well! Hello there!"

"Aw you a pwinces, Cowimay!" Rose gasped when she saw her dress. "Wear you cwown? You must has one if you aw."

Destan smiled, looking and feeling better as he walked up and gave Callimay a kiss, "As far as I'm concerned: she has one."

Rose tilted her head, confused by what he meant, but shook her head and blurted out, "Dis ez fwum Mammy."

"Why thank you for bringing it over." Callimay kneeled to take the box and give her a hug. "Tell Mrs. Manning we said thank you. Can you give her that hug from me?"

"I wiwl," she nodded; and then began fingering the jeweled band where the sparkly skirt flared out, "Aw dey wheel?"

She smiled as she stroked her hair in a longing way, "No. No, they're just pretty, fake ones."

"Oh. Otay."

Now came the awkward moment of silence.

"Umm. Rose?" Destan cleared his throat, nodding in the direction of her home. "Shouldn't you be going?"

"I tan go home. You no dat."

"Well then, off to Mrs. Manning's."

"All white. Buy, Cowimay! Buy, Desan! I see you waiter."

Right as they walked in, another knock came to the door, irritating Destan, "Everyone decides to visit 'right' as we're trying to leave."

"I take it I arrived as scheduled, Sir?" Rocher asked.

"Prompt as always. Let me go grab my cape and gloves… and hat. Ugh! — Calli? Is your stole upstairs?"

"Yes," she called out as she put the flowers Mrs. Manning sent in her hair. "Oh! Don't forget your keys."

*You remembered.* He laughed as he turned to go back up.

*I can remember sometimes.* "It's good to see you, Rocher."

"You look absolutely radiant, Milady. The evening's festivities will have a hostess of the highest caliber in the most elegant of arrays."

ℬ

When they arrived, Destan spoke with Graygoré and a few others while he allowed Callimay to inspect the finer details of the room. She glided from one cocktail table to another on the terrace portion of the room, thrilled with how the table design turned out: black linen cloths, silver brocade runners, and various mercury glass vessels for candles.

Once he was satisfied with his end of things, Destan joined Callimay as a certain song began to play. He took her hand as she perked up and guided her out to the dancefloor. Without missing a stride, he cut her quick objection off by kissing her.

As the other times, he slowed toward the end and only shuffled his feet while holding her close. She automatically leaned into his chest and closed her eyes while he leaned his chin on her head; sighing rather loud as they waited for the last notes to fade.

They jumped back from each other just as they were about to kiss; them hearing applause, "Redje? Tabitha?"

"You two dance beautifully." Tabitha offered a hug to Callimay.

"Now I'm gonna have to take lessons." Redje grumbled as he glared at his best friend. "Thanks, 'pal'."

Destan scratched his head, sounding a bit embarrassed, "Exactly how long have you two been here?"

"Long enough to give Tabby brilliant ideas."

She wagged her finger. "Now you hush. I never said a word."

"But you know you never do." Redje put his arm around her and pecked her cheek. "You know that, Tabby. I'm your fool, remember?"

"So that's why Rose said she couldn't go home. Oh! — Are they seated anywhere near us?" Callimay faded out, feeling how irritated Destan was. "It doesn't matter. I— I just am trying to figure out why you came. I don't remember seeing your—"

"Come here right— I mean… would you come with me?" Destan began to leave, but turned and asked in a gruff tone.

"Of course. — We'll be back in a bit."

"No rush." Redje nodded as he waved her on.

℥

Destan marched to the lounge, Callimay trying her best to keep up. She was so confused why he switched so suddenly, but then it dawned on her: guests weren't supposed to arrive for another three hours. He wasn't ready for "company". While this ball wasn't directly associated with his father, Callimay doubted he took the time to keep that distinction in his mind. She kept silent and followed him, paying close attention to his emotions.

He let go of her hand when they got in and stormed over to the window to stare at and bicker with the world; him tapping his fist at his side in a repetitive manner.

Once he had calmed, Destan came over and sat beside her, removing her glove so he could spin her rings around and around — his knee-jerk habit he developed when she was with him and he was deep in thought or concerned.

Callimay heard footsteps every now and again, but she saw a shadow at the bottom of the door this time. Redje cracked it open and poked his head in, getting ready to speak when she looked over wide-eyed and shook her head.

As the door closed, Destan sighed as he mumbled, "It's going to be a long night. Best you get some rest. They'll bring dinner up after a bit. I called them before we left about what you wanted."

"You need some, too."

"I'll be fine. I— I'm sorry. You're right, Calli. … Do you remember the first time I called you 'Calli'?"

*Where did this come from? You're usually the one who diverts like this when you're nervous or worried.* "Well… I know you were trying so hard 'not' to admit you said it. At least that's what it sounded like."

"Well that actually wasn't the first time. … But I don't know if you— I should've kept my mouth shut."

"It was when you caught me after I fell off of Lookout Point, right?" She nodded; explaining when he gasped, "I remember you saying it, though it didn't register until the next morning when you repeated it."

"I guess you don't remember anything about it, do you? It was when they took you to be processed. I… I couldn't hear your voice and so it just kinda slipped out that way." Destan admitted as he looked away. "I know that was really random. I… I'm sorry I said anyt—"

*I'm rubbing off on you.* "It's alright. I love that you use it. I know it's your term of endearment for me. Not that my given name isn't, but I know it's special to you. No one has ever called me that, even though it's the natural abbreviated form of my name. Abbreviating names is still frowned upon by those I know; so much of the Reeg culture clings to everyone. Not that it's bad, but—" she started to blush; and then asked after a bit, "Now it's my turn to be random: I know you said before we left, but… do you like my dress? Are you okay with it?"

"I like it," he smiled, not sounding too enthusiastic.

"Oh," she sighed as she slouched.

He clarified as he moved one of the ringlets of hair away from her face so he could see her eyes, "The woman wearing it is beautiful. And she makes whatever she's wearing beautiful. But I gotta say, this is a whole new level because of its special meaning."

ɓ

Redje came back before long and Destan arranged for them to have dinner as well. They took it separately; Redje and Tabitha wanting some much-desired alone time… that and Tabitha knew about the special meaning of Callimay's dress.

Not but a moment after they finished, Sonnie called. Guests were arriving. Callimay was expecting him to answer like he had last time, but he jumped up and was ready to go right then. They told Tabitha and Redje; them having a similar reaction as Destan.

As they started for the ballroom, the men lagged behind. It didn't seem obvious at first, but it became apparent they were finding a perfect opportunity to freely banter and poke fun at each other without being "scolded". That was all joy and competition until the water receded as the door opened. There stood Tabitha; eyes narrowed, hands planted on her hips, and this aura of frustration oozing from her.

"They really thought I was mad and going to say something! Oh when will they ever learn?" She busted out laughing as she watched the two of them scamper off. "I know I've said it at least a dozen times, but you do look stunning, Callimay."

"You do as well." She made over the chiffon-veiled evening gown that flowed in a way to make Tabitha look like a floating fairy.

"I was concerned it was going to be too small. I couldn't get a new one and this one was at its max already." She whispered as she put her hand over her now-noticeable baby bump. "I was silly to get this the second I found out about tonight, but when I— we originally planned to wait since Redje promised to help Destan. I just know God was laughing so hard when I broke the news to Redje."

Callimay glanced back at Destan and Redje who talked in hushed tones, "So you're helping greet? You didn't show up early to get some alone time?"

"Yes and no. — I'm surprised Destan didn't say anything. But… with everything else, it probably became a 'need-to-know' thing that he didn't think was needed. He can forget details just as good as any other man; it has nothing to do with being married."

"There was more to do than he anticipated when we finally found a good, solid resource. Our little 'treasure-trove' of information was hidden on the top shelf of my mother's book collection. I never recalled seeing it before, but there it was. One half of it was dedicated for the Vienna White Tie alone!"

"My part didn't seem so outrageous when I found out about what Redje had to do. I had to stop reading when I got halfway through the list; I was laughing so hard. — Good evening! It's so good to see you."

Guests arrived in rapid succession, it only taking fifteen minutes for the entire list to be checked off. Remembering each name she was inundated with was nothing short of overwhelming for Callimay; while it appeared Redje, Tabitha, and Destan knew everyone's full names.

It was rare for Callimay to offer her right hand and it be accepted. Everyone was conducting themselves as if there were no International Law at all! The horror! Aside from that, when the guests discovered Callimay was Destan's wife, they reacted with absolute shock, utter confusion, or complete amazement… and not in a good way. Not one question was asked of her, and sometimes she wouldn't even be acknowledged. If it would have been a couple of people doing that she could have excused it; but everyone? How was that any way to treat someone you didn't know… let alone the hostess for the evening?

All these abnormalities kept adding up and making her scared. She couldn't shake this feeling that something was wrong… that they were hiding something.

"What's wrong, Calli? You look worried."

She nodded to where their table was; not wanting to say anything aloud and needing some space from those they were around at the time. He followed; that awkward feeling of knowing what emotions she was feeling flaring up inside him.

When they got there she confronted him: *What is going on? Who are these people? I can't swear to it, but I get the impression every single person here is left-handed. Wh— we're out in the open! Why were you so worried about me while we were at the Society but not since we've gotten to Rayleen?*

Destan groaned as he rested his gloved hands on her shoulders and began to rub them, "I forgot to tell you. I'm sorry."

*Forgot what!* Callimay asked wide-eyed as she jerked away.

"Mrs. Jackman was a lefty just like us." He answered without fear as he panned his hand to the room. "Well, almost all of us. Her help with the balls was an 'extra' even though she enjoyed it. Her focus was providing a normal life for those oppressed by the 'devil law' as she called it. — Calli? Every person here is from somewhere in the world where there's a Safe Haven. We're not the only ones. All but a handful of these people are guards… like Redje, Tabitha, and myself are here in Rayleen. We're safe. We're around our own who love us."

His explanation didn't do much good, her eyes still stricken with fear as she grabbed his wrist: *But the servers!*

"Everyone you're going to see tonight — even the orchestra — are sympathizers, spouses, or relatives of lefties… or a lefty themselves." He calmed as he sat down and they looked around.

"But…"

"This is the safest place in the world." He reached over and turned her face toward him. "Please don't worry. Leave that to me. — Yes, I'm a bit nervous, but I trust every person in this room. You know I don't trust many people; but know that I 'do' trust them. — I want to enjoy tonight. You. Us. … This is our special night. Don't let this little detail I overlooked ruin it. Please? I'm sorry I forgot to tell you."

"How can you say they love us? They are quite clear about not being happy we're married. I know I'm not supposed to let others influence me emotionally, but it hurts that they don't approve of me. Right now I wouldn't trust them with anything. They're so cruel and c—"

"Have you been listening to them?" Destan asked worried.

Now sniffling, Callimay pulled her hand away, "I don't 'need' to and would rather not. It's written in their looks and voiced in their tones. Why make myself even more miserable by listening to what they're 'really' saying?"

He moved his chair closer and put his arm around her waist, "How do I put this? … Some — well, most — are work addicts. They don't put much value in what a marriage—"

"But they're married." She said agitated, gritting her teeth.

"Well, not everyone is. And those who are, aren't emotionally connected like we are. They're content with having someone around to talk to or ask for help: no emotional connection like we enjoy."

"That has to be a horrible way to function! How could you e—"

"That's exactly what they're thinking of us. They have their own ideas about what a marriage should look like and compare people to how 'they' function best. I'm not saying it's right, okay? But— do you understand, Calli?"

She grumbled, "Yes. But it's not how God designed marriage."

"Believe me, I know. — Let's focus on our little secret. Not ignore everyone, but make the effort to enjoy ourselves for what this is."

Callimay sighed as she looked down at the table.

"Let me offer to each and every one of you that it is of the utmost pleasurable experience to fellowship with you this eve." Rocher spoke out as everyone turned their attention to him and the few voices that were heard fell silent. "For the sake of formality and respect, let us begin by observing a solemn moment of time to remember Mrs. Vienna Jackman: the one who poured her body, soul, 'and' spirit into crafting this ever-growing Shadow of justice: the network of such individuals represented in but a fraction of their number here tonight. Let us not forget nor neglect the present reality that she was the one who single-handedly overran the blood-filled tide which was sweeping so many away; saving the lives of countless individuals and families during the Eradication. And then since that time expended everything at her disposal — including her life itself — in the most noble of efforts to preserve a facet of life which is still seen today in our society as nothing more than a disease and deplorable transgression."

A deafening hush fell over the ballroom as everyone bowed their heads. While everyone was reverent, there seemed to be something more attached to observing this moment of silence for Destan and Rocher… something more than the respect given to someone who was a friend and fellow "lefty". And here Callimay was, feeling awkward because she didn't have any connection at all. Yes, she now knew a little more about Mrs. Jackman; but she was still wrapping her mind around everything she was told. How could she properly give her the moment of respect that was expected under such circumstances?

The moment turned into a full minute; Rocher clearing his throat before he began again, "Usually, I am not the orator for such an event; not one to seek the gift of having such a place in the limelight… but I was compelled by Doyen himself to offer the opening remarks in light of my deeper relation to Mrs. Jackman. — Let me begin my remarks by singing her praises as I know we all would in insurmountable ways. She was a woman of women: refined and dignified. And yet she was a Commander: unrelenting and steadfast. She demanded nothing less than what potential she saw in everyone, regardless of what roll she was fulfilling: perfection. Tireless in her efforts to discover avenues of spurring others toward this goal — pushing herself at the same time so as to be a leader who truly led by example — she linked arms with those around her from eve till eve. She built an empire of lasting impact and grave importance which will never lose that foundation. Her attention to such detail is purely reflected in the style of tonight's gathering. I am confident every man can attest to this fact while it is visible through the color of all the ladies' attire. Building upon such symbolism comes the love of enjoying life which can be seen in the eyes of all those in this room; some of whom we all know would not be with us if it weren't for her work that is still continuing. … Losing her was a calamity of calamities; but her legacy refuses to die. It lives on as long as we allow it to. — Enjoy the evening of joining in the rest, though as abrupt and unlawful as it was, which she was granted from her relentless work. Use this evening as what she reminded as: 'an opportunity to gain strength in our fight against the devil law'."

Everyone applauded in a strict and formal manner as they rose from their seats in unison. Rocher turned on a dime and walked to Destan, looking very rigid and formal; pausing for a moment to whisper in his ear before leaving.

A few moments later, Rocher's voice could be heard as the orchestra began to play what was now Callimay and Destan's theme song… in a manner of speaking, "The Sir and Milady Nevrille have graciously agreed to open the ball for us this evening."

Everyone applauded with the same cadence, but Callimay could tell a difference: not one person stayed standing. Some leaned over to the person beside them and exchanged hushed words while they all but wagged their heads at her. — This was forced and almost a mockery.

Destan, on the other hand, popped up from his seat, glad to have this chance to show off his beautiful bride to another group of people he knew very well; and begin their secret reception. How he missed the fact she cowered from the overwhelming amount of people glaring can only be imagined.

Right as they got to the bottom step, she stopped. Destan tugged on her arm a bit and then turned back, seeing her flushed face: *Calli? Calli what's wrong?*

*I can't.* She barely got out in between sobs, twisting her hand to free herself. *Destan please. I can't do this. I can't enjoy myself. This— I want to go home. Please!*

He tapped into the other part of her ability only to be appalled and disgusted with what he heard. What he thought was Callimay reading too much into everyone's body language and vocal tones was, in reality, a conservative estimate.

When he heard her yelp, he realized he needed to keep himself from emotionally spiking further: *Calli I'm sorry. Please— don't let them ruin 'our' evening. I… I won't 'make' you stay, but I'm asking you to please try. Giving up will only fuel their contempt for you. You've got to fight this battle. I can't. I'm sorry. … Please Calli?*

She threw herself against his chest, doing everything to cry as quiet as possible: *I'm sorry. I'm not trying t—*

*I know you're not. — I wanna give them all a piece of my mind right now, but I know I wouldn't prove anything if I stooped to their level. — They can't control you. It's your choice. Everything's your choice, remember? Emotions and reactions are in your control, Calli. I know I'm guilty of not making that choice, so maybe I can't say this: but please 'choose' to prove them wrong. Do it in the right way like I know you can. You've done it before, Calli. … I know I can't shield you from their words or thoughts, but I 'can' make a statement that will remind them who you are to me and how devoted I am.* He lifted her face to him; giving her a long and slow kiss. *Everything's alright. I'm here. I'm not leaving. I promise. I love you.*

Those in the crowd were stunned while at the same time intrigued by this unplanned and quite public display of emotion and affection.

*Calli? I… I'll take you home if you need it.*

After she took a deep breath, she looked up to his worried yet loving face, *No. … No, you're right. I can't let them do this. What I do might be all I have control over, but it's more than enough.*

Fear which had crippled a young woman was now turned into a stronger and seemingly unbreakable trust in her husband. Rage which had kindled yet again in the heart of a young man now fueled the flame of devotion and protection; while recognizing the limits of such well-placed and fulfilling tasks.

His hold on her was so soft and tender while he led her. Even though he was angry, she saw that the loving look which had found its permanent home in his eyes and smile were pushing that monster aside. The battle inside of him was starting to end: he was winning. And in addition, what he said proved there was nothing he wasn't willing to protect her from… or no one.

This showed though, there were some things she had to do for herself. What she did at the Society she still had to do to some extent. She wasn't immune from having to stand up and fight. A time might come where she had to make that hard choice. Could she do it?

Everyone, now at peace with Destan's statement, joined them on the dance floor. The tension which poisoned the air was purified. Thoughts changed from condemnation to commendation. Expressions melted from sneering glares to awe-inspiring stares.

Redje and Tabitha stuck close, enabling the four of them to chat while they danced, "You're making my life miserable."

"Well Rej, if you'd come more you'd be better." Destan responded off the cuff. "'You' are making yourself miserable."

Tabitha warned, sounding very much like a mother, "Mind your manners. This is a ball, not your office."

"Yes Tabby."

"That guy," Destan chuckled and shook his head as the couples drifted apart. *Feeling better now, Calli? Able to enjoy yourself again?*

*Yes. I… I'm sorry I t—*

*Let's not think about it. It's done and gone.*

*H… how are you doing? Is this what you wanted it to be? Less my immature outburst, of course.*

*My only regret is you had to endure everyone's preconceived ideas for the time you did… and you didn't have anything like this when we got married.* He shifted his hold on her, resting his chin on her head. *You're so strong, Calli. So very strong. Don't 'ever' forget that.*

The dancing continued into the early hours of the morning; couples taking short breaks here and there. Those who traveled quite a distance had rooms in the hotel, allowing them to stay longer. So needless to say, those who lived closer were the first to go.

"You look exhausted, Tabitha." Callimay said concerned as she jogged over, seeing her rubbing her ankle.

"Redje is getting the car right now. I really wanted to stay for the whole thing, but I just— I can't. I'm sorry."

"They'll be another one next year." She said cheerful as she gave her a hug. "And I mean this with all the sisterly love possible, but I didn't think you'd make it this far. Are you sure you're alright?"

"I know you always mean well, Callimay. No worries. — This? I can get like this from standing in the shower for five minutes, I'm fine. … Do you want to know my secret for lasting this long?" Tabitha motioned for her to get closer. "I slept in until one. Unheard of for a mother of a five-year-old, I know; but Redje was a dear to let me do it. — On the flip side, you seem to be doing so well."

"Well I'm glad you think so. I'm ex-haust-ed." She admitted as she looked over at Destan who was talking with a small group of men. "I mean look: the men my husband is talking to look just like him. Who would say that let alone see that if they were fully rested?"

"I'll let Destan know we're leaving." Redje took Tabitha's hand and placed it over her baby bump. "Doing alright?"

She smiled and sighed as he gave her a hug, "We're just tired."

He wasn't bothered at all by Redje's comment; and with the first couple now gone, others began to follow suite.

Callimay walked over a while later, struggling to hide what were the ever-compounding signs of her exhaustion: she stashed her heels under their table a couple hours ago and even tried to freshen her makeup. But, things were getting out of hand — it still looked like the group of men he was with were nothing but carbon copies of him, "Destan? I— well I didn't mean to chase them off."

"Don't worry. What is it?" He smiled as he took her hand.

"A small group is getting ready to leave."

"Oh! Thank you for saying something. … Are you doing alright?"

*Do I tell him? ~ Please!* "I… I'm exhausted, Destan."

"Do you need to rest until it's time to go? I can finish—"

"It's not but another half hour until it's all over. I'll make it."

"It's four thirty already! Man, time's flown by!"

℔

The pavement was cold, helping her swollen feet get some relief as she leaned against Destan's shoulder; eyes barely open to see the sun's first rays bathing the cityscape. She made sure to hide her heels in her stole — unsure if she would be reprimanded for acting like the rural girl she still was deep down.

Destan was quite the opposite: so wide awake; chatting with a few others who were waiting with them, all the while checking around for anyone who might happen along like last time.

He helped Callimay in and took his normal seat, letting her curl up on his lap as best she could with the full skirt of her dress taking up so much room. It'd been a while since she was able to do that. Up until now, it had been one of them who drove when they went somewhere.

Rocher made the short drive to the house and then got in his car and left, "How does he always last longer than I do?"

"He told me it's because he drinks so much coffee." Destan laughed as he opened the front door.

℔

Everything hit him when he shut the door and looked at the stairs which were between him and his bed… he was exhausted now. What a change! Was he able to flip that fast or was this just him letting that feeling that had been there this whole time finally have its way since he was somewhere he considered safe?

Regardless of the answer to this trivial detail, they helped each other up to their bedroom and used the last bit of energy they had to rid themselves of as much of the evening and early morning's formalities as possible before passing out.

"This was — by far — the 'best' ball I've ever been to. Thanks for being a trooper and hanging in until the end, Calli. Sweet dreams."

"I love you. Goodnight, Destan."

# ~ 24 ~

He sounded like a broken record, Destan repeating his pleas for Callimay to wake up while he finished getting his clothes on. But then again, it could have very well been taken as a command because of the tone of his voice… the wild look of fear in his eyes suggested that wasn't the case though, "Callimay! Come on. Wake up."

For as much fun as his little jokes were, she was too tired to "participate". Destan had done this before: wake up super early and then bug her constantly, telling her to wake up. Why today of all days?

Irritated that she was now half awake, she lay there perfectly still and pretended to be asleep: *Let's see how long mister 'I'm wide awake' will last. Ugh!*

After him pestering her time and time again, not giving up on his little "joke", she replied groggy as she looked over and saw what time it was, "Destan it's only eight. We haven't had two hours o—"

"We've gotta go now." He ordered as he stormed to the window and pulled the blind back; sunshine spiking off the blade of the knife in his hand. "And be quiet!"

She stumbled to his side, rubbing her face and ignoring what he said, "Why do you have a knife?"

"Callimay Rose Nevrille, I 'need' you to wake up!" He grabbed and rushed her to the wall. "I know you're tired. I am too. But we've got to get out of here and we can't until I know you're awake."

"Destan what's wrong?" She quivered, still holding her head.

"There's no time for me to explain. You've just got to trust me." He demanded as he ran to the closet and threw some clothes at her. "Put these on. Now."

Her heart was racing and her head was pounding; she was awake but definitely not in the best of shape. Hearing him call her by her full name wasn't something he did. He hardly called her "Callimay" now.

She fumbled quite a bit, but got dressed as fast as she could and followed him downstairs to his office. Destan grabbed his duster along with his duffle bag, throwing a soft leather envelope in it that he took out of the locked drawer of his desk.

Just as he turned he heard a rapid round of shots. He threw her to the ground, covering her with his body.

After a minute and nothing happening, he scrambled to his feet and helped her up, racing down the hall and out the back door to the car. Destan only paused for a moment when they got in, now seeing who the shots were intended for and hit. Callimay couldn't get any words out; the sight she saw too horrific. He threw the knife on the dash, jammed the key in the ignition, and peeled out of there as fast as he could. There wasn't a vehicle around, let alone any human, but there'd been enough time since the shots for whoever it was to leave… or hide.

⌘

A few, agonizing minutes passed with no comfort or answers. They were out in the open countryside now; but the beauty of it couldn't erase what carnage they both just saw.

Destan shredded the speed limit before they were at the end of the first block — he didn't even stop at the signal. Callimay felt like they were flying, even though they were still on the ground. When she dared to look over, she saw Destan's eyes had a laser focus that couldn't be detoured for any reason. His jaw was firmly set; his right hand tight on the wheel while his white-knuckled left hand gripped the clutch. He was oblivious to Callimay who was frantically trying to catch her breath, "W— who did that!"

"Toreon," he growled as the leather steering wheel groaned and creaked from him gripping it tighter.

"W… what! I thought you said he was dead! H… how— why were Redje, Tabitha, 'and' Rose murdered? — I thought you said we were all safe there, Destan? What's happening!"

No response.

"Destan? Talk to me. What's going on? W… where are we going? Destan tell me! Please!" Callimay begged as she tugged on his sleeve, panic and hysteria poisoning her emotions.

Instead of a response there was an ear-splitting snap and crack. Callimay jumped in her seat and looked out, seeing a horrible storm barreling down on them. These were Kerogen's version of what she knew as howlers: the only difference being they had torrential rain fed to them by the nearby ocean.

At the speed Destan was going and the reality of a gale streaking ahead of the storm, she knew they were in danger of wrecking. She desperately tried to get him to listen, but realized: *You're in frenzy mode! I… I'm not synced with you! I'm sorry Destan!*

He was now going about one-twenty and still refused to listen. She braced herself for the pain and focused to reach him.

It wasn't any surprise she had to fight her way in, but nothing could've prepared her for the pain once she did make it. Things were bad enough with the migraine she had… now things were unbearable.

As if she'd been punched in the stomach, she doubled over and wheezed as she gripped his arm: *Destan! Destan you've got to slow down. You could kill us both. Destan please don't do this!*

Now she was the one begging and pleading over and over again while he ignored her… what cruel irony.

Finally! He came back to himself enough to realize he needed to slow down; pulling off onto the gravel shoulder when he stopped. Destan threw the door open and got out as fast as he could; dropping to the ground the second he put weight on his legs.

Callimay screamed as she fumbled to get her seatbelt unfastened; running around to see him wheezing and writhing as he tried to catch his breath. He hadn't used his ability, but being in frenzy mode was the equivalent of using it for the maximum amount of time his body could handle. She dropped to her knees and put her hands on either side of his face: *Just try to relax. Look at me.*

*I can't breathe!*

She yelped as she tried to keep herself calm, *I know it hurts.*

"Calli!" He gasped as he fixed his eyes on her; coming to his senses just then. "Calli I'm so sorry. Please… please tell me I didn't—"

"I'll be alright," she collapsed beside him, her trembling hand still touching the side of his face. "Just. Calm down. ... Okay?"

"I'm getting there." He put his hand over hers. "I'm getting there."

The gale tore across the area, its sound causing the ground to quake and the air to rumble so loud it penetrated to the heart. Destan rolled over and sheltered Callimay, the car doors slamming shut as it hit. He could feel her shaking and could tell she was in so much pain and terrified of what was all going on: *I'm right here, Calli. I'm sorry for not listening. We're gonna be alright. The wind will die down in a minute or so and then we can get to safety. ... It's okay, Calli.*

Using the car to steady himself, he got to his feet when the gale was gone. Hesitancy trying to save her from anymore hurt, Callimay refused his offer for help... at first. Feeling overwhelmed and terrified — him being her "safe place" — she reached up and let him help her. She clung to him as they looked around; the rain wall at the other end of the vast open field a couple miles off. And to make matters worse, she couldn't see any sign of Rayleen, "Where are we?"

"I... I don't know. Did you drive or did I?"

"What do you mean you don't remember!" She flew off the handle as she shoved him away. "I kept begging you to slow down so you wouldn't kill us; begging you to tell me where we were going. Why did you say Toreon killed them? You promised me he was dead!"

"I... I don't remember anything." Destan looked at her with his eyes wide-opened, voice stuttering and hesitating more than it ever had before. "Really, Calli. I... I guess because I was in frenzy mode I—"

"That was part of it," they heard a familiar voice interject.

"Baleck," he gritted his teeth as he grabbed Callimay and pulled her behind him. "You filthy, Syndicate scu—"

"There are ladies present, Mr. Nevrille. Let us conduct ourselves in such a manner becoming of her delicate ears."

Destan spat on the ground by his feet, "Falconer."

Baleck clapped his hands in an exaggerated fashion after he bowed; mocking, "I must bow to your unfathomable intelligence, Destan. I was worried sick that you wouldn't know. And may I offer yet another bit of intriguing information as yet more praise to your intellect: getting into your mind was about as hard as it was to get into Callimay's."

"You mean y—"

"I was only in Destan's right now, Callimay." He corrected as he shook his head and put a finger out to her. "I just needed to test you to make sure when the time was right I 'could' get in. … Did you ever wonder 'why' you agreed so quickly to go flying and never had the thought cross your mind that you would be terrified?"

"Leave her out of this." Destan snapped back as he gripped her hand. "You Syndicate scumbags are all alike. No respect or dignity for God, people, 'or' someone's privacy."

"You really should have left well enough alone when you were at the Society. You both would've become the Syndicate's greatest assets if you 'only' would have listened to reason."

Destan jerked back, his emotions spiking, "Syndicate?"

"I think you've known the connection for a while. I can't believe you never let the thought cross your mind." He continued to scoff as he turned and walked away; pausing and looking over his shoulder, "I'll be waiting whenever you're ready. … And please. Take your time."

As an immediate response, Destan looked around. It irritated him how puffed up and conceited Baleck was; strutting his ego by intentionally not having any backup. But then it struck him: Baleck came at this with formality and combat honor. At least it appeared so by him wanting to choose where they fought and not entertaining anything but it. Would he keep this up and truly leave Callimay alone? But was his word worth anything since he was a Falconer?

The more he looked at his uniform, the more disturbed Destan was… his was too close to Toreon and Webb's style.

Conclusion? He wasn't just "any" Falconer.

Who was he… really?

"Calli?" Destan said in a firm and deep voice as he took her by the shoulders and looked her square in the eye; keeping calm. "I need you to get in the car and do something for me. The top of the clutch flips up and there's a black button. Press it and stay in— I know the car won't keep you safe from any mental attack, but it'll keep you from whatever he might try physically." *Long enough for them to get here, anyway.*

She begged as he rushed her to the other side of the car, "I can't leave you."

"We've never come up against someone on his level. He's a different kind of evil. — Now whatever you do, make sure you hit that button! Promise you'll stay here no matter what."

"Destan please don't," she cried as he shut the door.

He touched the car, it turning the window into an interface. After keying in a code, he put his hand on the window as it scanned it.

She cried as she put her hand up to his, "Destan!"

"I love you, Calli. I love you with all of my heart. I won't ever leave you. You know that. … This is my choice. I know what I need to do. I can fight this battle for you. Trust me, okay?" He smiled as he pulled his hand away; finishing in a tone she only remembered hearing when they were in Faberton the time he went to find Webb, "Wolf? Don't let her out or anyone in."

The car's AI responded as he stepped back, "Affirmative, Doyen. Lockdown sequence initiated."

"Destan!" Callimay screamed as she pulled on the door handle.

He began walking but paused; closing his eyes and taking a deep breath to help him cope with the regret he was feeling when he heard her wailing. In a way, he felt he was tormenting her — he didn't want to treat her like he didn't care; he didn't even want to lock her in the car — but he knew this was what he had to do to keep her safe. He couldn't bear having her in harm's way like she was with Toreon. This was the only way.

As he stood there, he started bickering with himself: *I don't want to be stupid and put myself in a situation where I could get myself killed, but I can't stand her being in pain. Baleck's a seasoned fighter. He has to be. I'd only be asking for~ Just get it over with, Boon. Save her what pain you can. Even if Baleck is good, he's got to have a weak spot. And you've got more 'ammo' to pull from this time. ~ If I knew how to tap them. … Ugh!* *Calli? I… I know I said I'll always answer you, but I'm doing this to keep you safe. Be strong for me.*

It was difficult for him to figure out how to block her — him panicking for a moment and doubting he could — but he could "feel" the difference and so continued on his way.

While he was about a quarter mile off, Destan took a quick surveillance of the ground in the area and fumed. Baleck chose the muddiest part of the open field… which would only get worse with their fight and the rain that was beginning to fall: *Strategy is a strong point of his. Seasoned Falconers are. And since he has twin butterfly swords, that must mean he's a Hung Gar specialist. ~ No matter how good he is, if he doesn't have what is 'normal', he'll break. ~ They're still sheathed. He could be suckering me in with this whole 'honor' gig he's portraying: draw out the battle so I can't keep a good footing.*

"I said: take your time… 'Challenger'." Baleck smirked as Destan stopped about twenty feet from him.

"Why put this off any longer, Origin?"

"Ah! So Creigam let you know, did he? Or am I neglecting your own intelligence again?" Baleck countered, taking his stance.

*Hung Gar. I was right. ~ This'll be a 'nice' refresher, huh? ~ Strict method has no counter for the unpredictable… especially when it's an ability he won't be expecting.* He smiled as he took the appropriate defensive stance. "You've spent too much time with the Prince. His ill-timed banter isn't your style… nor is that ridiculous, fake, formal tone you're masquerading."

Destan knew it was coming, but didn't expect Baleck to see his way that soon and start things without another comment. What was that about strict method having no counter for the unpredictable?

Wait! Baleck disappeared?

A moment of panic set in, Destan quickly glancing around; but then he saw him coming straight at him. He was thrilled he'd cracked the code: *They work. Perfect.*

In one swift motion, he dodged while reaching out and grabbing Baleck's arm so he could pitch him to the side. After hitting the ground, he became visible to the unaided eye. While Baleck avoided the "embarrassment" of falling flat on his face in the mud, he did churn up quite a bit of muddied water as he skidded backward.

"How did you see me?"

"Good eyesight?" Destan joked as he lunged at him. *If I can lay one finger on him: his face, hand—I'll get something to add to my arsenal. Only thing is, I've got to make sure I know what emotion I'm feeling.*

Furious that he was able to fully engage him and actually land a few hits, Baleck became visible again and drew his swords. He was ready to end everything then and there, "This is the part of the serum's formula your father kept from me."

"He knew what you were doing."

Baleck shook his head as he lowered his swords, "No… no he didn't, Destan. He had no idea what was going on. Not even on the night I showed up to talk sense into him."

"You!"

The next moment, Baleck felt a blade right against his neck and Destan nowhere to be seen, "Is there anything you 'can't' do?"

"So 'you' were the one who murdered my parents… weren't you!" He bellowed; his eyes burning with anger. "Admit it Baleck!"

"And so, in epic fashion, your twenty-two-year quest has come to its haunting conclusion." He took a long breath and sighed… before kicking Destan's hand to dislodge the swords.

Their understanding of this ancient form of Kung Fu was — in a way — breathtaking. This was nothing like the brash, ruthless, and choppy style Toreon preferred. Blows were exchanged with such fluidity and yet were beyond powerful; and even if one of them took the final blow in a sequence, they were quick to recover. The rain "did" made footing a challenge, but both of them were subject to it. — Was Baleck smart about choosing this place?

This was starting to look like nothing but a stalemate the longer it was drawn out. And then a break! Destan was quicker to react in one moment and had enough time to grab the swords and have Baleck pinned again.

"Why are you working with the Syndicate?" He wiped the blood from his lip; his hand which held the swords starting to shake and his eyes beginning to dart back and forth.

"They have something I want and I have something they need."

"Cut the monologue. What is the deal you have with them?"

"Do you have a proposition for me that is more lucrative? — Fine. I want money and they need serums. There's nothing deep and twisted about it. Let it be known, though: I'm 'more' than willing to play with whatever side so that I am able to get the biggest payoff. Just like my niece Ingrid does."

"What! I— where is she?"

"You know I… I 'don't' know now that I think of it. She's quite more independent of ties than even 'I' am. — She hated being 'confined' at the Society. And in all honesty, I doubt this hunt would have been any type she would have preferred. She loves 'prowling' her prey."

"This 'hunt'. Is it a job from the Syndicate or personal?"

"It's both, actually." Baleck tossed his head back and forth a bit; becoming more relaxed and conversational. "I kept my cover intact too long to let you slip out, but the one who hired me was gracious enough to give me a second chance. … So, long story short: there 'is' a payoff coming for me in this from a high-profile individual. Though don't get the idea that they're part of the Syndicate. Let's not spread false intelligence concerning the Monarch. 'That' wouldn't be nice or fair."

⚏

Callimay was watching in horror this whole time. She was frantic and all but driven out of her mind — she hadn't done what Destan told her to. Every attempt she made to get the door to unlock didn't work, and then she couldn't break the block he'd put up.

Frustrated with her persistence and knowing she wasn't thinking clearly, he reminded, *Calli, make sure you hit the button!*

What in the world did he mean by "hit the button"? There wasn't any way for her to get the top of the clutch open in the first place.

Remembering the tone of his voice and seeing what was happening, she started working. Callimay broke a couple fingernails in the process of getting the stupid lid open. — All that hard work to get her nails "just so" now gone. — Inside this little steel trap of a compartment was exactly what Destan told her would be there. She stared at it… the button had some symbol on it she'd never seen before, and yet it was familiar for some reason: a spike with a ribbon flowing off it.

Why did Destan have this in the car? What was it for? And why wasn't it "easy" to get to?

She looked out and saw him with Baleck, knowing he had to be in pain. Was this the "only" way to get Baleck to stop? Would the door unlock if she did?

The second after she pressed it, the car's AI rattled off, "Closest Shadows and Veils notified: Confrere, Sentinel, Fidus, and Helpmate."

"Who… who was that!" She screamed as she pinned herself in the corner against the seat and door.

"The more accurate question would be 'what' was that." The car responded in its automaton, male voice. "Attempting to open the door is of no use, Callimay. Please remain calm."

"H… how do you know my name!"

"Doyen programed me to recognize your voice and know your name. — Please remain calm. Doyen secured you to keep you safe."

"Doyen? Who's Doyen? Or should I say 'what' is Doyen?"

"Doyen would be a 'who', have no fear. As to his secret identity, I am afraid I cannot further answer your question for security purposes. Though, your question is a strange one. You know him: he told me you are his wife. He was the one who locked the vehicle."

*Destan?* Callimay shrieked as she looked out, her eyes wild with terror; and then asked scared, "What is your name? Do you have one?"

"Wolf. Though I see no reason for it since it has no significance—"

"Wolf? What did you say you do?"

"I operate all the computer and security functions within this car. — Why are you asking such questions, Callimay?"

She started feeling the dashboard: *Destan turned you off. There was a button he— aha!*

"Doyen inst—" Wolf's voice died off as the computer shut down.

Callimay reached for the door handle, relieved it gave way. She saw the knife on the dash and grabbed it before jumping out.

It was difficult for her to see because of the torrential downpour. Part of her wanted to start running, but something held her back. She was still trying everything she knew to break the block he put up; her becoming more and more exhausted by the second. The pain was so numbing that she couldn't feel the rain pelting her.

Just as she thought she could break it, she froze with fear. What she saw was impossible: Destan having Baleck at the end of a sword while Baleck was sneaking up behind him, ready to run him through with the same type of sword.

"But— I— how!"

"This is easy." Ginger laughed as she put her hand on her shoulder. "And a source of amusement for me… as twisted as that might sound."

Callimay thrust the knife toward her and yelped, "Nightmare!"

"Calm down and quit waving that thing around. You could hurt someone. ... 'Thank' you. — Now. Look again. ... Go on." Ginger calmed as she gestured, not intimidated in the least by this show of supposed force; her dodging every effort with ease. "See it now?"

Destan was standing there, holding the sword at the air in front of him. Baleck was behind him this whole time!

She screamed as she started running, "Destan!"

"Calli?" He asked in fear as he whipped his head around.

"Destan! Behind you! That's not Mr. Willgun! Turn around!"

He yelled as he turned to her, "Get back in the car!"

"Turn around! Please! — No!" She screamed in a blood-curdling voice; running faster toward him as he fell to the ground.

Baleck was now leaning over him as he removed his sword from Destan's back; but vanished from sight as she rushed up. She slipped in the mud the two men churned up, losing the knife as she fell, but scrambled to her feet and kept going. It took her a bit of doing, but she eventually got him turned over so she could see his face.

"Destan?" Callimay wailed as she wiped the mud off his face and pushed his soaking wet hair out of the way. "Destan can you hear me? Oh please— you've got to be alright. Destan please. Destan! Destan don't leave me. I don't want to be alone! I want you back. You've got to come back. Please. — God, I— no!"

His shirt, though black, was visibly soaked with blood that ran down and onto his duster coat; eventually pooling on the ground in the standing water around them. He wasn't gasping for air, let alone his chest rising and falling from breathing. His eyes were open, a lifeless stare embedded in them. There was no doubt: he was gone. — He was most likely dead before he even hit the ground.

Completely hysterical now, she tried to get him to wake up by any means possible: shaking him, rocking him, and talking to him. She was trying to convince herself he was only in shock and needed help.

ᚼ

As this unfolded, Baleck looked on as Ginger came to his side; the most evil form of a content smile on both of their faces.

"Stop it! … Why are you torturing her!" Destan bellowed as he tried to move, doubling over from a shock. "Why are you doing this, Willgun? You're not just getting paid to torture my wife. Tell me!"

"The Syndicate has been trying to track you down for what feels like an eternity and a half." He began to explain as he walked over to where his prisoner was kneeling. "Well I use the term 'eternity' but it's only been what… five, maybe six years? — Anyway. When I found out about the payoff they were offering for what so many referred to as the 'Myth' — Doyen — I started searching. There were rumors concerning different people, but the most recent one sounded realistic and 'very' interesting. I got word where Toreon was and learned of his suspicions. I gave the Syndicate enough information to whet their appetite; upping the ante by turning Mr. Freigh over to them. — Yes. It was yours truly who organized all that. — I offered assistance to get Toreon out, but doing it so I could make sure to get the information 'I' needed. Of course Toreon wanted to go to the Monarch himself, but I… shall we say 'convinced him' that going through me was better. All that was left was to get you out in the open. Webb did well, but it seemed your guard dogs kept a closer watch on you than I was told or anticipated; even on such short notice. … Such a pity, but what can be done? — At that point, in my humble opinion, a frontal attack was going to lead nowhere of profit. Even though the Queen wasn't pleased, I 'assured' her that patience would reap greater benefits. — I do hope you enjoyed your 'leisure time'."

"Why are you torturing Callimay?" Destan gritted his teeth as he looked at his wife who was still screaming in agony as she held what she thought was his dead body. "What has she 'ever' done to you?"

"You 'are' dumber than I thought. … There is one way to make this stop, you know." Baleck offered as Ginger walked over.

"How?"

"Would you sign your own death-sentence?"

"Three simple words are all it takes for me to make her pain stop, Destan." Ginger smiled as she pointed back to Callimay. "She looks so grief stricken, the poor thing. I can only 'imagine' the migraine she'll have after this emotional roller coaster. — And I think she already had one. Such a shame you won't do what you can to help her."

"If I am who you say I am, would I be dumb enough to confess? That'd be putting Calli through the pain of losing me twice." Destan spat at their feet, glaring at these two greedy and self-centered people; then switched his focus and sounded so caring and worried, "Calli? I'm right here. I'm not dead. Ginger's toying with your mind. Wake up!"

"All this knowledge of your father's work and you still have 'no' idea." Ginger shook her head as she chuckled; kneeling and fingering his face. "She can't hear you, Destan. She can't even see you. You can't reach your precious 'Calli' anymore. She's mine and will continue to be so until I deem otherwise. I control what she sees and hears. You're naïve to think you can get to her."

"You're sick." He jerked back; shocking himself while at the same time receiving a strong punch to the face from an infuriated Baleck. *Not the way I intended to make contact… but it'll work. ~ Wait! ~ You're right!* *Calli? Calli can you hear me? Calli listen to me…*

ℬ

For a while, Callimay rocked back and forth as she wheezed. When the rain picked up again, she leaned over to shelter his face from it. There wasn't any love, frustration, hate, fear— there wasn't any emotion in his eyes at all. Her hand violently shook as she reached up to close them; but she stopped, sobbing as she fell on top of him and gripped his hair, "I can't. I can't believe— you can't be gone. This has to be some nightmare. … I want it to be. I want it so bad. If there were a way to— I'm just lying to myself. You're in my arms. I know this is real. I… I know I… I lost you. — God help me! Please!"

Amidst her wailing and screams, she heard a terrified voice call out to her: *Calli?*

"Destan?" She jumped back and looked at his face.

*Calli? Calli I'm not dead. Look around you. I'm to your right.*

She scrambled to her feet and looked around frantically at the empty field around her, "Destan? I— you're not to my right."

"How are you doing that?" Baleck sneered as he punched him.

"We're married… remember?" He chuckled even though he was in pain; somewhat relieved that he'd been able to get through to her. "Don't all husbands and wives read each other's minds?"

"How in the world is he mimicking her ability?" Ginger whispered as she came over and gripped Baleck's wrist; her focus bobbing between Callimay and him.

He was impressed and rather amused with this desperate effort. Yes, he had that momentary outburst, but the more he watched, the more it intrigued him what Destry was capable of formulating; both in respect to Liaison and Challenger.

After a few moments, he turned back, "So. You won't confess to keep Callimay from emotional 'wear and tear'. It's quite cruel, but admirable at the same time. … What would you say to a proposition of confessing to save her from killing herself?"

"She'd never do it." Destan growled under his breath.

"She could be— 'persuaded'." Baleck's long fingers interlocked in a conniving way as his eyes narrowed. "It only takes a suggestion for someone in such a weakened mental state to latch onto an idea and see it as their own."

*Calli!*

She hung her head as she laid him down — now closing his eyes — then turned and looked at the knife she dropped. Callimay trembled as she took his hand in hers and put it against her cheek; her silently crying as she looked at the blade. It didn't seem real for Destan to see this happening — she knew this was wrong. He was in such shock he didn't know what to do.

At one point, since it was so wet, the knife slipped out of her hand. She stared at it as she spiraled into madness; sounding so serious: *I said if it was your time to go that I wanted to go too. I can't do this again. I can't go through this loneliness. This will at least end the pain.*

*Callimay. Rose. Nevrille. Listen to me! I'm not dead!* Destan begged; trying everything he could to get up even though he was being shocked again and again. *Don't. Do this! You are stronger than this! Calli stop!*

"I just want to hear that!" She screamed as she thrust the knife into the ground and beat on the dead body's chest. "I want to hear your voice telling me you're still alive. I want to think this is all a nightmare. I want to think all of this is going to shatter; that I'll wake up and find you lying in bed next to me and it was all my imagination. I want it so bad that I can even hear your voice telling me so. — But I know the truth. I know Nightmare is toying with me to cause me more pain than I already have. She's that sick to do it."

*Calli it's not true.* He continued to plead, collapsing a foot from the dome she was in.

"Can you get him out?" Ginger began pacing. "I can't control that."

His admiration of seeing pure serums at work reached its breaking point; that, and he didn't actually think Destan would be able to do what it appeared he was. Baleck snapped as his eyes darted around, "I'm trying. I don't know where he is. This isn't as easy as Lylah was."

Destan looked at him with wild anger in his eyes, "Lylah?"

"Oh, that's right!" Baleck smiled as he switched his focus and kneeled next to him. "You never knew 'how' it happened, did you. — Truth be told, I only 'murdered' your father. In fact, he was my only target for that job. Your mother became necessary collateral damage… just like Callimay is. She took only a mere suggestion… just like Callimay is doing. She saw nothing but her husband lying dead on the floor… just like Callimay is seeing. She even had a weapon within reach. — Need I go on with the similarities? — With the hysterical state your mother was in, it didn't take much prodding to get her to kill herself… just like it is going to be for Callimay. Your father got free and ran to her like you just tried, but it was too late for him… just like it's going to be for you. — Like father, like son."

"You devil!"

Baleck laughed as he got up and turned, "I've been known by many names: the invisible man, demon ghost, manipulator… and so on."

For as much as he was panicking, Destan kept his wits about him enough to know he had one ace left in his hand: Baleck's appetite for monologue. If he kept him occupied long enough he could work his way in and talk Callimay down, "What did you mean, 'my father was your only target'?"

He took the bait like a duck to water, "As I said: I just want wealth. Your father was a very well-known and highly revered scientist. The extremist groups found out he was working with the government and saw him as a traitor. — How they knew you were a Derelict I haven't the foggiest, but that's beside the point. — I offered them the chance to… 'remove' this traitor. Of course it came with conditions: I would receive a handsome bounty and be allowed to ask favors in the future."

"It… it wasn't the Faberton government? The command—"

"The commander of government research only sent me to talk with him and bring him back in to show him that mixing the serums was successful; his agenda was nothing as heinous or violent as what happened. He was far too diplomatic to go 'that' route. Though don't think I never did anything for them. I did my fair share, and it all came with the same conditions. The Quaverly Mission was a specifically handsome deal, I recall. Quite fulfilling."

Ginger demanded as she stormed up and shoved him, "Could you get on with this? Destan's stalling, can't you see that?"

"You sly—" Baleck chuckled as he kicked him. "I take it back. You're not as dumb as I thought."

*Calli? Calli, please listen to me.* Destan begged; knowing he was able to break the block.

*Leave me alone, Ginger.* She cried as she curled up. *I just want to be with Destan.*

*You won't be with me if you do this.*

*I love you, Destan.* She closed her eyes and turned the knife.

*Stop it!* He yelled; causing her to flinch. *My Calli would 'never' do this. She knows it's wrong. She knows it's a sin to commit suicide.*

She dropped the knife and started sobbing again, *But I'm lonely.*

"How are you reaching her?" Baleck asked dumbfounded as he whipped his head around.

"You gave me the most powerful ability but didn't even know what it was? Who's the idiot now?"

Baleck rushed over and punched Destan again, now working him over to beat him unconscious.

*Calli you've got to believe me. I'm not dead. Well, not yet.*

"You are!" She screamed as she pushed him out. "I admit it! You're gone, Destan. I lost you. You're dead!"

"Calli!" He yelled before turning his attention to Baleck, his tone frantic, "Let her go!"

This comment caused a pause in the brutal assault; the chaos in his eyes thrilling Baleck, "There's only one way. … So. Are you Doyen?"

There was anticipation in the air that was about ready to burst the fabric of reality. It broke Destan first. He sighed as he hung his head, "I'm not just a Derelict. I 'am' Doyen: leader of the Shadows, head of the Veil. The 'Myth' is true. — Now let her go!"

"Oh, on the contrary." Baleck laughed as he let go; Destan falling to the ground and being shocked again. "My contract was to bring 'you' in alive. They said I could do whatever I wanted with her… even going so far as to say 'killing' her was encouraged. You really are an idiot to think I would abide by my word. What Falconer have you met that you can trust? Isn't that what all you Derelicts say?"

*Calli!* Destan put forth what energy he had left to fight her blocking him. *Calli you said a little while ago no one can make you do anything you didn't want to; that everything is your choice. You know this is wrong. What were we talking about just last week after we dropped Tand off? … Suicide is sin! I know you 'still' know that; you stopped when I told you to. Calli? You're letting Origin and Nightmare twist your mind and emotions. Stop; I'm begging you! Dig down deep and fight! I can't protect you. I'm sorry I can't. I wish for the life of me I could, but I know my limits now. I know I can't protect you every single moment of the day. It's my fault for trying so hard. I've protected you from so much that I made it so you don't know how to fight back… but you've got to. This is a battle you've got to fight in your mind and heart. Only you can do it. You've got to believe I'm not dead. You've got to believe what you're seeing isn't true. You've got to see what is actually going on. You've got to realize Origin and Nightmare are blinding you. You've got to push them out. I know you can. I know deep down in your heart you know I'm still here. I'm not breaking my promise: Calli, I'm answering you. You kept calling out for me and I'm answering. I'm begging and pleading… 'please' don't do this! I want to see you in Heaven. If you do this I won't 'ever' get that chance. I've lost my mother, please don't let me lose you too.*

That rocked her hard. Why would Ginger be so persistent about keeping her alive? She sat up and looked around, asking again with more hope, "Destan? Where are you?"

"How is she resisting?" Ginger asked terrified.

"I don't know! Just keep the illusion together. It's all we have."

*Find Ginger and push her out. You won't be able to until then.* Destan encouraged, sounding relieved. *You can do this, Calli. I know it's hard because you usually just take it and don't stand up to bullies… but you've got to. That's all Ginger is. That's all any of these people are. Please, Calli.*

She kneeled down and pulled the body close to her, sounding scared, "I… I don't know how to find 'or' fight her. I don't even know what fighting her means. Destan? Destan?"

"Well it's about time you knocked him out."

"I was— never mind." Baleck huffed as he got up; flicking his wrist and then rubbing it. "Good. It's holding. If you can hold it long enough, I should be able to slip back in and finish her. Then we can get him to the Monarch."

Ginger growled under her breath, "The things I do for you."

"Destan? Destan where are you?" Callimay cried as she curled up; wrapping her arms around her legs. "I… I don't know what to do. I need your help. I… I don't think I can do this. I'm not strong like you are. I couldn't even keep Webb from— Destan please!"

Too frightened to move, she sat there; soaked to the bone and bathed in mud. She began fighting within herself to believe it was him talking to her; and then trying to understand how to fight the battle she didn't know she was already fighting against Baleck and Ginger.

All the memories of seeing him say he would never leave her and no one would take her from him began replaying in her mind. And then memories of what he was saying to her: Tand, the ball, the jet flight— there were so many details that lined up. Too many. How could Ginger do that? How did she know so much? Could she?

No! No she couldn't! That wasn't her ability!

"Wait. How… how could Ginger— her ability doesn't allow her to pry thoughts." Callimay scrambled to get away from the body; heaving as she realized, "This is the nightmare! I've been pushing you out this whole time when I thought it was her! I'm sorry, Destan! I— I can still feel you. It's not like when we were in Faberton and I felt you leave. You 'are' still here. I just have to figure out how to get to you. You might be hurt and it's why you can't talk to me right now. … And I know you meant what you said: 'I'll always answer you'. — I… I'll fight. I don't know how to, but I'll learn to. I'm willing to do whatever I need to for you."

This whole time, the terrarium she was in began to fracture. Then, as she finished talking, she opened her eyes and the body in front of her burst into a million shards. Even the standing water around her became crystal-clear. She looked up in disbelief and saw the cracks and fissures in the sky and the field.

"Get out!" She screamed as she gripped her hair and closed her eyes to focus. "Get out of my mind! I know this isn't real!"

"What's happening?" Baleck asked shocked.

"I don't know. I've… I've never had someone— ah!"

"Ginger!" Baleck rushed over and caught her.

Callimay opened her eyes and saw the two of them in front of her, the man she loved lying on the ground behind them. She screamed as she started to run, only to smack into some invisible barrier.

"I'll get him away from here." Baleck finished after Ginger steadied herself; his voice sounding worried. "That is if you can manage."

"I can. Go."

It took her a minute — being laid out from such a hard hit like she took was painful and disorienting — but Callimay got to her feet. Being cautious, she kept her arms in front of her and eventually felt the invisible barrier that was keeping her from her injured husband.

Baleck had Destan by the handcuffs and was dragging him away, her seeing him mouthing something to Ginger but not hearing, "Keep it up for as long as you can and then join me. I'll be at the crossroads."

"Destan! Destan wake up! I can see you. Destan please! Answer me! — Let me out of here, Nightmare!"

"Just let him go. By the time I let you out, there won't be anything you can do to save him. But don't worry. They'll be someone else who will come along; I doubt you'll be prosecuted. And from what I've heard, it seems like there are quite a few high-profile young men you already know who find you attractive, and are champing at the bit to have you. … But, even if you don't; you've got all the money in the world. What more could you want?" Ginger, in her twisted way, tried to calm and appease her prisoner; and then snapped in a snarky tone, "I'm not letting you out so just shut up, you little brat. … Ah. The golden sound of submission and silence. Good. See how much better things go when you act civil and mature?"

"This isn't real." Callimay mumbled again and again as she tapped her fists on the sides of her face; her eyes being closed this whole time. "She's just trying to get me to think it's real. I can walk right through it. It's not there. It's not there…"

Ginger talked in a childish tone as she clasped her hands behind her and swayed back and forth, "If it makes you feel better, than yes, keep telling yourself that. … Oh certainly, be my guest and walk right through. It's nothing more than a sugar decoration that somehow let's rain through and you now have a mild concussion from hitting."

"Leave my husband alone and get. Out. Of my. Mind!" Callimay slammed her fists on the barrier, her screeching voice causing the birds in the trees over a quarter mile away to flee their roosting places.

♅

When she came to, it wasn't raining. And yet it was so dark she didn't know if it was because the storms were still in the area or she'd been out for so long that it was now evening. She groaned as she rolled over and got up, trying to focus as she stumbled around. At this point, she didn't even know what she was looking for. Something wasn't right, but she didn't know what.

Ginger was lying on the ground just to Callimay's right. She didn't recognize her at first and kneeled down beside her, trying to help.

Once she did, she jumped back and scrambled to get away.

Now remembering what was going on and where she was, she looked around for Destan.

Though she fell a couple times as she slid through the mud; Callimay made it to his side. She laid her head and hand on his chest, hearing his heart beat and feeling him breathe. Callimay started to cry as she touched his warm face, "You're alive. You really are. — God, thank you. I… I don't know w— thank you."

As she tried to move him, she heard a snapping sound and felt a faint shock. She looked down and saw the cuffs Destan had on. There were many things she was oblivious about as far as the world was concerned, but she "did" know of these and how heinous they were —

saved for the apprehension and "mild" interrogation of Derelicts. The Syndicate had a televised documentary one time which described these and how they worked: they had motion detectors which would send an electric shock if the person wearing them made any movement. There was a key to deactivate and unlock them like any handcuffs, but the key had to stay within a certain range for it to be active… and she had her suspicions about who held it.

After steadying herself, Callimay jogged over to Baleck… and then froze. What Destan told her about male Falconers popped in her mind. Was he still out, or did he just want her to believe he was? She picked up a rock nearby and then nudged him with her foot, doing it a couple times a bit harder.

Nothing.

Just to be sure, she tried to hear what he was saying to himself.

He was out cold.

She dropped to her knees and started searching for pockets as fast as she could. Did his outfit have any? What kind of person was he to not have even a single, small pocket for loose cleats?

Unwilling to give up, she found what she was looking for: *Of course it was hidden.*

Callimay started going through them, discouraged more and more after each one refused to fit. This whole time she kept talking with Destan, assuring him she was working as fast as she could; but her voice would become more and more broken the longer she tried. She went through the entire ring and nothing: *How could this be! I~ Just try it again, Rose Petal. ~ But I tried them all. ~ Maybe it was backward. Turn them around. ~ Why does he have so many keys?*

Sure enough, the key she felt was so promising the first time around slid all the way in and made that quarter turn to the right. The cuffs lit up and popped off Destan's raw and bleeding wrists. Callimay threw them as far away as she could, disgusted with them and what they'd done. She immediately moved him so his head was on her lap. His face was beaten worse than she'd ever seen. He needed medical help on that front alone.

While looking around she saw the car. She tried her best to pick him up: *I know Doctor Gerould was leaving for some meeting today, but Rocher's around. Destan said he would be for a couple days. If I could just get him to the car. ~ He's too heavy. ~ No he's not. I'm fine.*

It was nothing but struggle after struggle. She collapsed on top of him for the seventh time and cried, "Destan please wake up. I can't do this anymore. I'm scared. I… I need you."

Now she was the one begging and pleading.

This went on for a few minutes, her not realizing he was moving. He asked groggy; blinking slowly as he tried to sit up, "Huh?"

"Destan! Oh you're awake. I—"

"Calli behind you!"

Seeing Baleck standing over her with his swords drawn made her throw herself over Destan, "No! Please don't!"

Refusing to let go, it took him a few minutes to get her to loosen her hold enough so he could see what was going on. He wanted to know why nothing happened, "H… how did you do that, Calli?"

"Do what?" She shivered; not wanting to look up but doing so because he was pointing.

Around them was what looked like a semi-transparent terrarium. She got up and walked toward the edge since it was just about as large as the other one. Baleck ran toward her, causing her to jump back; but he couldn't get through. It was strange how just a while ago she was trapped inside one, but now she was generating one to protect herself and Destan. Callimay ran her hand across it, feeling a similar sensation in her mind as well.

Ginger panicked, grabbing Baleck's arm, "We need to leave. She—"

"Not without Doyen. Go get the car and bring it closer."

"She's not weak or inexperienced like you think she is. There's something else— fine! Get yourself killed. See if I care."

"So, you think you can protect Destan?" Baleck taunted as he ran his sword across the terrarium; Callimay eyeing him.

"I just did, didn't I?" *Why am I not feeling what he's doing out there but I can in here? What is this thing! How am I ma~ This must be what Destan's father talked about! ~ My offensive ability? How is this offensive? It's like a shield. They're defensive…*

"You may have 'developed' a new ability, but I know how this type of ability works at its fundamental level. You're not stronger."

"Maybe I am. You don't know."

There was a moment's pause before Baleck leaned back and busted out laughing, "Do you want to see?"

He moaned as he tried to get up, "Calli. Calli don't."

She gasped as he grimaced from the pain of putting weight on his wrists, "Destan!"

Baleck sneered as his eyes narrowed, watching the two of them fall, "You can't even help support him. How pathetic."

Mad at this belittling comment, she closed her eyes and hissed.

"Calli! Calli stop!" Destan grabbed her hand, wincing from even that much effort. "I know what you're doing. Don't!"

"I can't," she shook her head, not opening her eyes to look at him.

"You can. You can 'choose' to. As long as you pressed that button in the car we'll be fine. Just hold this a bit longer. Help is coming."

"I don't even know how I made this bubble. There's no guarantee." Callimay wrapped her arms around him and shielded him. "And look around. It's just us. Maybe someone will come, but we're out of time. You're too injured to fight. It's my turn. I love you."

"Calli? Calli don't talk like that." Destan said choked up as he saw the dome around them begin to crack. "Calli this isn't worth your life!"

"You are." She said teary-eyed as she gave him a kiss.

"I've been doing this for just over twenty years, but I must say that I've 'never' met someone as stubborn as you." Baleck applauded as Ginger crept up beside him, looking like she was cowering. "I'll give you one last chance: I was trained to use my abilities. You've only stumbled across things haphazard. There's 'no way' you can win."

"I know the purpose of my ability and everything about it from the man who made it. I know you're nothing but a toxic, weakened version of what the serums you manipulated were meant to be."

"My abilities are enhanced. Combined, they are unstoppable."

Callimay gripped Destan tight, trying not to succumb to the pain, "Your pride and selfishness and greed are keeping you from using your ability to its full potential."

"You're just trying to keep your sanity at this point. Take Destan's advice and stop. Even he knows how this will end." Baleck advised as he kicked in part of the crumbling dome and strutted toward her;

enjoying the sight of her yelping. "If you don't, you'll lose your mind; drive yourself insane. You'll never be the same. It's not pretty, believe me. The mind cannot be pieced back together once it's broken."

"I was never the same after I met you, Destan. And I don't see that as a bad thing at all." She whispered as she let him go.

"Calli." He cried as his falling hand streaked the blood coming from her nose. "Calli please!"

"You won't give up, will you?"

"I 'choose' not to. If I don't, you'll hurt other innocent people who have no ability. I'm 'choosing' to fight the battle they can't. I'll fight so they don't have to." She opened her eyes; her brown irises piercing in their gaze as she shoved him, "Now all of you get out and stay out!"

❦

Callimay slowly opened her eyes, unsure of what was going on. Destan was lying beside her, but he was unconscious. She saw they were outside, so she rolled over and tried to focus. Again, something didn't seem right. Something was missing… some "one" to be exact.

Off in the distance she saw a figure. It got larger over the next few seconds, Callimay now realizing it was a person walking across the field. She blinked a few times and then whipped her head around to look for Baleck. Neither he nor Ginger was anywhere!

This person kept walking toward them, but she couldn't make out who it was. Maybe it was Baleck! She was too weak to stand, so she pulled herself to Destan and took him in her arms; trying to shelter him from whomever this was.

When they were about fifty feet off, Callimay could see it was a man. She called out in a strained voice, "Who are you?"

He didn't answer. In fact, he didn't even pause when she called out.

Her heart started racing and she pulled Destan closer, worried who he was or what his intentions were, "Did you see where the other two people went? You did see them, right?"

Still no response!

Callimay all of a sudden realized something: his clothing was of the exact same styling as Destan's… it's just his coat had sleeves. Not only that, but he looked so similar; he even had green eyes!

"W… who are you?"

"I should be asking that question since you called me," he scoffed as he stopped about five feet from her; flinging mud in her face when he set his foot down with quite a bit of perturbed purpose. "Out with it. Who are you?"

"I never did any such thing. Tell me who you are!"

"You sent a flare from Wolf." The man said in the same tone as he pointed to the car which now had another one just like it next to it.

"I… I just did what Destan told me," she shivered as she glanced down to him and then back to the man. "Who are you?"

He finally answered, sounding extremely irritated as he huffed, "I'm Fidus: the second in command of the Shadows. The man you are 'protecting' is my superior — Doyen."

"W… why are you and the car calling Destan by that name? What are the Shadows?"

"As I understand it, Doyen's kept you in the dark to protect you. Needless to say, I think that 'brilliant' plan has backfired."

"Wait. Did you see where the other two went? A man and woman? Were they gone when you got here? Did you see what happened? How long have I b—"

"They've been disposed of." Fidus answered rather cold as he looked to his left and nodded.

"Disposed of?"

A pop and then whistling noise — though faint — could be heard right before Callimay lost her grip on Destan. She grabbed her neck and began gasping as she fell to the ground. Fidus walked up and leaned over to grab her arm, yanking her over so he could see her face.

She whimpered as she tried to get away, but it was too painful; she was having enough trouble trying to breathe.

"She's down and I have Doyen secured. He's still unconscious. It looks like he's at level three. Send in the extraction and recovery teams. Zone is secured. I repeat, threat is neutralized and zone is secured."

Callimay wheezed as she flailed; trying to reach his hand as tears streaking down her pain-ridden face, "Destan? I'm sorry. I trie…"

Fidus was about to push her hand away, but she closed her eyes and her hand splashed in a small puddle of water inches from Destan's.

The End

What. Just. Happened.

www.ingramcontent.com/pod-product-compliance
Lightning Source LLC
Chambersburg PA
CBHW070540310726
48982CB00010B/1416/J